P9-EGL-609

Ireland, pawn of England— no longer home to its sons...

The reign of Elizabeth I sounded the death knell for Irish independence. Ireland's proud earls were brought to their knees, their lands divided among the English, their sons and daughters scattered into England and France.

Rory O'Hara, exiled head of his clan, found life in the French court of Louis XIII infinitely more desirable than thoughts of returning to the pitiful rubble that was Ballylee—his home. And under the scheming patronage of Cardinal Richelieu, he made the most of his cavalier's life.

Then intrigue sent him back to England to spy. And destiny threw him into the arms of the ravishing highborn Brenna Coke, who insisted he must never leave England, must never leave her. But was she truly his destiny? Or did his future belong to Ireland, to Castle Ballylee—to fight to regain his heritage and continue the O'Hara Dynasty?

What the critics say about *THE DEFIANT*, Vol. I of The O'Hara Dynasty:

"Unusually...enjoyable historical saga."
—*Publishers Weekly*

"One of the most captivating novels of the year. It grips your heart and soul." **—*Affaire de Couer***

"An epic account...well researched and organized."
—*The Sunday Denver Post*

THE O'HARA DYNASTY

Volume 1 THE DEFIANT
Volume 2 THE SURVIVORS

MARY
CANON

TORONTO • LONDON • NEW YORK • SYDNEY

TO JACK
AN IRISHMAN WHO MAKES LIFE
A JOYOUS AND LOVING ADVENTURE

Published March 1982

Copyright © 1982 by Mary Canon.
Philippine copyright 1982. Australian copyright 1982.
All rights reserved. Except for use in any review, the reproduction or utilization of this work in whole or in part in any form by any electronic, mechanical or other means, now known or hereafter invented, including xerography, photocopying and recording, or in any information storage or retrieval system, is forbidden without the permission of the publisher, Worldwide Library, 225 Duncan Mill Road, Don Mills, Ontario, Canada M3B 3K9. Except for actual historic characters and events, all the characters in this book have no existence outside the imagination of the author.

The Worldwide trademark, consisting of a globe and the word WORLDWIDE in which the letter "O" is represented by a depiction of a globe, is registered in the United States Patent Office and in the Canada Trade Marks Office.

ISBN 0-373-89002-8

Printed in U.S.A.

Cast of Characters

THE O'HARAS

RORY O'HARA (THE O'HARA): Head of his clan, he has lived since childhood in exile on the continent. A musketeer in the service of the French court, he gradually reclaims his Irish heritage. Ancestral home is Ballylee.

SHANNA O'HARA: Sister to Rory, also raised in exile. Governess to the French princess Henrietta Maria, later returns to Ireland.

SHANE O'HARA: Father of Rory and Shanna, the head of his clan in his time. Imprisoned and sentenced by the English for his part in fomenting rebellion.

DEIRDRE O'HARA: Mother of Rory and Shanna, wife to Shane and daughter of an English lord, Henry Haskins.

THE COKES

BRENNA COKE: Daughter of Elizabeth Hatton and, secretly, Rory O'Donnell. Named daughter of Sir Edward Coke. Beautiful and with a considerable dowry, she is sold into marriage against her wishes. Mother of Robert Hubbard.

SIR EDWARD COKE: Barrister and member of the English Parliament. Second husband of Elizabeth, Lady Hatton, and named father of Brenna. Coke is continually embroiled in verbal battle with his wife and the English court.

ELIZABETH, LADY HATTON: Mother of Brenna and second wife to Sir Edward. Proud and tempestuous, she refuses to let her husband rule her purse or her heart.

CLEMENT COKE: Son of Sir Edward by his first wife, raised as half brother to Brenna. Nicknamed "the fighting Coke" for his love of battle.

THE TALBOTS

SIR DAVID TALBOT: A Scot by birth, David spies in England for Armand de Richelieu. Friend to Brenna Coke and Rory O'Hara, husband of Shanna O'Hara.

AILEEN TALBOT: Daughter of Sir David by a French mother. Determined and beautiful, Aileen grows to womanhood at Ballylee.

MAURA TALBOT: Daughter of David and Shanna.

PATRICK TALBOT: Son of David and Shanna.

THE VILLIERS FAMILY

GEORGE VILLIERS, DUKE OF BUCKINGHAM: Favorite of King James I of England, nicknamed "Steenie." Villiers schemes ruthlessly to advance his own and his family's position at court.

LADY COMPTON: Mother of George Villiers, manipulative and greedy.

SIR RAYMOND HUBBARD: Nephew of Lady Compton, cousin to Buckingham. Weak and ineffectual, Raymond is controlled by his family and forced to marry Brenna Coke.

★★★

SIR FRANCIS BACON: Philosopher, scientist and attorney general at King James I's court.

SISTER ANNA (ANNIE CAREY): Abbess of Fontevrault; companion to the young Rory and Shanna O'Hara during their exile in France.

ROBERT CARR, EARL OF SOMERSET: Favorite of King James I, supplanted by George Villiers. Husband of Frances Howard, he and his wife are tried and found guilty of murder.

CONCINO CONCINI: Italian advisor to the Queen Mother of France, Marie de Médicis. Hated by the populace and French nobility; eventually assassinated.

LEONORA CONCINI: Childhood friend of Marie de Médicis. Wife of Concino Concini.

RENE DE GRAMONT: Unacknowledged son of Henry IV of France. Childhood friend of Shanna and Rory O'Hara.

FRANCES HOWARD: First marriage to Earl of Essex annulled; then Frances marries Robert Carr to become Countess of Somerset. Tried and convicted of murder.

KING CHARLES I: Son of James I and ruler of England from 1625 to 1649. Married Henrietta Maria of France.

KING JAMES I OF ENGLAND: Reigned 1603 to 1625, married Anne of Denmark. Influenced greatly by his favorite, the Duke of Buckingham.

LOUIS XIII OF FRANCE: Ruled 1610 to 1643, after wresting the regency in 1617 from his mother, Marie de Médicis. Married Anne of Austria.

DUC DE LA MARDINE: Interested only in power, the duke aligns himself first with Concini, later with Buckingham. Skilled duellist.

CARLOTTA, DUCHESSE DE LA MARDINE: Wife to the duke; a temptress who uses her body to further her husband's intrigues.

MARIE DE MEDICIS: Wife of Henry IV of France and mother of Louis XIII. Rules as regent of France from 1610 to 1617 with her hated Italian associates, the Concinis.

RORY O'DONNELL (THE O'DONNELL): Head of his clan, he left Ireland during the flight of the earls in 1607 to live in exile in Italy and France. Godfather to Shanna and Rory O'Hara, father of Brenna Coke.

ARMAND DE RICHELIEU: Churchman and consummate statesman, he rises to ultimate power through Machiavellian scheming and deployment of spies. As cardinal, Richelieu becomes de facto ruler of France.

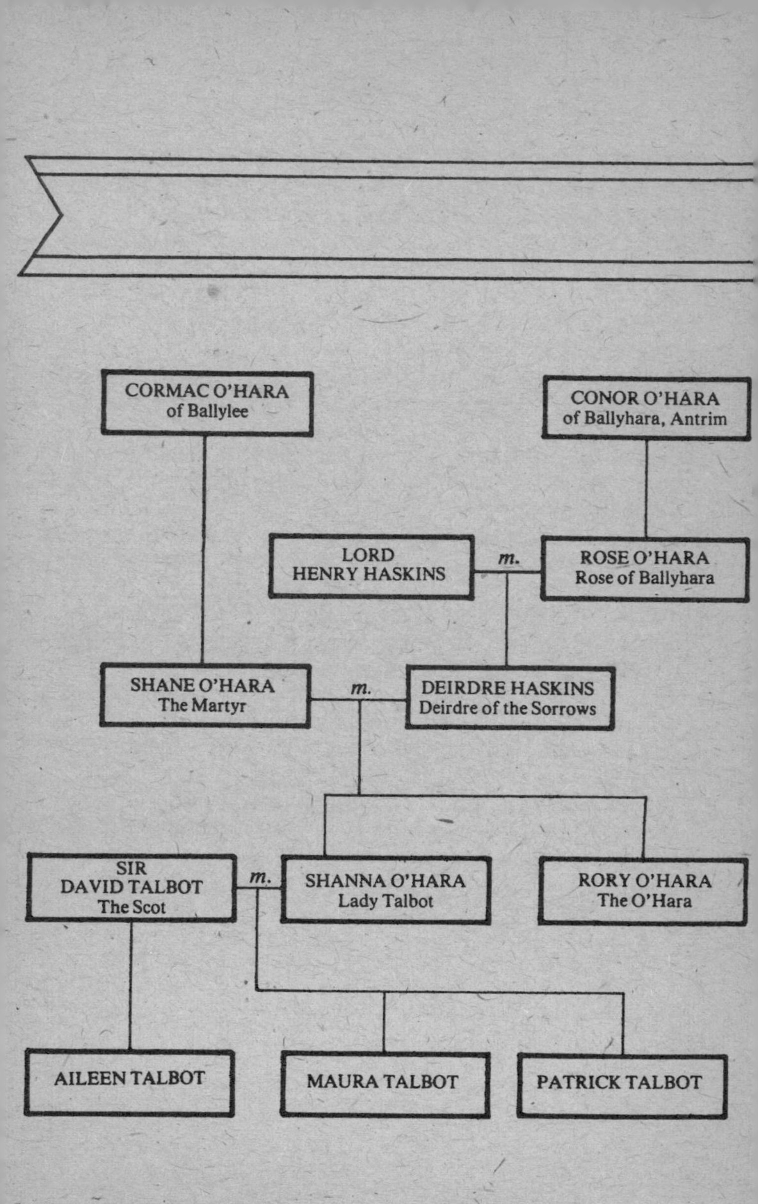
CORMAC O'HARA
of Ballylee
CONOR O'HARA
of Ballyhara, Antrim
LORD
HENRY HASKINS
m.
ROSE O'HARA
Rose of Ballyhara
SHANE O'HARA
The Martyr
m.
DEIRDRE HASKINS
Deirdre of the Sorrows
SIR
DAVID TALBOT
The Scot
m.
SHANNA O'HARA
Lady Talbot
RORY O'HARA
The O'Hara
AILEEN TALBOT
MAURA TALBOT
PATRICK TALBOT

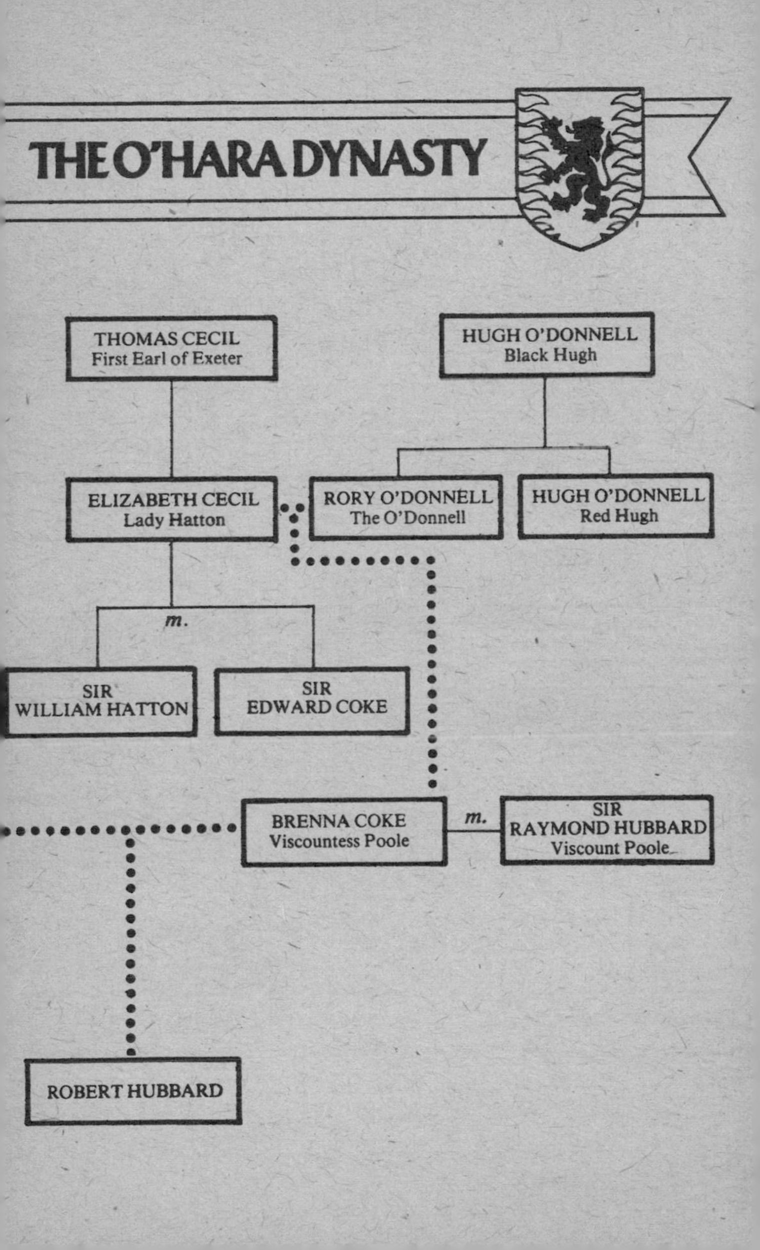
THE O'HARA DYNASTY
THOMAS CECIL
First Earl of Exeter
HUGH O'DONNELL
Black Hugh
ELIZABETH CECIL
Lady Hatton
RORY O'DONNELL
The O'Donnell
HUGH O'DONNELL
Red Hugh
m.
SIR
WILLIAM HATTON
SIR
EDWARD COKE
BRENNA COKE
Viscountess Poole
m.
SIR
RAYMOND HUBBARD
Viscount Poole
ROBERT HUBBARD

Part I
Spring 1616

CHAPTER ONE
PARIS

"WHAT THINK YOU on this point, Mademoiselle de Chinon? *Mademoiselle?* My dear Shanna, are you feeling quite all right?"

"What?" Shanna's thoughts were pulled instantly back to reality from the depths of her reverie, and her violet eyes struggled to focus on the woman who was leaning intently across the wide table toward her. "Forgive me, *madame*, I—I fear my mind was wandering. You were saying...?"

As the brilliant chatter flowed over her once again, Shanna de Chinon silently reminded herself that she usually reveled in the heady conversation bantered back and forth in the Rambouillet salon. Normally she was inquisitive and curiously attentive to the poetry, the theories of politics and the general gossip exchanged among the glamorous guests of Catherine, the Marquise de Rambouillet.

After all, it wasn't every Irish refugee girl who was invited to an exclusive salon to share wine and witty conversation with some of the wisest men and most beautiful, sought-after women in Paris.

But then, Shanna mused, she was not a normal Irish refugee girl. She was the granddaughter of an English lord, Henry, first Earl of Haskins, and the daughter of a prince of Ireland, Shane O'Hara, Baron of Ballylee. But to the French nobles around her in the glittering salon, Shanna's birth meant little. She was Shanna de Chinon, raised in L'Abbaye de Fontevrault by Capuchin nuns and brought to the court in Paris as companion and tutor to Henrietta Maria, youngest of the French King Henry IV's and Queen Marie de Médicis's three royal daughters.

Alone, that association with the court wouldn't have given her access to this salon, but Shanna's quick mind, her ready wit and her extraordinary beauty combined to make her a frequent and sought-after guest of the Marquise de Rambouillet.

On this spring evening, though, Shanna found it impossible to keep her mind on the topics of conversation whirling around her. The current court scandals, the misrule of Queen Mother Marie de Médicis's regency, the recent alliance with Spain and the attempted alliance with England, and the myriad other interests of Parisian society bored her.

Instead, her thoughts were occupied with the news that her papa, Rory, The O'Donnell, was returning from Rome. Her brother had told her the news earlier that evening as she had arrived at the salon. The O'Donnell, head of his Irish clan, was not really her father. But after the violent deaths of her real father, Shane O'Hara, and her saintly mother, Lady Deirdre, Shanna had always called Rory O'Donnell papa.

It was O'Donnell who had brought the children, Shanna and her brother, Rory O'Hara, to France after the flight in 1607 of the Irish earls from their Ulster homeland. And it was through O'Donnell's friendship with Father Joseph, prior of L'Abbaye de Fontevrault, that Annie Carey, Shanna's and Rory's nanny, had been accepted into the Capuchin order as Sister Anna. It was at Fontevrault that Shanna had been raised under Sister Anna's and the other nuns' watchful eyes.

Sister Anna, Shanna remembered, had taught her to be a lady, and O'Donnell had never let her forget her Irish heritage. But it was Father Joseph who had realized that the young, beautiful and high-spirited Irish girl was not destined to live her life sequestered in an abbey in the tiny village of Fontevrault.

The then Bishop of Luçon, Armand de Richelieu, had been a close friend of Father Joseph's. When Richelieu was summoned to Paris and the court to become secretary to the Queen Mother's household and spiritual advisor to Princess Elizabeth, Father Joseph had requested that Shanna be included in the bishop's retinue as tutor to Elizabeth's little sister, Henrietta Maria.

Though Sister Anna had hated to see Shanna go out into the world beyond Fontevrault's walls, it was she who had suggested the change in names. "Ah, lass," she had said, her French punctuated with her native English and her adopted Irish. "Believe me, I know. In the fancy halls of the Louvre palace, they'll look down on anyone with such an Irish name as O'Hara!"

And so Shanna O'Hara had become Shanna de Chinon. It had even been requested that she change her first name, as well, but that she stubbornly resisted. Shanna retained the memories of her early childhood and her pride in being Irish too much to forsake it all. Indeed, even now she could close her eyes and see the English troops storming Ballylee Castle. And she still shivered when she remembered the wild flight nine years ago with Annie and The O'Donnell after the castle fell at last.

How many times in all the years in France after the flight from Ireland had she thought about her brother Rory's childhood promise: "One day, little Shanna, I'll take you back to Ballylee!"

Would that ever happen, Shanna wondered, now that the years had so changed both her and her brother? For, even as the burning desire to return to Ireland had grown in Shanna's maturing breast, she knew that Rory had come to hate the thought that one day he might be forced back to his homeland.

"What think you of our new queen, Anne?"

"What...? Oh, I'm sorry, *madame*." A slight flush blossomed on Shanna's cheeks as she turned to the marquise.

"My dear, you haven't heard a word that has been said."

Shanna had accompanied the royal family on their trip several months before to Bordeaux, where the boy king Louis XIII had been married to the young Anne, infanta of Spain. At the same time, Louis's sister, Princess Elizabeth, had been pledged to young Phillip of Spain.

It had been a chaotic and hazardous trip, plagued by sickness, bad weather and marauding bands of Protestant Huguenots bent on disrupting the Catholic alliance the marriages would achieve.

It was not the trip that had occupied Shanna's mind, but reference to it was a nimble excuse for her rudeness in not paying adequate attention to the marquise's words.

"I daresay," Shanna replied, "that she is fair-skinned, with lovely, almond-shaped eyes and rosy cheeks as well as a delicate disposition."

The marquise chuckled and squeezed Shanna's arm. "My dear de Chinon, your verbal adroitness is wonderful. 'Tis a pity you are not a man and a politician; your tongue would take you far!" Then suddenly the older woman's features dropped their gay facade. "What I meant was, will this young girl have the spine to hold any sway over the lonely, sullen, bad-tempered child who is our king?"

Shanna knew only too well the meaning of the marquise's words. Would Anne have some power over her husband, King Louis XIII, and influence him to take more control of the government from his wretched mother, Marie de Médicis, and the corrupt marshal of France, Concino Concini?

Shanna doubted it, but she was too wise in the ways of court gossip to say so. Instead she chose to dwell on the pathos of the lives of the two youths. "I'm sorry to say, but our Queen Anne seems sad. And well she might. For to uproot such a young girl from her own land and plant her in a strange one as wifc to a boy king must be terrifying for her. I am certain our own Princess Elizabeth feels the same about Spain and her situation."

"True, but it is a thing that those of royal birth must do. How else could we barter for peace without waging another war first?" Here the marquise paused, chuckling. "And if it is her marital duties the young queen fears, I think she has no grounds. Our good King Louis would rather hunt and play with his toy cannon than romp in her bed!"

Shanna could only nod and feel disgust at the memory of that night in Bordeaux the year before. Louis and his new queen, both fourteen, had barely exchanged vows when the Queen Mother, Marie de Médicis, had bundled them into bed with instructions to Louis to do his kingly duty! Shanna didn't know what had occurred, but two hours later young Louis had emerged from the bedroom much the same as he had gone into it.

Poor little boy king and poor little girl queen, Shanna thought. Both rulers, yet ruled in turn by the overbearing Queen Mother, Marie de Médicis, who dreamed of greatness and wallowed in ignorance.

Other courtiers now joined the circle around the two women, and as if they could read the true thoughts behind Shanna and the marquise's banter, the conversation turned to the Queen Mother and her two hated advisors, Marshal Concino Concini and his swarthy, grasping wife, Leonora.

"And I say the Italian and his shrew will return to Rome only after they have completely raped the treasury of France!"

"One day King Louis will tire of Concini, and mother's favorite or not, the Italian will go."

"Perhaps, but before that happens we may have rebellion in the streets. The people know that these two are no longer merely a greedy couple but have become a robber band!"

Shanna listened and a chill went up her spine. In what odd ways the course of history could change!

Henry IV—for all his boudoir antics, his lusty appetite for youthful mistresses and his myriad bastard children—had been a good and just ruler. After his assassination in 1610, six years before, his wife, Marie de Médicis, became regent, ruling in their son Louis's stead even after Louis reached his majority.

Her regency was a terrible blow to France, and the blow had been made ten times worse when de Médicis chose as her personal advisors her former hairdresser, Leonora Galigai, and Leonora's gambler rake of a husband, Concino Concini.

In the years Concini and Leonora had wielded power, Henry IV's internal reforms had been dismantled, the foreign policy of France was reduced to chaos, and the couple had made themselves as wealthy as kings at the French people's expense.

Concini was also hated for his "Italian ways." Both he and his wife, whom the people called a sorceress because of her strange hold over Marie de Médicis, refused to adapt to the customs of the French court and flaunted their differences. As a result, neither of them could move outdoors without bodyguards. They were hated by the French nobles and were cursed and hissed by the common people wherever they went. But ever since young King Louis had reached maturity—his thirteenth birthday—talk in the salon had increasingly turned to open treason.

Such talk affected Shanna personally more than the others. She, too, was disgusted at the way the Queen Mother passed her royal power on to Concini and at the way he used it. But as a member of the royal household she felt duty bound to accept the situation. She also felt duty bound not to take part in such a conversation; she owed the Queen Mother that much.

And further, Shanna knew herself. She knew the Irish part of her nature to be rebellious. Too often she had spoken her mind without first cautioning her tongue. She was determined that, this night, she would heed that caution. She pleaded a sudden need of fresh air and excused herself from the gaggle of poets, philosophers and courtiers and moved through the crowded room.

As always, it was a colorful and stylish assemblage. The women were lavishly gowned in silks, satins, brocades and whispering taffeta. The men sported gaily colored long jackets, with gold and silver swagging and abundant lace at throat and wrists.

Shanna's moss-green dress with high-waisted bodice and linen collar trimmed in point lace was not as stylish and revealing as others in the room, but she wore it with regal bearing. When she had first come to Paris, her poverty in relation to other ladies of the court had galled her. Then she had realized how shallow were the women beneath the gaudy clothes and had paid less and less attention to keeping up with their constantly changing styles.

Now, as she moved lithely through the chattering people, Shanna sensed the cold stares of many of the women and the admiring glances of the men. Inwardly she smiled, knowing that no extravagance of clothes, jewels or cosmetics would make these women as beautiful as she was. She had been graced with exceptional beauty, Shanna knew, and she accepted it without conceit.

"Mademoiselle de Chinon."

A firm hand at her elbow stopped her abruptly. She turned, and immediately froze as she recognized the voice's owner. *"Monsieur le duc,"* she murmured politely.

The Duc de la Mardine released her, stepped back and executed a perfect leg, bowing slightly but gracefully.

Shanna silently cursed her luck. La Mardine was the last man in the room with whom she wanted to exchange conversation. Her eyes darted over her shoulder to the group she had just left. They, too, had noted the duke's arrival. Their conversation, Shanna knew, would now veer away from Concini. To utter such derogatory remarks in front of the duke, who was Concini's right hand and trusted aide, would be political suicide.

"I wonder, *mademoiselle*, if you have given any further thought to our previous discussion?" the duke said, his soft tone belied by the steely look in his eyes.

As a servant, yet more than a servant in the Queen Mother's household, Shanna was in a privileged position. She heard the servants' gossip as well as the conversations of the Queen Mother and the king. There was little intrigue throughout the Louvre and Tuileries palaces that Shanna didn't know about.

La Mardine had approached her several times, wanting to enlist her as another of his many spies at court. The duke, like Concini, was under the protection of the Queen Mother. But once Louis XIII reached the age of majority there was always the chance that the Italian and his co-conspirator in the rape of France could be usurped.

And there were other, unspoken reasons for the duke's interest, Shanna knew. She could sense the desire, nay, pure lust, in the man's dark eyes as they wandered down the fine column of her neck to rest on the swelling fullness of her breasts. Momentarily the darting pupils drank in the olive softness of her bosom and then moved down to the womanly curve of her hips only partly disguised by the wide sweep of her skirt.

As always, Shanna felt undressed under the man's gaze. Words were not needed to express La Mardine's desire. His eyes told her that he would be only too happy to add her to his endless string of Parisian mistresses.

"As I've told *monsieur le duc* so many times in the past," Shanna carefully replied at last, "I fear I have little taste for intrigue."

La Mardine shrugged. "You overhear much, and I need but a word here and there. Let me remind you, *mademoiselle*, improvement of one's station is an easy matter if the proper people are pleased. I am sure you desire more from life than a mere post as undergoverness to a royal brat."

Shanna's spine stiffened at the insult to Princess Henrietta Maria. She knew anger was flashing in her eyes and to prevent La Mardine from recognizing it as such, she tried to avoid his stare. It was impossible. The man's cold, cobalt-blue eyes held her gaze like a magnet. There were depths of cruelty in those eyes that Shanna had never witnessed in any other, man or woman.

They stared down at her now from a face framed by golden hair that was handsome but also cruel. La Mardine's lips, even in a smile, curled into an attitude of contempt. An aquiline nose seemed constantly to sniff the air, sensing any fear in those around him. And Shanna knew he would pounce upon that fear as a weakness he could use to his and his master's advantage.

She refused to bend and let him sense such fear in her. She was about to reply with a definite no to everything he had suggested when she was saved by the Marquise de Rambouillet.

Monsieur le duc was badly needed to settle a debate on a newly proposed tax that was raging across the room.

"Another time, *mademoiselle*," he said to Shanna, bowing, the eyes in his hawklike face never leaving hers. "Our business is not yet finished."

Shanna curtsied, biting her lip to hold back her anger, and directed her gaze to an intent study of the floor before her.

"I can be but a few moments, *madame*," La Mardine said to the marquise. "I would be early to bed this night, for the morrow is filled with duty."

"Even a few moments of your vast wisdom will be welcome, *monsieur*," the marquise lied smoothly.

Shanna sensed the two of them moving away at last. When she glanced up, the older woman was looking back at her, flashing an understanding smile. Shanna thanked the marquise with her eyes and then continued threading her way through the crowded room. She needed that fresh air more than ever now, and her destination was a balcony that overlooked part of the Rue St. Thomas and the Seine, offering a spectacular view of Paris.

Twice more she was stopped along the way and engaged in small talk. Both times she excused herself gracefully. After La Mardine, she had no stomach for conversation with anyone.

At last she reached the threshold and slipped through the tall, partly opened windows. It was a wide terrace with lavish, waist-high grillwork around the outer edge. Thankfully she found herself alone as she practically skipped to the railing and looked out over the city.

It was a clear moonswept night, with just enough breeze to push away the rancid scents created by the garbage Parisians insisted on throwing into the streets.

Instead of the smells of offal, the sweet aroma of honeysuckle wafted up from the garden below to delight her nostrils.

To her left, lanterns swayed gently on the Pont Neuf spanning the Seine River, casting a warm glow on the strollers in their multicolored costumes. Shouts and singing marked a few revelers celebrating the king's return from Bordeaux with his new bride. The poor, Shanna knew, wouldn't be singing, for they were aware that Louis's marriage would matter little in the scheme of things. Concini would still run the country, milking France dry, while the Queen Mother blithely looked the other way.

Shanna swung her attention to the right and the looming gray walls of the Louvre Palace. Lights blazed in the upper windows, the royal apartments. There the young king would be planning the next day's hunt with his big, oafish favorite, Charles d'Albert, Duc de Luynes. The Queen Mother would probably be dismissing her maids; Marie de Médicis retired early and slept late. The young queen, Anne, would very likely be sitting on her bed alone, weeping.

Signore Concini would be bidding his wife, Leonora, good-night and then retiring to his own apartments and one—or more—of his many mistresses.

And below, far below, in the servants' wings and in the cellars, two hundred and more cooks, valets, stable boys, iron workers, maids and dozens of other servants would be laying their heads down for the night. A few would be sleeping on soft goose down, but most would make do with a straw pallet and a rolled coat for a pillow.

Shanna's mouth curved into a sad smile when she thought of the poor lot of most of the king's servants.

She pitied them, but at the same time, she was glad her status in the household was more than that of a servant. She even had her own maid and rooms adjacent to the apartments of the royal princesses, Christine and Henrietta Maria.

Her gaze lifted to the Paris skyline, to the Hôtel de Ville, its immensity nearly as impressive as Notre-Dame. *Paris*, she thought, so beautiful yet still so foreign to her. It was far from Chinon, so far from Fontevrault and unthinkably distant from Ireland and Ballylee.

She had been but a child when she was torn from Ballylee's looming towers and graceful wide parapets. But the sights, sounds and smells of the castle and the Irish land had never left her. It was as if the wide heaths, so green they pained the eyes on sunny days, and the tall stately oaks had voices that called to her from far across the sea. Even the marshes and the bogs with their quiet moody silence, seemed to cry out to her soul.

And where was she now? A foreigner in a foreign court, hating those she served but powerless to break away from the only position she had. Her restless thoughts flew back to her first meeting with Armand de Richelieu, Bishop of Luçon. Proudly Shanna had voiced her distaste that she, the daughter of an Irish lord, should be nothing but an undergoverness, even if her charge were a princess.

"Many of us, my child, must bend and flow with the winds of chance. You and your brave brother have been children of misfortune. Now 'tis time to forget the life you had or might have had and ride a new road where you are," the bishop had counseled.

She would never forget Richelieu standing over her,

lean and majestic in his purple robes, puncturing every argument she could muster. He was a compelling man, with an arched nose like the prow of a ship and heavy eyebrows that accentuated a steep scholar's forehead.

But it was his sonorous voice and his dark metallic eyes that had transfixed her. They were shrewd eyes that seemed to read her thoughts and bare her soul. In the end it was the imperial quality of those eyes that had made Shanna relent and agree to follow Richelieu to Paris.

And, later, it had been the driving force of Richelieu's personality that had drawn her into his service even while she was serving the court. Here had been another reason for turning down La Mardine when he previously had approached her. Being a court spy for Richelieu was dangerous enough. Performing the same service for Richelieu's rival in the Concini group would have been suicide. So when La Mardine had first approached her, Shanna had gone to Richelieu.

"The tools of power in the hands of fools," he had told her, "are the machines that bring government to its knees. Follow the dictates of your own ambition, my child, but remember that one day France will be the leader of all Christendom."

Shanna was intelligent enough to discern what Richelieu had left unsaid. If France was to be the leader of Christendom, Richelieu planned to be leader of France. She chose to let her allegiance remain with the wily bishop, firmly believing that one day Armand de Richelieu would have ultimate power. And when that day came, Shanna would use her association with that power to return to Ireland and claim what was hers.

Suddenly the breeze felt chill and the moonlight dancing on the Seine almost ominous. She curled her fingers over her arms and hugged herself as a shiver passed through her body. She was about to return to the warmth of the salon when she sensed a presence behind her.

"I think, *mademoiselle*, that the moon dances merrier over the Seine now that you have returned to Paris!"

The lilting baritone voice was right at her ear, a warm breath barely rustling the dark curls of her hair. Shanna smiled, not bothering to turn, for she knew well the voice's owner. "Why, sir, I believe you do aspire to poetry."

"Only when I am near enough to you that your scent fills my nostrils and your radiance dazzles my eyes."

René de Gramont, his handsome head crowned with golden curls, appeared next to her. Shanna lifted her face toward his, but instead of brushing her cheek with his lips, René whirled her into his arms with a low, guttural laugh.

His azure blue eyes, full of life and gaiety, gleamed down at her from his enormous height. His white, even teeth shone equally bright in the fine line of his chiseled jaw. His smile, as always, was one of mockery as well as tenderness.

"Nay," he chuckled, "I'll not kiss you like the gallants who swarm around you daily over there."

René de Gramont inclined his head in the direction of the Louvre and then tensed the muscles in his strong arms, bringing Shanna's body, like a feather, to the toes of her embroidered slippers. Even then he had to bend from his towering height to bring his face near hers. Gently but firmly their lips met in a caressing kiss.

For an instant Shanna responded, letting that familiar giddy feeling embrace her. She swayed forward, momentarily pressing against the hardness of his chest. She felt his hands move down her back, pulling, tugging her hips closer to his. His kiss became more insistent, his tongue probing between her lips.

And then his hands moved to her sides and up toward her breasts. Her body tensed and her own hands came up between his. She flattened her palms on his unyielding chest and began to squirm in his arms. "No... René," she mumbled, pulling her lips from his and turning her face aside.

But he was insistent. His lips nibbled at her ear and he buried his face in the thick softness of her scented hair. "You would make the finest mistress in France," he groaned.

"A better wife," she replied with a chuckle.

"All right... wife. Say when!"

"No," she said, turning from him, the humor leaving her voice.

"All Paris supposes us lovers already."

"That's because the court and all of Paris is so full of lovers, no one can imagine anyone else sleeping alone!"

"If not mistress or wife, what then?"

"Friend."

"I'll be your friend as well in bed. Damn it, Shanna, I love you!"

"And I love you, René... as a friend."

His arms tightened like a padded vise around her body. She could feel his tall lean length from her toes to her shoulders; so close that even though there was a corselet, a huge flowing skirt and voluminous petticoats between them, Shanna could feel his maleness.

"I'm your brother's friend," he whispered into her hair. "I wench with him, drink with him and fight with him. He's the best friend I have ever had, as are you. But with you, dearest Shanna, I would be more. I would be your lover."

"And where would you bed me? In the quarters of the king's musketeers?"

The gibe at his lack of wealth deterred René not a whit. Again his hand slid upward. He cupped her breast for an instant and went on to the bare flesh rising above the material. He was about to slide his hand into her bodice when Shanna caught it and brought it back to her waist.

"It—it would be like incest."

"Mon Dieu!" he cried. "That again!"

They had both been twelve when they had met at Fontevrault, Shanna the orphan of an Irish warlord and René a bastard son sired by King Henry IV and Corisande, Countess of Gramont. Unlike most of Henry's other bastards, René had never been claimed by the king and therefore had never attained a title. That fact, as well as being the unwanted son of a countess with little wealth herself, had turned René practically into the streets. Only kindly Father Joseph's intervention had saved him from a wastrel's life. For the first time in his young life René had the security of being wanted, at least, if not loved, where he was living.

The attraction between René and Shanna had been immediate even if it was, at first, slightly one-sided. Even at twelve Shanna had been beautiful, with darkly violet, flashing eyes, ebony tresses and a blossoming figure.

René de Gramont had been smitten.

Within a very short time, Shanna had begun to feel more than a childhood interest in René. His easy laughter, his apparently carefree manner, his blond good looks and his quick wit had intrigued her from the first. As the months had passed, she had begun to look upon him with womanly eyes.

But even with the gentle stirrings of young love and womanhood rippling in Shanna's breast, she had held back. For a long time she hadn't known why. And then, slowly, she had begun to realize. René had taken the place of her brother. Rory O'Hara had gone on to Rome after the flight from Ireland, and she had missed him sorely. If she thought of René as her brother, how then could she feel anything but sisterly love for him?

But Shanna hadn't taken into account the narrow confines of Fontevrault. She and René had been thrown together constantly. They had been tutored as one. Their chores at the abbey had been done together. They had ridden and talked and dreamed together until, by the time they were seventeen, they were inseparable.

"Tell me the gossip of Paris in my absence," she now said lightly, trying desperately to shift the conversation away from dangerous ground. "Is the Countess Boudine still sleeping with her footman?"

"I'm sure she is. All of them. But don't change the subject! Is it because I have no future as a king's musketeer that you won't marry me or even sleep with me?" He squeezed her tighter. "After all, it isn't as if we haven't made love before."

Shanna was glad her face was turned away. She could feel the flush of embarrassment creeping up to suffuse her cheeks. "A childish mistake," she whispered.

"Not so childish, I think," he replied. "And I hope to prove one day that it was not a mistake."

There was such tenderness and pleading in his voice that it brought a lump to Shanna's throat. No, she thought, it hadn't been a mistake, or if a mistake, a wonderful one.

It had been a brilliant day with hardly a cloud in the sky when they had ridden into the low, rolling green hills between Chinon and the River Vienne for a picnic. A coverlet spread upon the ground had been their table, a good wine from the Chinon vineyards, cheeses and fresh bread from the abbey ovens their fare.

They had talked of books and poetry, for both were avid readers. They had discussed Cicero and Montaigne and bantered tidbits of gossip concerning the royal court in Paris. They had mused with both laughter and sadness upon what would become of them, two orphans with few expectations.

They had talked of one day returning to the lands that were rightfully theirs; he to the château of Gramont, she to Ireland and Ballylee. And eventually, as it had so often lately, the conversation had turned to love and marriage. Carefully they had skirted any reference to each other. It had become a ritual since they had both begun to feel the stirrings of maturity in their bodies.

Shanna had never known what had brought about the change in their attitudes, the sudden realization that this was a day unlike other days they had spent together. Much later she had blamed the beauty of the countryside, the scent of spring in the air and the rippling sound of the flowing river so near. She had attributed it to the security of the grassy depression where they had lain, secluded, it seemed, from the whole world, by a thick grove of trees.

The memory of that moment when she had known it was going to happen would never leave her. In mid-sentence their eyes had met and René's hand had reached to cup tenderly her delicate chin. He had leaned forward and kissed her soft lips. Shanna's response had been immediate. The ardent way she returned his kiss had surprised her, but she was powerless to stop it. It was as if time had stopped, and for the first time in her life, caution was thrown to the winds. She had been swept up in an impetuous burst of passion born of the moment.

"I love you," René had said very calmly, and had gently pushed her back until her shoulders found the soft grass.

"René, we can't. We must think—"

His lips had silenced hers and she had found herself amazed at how deftly his fingers worked at the ties of her leather riding blouse. The cambric underblouse had opened as if by magic, and then his lips were at her breasts, sending searing tongues of fire through her body.

His exclamations had been of awe and reverence as the riding skirt and petticoats fell away to bare her body before his eyes. Only sounds had told her that he, too, was discarding his clothing. Shanna had tightly closed her eyes, as if to block out reality.

But the feel of his hard male body pressing down over hers, naked flesh to naked flesh, had been all too real. Willingly, she had moved into his arms and fervently surrendered her feverish body to his exploring hands.

With each fiery touch, more and more of her caution had been washed away by unabashed desire, until she had wantonly implored him to take her.

Near unearthly thrills had coursed through her as his hand found the soft flesh of her inner thigh and moved upward. Her legs fell open and he moved between them. Though she was completely inexperienced, instinct had boiled up from some well of passion buried so long and so deeply in Shanna's body. Her hand found his hardness, and caressed. René's moans had matched her sighs as, without embarrassment, she had guided him deftly.

Again surprise had overwhelmed her when, ever so gently, their bodies were joined and there was little or no pain. Instead, excitement had rippled through her body like a brushfire fanned by a high wind.

And then she was moving, matching his thrusts with rising lunges of her own. For a brief second she was embarrassed by her abandon. But then the driving passion that had erupted erased everything outside the aura of their joined bodies.

Suddenly a spasmodic seizure had turned her whole being inside out. It was as if her mind and her body had exploded as one. She had cried out and clutched him to her, willing the ecstasy of the moment to go on and on.

They had lain silently until dusk faded the blue from the sky. Then, just as silently, they had bathed in the river, each carefully avoiding the other's gaze.

Not one word had been spoken on the ride back to Chinon, and it had been the next morning before the full impact of what they had done clutched at her heart.

Was she with child? No, she couldn't be.... René had not—or had he?

She had committed a mortal sin—or had she? How glorious it had been. Then yes, it had been sinful. But would she be damned to hell for it? Should she confess? Would she be cast out?

She would tell Sister Anna. Her dear nanny and teacher had often hinted that, in her own youth in England, she hadn't always been so saintly. But when she appeared before Sister Anna, fear had made Shanna speak only of the weather.

She hadn't eaten for days and had taken to her bed for nearly a week with fever. Her every waking moment had been one of fear and self-deprecation. Her every sleeping moment had been filled with nightmares of her body burning in hell.

Finally, her superior intelligence and common sense had taken over. What was done was done and could not be undone. And if what she had done had been so bad, then over half the women in France would probably burn in hell with her.

After some time she had even started speaking to René again. Their friendship had returned, but Shanna had vowed never to let it reach such intimacy as had occurred that day beside the River Vienne.

The situation had been difficult, well-nigh impossible, for René. He was truly in love with Shanna and had told her so every chance he could. Many times he had tried to repeat the afternoon, but always Shanna had held him at bay.

Soon afterward, he had left Chinon to attend the College of Navarre in Paris. He had written constantly, always expressing his undying love. Shanna's brother, Rory O'Hara, had been at the time a senior cadet at Navarre. He had taken René under his wing and they had become inseparable friends. René had begged Rory to intercede for him, and Rory had tried, to no avail.

"I fear I love René as I do you, dear brother. How, then, could there be anything more than lasting friendship?" Shanna had written.

Slowly she had realized that through the experience she had become not only more of a woman, but wise beyond her years. She had learned that it had been passion, uncontrollable physical desire, and not love, that had allowed that afternoon to happen. And to let it happen again would only hurt René one day when she would have to tell him that she could never love him, deep in her heart, as more than a friend.

At last O'Hara had told René to settle his own problems of romance.

Once, while visiting Paris and her brother, Shanna had seen René with his cadet sword and his plumed hat, looking like a blond god of war in his slashed doublet, jaunty cape and spurred boots. His tall, gangly body had acquired grace. He had muscled into a giant with even more mischief in his merry eyes and a quicker wit upon his tongue. She had nearly acquiesced.

But this time her mind had managed to control her body. She had fled back to Chinon, to her books and the abbey, wondering if there was a man anywhere to create in her a love to match the unbridled passion she now knew existed.

"I ask you again.... Was it such a mistake?" René whispered.

Shanna's hands covered his at her waist. She squeezed them tightly and leaned her head back from his chest. "No, my dear, sweet René, it was not a mistake. It was a warm and glorious afternoon for us both. It awakened us and made a man of you and a woman of me. It—"

"Ah-ha, you admit it then!" he said, the lightness returning to his voice as he spun her in his arms until she again faced him.

"Of course I admit it, but—"

"Then run away with me to Burgundy, where I will become a gentleman farmer and fill your belly with babies and your mind with all the carnal lust I have learned in Paris!"

"Nay," she replied, "you run away with me to Ireland. Help me find an army and make me queen of Ballylee!"

René's face fell. Like all Frenchmen of blood, he felt that any place outside France was anathema, particularly barren Ireland and bloody England. But he managed to make light of it. "Nay, like your brother, wars and rebellion bore me. I would live my life making love!"

He began to draw her toward him for another kiss, but a footman appeared to interrupt them.

"Mademoiselle de Chinon?"

"Oui."

The red-liveried footman handed her a note, bowed and backed through the door.

Quickly Shanna skimmed the missive and turned a smiling face to René. "It is from papa, The O'Donnell. He is at the abbey and would see us at once. I must tell Rory!"

He caught her arm. "Uh...Shanna...Rory's gone."

"Gone?"

"Yes, I saw him slip away about an hour ago."

"To where? I must find him."

René shrugged and turned his face away. Shanna saw his lips curl into an impish smile.

"René. . . ."

"He won't want to be disturbed for a while," René replied with a chuckle.

"René, he *slipped* away, you said. To whom did he slip away?"

"Shanna. . . ."

"René!"

Another shrug as his lips opened into the boyish grin she knew so well. "La Mardine."

"*Mon Dieu*. Come, we must hurry! Damn my hot-blooded brother for a fool!"

"What?" René stammered, holding back. "Why?"

Shanna stopped and whirled on him, her eyes flashing fire. "René, use the brain beneath all those blond curls. Think! Who is the deadliest swordsman in all France?"

"The Duc de La Mardine," René replied.

"And where is Rory?"

René suppressed a laugh. "Very likely between the Duchesse de La Mardine's long legs."

"And the duke?"

"In there," René replied, swinging his arm upward and pointing toward the interior of the salon.

"He isn't," Shanna hissed, real worry now furrowing her brow. "Minutes before I came out here I heard the duke excuse himself to the Marquise de Rambouillet, pleading that he must to bed early this evening in order to rise early tomorrow."

CHAPTER TWO

The Duchesse de La Mardine threw her long tapering legs wide and then drew them tightly around the lunging body above her. There was a blazing crimson haze before her eyes, and her body was a writhing mass of unbridled desire. It had been so for nearly an hour, ever since they had stepped into her bedroom and immediately began discarding their clothes.

She had never known a man like this. He had virtually attacked her. There had been no time for the coy games she usually employed before her many other infidelities.

And now she didn't care. His lovemaking was forceful, demanding, yet deliciously satisfying at the same time.

"Oh, Rory, my lover... my lover...."

Built like a horse, she thought, *with the lust of a bull! All this besides being the handsomest of the Marshal Concini's guards!*

"Carlotta, *ma* Carlotta, you are not only the most beautiful wanton in France, but the most wanton of wantons."

His French was so delightfully accented with the lilting cadence of his native Ireland that it almost brought a giggle to her lips.

I'll keep him for a lover until eternity, she thought.

Rory O'Hara looked down out of his dark eyes at the woman beneath him. Normally her face was a vacant picture of contrived innocence. Now it was contorted into a mask of passionate lust. Her blond hair, always carefully rolled into a mass of stylish curls, was now in total disarray, its combs loosened and scattered on the pillow.

Even in the midst of his own passion, laughter danced in his eyes and threatened to bubble from his throat. It was Rory's nature to be excited by intrigue and inflamed by danger. He had both with Carlotta, wife of the Duc de La Mardine.

Rory was captain of Concini's guards. He had command over the troop of Swiss mercenaries that guarded the fat Italian's belly from a blade or bullet. As Concini's right hand, La Mardine was Rory's direct superior. Rory hated La Mardine almost as much as he did Concini.

What better way to satisfy all his desires—court danger, experience intrigue, satiate his loins and vent his dislike of La Mardine—than to bed down his wife, the duchess?

Not that it wasn't a pleasant tryst, for Carlotta became an animal beneath a man. But Rory had tumbled serving wenches who reacted the same. No, it was different with Carlotta only because she was married to La Mardine.

"Oh! *Mon Dieu, mon Dieu, mon Dieu!*" she cried aloud, forgetting that there were servants in the house. Her nails clawed at Rory's broad, powerful shoulders and on down the strong arms, leaving red gouges.

His wide upper torso lifted from her breasts. The features in his darkly handsome face contorted, and his coal-black eyes flashed ebony fire down at her. His lips formed an O, and then his throat made the sound in a long, low growl.

And then it was over. His massive chest heaved once,

and his weight covered her body. Together they gasped until speech was possible.

"You may be Irish," Carlotta sighed at last, "but, Rory O'Hara, you're a Frenchman at heart!"

He chuckled, his voice of a rolling timbre that, even whispering, sounded like thunder in her ears. "That, m'lady, is the reason every young lad should have Italian ladies for tutors at an early age!"

"You're a devil," she hissed, her tiny fists pounding at his shoulders. "You bed me and then taunt me with your cheap conquests!"

"Conquests, m'lady?" he quipped, nuzzling his face in the blond disarray of her hair. "Cheap? Nay, m'lady. For each, though there must have been a hundred, were all deep affairs of the heart—like you."

"You are a devil!" Her fists became claws again, wrapping around his neck and holding him close.

And what of your affairs, Rory thought, feeling the flicker of her long eyelashes against his cheek. Rory knew the Duchesse de La Mardine's past, as did everyone else in the court. She had been Carlotta of Savoy until three years ago, when she had married the Duc de La Mardine. Before him, there had been the Duc de Vendôme, the Duc de Carlisle, even the youthful Duc de Conde, plus countless other casual lovers.

And all had been stepping-stones to her present place of power near Concini, through her husband.

It was rumored that La Mardine had known full well his bride's tempestuous past when he had married her, but the size of her dowry—and her beauty—had made him overlook it. It was also rumored that on their wedding night he had told her that if ever she should be tempted to place horns upon *his* head, he would take great pleasure in killing both her and her lover.

To Rory O'Hara, such a challenge could not go unmet. "Now that we have begun, my sweet," he whispered, "I hope you have plans for another meeting."

"I don't know," she said lightly, refusing to give him the upper hand. "I'll have to think about it."

"Do that," he countered with another chuckle. "But pray do not tarry too long with your decision, lest I lose my heart to a wench at Picard's."

The insult, even in jest, was made worse by the mockery in his voice. Picard's was the most notorious bawdy house in Paris, full of scheming women hungry for favor from their high-placed customers. Carlotta might be scheming, but after all, she was a duchess.

"You insolent beast!" she cried, clenching her fists for another attack on his shoulders. But before she could strike, her attention was diverted by a sound in the courtyard. "Listen!"

"What?" Rory mumbled.

"I heard a sound. . . ."

He lifted his head from her shoulder and cocked his ear toward the window. "A carriage, I do believe," he said, rolling to her side.

"Mon Dieu!"

The words barely left her lips before she wriggled out of the bed and lurched wildly toward the windows. Carefully she parted the draperies, letting a stream of lantern light spray across her body as she peered out and down into the courtyard.

Rory languidly stretched his now-satiated body and watched the nude perfection of Carlotta's in the slanting light.

"Oh, no," she gasped, her voice shrill with fear. " 'Tis the duke!"

Suddenly she was a flurry of motion, dashing about

the room gathering suitable dress for herself and throwing Rory's clothes toward the bed.

Rory didn't move. He lay quietly, watching her with the eye of a scholar. The duchess had a lithe, angular body, narrow at the waist and rounded at the hip. Her breasts were not large, but just full enough, with a lovely upward tilt. The effort she now exerted trying to throw herself into a stark white chemise made her seem innocently enticing.

Suddenly she realized he hadn't moved. "What's wrong?" she cried in a fearful voice.

"Nothing," he replied, his white even teeth flashing in a smile. "I was just admiring your legs. You have very long, very beautiful legs—"

"Damn you, be quick! Are you mad? 'Tis my husband, you fool! Would you ruin us both?"

"Nay," Rory laughed, rolling from the bed and reaching for his drawers. "I would explain to m'lord the duke that I am but taking lessons in the ways of the French to improve my fortunes."

Carlotta's eyes flashed fire as well as fear when she looked at him. But the impudent grin on his handsome face brought a smile to her lips as well.

"If you had the skill of a swordsman to match the skill of your tongue, I would say stay and provide me with further entertainment. But—"

"But I haven't," he chuckled, struggling into his breeches and boots. Loud voices in the courtyard rushed him into his cambric shirt and uniform jacket. Over his right shoulder went the sash to hold his sword at his left hip.

"Hurry!" Carlotta gasped, as the sound of footsteps reached them from the lower landing.

Rory whirled the guardsman's cape over his shoulder and fixed its clasp as he threw one leg over the window-sill. The duchess frantically tried to push him on.

"Another time, my sweet?" Rory teased.

"Yes, yes. Now go, you idiot!"

But instead of moving farther, Rory leaned back against the sill and appraised her with another wide grin. "When?"

"*Mon Dieu*—I wish I had never met you!"

"Yes, you do. When?" he asked again, his lips curling into an even wider smile.

Her eyes were saucerlike now, and her face was as white as the chemise, which hung open in disarray. "In a month's time.... I'll be in the country—at the château in Mardine."

He leaned forward and lightly grazed her upturned lips with his. "Till then," he said, and dropped into the darkness.

Quickly Carlotta closed the windows and pulled the draperies taut. At the bed, she ignored the candle snuffer, wet her thumb and forefinger and threw the room into darkness.

"Owww! Ouch! Damme for a fool!"

With her heart in her mouth and her legs quaking with fear, she scrambled beneath the coverlet. She jammed both burned fingers into her mouth and listened as the footsteps came closer and closer to her door.

Oh, dear God, she thought, *not tonight of all nights. Let him have visited one of his mistresses already this night. Let him go on to his own apartments. Please, God, let him be weary... let him be drunk... let him be anything but in need of my body.*

The footsteps slowly stopped. Carlotta curled herself into the smallest possible ball and pulled the coverlet over the tangle of her hair. She felt faint, unable to breathe.

Then the footsteps sounded again, moving on down the hall into another wing of the sprawling house. Before they had completely faded away, Carlotta, Duchesse de La Mardine, had already forgotten her pleas and prayers to God. Her agile mind had already changed. Now it was a prayer that the time pass quickly until she could spend another evening in the bull-like arms of that impudent Irishman, Rory O'Hara.

RENE CLAMBERED INTO THE COACH and threw himself down beside Shanna with a sigh. "I could detain His Grace the duke no longer at the gate. It was a weak excuse I had at best."

"No matter," Shanna replied, the tone of exasperation clearly evident in her voice. "I saw Rory drop from the slut's window. Od's blood, probably half of Paris saw him." Shanna raised her arm and pointed a long delicate finger toward the rear of the huge hotel. René leaned, squinting and searching until at last he saw his dear friend.

Together they watched him run in a crouch along the top of the garden wall. Even though clouds partly covered the moon, there was still enough light to see the gold braid on the cape and the red-and-gold guardsman's piping on the uniform jacket.

René shook his head.

"What?" Shanna asked, seeing the movement.

"I would say 'tis daring enough to visit La Mardine's wife at such an hour, but to do so wearing a guardsman's uniform is near to the fly casting the spider's web over himself!"

"Nay, 'tis not daring," Shanna replied, in a barely controlled whisper. " 'Tis merely foolhardy!"

In his mind, René firmly agreed. He held his breath as the figure neared the corner of the wall and then released it in a long sigh as Rory dropped to safety.

Less than a minute later they saw him round the corner and enter the Rue de Mauconseil. He wore his wide-brimmed cavalier's hat now, and the plumes bounced with a jaunty air, as if the owner had just come out to take an evening stroll.

When he neared the carriage, Shanna threw open the door. "Pssst! Here, you fool!"

Rory's eyes widened and his dark face broke into a mischievous grin when he recognized the coach's occupants. "*Allô!* And what brings my beautiful sister into the Rue de Mauconseil so late in the evening?"

"A wayward brother with the morals of an alley cat. Get in. . . *dépêche-toi!*"

With a guttural laugh, Rory grabbed the handrail and swung into the coach. Shanna rapped her knuckles on the overhead and they lurched forward, the unpadded wheels clattering loudly on the rough cobblestones. The movement threw Rory across René's lap and into the seat beside him.

"Ah, René. . .*bonsoir*! What are you up to this evening?"

"Not nearly as much as you, *mon ami.*"

"Me?" Rory replied, a look of assumed innocence spreading across his wide, rugged features. "I have been merely doing my duty, inspecting the security at *monsieur le duc*'s town house."

Even Shanna had to smile, but she hid the fact behind a fan. "And how did you find it?" she inquired archly.

Rory threw back his head and his rumbling laugh filled the carriage. "Very bad. I do believe a rogue could enter and leave with no one the wiser after having obtained the duke's prize possession."

"And what would that be?" René asked, his own laughter joining Rory's.

"*Mon ami*, I am surprised at you. That is a thing two gentlemen do not discuss—especially in front of a convent-bred lady."

Rory leaned across the coach and, before she could turn away, lightly kissed the tip of his sister's nose above her fan.

"*Mon Dieu*, but you have become completely French," she said. "All bluster and false facade with no mettle!"

"Nay, sweet sister. Bluster, perhaps...but had you recently heard Madame de La Mardine's caterwauling, you would agree I retain my Irish mettle!"

Shanna's blush was instant. She raised her fan to hide it as Rory rolled back into the coach's cushions, convulsed with laughter.

How like two boys they are, she thought, *these two men I adore...and who adore me.*

Playfully, Rory and René joshed one another about the relationship and rivalry between Concini's guardsmen and the king's musketeers, of which René was one.

Shanna listened with half an ear. How close the three of them had become, and how easy was their relationship. Would it always be so? With her yearning for something in her life besides court intrigues, and her inability to return René's puppylike love, how close could the three of them remain? With the rift ever widening between King Louis XIII and Concini, the Queen Mother's favorite, would René and Rory one day find themselves on opposite sides of a war for power?

If the boiling animosity should erupt into a full-scale struggle for power, would Rory and René—as officers in the opposite camps—be forced to draw their swords against each other?

The thought sent a momentary chill through Shanna's body, but another burst of exultant laughter from across the coach brought her attention back to the men.

How alike they are, she thought, *and yet different in so many ways.* Rory's dark skin and black hair contrasted with René's pale complexion and blond locks. Her brother's shorter, more wide and powerful body seemed to exude awesome strength as compared with René's lighter form, even with its towering height. René had the narrow features and sad eyes of a poet, while Rory had a wide, rugged face that seemed chiseled from dark stone. Even their voices were different in calm conversation; the one gentle as a rippling stream, the other rumbling like thunder from a mountaintop.

But they were alike in one thing: their carefree lust for life, with Rory usually prompting their wild escapades and René following sheepishly and adoringly along.

How women did flock to her brother! And Shanna, as a woman, could see why. There was something terrifying and fascinating about him, all at the same time. Unlike René, whose calm was rarely ruffled, even to an unnatural extent, Rory could erupt with a volcanic temper one moment and in the next charm all around him with the beguiling smile of a child. He was mercurial in all of his emotions, and rarely did he keep them in rein.

It was because of this that Shanna often feared for him. Tact and diplomacy were necessary ingredients for both the O'Haras as Irish nationals in the service of a French court. Rory exhibited little of either.

If he thought something, he said it. If he felt something, he expressed it. If he wanted something, he went after it—and usually got it.

When she would beg him to give more attention to his future, to ready himself for the day when the two of them could return to Ireland and claim what was rightfully theirs, Rory would only repeat, "When will you realize, Shanna, that Ireland is lost? Ballylee is rubble, and we are destined to be French, like it or not."

And, as if to match his actions to his words, he cared about nothing but enhancing his skill with a sword, overseeing the fine cut of the clothes that made him a cavalier gentleman and pursuing an enticing figure in a satin ball gown.

There was no doubting it. Her brother was a beguiling rogue, a lovable rake, and yet she loved him with all her heart. She could only hope that one day the boy in the man's body would mature. How often she had prayed that something would happen in her brother's life that would make him accept responsibility. Rory admired Richelieu but refused to emulate him. He adored women but let not a one break through the veneer he showed the world and reach the well of his emotions.

How often, since they had been reunited in Paris, had

Shanna herself tried to reach the core of his soul. "If 'tis position you want, dear brother, then what better position than master of your own Irish lands?"

Rory would scoff in reply, only once in a great while letting the window to his deepest thoughts open a crack to reveal his torment. "You were too young, sweet sister, to sit at old O'Neill's knee and hear him rail against the treachery of the clan chiefs in the days of his great rebellion. You don't remember O'Donnell in the years right after the flight, before nostalgia fogged his eyes to reality. I do. I remember his words when he spoke of lost causes, of dying men still walking, just waiting like dumb oxen for the sword to fall.

"And, sweet sister, do you not ever wonder how just was a cause that drove our mother to murder our father and die doing the deed?"

"'Twas not murder!" Shanna had hotly retorted. "'Twas an act of grace—and love. The Lady Deirdre would not have the legend of The O'Hara end in the mud by such a death as quartering!"

To this Rory would shrug and answer, "You have your thoughts and your demons, I have mine. So be it!"

And so Rory chose to live his life in the pursuit of pleasure and to reveal to no one the inner turmoil the choice might have cost him. That thought brought Shanna's mind back to the evening's foolish escapade.

"What think you," she asked, interrupting their conversation, "would have been the outcome had you been caught tonight by the duke in his lady's boudoir?"

"I think...." Rory began, his dark eyes flashing in mock seriousness as they met hers.

"Well?"

"I think I would most assuredly have been skewered."

This was accompanied by another round of raucous laughter, which Shanna didn't join.

"Can you never be serious?"

"Oh, I'm quite serious. *Monsieur le duc* would have put a sword through me as surely as I'm sitting here!"

He was exasperating her, and worse, enjoying it. "Why, then, did you do it?" she asked.

"Because," Rory said, his wide, sensuous lips curving into a narrow line of intense seriousness that caught his sister off guard, "it's been rumored that the lady has two dimples." He rolled to his side and indicated their position with his thumb. "Here...and here. My curiosity merely got the better of me and I had to find out."

"And...?" René asked.

Rory rolled back over and looked directly into his friend's face. " 'Tis no rumor!"

More laughter caused Shanna to snap her fan shut like a clap of thunder. "Perhaps 'tis good that our summons has come. It may prove to save you from being the victim of a jealous husband's wrath."

"What summons?"

"Papa—The O'Donnell," she amended, for Rory never called O'Donnell papa. "He has returned from Rome. He would see us posthaste at L'Abbaye de Fontevrault."

The cloud that had covered Rory's face at her words wasn't feigned. Suddenly he sat back in the seat and peered through the coach window at the outskirts of Paris. His eyes narrowed and his lips compressed into a taut line. The hilarity of moments before vanished from his eyes, and his forehead furrowed in deep concentration.

Perhaps, he thought, *O'Donnell's scheming has got results this time.* Rory feared it would, each time he was summoned to Fontevrault. Each time he feared that O'Donnell would at last have opened the way for their return to Ireland.

And Rory O'Hara had no wish to return to his native land.

CHAPTER THREE
LONDON

NO STATE TRIAL AT WESTMINSTER HALL had ever created such a frenzy of anticipation and excitement. But then, never in English history had an earl—the king's favorite—and his beautiful wife been tried for murder.

For two days, on the river's steps outside the great hall, people had been bartering for seats. For the past week, the realm's peers had been flowing into London from the countryside. A special stage had been built at one end of Westminster to accommodate them. Lesser nobles and gentry would sit in newly erected scaffolds above the main floor. Even these seats were costly, bringing up to five pieces of gold each.

It was late May 1616, and outside, the towns of Westminster and London, as well as the surrounding countryside, blossomed with spring. Inside, the air was already hot and sultry with the heat of packed bodies. It seemed to rise in waves from the sea of colorful dresses and richly embroidered doublets of silk and satin that crowded the huge room.

In one of the highest tiers Lady Elizabeth Hatton sat with her daughter, Brenna. The lady held a scented kerchief to her nose with one hand and with the other lightly fingered a pearl pendant that hung between her breasts. The pendant was the size of an egg and had been a gift from the very lady who would this day stand trial for her life. It was this gift, and the reason it had been given, that now caused Lady Hatton's fingers to tremble.

Now and then heads turned to cast quick, furtive glances at Lady Hatton and her beautiful daughter. Whereas Lady Hatton was fair, with auburn hair and green eyes, her daughter was dark. Brenna's hair, coiled like her mother's in the latest style from France, was black as a raven's feather. Her eyes, too, were dark, and though she was but seventeen, they seemed to brood and smolder with a strange sultriness far beyond her years.

Both were dressed to fit their station, for Lady Hatton was a very rich woman. This day, Elizabeth had chosen a black overdress with slashed leg-of-mutton sleeves. The outer skirt was pulled up and caught in gathers at the hips, to expose gray satin petticoats. The petticoats themselves were lined with red and trimmed with costly gold lace. The V-shaped bodice was cut low and trimmed with gold thread. In view of the occasion, Elizabeth, unlike many of the women around her, had decided to fill in the V of the plunging neckline with a simple arrangement of sheer red silk that matched her petticoat lining.

Like her mother, Brenna had chosen dark colors, a midnight blue with burgundy trim. Unlike Elizabeth, Brenna's bodice was square cut but also low on her breasts; so low as to skirt the bounds of decency. Necessity and comfort, rather than style, always regulated Brenna's choice of dress, and she had declared that it would be too hot in the hall to wear any more than necessary. If the swell of her breasts attracted more leering stares than those given to other women, Brenna never cared nor noticed.

There were many other differences between mother and daughter that went too deep for the eye of the casual observer to discern. Lady Hatton was a strong-willed, independent woman with a violent temper. Brenna, too, had a strong will and an independent nature. But the daughter had an aura of sweet serenity about her that made her instantly admired, even adored, by all those who knew her.

Even in the midst of one of Elizabeth's tirades against the king's injustices, or her husband's devious ways, or the cruelties in general that men perpetrate against women, Brenna's voice often sounded a calming note. Whereas Lady Hatton was often irascible and tempestuous, her beautiful daughter was patient and serene; whereas Elizabeth was ambitious to the point of desperation, Brenna was content to observe the society of London life and the court with a calm placidness and a wry wit.

From an early age, Brenna had been exposed to corruption in the court of King James I. But instead of railing against it, she had exhibited a depth of intelligence far beyond her years and chosen to forgive the frailties of those in power.

"Oyez...oyez!" came the sergeant crier's voice from the floor below. "All quiet for m'lord's entrance!"

The huge hall fell silent as six sergeants-at-arms, maces in hand, their red-and-gold velvet cloaks gleaming, escorted the lord high steward of England to his seat at the upper end of the court. When he was seated beneath the cloth of estate, the sergeant crier again turned to the assembly.

"Oyez. . . oyez, all silent while His Majesty's commission to the court and indictments of the prisoner be read!"

The clerk of the crown stood and, in a droning voice, began to read the orders of justice prescribed by King James I of England to his court of nobles and judges.

Lady Hatton's gaze wandered around the hall, taking in the darkly clad peers and, below them, the scarlet-robed judges. The faces beneath the bewigged heads were lively and animated, and well they should have been, for the depth of the scandal that would be revealed that day could well rock the foundations of an already somewhat unsteady crown.

Elizabeth's gaze found the Villiers clan, the stern-faced mother, Lady Compton, with her three sons. Seated most prominently among them was George Villiers, imperious, with an only recently assumed regal bearing. His lean handsome face framed a haughty smile beneath a thin aristocratic nose and eyes that seemed to look piercingly at the spectacle below.

And well he should smile, Elizabeth thought, for should Robert Carr, Earl of Somerset, be convicted of murder, George Villiers alone would be the king's favorite.

Swift had been the mercurial young man's rise to favor. Less than two years before he had been a penniless adventurer, the youngest son in a family without lands or fortune. And then he had been spotted by

King James among a host of other gallants at court trying to curry the king's favor. Over Carr's objections, the youthful George Villiers had soon received a knighthood. Carr, the reigning favorite, was then pushed near apoplexy when his rival was further given the Order of the Garter and made a Gentleman of the Bedchamber.

Ah, Elizabeth thought with a mental groan, if only the commoners knew, as the court knew, how favorites came and went in those royal chambers. . .and how favor was gained there!

No wonder now the smile on Villiers's face, for Carr's doom was almost a surety. It was even rumored that, once Carr's fate was set, George Villiers would become a viscount.

A shiver ran through Lady Hatton's body when she remembered the day she had made the decision to attach her own future to that of Robert Carr, his wife, Frances Howard, and the Howard family.

It had been a cold, blustery, rainy spring day in 1613 when the beautiful young girl had called at Hatton House. Then Frances had been Lady Essex, and Elizabeth had addressed her as such. . . .

•

"PRAY YOU, LADY HATTON, let us not be so formal, for I would be on more intimate terms with one from whom I so badly need a favor."

"A favor?" A tingle of apprehension rippled up Elizabeth's spine and disturbed the hair on the back of her neck. She knew the Howards. Thomas, first Earl of Suffolk, and his lady, Frances's mother, were a wily couple who had unscrupulously used their patronage under King James to gain enormous profits. Their appetite for gold and the shameless way they had acquired it were common knowledge. It was widely supposed that young Frances, brought up in the direct shadow of this greed for money and power, was very much her parents' child.

Why, then, would Frances seek a favor from Lady Hatton? Elizabeth had lost much favor at court because her husband, Sir Edward Coke, insisted on loosing his barrister's tongue and challenging the king's divine right to rule. What on earth could Frances hope to gain from an alliance with a woman like herself, who was out of favor with both King James and Queen Anne?

And, if the gossip were true, there was a second, powerful reason Frances would not need aid outside her own circle.

Lady Hatton's tongue briefly moistened her lips before she spoke. "If I can be of any service, it will be my pleasure. But I must confess I am surprised. I have heard rumors, Frances, that you are close to one who can grant any and all favors."

From the girl's reaction, Elizabeth knew that the rumors she had heard of an affair between Frances and the king's favorite, Robert Carr, were true.

The girl demurred, however. "Once that was true, but no longer," she replied. Then she paused, as if assembling the words she would say in her mind before speaking them. A chill entered the glassy blue eyes that reminded Elizabeth of the many rumors and tidbits of gossip she had heard about this girl, so young in years but already so well versed in the intrigues of court life. It was a calculated look, one of hardness, a look that said its owner would have her way in the world, no matter the price.

They had remained standing. Now Elizabeth motioned Frances toward the crackling fire and two high-backed farthingale chairs. Carefully the women lowered themselves into the uncomfortable seats that had been designed to accommodate the enormous, tentlike skirts.

Elizabeth hated them, but they were a necessity. The huge hooped skirts had waned in fashion during the last years of Queen Elizabeth's reign, but when James came to the throne, his queen, Anne, had brought back the style with a vengeance. So much had the fad taken hold that furniture had had to be designed for skirts that had grown ever wider.

At last they were settled. Elizabeth poured wine for both of them and then looked apprehensively at her young visitor.

With a deep breath that strained the fabric of her well-filled lacy bodice, Frances, the Lady Essex, spoke. "I will be truthful and blunt. What started as a mere flirtation with Robert Carr has grown into a great deal more." She leaned forward conspiratorially. "My dear Elizabeth, I would marry Sir Robert."

This revelation nearly caused Lady Hatton to dribble wine from the glass at her lips, threatening a stain to the newly made satin skirt spread in yards around her.

Was this girl mad?

At thirteen, six years before, Frances Howard, the most beautiful of the powerful Howard family offspring, had been married to the fifteen-year-old Robert Devereux, third Earl of Essex. Young Robert was the son of Queen Elizabeth's favorite, who had lost his head on Gallow's Green for his ambitions. When the younger Robert's lands had been restored to him, he had been properly nurtured *not* to follow in his father's footsteps. The early marriage to combine the

Essex and the Howard families had been part of this purpose.

Because they were so young, Essex had been sent abroad to learn soldiering, and Frances had been sent to Suffolk to wait for his return and the consummation of their marriage.

But Frances, not unlike the Lady Hatton herself years before, had been strong willed, independent and not content to spend the days of her youth outside London amid the mud and bumpkins of the countryside. The country, with the exception of Tunbridge Wells and Bath, bored her. Only London, the great town on the Thames, offered the amenities of wits, beaux, fops, theaters, gossip, crowds and scandal; in short, everything a young girl adored.

And so to London and the court she had come. It was only natural that, with her great beauty, Frances had caught the eye of every gallant and courtier at Whitehall. But Frances hadn't settled for just any gallant. Only King James's son, the popular Henry, Prince of Wales, would satisfy her.

The affair had set tongues wagging, but no more than usual in a dissolute court ruled by a king who adored men and women alike and made scandal with his own affairs.

But then young Henry had taken ill and died. Now Frances had cast her net again and caught a fish nearly as big.

When Elizabeth replied, the words came haltingly. "From the king's son, you would go to the king's favorite? And all the while *still married*? Methinks, Frances, that you are taken with a slight madness!"

"Aye, mad with love," Frances replied, the semblance of a demure smile on her lips.

"And does Sir Robert return this love?"

"Aye, but he balks at commitment because of my status." For the first time during their conversation, the girl averted her steely-cold eyes from Elizabeth's. "Also, his friend and advisor, Sir Thomas Overbury, is deadly set against the marriage."

"Overbury?" Lady Hatton questioned.

"Aye, but he can be taken care of...somehow." Frances waved her bejeweled fingers in a fluttering motion as if to dismiss the thought of Overbury. "Elizabeth, I would annul my childhood marriage to m'Lord Essex."

Elizabeth shook her head in wonder and awe. Already the sense of foreboding she had had about this afternoon's visit had grown into fear. "To annul such a highly placed marriage is well nigh impossible, Frances."

"I know that," the girl replied, her mouth again curling into that smile that didn't detract from her beauty but added a craftiness to her features and suggested a lack of true nobility in her character. "But there is a way. Should m'Lord Essex, upon his return, prove to be impotent, I would be well within my rights to demand my freedom from the marriage."

"But...to make stand such a claim your virginity would have to be proved."

"Exactly, Lady Hatton, and that is where I need your aid!"

In detail the girl put forth her plan. Elizabeth was at first shocked and then appalled. In her own lifetime, Lady Hatton had been far from saintly, but never in her wildest dreams had she envisioned doing such a deed as she now heard from this girl's lips.

So aghast was Elizabeth that she could only mutter feeble excuses when pressed for an answer. At last she bid the girl goodday, with a promise that she would tender a yea or nay within a month's time. And if the answer be nay, Elizabeth further promised to never reveal the afternoon's conversation.

Soon after the Earl of Essex did return to England and did take his bride off to his Chartley estates for the consummation of their marriage.

From afar, Lady Hatton watched Frances put her plan into action. The girl denied her husband while passing rumors that he would have none of her. Essex, being a proud man, refused to deny the gossip. Indeed, he kept silent altogether about is wife's strange behavior.

Message after message flew from Frances at Chartley to Elizabeth at Hatton House.

"Pray, find a way, dear Elizabeth, to come to my aid when the time comes. I am sure that you have heard that my beloved Robert may soon be rewarded with an earldom, it is said, of Somerset. I assure you, dear Elizabeth, that as the Countess of Somerset I would be in a position to aid the fortunes of my good friend Lady Hatton."

The inference was clear. As a countess and wife of the king's favorite, Frances could indeed solve many of Lady Hatton's problems.

And problems Elizabeth had, in abundance. Not the least of which was the continuation of the war over property and monies with her husband, Sir Edward Coke; a war that had started on the day of her marriage years before.

On that day, Coke had begun to manipulate her considerable holdings so that they would fall under his control, and Elizabeth herself would be forced to live like a slave to his every whim. Because of this they had rarely lived as man and wife, and Elizabeth had retained the name of her first husband, Sir William Hatton, from spite.

Her uncle, Sir Robert Cecil, had been her protector at court, as well as a shield against Coke. But now the little hunchback—her favorite relative and the only man to have shared the darkest secrets of her life—was dead.

Racked with illness from his long service to Queen Elizabeth, and embittered by the degeneracy and wastefulness of the king he had helped to place on the throne, Cecil had seemed to court death. He had driven himself with work until, during his last week, there had seemed to be nothing left of the already tiny body.

Cecil's funeral had been a travesty. The base and flattering courtiers surrounding King James could hardly wait to place the little hunchback's emaciated body in its marble tomb at Hatfield House before rushing back to London to pluck the plums of government that Cecil had wisely kept from their greedy hands while he lived.

Elizabeth had been the last to leave the little chapel in Hatfield Garden. For hours she had stood by the crypt. For all of the strife there had been between them, for all the heartaches her uncle had caused her in what Cecil had termed his "duty to crown and state," Elizabeth had still loved him more than any other of her blood. Their minds, more often than not, had been as one. Cecil might frequently have used her to gain his ends, but he had never stopped being her buffer and protector at court and her lifeline to influence. But now he was gone.

With Cecil's death, the star of Sir Francis Bacon—Coke's old enemy—had begun to rise. Because Bacon was her husband's rival, Elizabeth often sought his aid and advice. She was uncomfortable around the little man with the ferretlike face and viper's eyes, but *any* man who could stand against Sir Edward Coke was an aid to Elizabeth. Even then, one man, one friend at court, wasn't enough.

The enormity, however, of Frances Howard's request gave her fearful pause. So much so, that months passed and still she sent no answer to Chartley.

> Dear Elizabeth, I beseech you, for the time draws near. Think of yourself, and the marriage—nay, two—that were forced upon you. Think of the many times you have publicly said that never would your own daughter, Brenna, be forced into a marriage not of her own choosing. Think of me, I pray you, as a second daughter, who would but make her own choice. Even my parents are in agreement of this thing I do and have secretly bargained with the king to have Sir Thomas Overbury placed in the Tower to remove his objections to the marriage of dear Robert and myself. . . .

Elizabeth was in turmoil. Even the *king* was involved! And to such an extent that he would have his own favorite's former advisor, Overbury, placed in the Tower so his loud objections to the marriage between Frances Howard and Robert Carr would never be heard!

Ah, Elizabeth thought, *to what lengths we go to curry power and favor, and what we will do to keep them, once attained.*

Overbury knew that his seat of power close to the inept Carr would be usurped by the wily Frances. Thus he railed against her divorce from Essex and her marriage to Carr.

Lady Hatton knew well she could vacillate until she was no longer in a position to give or deny her aid to Frances Howard. Indeed, she intended as much, leaving herself neutral. But her husband, Sir Edward Coke, arrived at Hatton House with yet another petition designed to infuriate her and to deny her rights. Little did Elizabeth then guess how much Coke's visit would influence her eventual decision.

"Madam, I would ask you to be civil enough to at least treat me as a guest. . .if not as a husband!" Coke blustered.

"Sir, you may continue to stand, for I would treat you as neither guest nor husband but as a petitioner! I'm sure the only reason for your presence here is the fact that you want something from me. Now, what is it?"

Fury flashed in Sir Edward's eyes to match the flush that reddened his cheeks. What she said was true, but it always galled him to admit it, even to himself.

Why, Sir Edward thought, could not this shrew be like his sweet first wife, Bridget? She had tended his house, borne his children and kept her peace as a dutiful wife. Not only did Elizabeth not conduct herself with servility, but she had retained her own name upon their marriage and since had refused to live with him.

"Well?" Lady Hatton demanded.

Sir Edward quickly shuffled through the papers he held, and passed a portion of them to her.

One by one, Elizabeth read them over, signed and passed them back. All but one.

"Pray, sir, what is this?"

"A writ, madam," Coke replied, gazing over her head. His concentration was suddenly taken by a tapestry on the far wall of the great hall.

It was a tapestry he had seen a hundred times, and the reason for his sudden interest in it did not escape the Lady Hatton. She was an astute woman who, upon the death of her first husband, had wisely invested and expanded the inheritance left her.

"I see 'tis a writ, Sir Edward, and not a complete one, at that."

His eyes flickered downward for a brief second to the papers remaining in his hand. Then, just as quickly, they snapped back to the wall.

"I would see the rest of it," Elizabeth insisted.

"There is no need. . . ."

"Damme if there is no need, sir!" she rasped, rising and demanding attention from his eyes with her own.

"Od's blood, woman, you are the wife and I am the husband—in fact, if not in deed! 'Tis *I* who will run the family affairs!"

"Not until I know whereof those affairs stray!" she interrupted, matching his tone in volume, with even more steel.

Across the desk they stared at one another: Elizabeth, tight-lipped with an unbending spine, Coke with beard bristling and dark eyes flashing in fury.

In a small corner of her mind Elizabeth viewed the scene dispassionately. Anyone watching them at that moment would have indeed realized how mismatched a pair they were. They had been thrust together out of personal greed on Coke's side and urgent necessity on

Elizabeth's. Coke had long coveted the Hatton holdings but Elizabeth had remained a widow for years after her first husband, Sir Christopher Hatton, had died. And she would have stayed in that state had not fate intervened.

From a wild, tempestuous affair, which had proved to be the one real love of her life, Elizabeth had found herself pregnant. Because marriage to her rebel Irish lover had been impossible, she was forced to choose from among the suitors available.

Coke had been the best of a bad lot.

He was a large gruff man with an abrupt manner and little or no tact. Soon after the marriage, she had discovered a cruel streak in him that bordered on brutality. Often this facet of his character would emerge in towering rages, and he would go so far as to threaten Elizabeth and her household with physical violence.

Standing before her now, his eyebrows furrowed to a dark V over his stormy eyes, Elizabeth reckoned that he was on the verge of such a rage.

"Madam, you are the most insolent—"

"And you, sir, are the most knavish rogue for your total disregard for my wishes in all—"

"You will sign."

"I will not sign until I know to what I am putting my signature."

Their eyes met, still glaring, his a smoky gray, hers an icy emerald green. For a full minute it was an impasse. Then Sir Edward stomped his foot, whirled and stalked to the window. There, with his hands knit tightly at the small of his back, he glared out across the blossoming colors of Hatton Gardens to the open meadows reaching to Turnmill Brook. But he saw no colorful flowers, regal boxwood trees, nor azure blue sky. He saw only a red haze of anger as he tensed the muscles in his big body in an effort to compose himself.

Elizabeth stared at his broad back encased in an inexpensive broadcloth cut in an out-of-date style. She knew his thoughts, for they rarely varied. Sir Edward had married her for her wealth and for the power she could bring him through the Cecil family name. He had scoffed at her willfulness and her independence then, stating that he would be her master just as he had been the master of her predecessor, his first wife, the simple Bridget.

Though they had now been married for seventeen years, he still refused to admit that he had met his match. Often in those years she had wondered, as she wondered now, if her husband was ever lonely. Elizabeth was, though she would never admit it, least of all to this man she had grown to hate and fear.

"Elizabeth?"

"Yes?"

"'Tis a writ for the release of deed to the manor of North Elmeham in Norfolk."

She gasped. "Surely you jest! Elmeham is the only source of personal income you have left me and the basis for Brenna's dowry when the day arrives for her marriage!"

"Other arrangements will be made for the dowry, and I give you my word that your portion from our other properties will be increased."

"Your word, Sir Edward, *your word?*"

"Aye."

"Your word, sir," she replied coldly, "is like your allegiances. . . they sway like the rear end of an ass."

Coke turned and moved back to the desk to face her. This time when he spoke, it was through clenched teeth. "As you know, madam, my appointment as chief justice of the king's bench was a promotion in prestige but quite hollow in funds."

Elizabeth knew well that his previous post, as attorney general, had been much more lucrative. That was why it had been coveted and eventually attained in 1613 by his old enemy, Sir Francis Bacon. Secretly she had urged Bacon on in his battle with her husband.

Now it appeared as though Coke were trying to wreak revenge upon her for his present penury. It gave her second thoughts about her connivances with Bacon.

She chose a different tack.

It was common knowledge that Coke and the king had come to verbal blows over James's divine right to rule. Coke, in his usual tactless way, had said too much, not caring who heard his words.

"Methinks King James a man with a wonderful capacity for doing harm to himself, our country and the law. He considers himself too much the lord of life and death. Witness his first entry into England, when he presumed to have a thief hung without trial."

Not content to merely border on treason, Coke had persisted in openly and blatantly railing against the king's divine right.

King James had replied in kind.

"Mark you well, Sir Edward Coke, it is not lawful to dispute the king's power. The absolute prerogative of the crown is not a fit subject for the tongue of a lawyer, nor is it lawful for our word to be disputed. It is atheism and blasphemy to dispute what God can do. And since our rule is God's will, it is high contempt for a subject such as yourself to dispute what God has deemed the king can do!"

Sir Francis Bacon, now close to James, had used Coke's stubbornness time and time again to lower Coke's prestige with the crown. Now Elizabeth hurled this fact cross the desk at him.

"Had you not been so adamant and so open in your condemnation of the king's proclamation of the right of divine rule, perhaps you would find yourself in better favor at the court and not make yourself so vulnerable to the wily Bacon."

"Elizabeth, my problems with the nefarious gentleman in question is neither here nor there. Because of what has happened, I find our family is in need of further revenues."

"Don't you mean, sir, that *you* are in need of further revenues?"

"We are husband and wife."

"In name only."

"Damme, madam, we may mix like fire and water, but having the law on my side will make *me* the water that will extinguish the fire of your insolence! Now will you sign, or must we again make of ourselves the laughingstock of all London by settling our differences before council!"

Elizabeth planted her hands palms down on the desk before her. "Sir Edward," she said calmly, "in the years of our marriage you have robbed me of the Stoke Poges estates, you have used the revenues from Purbeck for your own ends, you have sold Holdenby out from under me, you continue to provide me with barely enough funds to run Hatton House, and you control revenues from all my other lands. And now you would have me sign away the one thing I can count on for our daughter's future. . . ."

"*Our* daughter, Elizabeth?"

She started to rise in anger, thought better of it and settled back in the chair with a smile on her face. "She bears your name, Sir Edward, and I do think it was the one thing you have given her willingly."

"Then you refuse."

"I will think on it. Good day, Sir Edward."

Elizabeth could swear she saw a smile of satisfaction on his face as he shuffled from the room. He had unnerved her with his reference to the circumstances surrounding Brenna's birth, and he knew it. There was always the threat, unspoken of course, that he would sit the girl down one day and tell her that she was in her mother's belly a full three months before Elizabeth married Edward Coke.

Brenna would be crushed. For all of the disputes and bitterness between her parents, Brenna had been taught by Elizabeth to respect Sir Edward. It would shock and hurt her to know that Coke was not her father. And how would she, Elizabeth, then appear in her daughter's eyes?

Lady Hatton's shoulders shook and her eyes misted at the thought, for Brenna was all the world to her. . . and Elizabeth would not have her hurt no matter the consequence to herself.

But neither would she give in to Sir Edward's latest demands without a fight.

Early the following morning, she took her newest problem to Sir Francis Bacon. Elizabeth didn't completely trust the man, but he was the only person to whom she could turn. She related the bulk of the previous day's conversation with Coke, and the reason for it.

It took two days for Bacon to ferret out the real interest of Sir Edward's writ.

Unknown to Elizabeth, there was a debt owed to the crown on the North Elmeham property. Thinking to eventually wrest the property from Elizabeth through foreclosure, Coke had previously transferred the debt to himself. But now the crown was calling up the note and Coke was without funds to pay. Therefore, in lieu of crown foreclosure and loss of the whole property, he sought to sell it, pay the debt due and, at the same time, hide the illegality of his former act.

Elizabeth was outraged. She went back to Bacon. Wasn't there something she could do?

"My dear Elizabeth, Sir Edward's act was indeed rash and not totally legal, but he is within his rights to do with the property as he sees fit."

"Very well, then," she raged, her anger instantly at the boiling point, "I will take him to Star Chamber. Surely the king's council will see what he has done and find for me!"

"The king's council will see, rightly enough," Sir Francis said, chuckling in the manner that disturbed Elizabeth so much, "but I fear they will find for Sir Edward, anyway. He is the husband, Elizabeth...'tis the law."

"Damn the law!"

Bacon shrugged. "Even I cannot change it."

"But the king could."

"Perhaps...but I doubt that he would."

"Perhaps," Elizabeth stonily replied, "there is someone who could convince him to change it."

When the next missive arrived from Chartley Estates and Frances Howard, begging the Lady Hatton's aid, Elizabeth replied in the affirmative.

Less than a week later, Elizabeth made the short journey down the Thames to Lambeth Palace. With her were three other ladies of the court, chosen by the bishops' board hearing Frances's plea for divorce.

There was one crucial point at issue in Frances's suit—was Frances, the Lady Essex, still a virgin? If upon examination she was, her claim of Essex's impotence would be considered valid and the marriage annulled. Any whispers of Frances's other affairs hopefully would not reach the bishops' ears.

Knowing full well the dangerous ground she tread that day, Elizabeth entered the bedroom that had been set aside for Frances's examination with the three other women.

Minutes later a female figure, gowned entirely in black from her head to her toes, joined them.

"Because I would be so embarrassed to have it any other way," Frances had told the bishops.

Only Elizabeth knew that the girl who was being examined was not Frances Howard but the daughter of Sir Thomas Monson, a staunch ally of the Howard family. It was Elizabeth alone who verified Frances's identity by lifting the heavy dark cambric veil that hid the girl's face.

"'Tis indeed Frances, the Lady Essex," she said, with only the slightest of tremors in her voice.

The girl was then placed on a bed for the rest of the examination. Carefully the heavy skirts were lifted. Her petticoats and other undergarments were removed. Then, when all was in readiness, one by one the four women made their examination and rendered their verdicts.

One hour later Elizabeth, as spokeswoman, entered the great hall of Lambeth Palace on watery knees. The swishing sounds made by her huge skirt seemed to echo loudly in the stillness. She was glad she wore the elbow-length white kid gloves, and she was equally thankful she had chosen a somber gray doublet. She was sure the perspiration was flowing like a small river down her back as well as puddling in her palms.

Her auburn hair was completely covered by a jeweled cap, a stylish *chaperon*, and perched atop it was a small cupcake hat with a veil attached. The veil seemed to dance in front of her face, disturbed continually by her deep breathing. But it did reach her chin and thus hid the way her teeth gnawed at her lower lip.

At last she was standing before the bishops' jury, eight crimson-and-black-robed figures with solemn faces and beady eyes. Elizabeth was positive those eyes could see right through the veil, indeed peer right into her mind and read the truth.

"Lady Hatton."

"M'lords."

"You have examined Frances Howard Devereux, Countess of Essex?"

"We have, m'lords."

"And your determination?"

"We deem her a virgin," she replied.

The eight solemn heads nodded and Elizabeth, breathing a long sigh of relief, turned and walked from the great hall.

At least upon the last I am not lying, she thought. For the girl who was examined had indeed been a virgin!

Three weeks later, Frances's decree of nullity from the Earl of Essex was granted by the bench of bishops on the grounds of her husband's impotence. The following day, Frances and Robert Carr were married with the king's blessing.

But before that, the only voice ringing out against the marriage had been silenced forever. Sir Thomas Overbury, while still incarcerated in the Tower of London, had died of an unknown malady.

THE CLERK'S DRONING VOICE changed to a new tone, jerking Elizabeth's thoughts back to the present. The king's order of justice had been read, and now the clerk was starting on the indictment.

"... that said person, Frances, Countess of Somerset, while still Countess of Essex, did enlist and conspire with persons Elways, Turner and Weston to murder by the administration of poison the knight, Sir Thomas Overbury...."

The clerk read on, but Elizabeth heard little else of what was said. A mist developed in front of her eyes and she thought she might swoon.

Murder.

Had it been murder Elizabeth had seen in Frances's eyes that long ago afternoon at Hatton House?

Frances had indeed enlisted the aid of Mrs. Turner, the necromancer and seller of love potions. She had in turn bribed Elways, the lieutenant of the Tower, and Weston, Sir Thomas Overbury's Tower keeper, to administer the fatal poison.

All three had confessed. They had already been tried and hanged.

Dear God, Elizabeth thought, *how much we depend upon astrologers, necromancers, fortune-tellers and sellers of potions for our worldly ambitions. Nearly as much as we depend on leeches, midwives and nurses for the running of our bodies!*

She wondered again if, on that first afternoon, Frances had already made the pact with Mrs. Turner to still Overbury's tongue with aquafortis, white arsenic, mercury or one of a dozen other delicate potions available to do away with one's enemy.

There had been subtle rumors that the king had used a potion to end the life of his firstborn, Henry, who early on had grown much more popular than James.

The thought made Elizabeth shudder, and again her nervous fingers went to the pearl pendant. What price would she have to pay for that gift and Frances's intercession with the king on her behalf? She, too, had been enlisted by Frances to play a role in this scandal. Would her lie about Frances's virginity be found out during the day's trial? And if so, what would her punishment be?

"Oyez. . .oyez, have the prisoner brought to the bar!"

There was a ripple of muted voices, and then hushed quiet, broken only by a single gasp when the Countess of Somerset appeared in the aisle before the bar.

Frances was led slowly forward by the newly appointed Lieutenant of the Tower, Sir George More. While her steps weren't faltering, her carriage was far from being the confident pose Elizabeth was accustomed to seeing in her.

She was a petite, slim figure in a matching black taminy doublet and skirt. The wrist-length sleeves of her underblouse were less full than the fashion, and unslashed. The dark *chaperon* that completely covered her head was unadorned with lace or jewels. *All a nod to the Puritans among her judges and peers,* Elizabeth thought wryly.

Frances reached the bar and made three low curtsies to the lord high steward, the judges and the peers. Then she stood, her hands folded before her.

Elizabeth gasped and drew her lower lip slightly between her teeth when Frances's eyes rolled upward and met hers for an instant.

There was a muffled sob beside her, and then Brenna's whispered voice. "Oh, mother, she is so beautiful, and she looks so innocent!"

Elizabeth could only nod. It was true. Frances's stark white face staring out from the dark frame of the *chaperon* looked beguilingly innocent. Yet in those large almond eyes, Elizabeth detected the look that had bewitched so many men and caused the vile murder of one.

It was unplanned but ironic that the family seat of Essex was located directly in front of the bar. In that seat now sat the tall trim figure of Frances's former husband. Rather than satisfaction, however, there was melancholy on his handsome features and gloom in his eyes.

What must be in the poor man's mind, Elizabeth wondered, and then gave a start when the lord high steward's voice rang out, loudly addressing the court.

"M'lords, you have been called forth this day to sit as peers in judgment on Frances, Countess of Somerset."

Even louder came the clerk's voice. "Frances, Countess of Somerset, make thyself known!"

Slowly she raised her ungloved hand up, up, until it was high over her head. There was only the slightest of tremors in the long tapering fingers.

Elizabeth heard a wag's muffled whisper from somewhere behind her: "Methinks the winsome bitch shows much confidence for one in such distress!"

Again the indictment was read. Frances's lips began to tremble. A tear squeezed from the corner of one eye and rolled down her cheek. One trembling hand lifted a fan to cover her face.

The clerk finished and the lord high steward stood.

"So stand the charges. Is there anyone present who would add to this tale?"

Elizabeth held her breath. Her heart was pounding so hard beneath her breast that she was sure it could be heard throughout the great hall. Now was the moment when her part in the affair would come out, if it was to be revealed at all.

Her eyes moved to Robert Devereux, Lord Essex. Would he stand and insist that the true facts of his divorce be aired and thereby clear his name and reputation?

Essex sat, immobile, his eyes vacant and unseeing.

"Lord Essex?" said the steward.

Another long pause. Elizabeth felt like screaming to relieve the tension in her taut body.

"Nay, sir," Essex mumbled. "I would remain, as I have before, mute."

Elizabeth sighed in relief. Her shoulders sagged and her head slumped forward.

"Mother, you've torn your kerchief to shreds," Brenna said with some surprise.

"So be it," intoned the steward and regained his seat.

"Frances, Countess of Somerset," the clerk said, "how dost thou plead, guilty or not guilty, to this felony and murder?"

There was a long moment's pause. The scaffolds creaked audibly as everyone leaned forward to hear the lady's whispered, "Guilty, sir."

Elizabeth mopped her damp face with the tattered remnants of her kerchief. So relieved was she that she barely heard her husband, Coke, rise and speak of veiled accusations, that perhaps there was more to this conspiracy than met the eye. Only when she saw Frances's hand raised again, this time to receive sentence, did Elizabeth shake her head and regain some degree of clarity in her mind.

The steward received his white staff of office and leaned forward.

"Frances, Countess of Somerset, whereas thou hast been indicted, arraigned and pleaded guilty, and that thou hast nothing to say for thyself, it is now my duty to pronounce judgment upon thee. . . ."

All eyes turned upon the timid white face of the woman at the bar.

"You shall be carried from hence to the Tower of London. From there you shall be carried to the place of execution, where you shall be hanged by the neck until you be dead. Frances, Countess of Somerset, may God have mercy upon your soul."

Beside her mother, Brenna was openly weeping, the tears of pity running in tiny rivers down her cheeks.

How you would weep, my little darling, Elizabeth thought, *if you knew the full of it.*

CHAPTER FOUR
FRANCE

THE NIGHT OUTSIDE FONTEVRAULT ABBEY was alive with the chirp of crickets and the scurrying sound of small furry animals. Rory, The O'Donnell, stood silhouetted in a high window staring down at the marshy lowlands and stunted trees of this land that, to him, was so foreign.

Even though it pained him to do so, he couldn't help but compare this place he now called home to the Ireland he loved. Though it could never be, and O'Donnell knew it, he longed to smell the fresh scent of spring heather and let his eyes again drink in the emerald brightness of the Irish lowlands or the bogs, brown with windblown grasses. He yearned to stand atop the keep of Donegal Castle with the ocean wind in his face and gaze down the ragged cliffs to Donegal Bay.

How long had it been.... Eight?...no, nine. Nine long years since the flight. Rory O'Donnell could still close his eyes and bring it all back as though the memory were but a day old. Standing beside The O'Neill on the gunwale, the ship slowly sailing outward from Lough Swilly, the multicolored cliffs of Malin Head disappearing in the mists.

And the old earl's words, said through trembling lips with tears in his weary eyes. "Oh, my Ireland, tonight you are a desolate land. If there is a God, let him keep faith with you and one day bring back your sons."

O'Donnell had turned away that night. His thoughts then had been only on the fruitlessness of this rebellion and the total loss of everything they had owned upon their defeat.

But in the years since, The O'Neill's words had constantly returned until they were burned into his memory: "one day bring back your sons."

Now there were precious few sons left to return. Maguire and most of his kin were dead in Geneva. Sullivan had been assassinated in Rome, probably by the same agents from Dublin Castle who had stabbed Cahir O'Dogherty to death in Ireland before he could flee.

Nearly all the clan leaders from before the earls' flight, from the wars of rebellion with Queen Elizabeth's England, were dead now. And those that weren't were like O'Donnell, too old and broken to make rebellion again. Rory O'Donnell was forty-seven now, but his flesh bore the scars and his bones the ache of twice that time.

And the great O'Neill, the genius himself who had come the closest of all to pushing the English back across the bitter Irish Sea, was gone. O'Neill, the only man who had been able to unite most of the warring Irish clans into one to fight the common enemy, England.

Would it ever happen again? Would there ever be another O'Neill to step into the breach and heal the Irish wound?

O'Donnell blinked back a tear, surprised that he could still create one. The O'Neill, old, blind, weary of war and life and all but alone, had finally succumbed. Within two days, his last son had also died of the fever. O'Donnell himself had buried them in Rome.

There had been the proper condolences from the King of Spain; an emissary brought the papal blessing from Pope Paul V; and there had been due pomp and circumstance for the interment of the man who had nearly saved Ireland for the true faith against the English Protestants.

Much of it had disgusted O'Donnell. They had acclaimed and martyred O'Neill in death, but in life they had forsaken him when they hadn't sent the arms and men he had needed so desperately. Instead, they had waited until he was defeated and then granted him small pensions for his support. At his death they had salved their own consciences with eulogies to his greatness.

"Let my bones rest one day in the sod of Ireland!"

They had been the old soldier's last words as he lay dying, clutching the tiny pouch containing a bit of Irish soil and pebbles from the O'Neill clan coronation stone at Tullaghogue, the stone that had been battered into nothingness by the hammers of Lord Mountjoy's English soldiers.

O'Donnell wondered if he would ever be able to keep his promise to O'Neill. He doubted it. But there might be one, some day, who could, one of those sons O'Neill had begged God to help return him to his homeland.

A door creaked open behind him and then closed again. O'Donnell didn't turn. He knew who it was. Vespers had just ended and Sister Anna had climbed the stairs, as she did every night, to join O'Donnell in her study for a glass of light wine and conversation.

He heard the top being removed from the decanter and then the gurgling sound of the wine as she poured.

"It smells like rain. There's a bit of a chill in the air," he said.

"All the more reason you shouldn't stand at an open window taking so much of the night air!"

O'Donnell smiled. He had spoken in French but she had replied in Gaelic. Her native tongue was English, and she had acquired the Gaelic in Ireland, but she had learned Latin as well as French before taking her vows. O'Donnell wondered if she ever confused her languages when she prayed.

God knows she prays enough to use all four languages, he thought.

Suddenly, as if her words about the chill night air had prompted it, O'Donnell's tall lean frame exploded in racking coughs. Sister Anna's tiny black-clad form was at his side in an instant, closing both shutters and tugging him toward the fire.

"I told you," she rasped.

"'Tis momentary. . ." he replied.

"'Tis not momentary," she said. "Methinks you've caught a touch of the Roman fever yourself!"

Before letting him sit, she plucked a velvet mantle from the chair behind her and lovingly wrapped it around his shoulders. Her hands lingered for a time on the worn fur of the collar and the nearly smooth velvet covering his shoulder.

"You should let me have the sisters build you a new mantle," she said. "'Tis near tatters, this one."

"Aye, 'tis, and well it should be," he replied somewhat gruffly.

"Then—"

"Nay. 'Tis the mantle of The O'Donnell and it looks as it should, tattered and rent, like the clan it signifies. 'Twas worn by my father and my brother before me, and since there will be none to pass it on, I'll wear it till I die. It will make my bones a kindly shroud."

The tiny hand on his shoulder clenched and then went to her breast. "Sure an' 'tis not the wild, fighting O'Donnell I once knew who sits here now with his only talk that of dyin'!"

He looked up, his dark eyes meeting the clarity of hers. And, for just a moment, the years disappeared. Briefly they were both young and full of life and fight again, full of hatred of the English. They were once again in the great hall of O'Neill's Dungannon Castle, before a much larger fireplace than this, and little Annie Carey was offering herself to him in lieu of the love he had lost.

"You'll not speak more of it. . . this dyin'," she said, her elfin, ageless face peering down at him. "Promise me!"

"I promise, little Annie," he replied, letting some of the old O'Donnell creep into the grin that spread his leathery features.

Her face colored and she quickly turned to fetch the wine. Only O'Donnell would have the temerity to use her given name now. Every time he did it, memories washed over her, not all of them bad but not in tune with the cowl she now wore and her marriage to her Christ.

"Here," she said, handing him the wine. "Warm your belly with this. It'll help your chest as well."

"I would have some good Irish uisquebaugh instead!" he protested.

"Aye, I'm sure you would," she said, and chuckled to herself as she wadded her huge black skirts into the chair opposite his. Raising her glass, she said, "To m'Lady Deirdre."

"And to her male offspring, whom I shall flail to within an inch of his life if he isn't here within the hour."

Sister Anna made a wry, tight-lipped face and crossed herself before sipping the wine.

O'Donnell watched the glass lower from her lips and studied her face in the firelight. There was still some of the same fire in her eyes that he had recognized when he had first met her in a Southwark tavern across the

Thames from London town so many years before. She had been a thirteen-year-old waif of the streets then and a mistress of the highwayman, Ned Bull.

Dear Ned had died because of his loyalty to Rory O'Donnell. But Annie Carey had survived and had fought the English at O'Donnell's side. How things changed. Her hatred had disappeared. She had adopted the religion of the mistress she had loved, the Lady Deirdre, and had taken vows. Now, instead of a wild young rebel, she was about to become the abbess of Fontevrault.

Rory O'Donnell thanked God in many ways for that. He had promised Ned before the man's trip to Tyburn Tree gallows that he would care for Annie and see that she was safe. Now she was not only safe but serene and happy.

He couldn't suppress a quiet laugh.

"What?"

"Thinking," he replied. "I couldn't help wondering what Ned would be thinking from up there if he's looking down on his little Annie about to be an abbess."

"I think he would be proud."

"Aye," O'Donnell nodded, matching the calm tremor in her voice, "I think he would."

They sat for a time staring into the fire before O'Donnell spoke again. "Think you The O'Hara will take the latest news from England to heart?"

"I think little of what your wild godson does and know less what he will do now that the time has come to claim his right."

O'Donnell shook his head and muttered in a low voice, "Would that Shanna had been born Rory, and Rory, Shanna."

"What?"

Louder, he replied, "Methinks if it came to Shanna, this recent news, the lass would be off to Calais and London in the twinkling of an eye. 'Tis Rory who has become so Frenchified that he's lost the fever of Ireland in his blood!"

"Perhaps, O'Donnell, 'tis better that he stay in France and make his life."

"In the service of the Italian bastard?" he raged, and came up short when he saw Annie's eyes flash scorn in his direction. "Your pardon. . . sister."

" 'Twas you, O'Donnell," she said, her voice plaintive now, for she hated to see the rift that had arisen between these two men she cared for so much. "Yes, it was you who spoke to Richelieu and convinced him of Rory's worth. It was through you he went to Navarre and learned soldiering."

" 'Tis an honorable trade," O'Donnell shrugged.

"Then if Richelieu placed him in Concini's guardsmen, 'tis partially your fault he's found a home there."

"Aye, I know. But I wanted him to learn at Navarre so one day he could fight for his birthright and Ireland. Now I've rued the day I brought him from Italy, for I've created a swaggering popinjay with a plume covering his loss of brain! I should have sent him to Spain. Even now, Owen Roe O'Neill distinguishes himself in the Spanish army. He would soon be a general, and he's but a year Rory's senior. And what does the owner of The O'Hara mantle do? He—"

Again O'Donnell gasped and broke into a cough that threatened to unseat him. A hurried rustle of skirts and his hand held a fresh glass of wine. He let the cough run its course and then soothed the burning pain in his throat and chest with the wine.

"You do have a fever," Sister Anna stated, concern and anxiety apparent in her voice.

"A touch," he said, waving her back to her chair and returning his eyes to the fire.

A knot of remorse balled in his belly and threatened to rise. He checked it with more wine and let his free hand fumble at the laces of his shirt beneath the heavy mantle. He found the locket and furrowed his weary brows into a straight line of concentration.

It was a habit. Merely touching the locket seemed to help him think.

They said Gaelic Ireland was broken and doomed. English plantationers, the so-called "undertakers," had flocked to the north of Erin after the flight. Proclamations had begun to fly the moment word had reached London that the earls of Ulster had left their native soil. Since then, plantationing had begun with a vengeance. Nearly all the lands in the counties of Armagh, Tyrone, Coleraine, Donegal, Fermanagh and Cavan had been escheated to men deemed civil and well effected in religion by the English Crown and Dublin Castle.

O'Donnell's own lands of Donegal, even his beloved Donegal Castle, had passed by crown order into the hands of one Sir Basil Brooke.

"A bloody Englishman, a sassenach, striding the ramparts of Donegal!"

"What?" Sister Anna queried.

"I—nothing," O'Donnell replied, thinking how often he talked aloud to himself of late.

His eyes returned to the fire, and his mind to Ireland. Now, with The O'Neill dead, was it all over? Now, after the fierce wars of more than four hundred years' duration, from the time of Richard de Clare, called Strongbow who began the English conquest, were Ireland and her people at last reduced completely to the station of vassals to the English Crown? Would there ever again be a movement for independence?

Perhaps not. But if not, at least one Irishman could claim his birthright and inherit something from the shambles of what once was.

"Damme, and he will!" O'Donnell thought aloud again.

"Who will?"

"Our Rory. . . uh, I was thinking aloud."

"I see," Sister Anna said, drawing a look from O'Donnell by the tone of her voice.

She was looking directly at the locket in his fingers. Without realizing it, O'Donnell had snapped it open.

"She would be a young lady now."

"Aye, just seventeen," he replied, wistfulness in his voice as he looked down at the miniature portraits the locket held. Suddenly his eyes looked back up to meet Sister Anna's. He felt a momentary flush of embarrassment at the fact that she had read his emotions so well.

"Do you think of her often?"

It was not Sister Anna talking now, but Annie Carey who knew all and spoke of it as a friend.

"Aye," he replied, his eyes wandering again to the miniature of the auburn-haired beauty with her wide emerald eyes and the little raven-haired girl who looked so much like himself that he could still gasp at the likeness. "More than I should, probably."

"I'll wager she's a beauty."

"She was, even as a child. I can't forget that last meeting at Holdenby. I looked at her and saw Elizabeth, and yet still saw myself."

"'Tis the wonder of birth and blood."

"Aye." He heard her chuckle and again felt embarrassment at his maudlin tone. "And nuns don't wager."

"'Tis a habit I've never been able to lose," she said, grinning and again raising her glass. "In God's eyes true love isn't a sin. To the Lady Hatton and your daughter."

O'Donnell nodded and raised his glass as well. "Aye, I hope the lass finds what her mother missed. To Brenna Coke—would that I could call her O'Donnell."

CHAPTER FIVE

ARMAND DE RICHELIEU DREW THE PURPLE FOLDS of his bishop's robes closer around his thin body as he paced. With an effort he managed to blink away the pain that throbbed behind his eyes. Even though it was a warm evening and the air inside his quarters above the Rue des Mauvaises-Paroles was close, Richelieu felt a chill, caused by a recurring fever he had contracted as a youth from the damp marshes around his native Poitou.

The throbbing headaches had grown worse with each year. Such constant pain would have driven a lesser man to his bed, but the Bishop of Luçon chose to ignore it. Richelieu was a man with a mission, and the pursuance of that mission left no time for rest or self-pity.

"The news you bring weighs heavily." The bishop's voice was majestically sonorous as he turned and addressed the darkly clad man near the open window. "How certain are you of its truth?"

"Sure enough to bring it across the Channel myself rather than trust a messenger," the man replied. "The tongues of our noble courtiers in London grow exceedingly loose the moment they seat themselves at a gaming table. Believe me, Armand, 'tis a fact I tell you."

The man's French was excellent, marred only slightly by the burr of his native Scots brogue.

Richelieu's noble face fell and the nostrils in the prowlike nose twitched. "So James would further his alliance with Spain through marriage, much as our stupid Queen Mother Marie de Médicis has done."

The man by the window chuckled. "'Tis a pity the Spanish kings are so fertile. They breed infantas like rabbits—one for France, and now another takes her place in the marriage market."

Richelieu's dark, all-seeing eyes probed the darkness but failed to find those of his guest. "I'm sorry I cannot share your mirth. Because of de Médicis's foolishness, Spain is a greater yoke around our neck in the south. The Hapsburgs surround us to the north. Should England solve her problems with Spain, I fear France would be in a vise for the next fifty years."

"And that is why I would be out of it," the man replied, moving into the room to stand at Richelieu's shoulder. "Five years now I have been your ears across the Channel, Armand. My debt is paid. I would be released and claim what is mine."

"You stopped at Poitou on your way to Paris?"

"Aye."

"And spoke to the child?"

"Aye."

Richelieu sighed. "I should never have agreed to let you see her in the first place."

"But you did, and the bond is cemented between us."

"And will you care for her growth into womanhood, rake and gambler that you are?" the bishop challenged.

"No, I have plans."

"To do what?" Richelieu replied, purposely letting a harsh note of cynicism creep into his voice.

The man leaned down until Richelieu could smell the drink on his breath. "To remove myself from these intrigues for power. I know you, Armand, for I have been like you, cunning and treacherous, and I would have no more of it."

The bishop's stern face broke into a rare smile. "I think you would wither and die, away from what you call these petty intrigues. But 'tis true, you have kept your part of the bargain, and I will keep mine. So be it. I ask but one thing."

"What is it?"

"That you continue as you are until I can find a suitable replacement."

"You mean until someone else falls into your web and has no choice but to do your bidding."

The thin shoulders in the purple robe shrugged and a long-fingered hand brushed the air. "What appears to you as the manipulation of men, yea, even unfeeling cruelty in my person, is a necessity of rule. Men are not managed by kindness any more than great states are created by weaklings."

Richelieu's words were greeted by a mirthless, sardonic laugh. "And so speaks the purveyor of Christianity!"

"Aye, I do. But, like Machiavelli, I believe Christ's ethics alone will not create a strong state. And, with God's help, France will be strong!"

"Then by God it will be so without me, for I've served you and France long enough. Now I will serve myself!"

"So be it," Richelieu repeated, raising his long, tapered fingers and applying their tips to his burning eyes.

Ever since he had first begun his service to the state, Richelieu had found many men, much like the one who stood before him now, to serve as his eyes and ears abroad.

With the information they gave him, the bishop had been able to follow in the wake of Concini's foolishness and repair many of the marshal's mistakes in foreign policy.

How much longer could he do it?

Through flattery and a deft manipulation of underlings in the Queen Mother's retinue, Richelieu continued to hold Marie de Médicis's favor. In the same manner, inroads had also been made with Leonora Concini.

But there was no breaching the power of the marshal himself. Concini's self-esteem and conceit now knew no bounds, and he had come to think of himself as king, in fact if not in name.

The bishop sighed, now using his delicate fingers to massage his throbbing temples.

Time, he thought. *Given enough time perhaps Concini will bring about his own downfall.* Meanwhile,

Richelieu knew that it was he alone who was keeping the fabric of France together. And he was doing it with the help of men like this Scotsman who had insinuated himself into the English court.

A trick of fate had given Richelieu a hold over the Scot. Years before, there had been a foolish love affair between the man and a young novitiate in the Abbey of Poitou. By the time the girl had found herself with child, her lover had been recalled to Ireland and his regiment.

The issue had been a girl child. Immediately after the birth, the mother had fallen into a frightful state of depression. Daily the weight of her sin had drawn her closer and closer to a state of madness. Thankfully, her soul had deserted her body before her mind was completely lost.

It was Richelieu's own mother who had cared for the child and named her Aileen, and Richelieu himself who had carefully conveyed the news to the child's father when he had sent for his former love. The Scot by this time had forsaken the English army and established himself in London.

Richelieu's estimate of the Scotsman's character proved correct. Upon hearing the news of his lover's death and the existence of a daughter, the Scot had rushed to Poitou.

It wasn't for naught that Pope Paul V had predicted that young Armand de Richelieu would one day make a fine scoundrel.

"'Tis grievous, this thing you have done," Richelieu had said. "And now you would have me hand over its issue into your care? Impossible! Unless... You will serve the church and France through me for five years' time. Then and only then shall I give you the opportunity to claim the child—and only if she so chooses."

The Scot had agreed to the pact. He could do little else.

And now the five years had passed. A pity, Richelieu thought, for the man had proved to be an uncommonly good spy.

But already Richelieu had a replacement in mind. That is, if O'Donnell could convince his headstrong nephew, Rory O'Hara, to leave France's shores.

CHAPTER SIX

OUTSIDE IT HAD BEGUN TO RAIN. In the distance there was an occasional roll of thunder, and through the partially opened shutters water could be heard rolling down over the stones of the old abbey walls.

Inside, the tension was as heavy as the silence between the room's three occupants.

Shanna sat stiffly at the table, still wearing her dark-blue velvet riding costume. Her cloak, of the same material and color, was draped near the fire over a chair that had been vacated by Sister Anna when they had arrived. The cloak steamed slightly as it dried, for they had ridden the last mile in the rain.

Her hands nervously twisted the velvet-and-satin riding mask they held. Her gaze was uneasy but intent as she stared at her brother across the table.

Rory stood leaning forward with his palms flat on the plank table top. His gaze danced back and forth across the documents before him, and as he read and absorbed their content, the scowl on his dark face grew in intensity.

It had been a hard four-day ride from Paris. After René had secured them horses outside the city and Rory had received leave permission, they had left immediately. During those four days they had barely stopped for food and sleep, much less a barber. Consequently, a heavy black stubble lined Rory's cheeks and jawline. The effect of the dim candlelight wavering across his stern features made Shanna feel that inside him a storm was brewing.

O'Donnell sat silently by the fire, still wrapped in his mantle. Now and then his eyes flickered up to appraise one or both of his godchildren.

The hard lines in his leathery, weather-beaten face softened as he admired Shanna. *How beautiful a woman she has become,* he thought, taking in the girl's high cheekbones and softly violet eyes. The dampness had made her shining hair a crown of black curls. As they cascaded down the sides of her face, the blackness seemed to frame her features like a madonna.

As Rory shifted his weight and coughed slightly, O'Donnell's eyes moved from Shanna across the table to her brother. The seriousness on the young man's face and the way he stood, feet wide apart, his cape draped rakishly over one shoulder, made O'Donnell shake his head and blink.

With Irish dress and a full month's growth of heavy beard, it could be The O'Hara, Shane, standing there. The younger O'Hara's facial features were slightly softened—a legacy from his mother—but still square and rugged. It was his body—stocky, powerful, with wide shoulders and a barrellike chest—that was like Shane, and Shane alone.

Like his father before him, Rory had grown into a dark, lusty stallion of a man. A man, O'Donnell thought, who could take a stand with any man...if he would.

"How long?" Rory said, gathering the papers in his huge hands and moving to the end of the table. He sat on its edge in such a way that he could see his sister as well as O'Donnell.

"What?"

"How long have you had these?" Rory shuffled the papers in O'Donnell's direction.

"Years," O'Donnell sighed.

"And you never mentioned them?"

"There was no need—until now."

Rory dropped the papers to the table's plank top and raised his hands to his head. Gently he rubbed his eyes and then his temples, as if the friction of his own fingers could clarify his thoughts and miraculously give him a better understanding of what he had just read.

Robert Cecil, Earl of Salisbury—and, if legend were true, anti-Irish, anti-Catholic and an enemy of O'Donnell, O'Hara and O'Neill—had paved the way for the O'Hara heir, Rory, to gain his birthright.

"Evidently my mind is thick," Rory said at last. "Why would Cecil, before his death, draw up documents that would one day restore my grandfather's lands in England and my father's lands in Ireland to me?"

Shanna gasped at those words, stood, and flew to O'Donnell's side. As yet she hadn't read the papers, and now, knowing what they contained, she was filled with joy and anticipation.

"Oh, papa, is it true? Is it really true?"

O'Donnell smiled at the sudden rush of excitement in her face. "Would you like again to be Shanna O'Hara of Ballylee instead of Chinon?"

"You know that I would," she said decisively, and swept her glance back over her shoulder toward her brother.

Rory waved her to the chair across from O'Donnell and moved himself to stand with his backside to the fire.

"Well?"

O'Donnell met Rory's gaze and shrugged his shoulders inside the heavy mantle. "I've told you of Cecil's deviousness, his cunning and his unquestioned power after the death of his father, Lord Burghley, First Secretary to Queen Elizabeth."

"Aye, many times." There was a slight edge of boredom in Rory's voice that brought a darting flash of scorn from his sister's eyes.

O'Donnell continued, his voice almost wistful. "Cecil was a strange, deformed little man with a brilliant mind. Our friend here in France now, Armand de Richelieu, reminds me a great deal of Robert Cecil. Richelieu, as you know, is not above any betrayal to gain his objectives. He has no shame nor conscience when it comes to accumulating power. Robert Cecil was of the same mold, but as Richelieu is now, Cecil was a lonely man and did in the end try to rectify some of the harm he had inflicted on others. Though I hated him, I have come to call Cecil friend."

"I could call no man friend who was ever my enemy!" Rory growled.

"Nor could any other youth," O'Donnell intoned.

The two men's eyes met. Neither blinked. For years these two wills had been at loggerheads, unable to see past the framework of personal beliefs, beliefs that had grown into an impregnable wall between them.

At last O'Donnell nodded and broke the silence. "But I digress."

"You do," Rory agreed.

A brief flash of anger shone in O'Donnell's eyes at the younger man's impertinence, but he pushed it aside and continued to explain, at his own pace and in his own way.

"Cecil wanted peace. He wanted conciliation with Ireland rather than war. He went to any lengths to achieve it."

Here O'Donnell smiled wryly and fingered the locket at his chest. *Any lengths indeed,* he thought, *even throwing his married niece into my arms to gain his and England's ends.* But how could Cecil have known that Elizabeth and O'Donnell would fall so deeply in love, or that the result of that love would be a beautiful girl child. And how could Cecil have known that, just as he had put them together, he would, in the interests of his queen and country, have to force the two lovers apart forever?

But that personal part of O'Donnell's life was his secret; his and Elizabeth's, and the dead Cecil. It wasn't necessary for Rory O'Hara to know of it.

He sighed and looked again into his godson's scowling face. "Enough to say that Cecil felt he had done us all—myself, you and Shanna—a grave wrong. Perhaps this was his way of repairing that wrong. After Lord Haskins died, it would have been impossible because of your youth to fight for your grandfather's lands and title. That was why I spirited the both of you, with Cecil's help, out of England.

"When the Haskins lands and Ballylee in Ireland went to the crown and in turn were given to King James's favorite, Robert Carr, Cecil must have seen a way to right some of his wrongs to us. Thus, those documents."

Rory's frown turned into a look of puzzlement. He retrieved the papers and talked as he perused them yet a second time. "I fear I still don't understand. This is a right of forfeiture from the crown to me should the lands of Haskins and the barony of Ballylee ever be lost to Carr."

"Exactly," O'Donnell nodded.

"How in God's name did Cecil get James to put his signature to such a paper?"

"I can only guess 'twas done by sheer cunning," O'Donnell replied, chuckling. "In those days James would rather hunt, muddle himself with strong drink and dally with his favorites than attend to state matters. During one of those times, I imagine, Cecil slipped those documents in with more important state papers to be signed."

"Still—" Rory shrugged, again ridding himself of the papers "—there's nothing for it. 'Tis well known that Robert Carr is firmly entrenched as favorite to the spindly-legged James."

O'Donnell slowly turned his body in the chair to face Rory. "Not is—was. Robert Carr, Earl of Somerset, and his countess were convicted of murder by a jury of their peers a fortnight ago. They were saved from death by the king's grace, but all their lands save one—a manor at Cheswick—were stripped from them."

Shanna gasped and leaped to her feet. "That means that by the king's own hand our lands are ours again!"

"I think not, sister, for James is a greedy and spendthrift king. He'll want Haskins House and the wealthy lands around it for his own." In disgust, Rory poured brandy into a silver goblet and made to rise.

With his bones aching from so long in the chair, O'Donnell lurched to his feet and moved to block Rory's movement.

"Aye, that's right, lad. Already there is word that the lands will be given to the new favorite, George Villiers."

"There you are," Rory shrugged.

"The Haskins lands, lad, don't you see?" O'Donnell growled, the strain in his voice showing in his face. "But not Ballylee! By the king's own hand you can once again be Baron of Ballylee! You've not a price on your head like the rest of us. You were but a child when the last troubles ended. You and Shanna can go back to Ireland. . . back to your own lands!"

The following silence was awkward, with the two men staring straight at each other. Rory's face was troubled, a little sad. O'Donnell's was full of light, his eyes radiating a look of pleading mixed with joy, hopeful that one of Ireland's sons would return to his home.

Rory's thoughts were of a different nature. He knew the plight of those titled native Irish who had stayed on their lands. Daily they feared confiscation from unscrupulous crown representatives. And even those who had professed loyalty to James were practically taxed into a state of serfdom.

Ulster, like all Ireland now, was fragmented into unequal groups of power. There were the Old English, still Catholic but loyal to the crown, now reduced to the status of tenant servants on their own lands. The New Irish, made up of Scottish and Irish Protestants, were willing to do anything, even change their religion, to share in the spoils of Irish land.

And the only group with real power, the New English, the Protestants, were undertakers who would turn green Ireland black under the plow, rape her forests until the land was bare and use any loophole in the law to gain power and ensure Irish servitude.

Where, Rory thought, would he fit in if he returned to Ireland? He knew naught of the law to outwit the English scoundrels, and he had no taste for servitude if he failed.

Shanna broke the silence. She moved to her brother and threw her arms around his broad shoulders. When she looked up into his face there were tears in her eyes. "Rory, oh, Rory, don't you see? It's come at last, what we've dreamed of—we can go back to Ballylee!"

"Can we, Shanna?" his voice rumbled.

The tone in his voice, the look in his eyes, spoke the unspeakable. She flung her arms from him and stepped back. "Yes! You heard The O'Donnell—"

"'Tis true, Rory," O'Donnell urged. "Haskins House may be lost, yes, but by the laws of the land he governs, James must abide by what he has writ. He must give you back Ballylee—and the bulk of ten thousand acres in the bargain."

"Ballylee—home," Shanna cried.

Rory's gaze hadn't left his sister's eyes. "Methinks, dear sister, that for all your reading and your time at court and in Paris, you still have been too long in a convent to see truly the ways of the world."

"And you were too long in Italy!" she angrily retorted, not understanding his words. "And too long now in Paris, dancing the pavane and playing the cavalier!"

"Shanna," Rory said, his voice calm, "even if

James were to honor these papers, if he were to give me the barony of Ballylee, which by law is mine, to attain it I would have to pledge the oath of supremacy to claim."

Shanna's hands balled into fists as a tiny, painful gasp escaped her lips. "Oh, no," she said, whirling on O'Donnell. " 'Tis not true."

O'Donnell only nodded. "I fear 'tis true, lass. Rory would have to become a Protestant. He would have to throw off the religion of our fathers and adopt the English church of Ireland."

"And what does my arch-Catholic, convent-raised sister say to that?"

The fear in Shanna's eyes and the pain on her face faded away, and in its place there appeared tight-lipped resolution. Neither man was prepared for her reply. "I think of myself as Catholic by baptism and French by cultural background. But by desire and birth I am Irish."

Rory could only stare in awe, unable to believe his ears. "Shanna, you mean you would—"

"Even the former king of France, Henry IV, changed religions as he did clothes. He was raised a Protestant—that helped him gain part of a kingdom, and he became a Catholic to get it all. When besieging Paris, it is said that he turned to his mistress and remarked, 'Paris, Mademoiselle Gabrielle, is surely worth a Mass!' "

The men exchanged quick glances. Rory looked away first and studied the silver goblet rolling between his huge hands. "Sister Anna should hear your heresy."

" 'Tis not heresy!" Shanna barked, her hands on her hips now, her face full of fire. "What is heresy? One man insists his religion is the only religion. Another of a different faith says the same. I say Lutherans, Huguenots, Protestants, Catholics are all names...tags. Be done with them all and let us all be Christians. And I would be a Christian in Ireland!"

"Damme, woman, your mind shifts like the wind."

"Mayhap. But like the philosopher Montaigne, I think I change my opinions with my years."

"Well, philosopher I am not," Rory retorted. "Nor am I poet, scholar or politician. I am but a soldier and understand damn little beyond my sword."

His voice was rough and his knuckles, where they gripped the wine goblet, were white. Suddenly he whirled. His boots echoed in the room as he stomped to the window. He wrenched open the shutters and let the rain pelt his face. A sharp gust of wind made the room's candles flicker eerily. The shadows they cast upon Rory's broad back gave him the appearance of an ogre about to fly into the dark night.

"I've not learned to plead nor speechify," he said, his voice more controlled now. "Nor do I politic well. And I've no knowledge to husband the land. 'Twas you, O'Donnell, and Richelieu, who put me in the academy at Navarre. There I learned the gentle arts of musketry, artillery fire, horsemanship and fencing. I learned to kill as well as the next man. I am a soldier; 'tis all I know."

"Aye, that you are," O'Donnell replied, his voice low, matching Rory's. "But I would have you be a soldier of Ireland. I would have you fight for your own land and yourself rather than a fat Italian thief."

"Concini will be gone one day."

"Aye," O'Donnell said, "and then where will you be?"

Rory turned. "'Tis yourself who has said that when that day comes Richelieu will step in. The guardsmen will be his and I'll get a generalship."

O'Donnell winced noticeably, for he knew the truth in Rory's words. He tried a different tack, again letting the pleading tone creep into his voice. "Rory, lad, 'tis for yourself I'm thinking. Some of the Irish chiefs have received re-grants from the Crown. You could take your place among them. . . ."

"Is that what you would have for me? A few sheep to herd, a bit of land to till, a sullen wench when I'm too tired to drag myself from a forest booley house? That is what you would desire for The O'Hara?"

"I think it better than the fat life you have here," O'Donnell rasped, his anger beginning to seethe. "There are men in Ulster even now waiting for another leader, another O'Neill."

"Aye," came Rory's thundering reply, "and they'll wait till the Pope marries before they'll get one! Where are the O'Haras of Ballyhara, my distant cousins? Are they proud landowners on the plains of Antrim? Nay, they are wretches struggling between the Presbyterian Scots and the Protestant English for survival."

"But, damme, they struggle!" O'Donnell roared back, unable now to keep his wrath in check. "Would you have James turn all of Ulster into a playground for his fellow Scots, with not a strong Irishman to say them nay?"

"Aye, that I would, and they can use Ballylee for their sewer for all I care!"

Shanna and Rory were both surprised at the speed of the older man's movement. He stepped forward and swung his arm in a wide arc. The blow from the flat of his hand against Rory's cheek was like a thunderclap in the room. The younger man's head snapped around and his big body crashed against the window casement. With an animallike growl, Rory bounded back. He raised his arm above O'Donnell to strike. O'Donnell didn't flinch or move, even though he knew that in that arm was the power to fell an ox.

Shanna knew it as well. She hurled herself between them and, screaming her brother's name, threw her full weight on Rory's upraised arm.

"Would you strike down *all* that is dear to you?"

Slowly the tenseness flowed from Rory's arm and then from his body. Shanna released him and stepped back. Tears streamed down her cheeks and the tension of the moment reverberated through her body. Calm replaced the anger in Rory's face, and then he brushed by them both, stomping toward the door. He flung it open, but before he could exit, O'Donnell's voice stopped him.

"There was a time, lad, when we Gaels were famous eaters of meat. A time when we stood on our own castle keeps and fed from our own land. . . a land that grew proud men with big bones and comely, round-bosomed women."

"Aye," Rory replied, his voice flat and toneless, "even now every village in Ireland has its castle and keep—and they're all in ruins." He partially turned, fixing the twin coals of his eyes on O'Donnell. "And as for my bones, I think they are as big as yours once were and my sinews as lusty."

So saying, he raised the silver goblet he still held. The muscles in his arm tensed and the goblet melted in his fist. "I'll not to Ireland and I'll not to England. I'll be for Paris with dawn's first light." The goblet struck the stone floor with a hollow, clanking sound, and he was gone.

"By God's blood," Shanna rasped, "were I only a man!"

CHAPTER SEVEN
ENGLAND

THROUGH THE SUMMER OF 1616 the Whitehall government stumbled along in mindless luxury. Fueled by graft, corruption and petty subterfuges, the court of King James I seemed blind to any happenings beyond the palace walls.

The poet and playwright William Shakespeare had died and was buried at Stratford. All London watched as Sir Walter Raleigh's flagship, *Destiny*, was being readied for his expedition to the golden city of El Dorado.

By fall, the Somerset trial and its aftermath was still on everyone's lips. Robert Carr was a broken man. But many thought that London had not seen the last of his wife, Frances. She was still a young and beautiful woman, and it was gossiped that the boredom of house arrest at Cheswick would soon become more than she could bear.

With the Earl of Somerset and his wife exiled from London and the court, Sir George Villiers had quickly moved into the void. Villiers made himself indispensable to the king, both in and out of the bedchamber, and was amply rewarded for it. Already he had been made a viscount, and there was a dukedom in the offing.

To many in the government Villiers was like a fresh breeze, a relief after the arrogance of Somerset. But as his power spread and the stream of applicants and ambitious men flowed toward him, another facet of his character emerged. He became more and more capricious in his dealings. More than one who had counted Villiers as friend experienced the wrath of that saturnine face when its owner would suddenly turn on them for little or no reason and, with a single word to the king, ruin them.

From these actions a few sensed storm warnings on the horizon. Queen Anne herself was one and declared it openly. The queen, who had been no friend to Somerset, saw an even worse advisor in the young viscount. "Mark ye my word, this young man will prove far more intolerable in time than any that have gone before him."

The Villiers family—the grasping Lady Compton, her other sons and their ambitious cousins—lost no time in capitalizing on their good fortune. The mother used her son's influence to arrange marriages for his brothers that would previously have been far above their stations. Fathers of families who had wealth but had lost their influence at court since James's coronation saw a way, through their daughters, to regain favor.

Sir Francis Bacon, always sensing which way the king's favor flowed, quickly allied himself with the new favorite. And with that alliance, Bacon was at last able to strike a telling blow against his old enemy, Sir Edward Coke.

Coke had held his peace during the trial of Frances Howard. The king had instructed him to do the same during the second trial, that of Robert Carr.

"I command you," James wrote, "not to expatiate

nor digress upon any other points that may not serve clear to that point whereof Sir Robert Carr is accused."

Sir Edward did just the opposite. He arose and delivered a tirade, inciting the court to think about just the things James did not want aired. It amounted to an accusation that there had been treasonous elements behind Overbury's murder and that they might be of Spanish origin.

Since the king was secretly negotiating a marriage between his son Charles and the Spanish infanta, Coke's railing about popish plots and Spanish spies in league with English peers proved too embarrassing for the crown to bear.

Even Lady Hatton saw the stupidity of her husband's belligerence. "Sir," she wrote, "should the king see fit to hang you, I assure you I would care little. But in London and with the court I would live. So, sir, I would have you desist with your railing tongue!"

"Madam," Coke replied in a caustic note, "should His Majesty see fit to hang me, I plan on forcing him to do it with a silken noose."

Coke's bravery and sense of duty were commendable, but his methods and stupidity were deplorable. Bacon realized this and seized upon Coke's weakened status. With Villiers's help, he convinced King James to relieve Sir Edward of his post.

> Be it known that on this day, 16 November 1616, for certain causes having moved us, that you, Sir Edward Coke, shall no longer be our Chief Justice; and we command that you no longer interfere in that office. By virtue of this presence we at once remove and exonerate you from same.
>
> James R.

Coke's hands shook and his knees turned to water as he read. Tears, the first he had shed in his life, squeezed from his reddened eyes. But they soon became tears of anger when yet another order came instructing him to withdraw to the country.

Railing against the injustice of it all after his long years of service, Coke finally accepted the king's judgment and rode to his country home at Stoke Poges. There he sequestered himself but not in retirement. Carefully and deliberately he made plans and mapped out a campaign to reinstate himself in the crown's favor.

By January 1617, with ice floating in the Thames and white snow blanketing the countryside, those plans were ready to be set into motion.

Proving truth to the rumor, the Viscount Villiers was made Earl of Buckingham and a member of the Privy Council. He had married his brothers well and had gained for himself the annual income of a prince. Now he and his mother, the Lady Compton, had begun to cast around in hopes of furthering the status and wealth of the rest of their family.

First on the list was one of Buckingham's cousins, Sir Raymond Hubbard, an undistinguished man with a handsome but somewhat dour face and sad eyes. They were a dull brown and deep set beneath brows that seemed constantly to be knitted in wonder as events unfolded around him.

The fact that his cousin was now the Earl of Buckingham and had risen to such heights totally overwhelmed Sir Raymond. The idea that he might profit from this rise had never entered his mind until Lady Compton put it there.

"As my sister's son, you shall marry well, Raymond."

"I will? But who?" Women rarely cast a flirtatious eye at Sir Raymond, and when they did he was either too nonplussed to do anything about it or they were old enough to be his mother.

"That," Lady Compton declared, "is what we must decide."

Soon after, she was intrigued and Sir Raymond was overjoyed when a letter arrived from Sir Edward Coke inviting them to Stoke Poges. The letter hinted at a possible match between Sir Raymond and the rich, darkly beautiful daughter of Sir Edward and the Lady Hatton—Brenna Coke.

CHAPTER EIGHT

BRENNA RODE MORE LIKE A MAN THAN WOMAN, with her body bent low over the straining neck of the big chestnut mare. Her *chaperon* had long since been pulled from her head by the rushing wind, and now her long black hair flowed straight out behind her, as did the mare's streaming mane and tail.

The power of the horse beneath her and the crisp winter air against her face fitted her mood. Her father had sent word requesting that Brenna spend the Candlemas holiday with him at Stoke Poges. That morning she had taken the request to her mother and a violent argument had ensued.

Lady Hatton was currently embroiled in yet another dispute with Sir Edward over his recent exile. Brenna's father had wanted her mother to intercede with Queen Anne on his behalf. Elizabeth had refused, with the excuse that she had barely regained her own place at court.

Sir Edward had promptly retaliated by firing half of Elizabeth's servants at Hatton House and threatened to withhold the monies to pay the other half.

Elizabeth had flown into a frenzied rage. "I swear by God in heaven I will stop the man's high tyrannical ways! I have suffered beyond the measure of any wife, mother, nay, of any ordinary woman in this kingdom. 'Tis my birth and family influence he sought when he wed me, and 'tis my fortune that has raised him now so high. I'll see him in hell before I'll aid him one whit in his attempts to make a greater fool of himself!"

Brenna had escaped before she could be drawn into it further and forced to take a stand. *Poor father,* she had thought, *poor mother and poor me.*

It was just another instance of Brenna's being forced to play devil's advocate in the strife between her parents. She had grown up in the shadow of their constant battles. During her early years the situation had been more humorous than sad. But of late Brenna had grown tired of it.

She admired her father's reputation as a forthright barrister and judge in the same way that she admired her mother's self-willed independence and pride in being a woman, a woman who had prospered in a man's world. The one thing Brenna did not admire in either one of her parents was their passionate ambition. It seemed to control every thought and movement of their lives.

Long ago Brenna had vowed to herself to ignore the animosity between her parents and to look toward her own life. She had vowed to place love and happiness above ambition, to be sure that her own life would be happier than her mother's.

Lately Brenna had felt more and more the need to escape from them both. But the only way she could do that was through marriage, and she felt far from ready to take a husband.

Thus far she had met no man who had inflamed her passion enough to make her want to spend the rest of her days in his company, least of all his bed.

Not that there weren't beaux aplenty for her to choose from. There were. Besides the rich dowry Brenna would bring to her marriage, there was the breathtaking face and figure she had inherited from her mother. She was a girl graced with differences. Her olive skin and sultry dark eyes gave her an aura of underlying, smoldering passion, while her sunny smile, her wit and her gaiety made her seem like she would be the adorable little girl forever.

But I'm not a little girl anymore, she thought, running a free hand over the horse's lathered neck. *I'm a woman, and in many ways, it's sad not being able to hide behind innocence any longer.*

The mare's hooves thundered across a narrow wooden bridge of the "New River," which had been dug to bring badly needed fresh water into overcrowded London. Brenna reined to the right, toward St. Martin's and the Tarter Oaks.

An odd thought brought a smile to her lips, then a low laugh from the long column of her throat. It had been at this spot, weeks before, that King James had been inspecting the "New River." In the midst of the inspection, the king had fallen from his horse, right into the water. Gossips had quickly repeated the story, and everyone laughed, for it was not the first instance of its kind. It was one of the things King James was known for—falling off his horse.

"Brenna!" Sir David Talbot shouted from behind her.

She waved a gauntleted hand in answer but didn't turn.

Fifty yards in front of her loomed a tall hedgerow, with the Inn of the Three Ravens beyond. She spurred the mare on, directly toward the hedgerow.

Her riding companion, desperately trying to keep up with her, saw her intent. "No, Brenna!" he shouted. " 'Tis too high. Veer around, toward the gate!"

Brenna paid no attention. She smiled into the wind and gently urged the mare on with her spurs. The horse's long graceful legs stretched over the ground until their motion became a blur. Brenna bent even lower over the proud curve of the mare's neck until her own black mane seemed to mingle with the animal's. Closer and closer came the hedgerow.

"Up, up, girl!" Brenna cooed.

The mare's ears pricked and bent forward at the sound of her mistress's voice. The powerful withers bunched; the front legs bent and lifted. Brenna gave a shriek of glee as they cleared the foliage by a foot and sailed over to settle back to the ground in a smooth gallop.

Seconds later she thundered into the inn yard and reined around to watch Sir David Talbot ride through the break in the hedgerow and canter up the narrow lane to join her.

She assailed him with a high, taunting laugh when he turned into the yard and slid to the ground. "You amaze me, David!"

"How so?" he growled, turning his horse over to a groom and reaching up to help her dismount.

"You live so recklessly by night, yet by day you are the very picture of caution."

He set her on the grass before him and scowled down into her laughing eyes. "I could say that you are as foolhardy as you are beautiful, but it would only feed your recklessness. Suffice it to say 'tis too early in the day for me to have imbibed enough strong tankards to risk my neck."

"Then come, my gallant, and I'll warm my bones with a toddy while you begin the day's serious drinking!"

Brenna laughed as Sir David's usually hooded eyes opened wide in agreement and his dour lips curved in a light smile.

Sir David Talbot seemed to have two passions in his life, and drinking was one of them. The other was gambling, which he indulged at every opportunity, sometimes for days at a time. His name was legendary in the gaming rooms of London. It wasn't unheard of for him to rise from a marathon sitting of the dice game hazard with a profit of twenty thousand pounds. He was equally adept when betting at bowls, and there were few fops and gallants in London town who would even approach a billiard table with him.

Talbot's habits had given him the wild reputation of a wastrel and rake, but Brenna knew better. With her he was kind and gentle and caring. She had known for a long time that David cared a great deal for her, perhaps even loved her. But she also knew that his love would never go beyond a light kiss on the forehead or a gentle arm about her waist during an afternoon stroll on a warm summer's eve.

For that was his way. To the world he was aloof, sarcastic, cynical and an alcoholic. To Brenna he was a surrogate brother, father and an undemanding beau. They had known each other less than a year, but in that time Brenna had come to think of him as her one true friend in the world. His background was slightly mysterious, and that made his company all the more interesting to Brenna. He had lived in France and visited Italy and Spain. He had even been to Persia and to Turkey, the seat of the Ottoman Empire.

Once, when he had been tippling more than usual before visiting her, he had told her hair-raising tales of the Saadian dynasty in Marrakesh, the capital of Morocco. His stories had thrilled Brenna, making her ache for the freedom to travel and the feel of exotic silks and spices.

Many of the wilder tales Brenna heard about Talbot she knew to be hearsay. Most of what Sir David himself told her she believed. He had taken a captaincy in the king's Irish army but had found the pay too low to give him the style of life he desired. So he had taken to cards and dice. When he found his fellow officers reluctant to lose enough of their money to meet his extravagances, he had resigned his commission and come to London where the pickings were better.

He soon found himself winning enough to buy his way into the higher ranks. Being a Scot by birth and now able to afford the price, he had purchased a knighthood from the crown. More winnings allowed him a fully staffed London house and the lease, from Brenna's mother, of the manor of North Elmeham House in Norfolk. He lived a gracious mode of life, which included eating and drinking well and playing the gentleman of leisure at all times.

As David and Brenna blinked at the sudden gloom of the interior, a young maid met them at the timbered arch of the inn's main room. "A chamber, sar?"

"Nay, 'tis a pity, but the lady is neither my mistress nor my wife," he replied with a grin. "We'll have a common table, but alone."

"Aye, sar." The girl guided them to a plank-top table near one of the inn's front windows. "An ale, sar?"

"Nay, two tankards good and strong, to begin with. A man needs brandy on such a day, and the lady will have a rum toddy. And be sure, girl, that the damn brew is over two days old!" So saying, Sir David leaned forward, bussed the plump girl on the cheek and threw off his cloak.

Giggling, the maid ran off.

Brenna draped her own satin-lined woolen riding cloak over the back of her chair before sitting down. David loosened his cravat and the top laces of his fine linen shirt before moving to a chair across from her.

As he settled into the chair, Brenna noticed his hands. One couldn't help noticing David Talbot's hands. They were pale, with hardly any pigment at all, and narrow with long, agile fingers. They were the distinctive hands of a professional gambler, and right now they were shaking.

Drink, she thought, at the same time wishing she could talk to him of his troubles as quickly and with as much ease as she seemed to speak of her own. She often wondered what it was that drove him to his excesses.

He followed her gaze and moved his hands beneath the table, to his lap. " 'Tis the bitter cold. An awful day for a ride. I don't know why I agreed."

"'Twas you who suggested it," Brenna rejoined smartly.

"Oh?"

"And 'tis not the cold. 'Tis the lack of spirits in your belly."

He shrugged. "Perhaps, but if I didn't drink my daily ration, how else could I put any color in this pallid face?" He pinched his already reddened nose to make it grow brighter, and laughed.

As he always did, David Talbot made light of Brenna's efforts to mother him and chastise him for his habits. She joined in his laughter, and then abruptly changed the subject.

"How was France?"

"Very French, as usual," he replied dryly.

"Always your answer," she said. "Did you go to Paris?"

"Yes."

"Oh, how I would love to see Paris," Brenna sighed, her eyes sparkling with visions of that most romantic of places. "Why will you never take me on one of your trips?"

"Because you are too young and innocent to be the traveling companion of an old rake like myself," David chuckled.

"On with you!" Brenna cried, flashing him a mischievous smile. "Tell me the truth, you've a doxy in Paris, haven't you—one you don't want me to know about. That's why you make the trip so often!"

"Aye, lass, you've found me out at last. But not just one. . .three! All toothless hags with enormous, soft bodies who pander to the seamier side of my nature."

As usual, he had put her off. Brenna's curiosity was more than piqued about his frequent trips, but David always evaded a straightforward answer on the subject. There was a mystery here, Brenna knew, and she was determined to unravel it. But just then the serving girl returned to the table, preventing Brenna from probing further.

"Will you be eatin', sar?" the girl asked, setting pewter tankards in front of him and a glass at Brenna's hand.

"Aye, a meat pie for the both of us, if the marchpane is fresh."

"Just this mornin'," the girl assured him. "'Tis always the case at the Three Ravens, sar."

"Good then, and liquor it well with butter and verjuice before you serve it!"

As David was ordering and making light with the serving girl, Brenna looked around the room. She liked the warmth of the old beams in the high ceiling, their natural wood color darkened by years of tobacco smoke combined with that from the open brick hearth. She liked as well the long, rough-hewn plank tables and the bar at the far end of the long room. Behind it, oaken kegs rested on trestles, ready for tapping, and above them gleaming pewter tankards hung in readiness on wooden wall pegs.

She breathed deeply the aromatic smells coming from the kitchen and was glad David had no qualms about escorting her to such a place.

"M'lady," her beaux would say, "you cannot be seen in an ale house!"

"'Tis not an ale house, 'tis an inn," she would protest.

"'Tis a place of rough fellows!"

Rough fellows, she thought, mentally scoffing as she

looked at the men by the fire in their untanned leather jerkins and coarse woolens, obviously men used to hard work. Brenna was sure that if a hand was needed to fend off a real brigand, these "rough" fellows would be the first to lend it.

It was one of the reasons she loved to be with David. Though he was far from a beau, he would happily take her where she pleased to go. She was even sure he would show her the inside of a Southwark brothel if she expressed an interest in seeing one. Social conventions and place of birth, whether high, low or bastard, meant little to David Talbot.

Brenna watched the girl flounce off in the direction of the kitchen and turned back to face David. He was staring out the window, deep in thought, as his eyes took in the harsh winter landscape.

How handsome he is, she thought, and yet in such a strange way. She guessed that he was only a few years past thirty, but the dissipated life he led had so ravaged his face that it had some of the lines of a man well past forty. And yet they were good, kind lines, etched in the well-wrought mold of his fine features. His face, in repose as it was now, showed the weariness of perhaps too much life already lived. It wrenched her heart to think what that face would look like in a few more years if he continued as he did now.

His skin had the classic pallor of one who spends nearly all his time indoors. His hair was a tangled mass, dark but splashed here and there with strands of premature gray. Where it fell nearly to his shoulders, its darkness accentuated the starkness of his face. And in the face itself, his hooded eyes were set wide above a lean Scots nose. Brenna had seen him angry only once, and then those aristocratic nostrils had flared wide and it had seemed that the blackness of his eyes had bored right through the hooded lids into the object of his anger.

He was tall, his lean body as supple as a willow, and though he seemed always to be laconic, Brenna had seen him move like a striking asp when it was necessary.

Sir David Talbot was the kind of man few women took a second look at and men would shy away from. For men could sense danger in him, that he was a man too ready to bare the sword at his side or draw the pistol in his belt.

Suddenly she chuckled, drawing his attention.

"What is it?"

"I was just thinking how devastatingly handsome you are."

"I quite agree," he replied, and downed a third of the tankard's contents.

"And how worldly you make me feel when I am with you."

He leaned forward, and when he spoke there was the cynicism and caustic quality in his voice that Brenna had come to know so well. "My nose is too big, as well as being like a beacon on a dark night. I drink too much. I while away my time at dice and cards, and still you say you love me?"

"I didn't say I love you. I said I find you fascinating."

"I find me boring."

Brenna leaned forward until her face was inches from his and placed her chin in her hands. "David, do you ever desire me?"

"Night and day."

"Damn you, I mean it."

"Do you?"

"Yes!"

"I would answer you, but I know you are only testing your ability as a seductress."

"No, as a woman," she replied, leaning back and turning slightly sideways in the chair. The lids of her eyes dropped until the long black lashes nearly met, and she drew her cerised lips into a pout. "Some men would call this a look of bold invitation."

"And what do some men do when you cast this bold invitation their way?" he chuckled.

"Why, they melt before my imposing stare, of course," she said in a perfect imitation of her mother's haughtiness.

David Talbot drank, staring at her over the tankard's rim. "If they melt, my dearest Brenna, it means but one thing. You have picked your men to stare at with an eye to their lack of boldness. No wonder they think you so imposing."

Brenna's face flushed at once, and she immediately dropped the pose. No other person on earth saw through her like David nor had the cheek to say so.

"You're impossible. 'Tis impossible to make conversation with you!"

Talbot smiled at the way Brenna was able to shift her facial expressions as well as her attitude, from the sultry seductress to a winsome lass.

"Aye," he said, " 'tis truly impossible when the conversation is pale, romantic and of little weight. I believe I'll wait to marry you until you become more of a woman in years and experience."

She couldn't mistake the impudent mockery in his voice and in his smile, but from him she didn't mind.

"Sometimes I wonder," she sighed, "if indeed I don't love you. It seems that I would rather avoid all the other men drawn to me."

"'Tis the occupational hazard of genteel birth—having too much beauty mixed with a goodly amount of brains. But come, this talk of young love is boring. Let us concern ourselves with higher thoughts. Why doesn't such a beautiful woman as your mother, for instance, have affairs?"

Brenna couldn't suppress the giggle his words brought to her lips. "I imagine it's because she's past such things at forty-three."

Talbot roared with laughter. "Only a lass of seventeen could express such a view and believe it."

"And," Brenna added, "because she is married."

"That doesn't stop most of the women I know."

"But they are not married to Sir Edward Coke," Brenna replied knowingly. "If he had adultery to punish her with, there would be even more of his legal maneuverings to control her income. How can a woman with such a brilliant scallywag of a husband have affairs?"

"True, I suppose," David replied, flashing her another tight-lipped grin. "Your father is probably the most intelligent and boring man I've ever met. If I were married to him I would have daily affairs...perhaps hourly."

He finished the first tankard and immediately shifted his attention to the second, then continued his bantering. "What will you do when he decides to marry you off to Lord Fop from Wales, or Lord Fancy Feathers, the Scot from Edinburgh with the burry twang in his speech?"

"He won't. My mother will see to that. She has promised me since I was a child it wouldn't happen. When the time for marriage comes, it will be my choice to make."

Talbot rolled his eyes to stare at the beams above and his lips curled downward in a mockery of a smile. "Od's blood, young maids choosing their own husbands before marriage—'twill be the ruin of the land!"

"What if I choose you?" Brenna said, her laugh erupting like tinkling bells and momentarily arresting other conversation in the room.

"I would say, 'Have to,' and I would carry you off to my castle in Ireland. There I would have you on your knees scrubbing the stones like a scullery maid until you begged me for divorce."

Even though Brenna knew Talbot was joking, she detected a note of seriousness in his voice. And in their meetings in recent weeks he had alluded more and more to Ireland.

"A strange tone comes into your voice when you speak of Ireland lately. Why so?" she urged.

"I served there," he shrugged.

"No, 'tis more. Tell me."

He fixed his eyes on Brenna in a sudden, icy stare. His dark browline knitted in concentration, as if he were weighing carefully the answer to her question.

"Why do you speak of Ireland?" he countered.

"No pure reason," she said, throwing her hands upward and shrugging slightly. "'Tis you who seems to bring it up."

"Aye, I suppose I do. It's been a lot on my mind of late." Again his eyes moved to the scene outside the window. Brenna sensed that he was seeing something far beyond the bare oaks and brown hedgerows of St.-Martins-in-the-Fields.

"Ohhh, comes such seriousness in his tone. Perhaps you have a wench you miss in Ireland, as well as one in France?" His eyes darted back immediately, meeting hers with a piercing stare. There was something in the look that made Brenna feel she had struck a personal chord, perhaps one from his past. "Aye, that's it, a wench! It must be, for you philander little in London."

A chill seemed to run through his body, shaking it much the same as his hands had shook before. Then the moment had passed.

"Don't you know, lass, that all Ireland is a wench?" He waved his tankard in the air for more brandy. "Girl! I say, girl—more brandy here! Damme, a man could die sober in this establishment!"

The plump serving maid quickly refilled the tankard and brought their dishes of meat pie.

Talbot pulled two small leather sheaths from his doublet. From them he took a pair of knives with steel blades set in ivory shafts, and two forks with agate handles arabesqued with silver.

"For you," he said, passing Brenna one pair.

"My, such *savoir vivre*."

"Why not? After all, I'm dining in such grand surroundings—" he replied, gracing the room with a sweeping arm "—and with such a fine lady, only the latest in dining utensils should be employed."

"Bon appétit, monsieur," Brenna grinned, and applied her elaborate knife and fork to the pie.

It was prepared perfectly in rose water, with just the right amount of saffron and grated manchet or bread-crumb seasoning. Gooseberries and barberries for sweetness and a liberal amount of the tart verjuice over the top made it delicious.

Brenna hadn't realized how much of an appetite the chill afternoon ride had given her. She ate with gusto, and it was several minutes before she realized that David had taken only a few bites from his portion before pushing it away and returning to the brandy.

"If you only drink and don't eat, you'll not be able to sit your horse all the way back to Hatton House," she teased.

"I ride better drunk than sober—I've had more practice at it," he replied in his usual jocular fashion. But then she sensed a strange new look in his eyes as they studied every plane in her face. "Brenna?"

Now she pushed her own plate away and dabbed at the corners of her lips with a lace kerchief. "I know that tone, David. You're either going to impart some of your worldly wisdom or you're going to pontificate on the current debauched status of London society."

Usually David would laugh and quickly respond with a glib reply to such a gibe, but he didn't. He only stared, a strange new intentness in his eyes.

"I'll give you a little of both," he replied, "and perhaps much more."

He leaned across the table toward her, placing his elbows on the rough planks, and curled his long delicate fingers around the pewter tankard. There was such an intensity in his stare and manner that Brenna felt a ripple of both fear and odd anticipation thrill up her spine.

"I've a mind, at last, to give up this rakish life of dice and cards that you're constantly telling me will one day kill me."

"And drink?"

"Nay, lass," he chuckled, "I'll not become a saint. But I would, perhaps, become a country gentleman... in Ireland."

"Ireland!" Brenna exclaimed. "'Tis a heathen land—" And stopped in mid-sentence as David held up his hand, palm outward, to halt her.

"'Tis a savage land, yes, but with space where a man can breathe. You've not seen it through my eyes, little Brenna, so you cannot know. Look you there!"

He pointed out the window at London in the distance.

"'Tis London," she said, not following his meaning.

"Aye, sprawling London town, already grown in the last ten years twice its size outside the walls. Soon its edges will be creeping past the Strand. In fact, its sordidness may very soon be eating up the greenery right here at St.-Martins-in-the-Fields. And inside the old town walls it is congested with animal and man alike. There is random building over old stables, and gardens disappear daily. A shack is thrown up in any corner where a tumbledown roof can house bodies and produce rents."

Brenna didn't like the direction of his words. Was he suggesting he might leave England? Was she about to lose the one friend she needed and could depend on?

"Then—then leave London and be a grand country gentleman in Norfolk at North Elmeham!"

"I suppose I could do that...until you marry," he replied softly. "My lease states that I must vacate when you need your dowry."

Wildly Brenna searched her mind for other objections. "There are other manors—"

"Nay, not to my liking. I find myself railing more and more at the English around me, perhaps because I know them too well. I won't to France, because I believe the French are too enamored of themselves and their own lust. The Irish are a better-natured people than the English or the Scots. Daily I think it harder to find the life I want in this hellish land of England."

Brenna's eyes widened in prickly anger and her spine straightened. But before she could speak, he again held up a hand.

"Come, lass, come—let me speak! You see, I've grown to dislike the English gentleman under our good King James. Robert Carr was bad enough, but I think now with this Villiers so recently made Earl of Buckingham, the English gentleman will become even worse. When he doesn't hunt, he hawks. He does little in a day but rise up to play, eat and drink. An English gentleman will spend near all his other time at bowls or tennis or at cheating one of his peers at chess or dice."

"Aye, that they do," she said somberly. "You should know."

He nodded, his face wrinkling with an ironic smile. "Aye, I do, because I've become one of them and liked myself less each day because of it. And more, I'm a foreigner, a Scot."

"The king is a Scot."

"Aye, and if he weren't the king he would be detested more than he is."

"Od's blood, you sound like my father!"

"Your father speaks the truth, be it in a tactless way that has brought him much harm. There are things, lass, you never see or feel because of your birth. In London as well as the countryside, people of different ranks intermingle with ease. That is, as long as they are all Englishmen."

Suddenly Brenna was glimpsing another side of David Talbot, seeing a reason for his caustic attitude and biting cynicism—he was an outsider.

She felt tears well in her eyes, and held them back as she placed her hands on his. "But Ireland, David, is a lost and desolate land. 'Tis said it will be years before the ravages of the Munster and Ulster wars are erased."

"I see you know your history," he replied dryly. "What you say is true, but I see a solution. Do you know what I mean when I refer to English undertakers on Irish soil?"

She shook her head.

"I'll tell you. These English are unscrupulous men who wrested great grants of land from the crown through their influence at court. They are then bound to work and improve that land by bringing settlers over from England and Scotland. But importing that labor would be unprofitable and would require that they—the English undertakers—oversee their properties themselves. This they don't want to do. They can use Irish peasant labor cheaper and Irish overseers to do their own work while they sit on their fat arses in London and gamble away the Irishmen's sweat."

As he spoke, Brenna recognized a new kind of anger in his voice and a sense of commitment, something that she had never before heard from David Talbot. And, as he continued to speak, the dull veneer of laconic cynicism disappeared. In its place she saw a man with a dream.

"The English undertaker, while plantationing Ireland in such a way, has created chaos, pitting the Irish against themselves. Out of that chaos has come confusion, which will help breed more greed and even more corruption. I would buy me a piece of Ireland and end that confusion and corruption."

"I—I don't understand. 'Tis beyond me. . . ."

David's hands slid from hers, only to return and grasp them even harder. His voice took on a fervency that frightened her. "In any English port of entry you will find Irishmen who are trying to escape the famine and persecution in their own land. It is the same in France."

"And you think you can change that?" Brenna gasped in amazement. "You are mad!"

"Nay, crafty," he replied. "I can't stop them leaving, but if I can keep enough Irishmen on the land by giving them a fair share of their own labor, I'll be the only landowner in Ireland to grow rich and be secure at the same time."

Brenna shook her head in disbelief. His words came too fast, and they were too foreign for her to comprehend completely. "I know naught of it, but it sounds sensible and noble."

"Come, lass, don't ever accuse me of being noble!"

Brenna lowered her eyes to the table. She suddenly felt a great weight descending upon her shoulders. What would she do in the months to come without David's shoulder to weep on, his wise words to hear when confusion frustrated her, his witty humor to lift her spirits when depression engulfed her?

"It—it sounds as if you have already made plans to leave."

She turned from him, for now she found it impossible to keep the tears from spilling down her cheeks, and it wouldn't do for him to see her weep.

"Aye, lass, but not soon. 'Twill take time to settle the portion of land I want. 'Tis only recently come to the crown, since Somerset's scandal."

"I know not the geography of Ireland," Brenna said, a husky quality in her voice. Then she curled her lower lip between her teeth to keep the tears in place.

Talbot's voice when he replied was full of a gaiety and a joy that she had never heard before. " 'Tis a place in the west. Beautiful it is, with rich lands...called Ballylee."

CHAPTER NINE

THE KING AND BUCKINGHAM LEFT FOR SCOTLAND with a retinue of three hundred. In their absence Sir Francis Bacon, recently made lord keeper, was acting head of state.

At Stoke Poges, Sir Edward Coke fumed as stories reached him of Bacon riding through the streets of London in his velvet cloak and high steeple hat. The cloak was trimmed with gold lace, and his retinue of valets, footmen and hangers-on were equipped with sumptuous livery.

Bacon's extravagance in banquets and revelry were also kinglike. It was said that hardly a day went by that the new lord keeper didn't remind London and Parliament, as well, of his exalted position.

All this while Coke boiled with rage and railed at the paneled walls and expensive tapestries in Stoke Poges's great room.

At last, two weeks after he had issued the invitation,

his day came. It was late afternoon of a gray, rain-threatening day, when Lady Compton's black-and-gilt coach-and-four clattered up the long avenue to the door of Stoke Poges.

The grande dame of the Villiers clan travels nearly as well as the queen herself, Sir Edward thought, as he stepped out onto the stone-paved walk-around and awaited the four prancing horses in their jeweled harness.

Two additional wagons carrying baggage, personal plate, linen and servants moved down the manor's side lane to another entrance. There Coke's servants would scurry to sort out the contents.

In the time it would take the lady to exit her coach and mount Stoke's wide stairway to the apartment she would use, all would be in readiness. That very morning, Coke had drilled his servants himself, to be sure of it.

The coach rocked to a halt. Six maroon-liveried footmen leaped from the rear and side steps to fling the door wide and offer their arms.

Coke watched, stony-eyed, as Lady Compton emerged from the burgundy-velvet opulence of the coach's interior. A light, gauzy *chaperon* barely covered her frizzy, short hair and failed to soften the sternness of her formidable features. An enormous starched ruff wound around her neck and extended far above her head in the back and to the center of her chest in the front.

The dress was black, matching the ominous scowl on her face. It had enormous puffed sleeves, slashed and inlaid with yet a deeper black satin. Large pearls were sewn in even lines down both sleeves, ending in rolled-back gauntlet cuffs adorned with lace.

At last her black-slippered foot found the stones and

her considerable bulk followed. Sir Raymond Hubbard's moody, solemn face appeared in the coach door behind her, but Coke paid the nephew little attention as he stepped forward.

"M'lady," he said, making a slight leg and accepting her hand covered with soft doeskin.

"Sir Edward." The voice was breathy from the exertion of exiting the carriage.

"My house and myself are honored, m'lady, to welcome you."

"And we are honored to accept your kind invitation, Sir Edward."

Coke didn't miss the use of the royal "we" and inwardly smiled at the audacity and pomposity of this scheming woman. Thrice married and thrice widowed, Lady Compton had finally risen, through her son, the Duke of Buckingham, to the heights she had set for herself when starting life as the daughter of an untitled merchant.

He stepped to the side and crooked his arm. She laid her gloved hand lightly upon it and together they entered the house. From the corner of his eye, Coke noted the approval in hers when she assessed the great hall with its high vaulted ceiling and enormous hearth of chiseled marble.

The room and its furnishings told the tale of the rest of the house. Stoke Poges offered everything money could buy for comfort and luxury, and Lady Compton missed none of it.

"The house is as beautiful and gracious as I've heard, Sir Edward."

"Many thanks, m'lady," Coke replied, turning his head so their eyes could meet. "Let us hope your stay is pleasant."

"And profitable, Sir Edward, to us both."

She had served warning, with both her eyes and her tongue, that she would be a formidable opponent and a hard bargainer. It was all Sir Edward could do to keep from wringing his hands in anticipation of the battle to come.

Lady Compton offered the kind of challenge he enjoyed.

It was early evening, after Lady Compton had rested, when they met in the manor's smaller dining room to sup. Silver candlesticks, embossed plates and jeweled goblets from Venice decorated the long table. After a light meal of mutton, veal and various sweet confections, they adjourned to Coke's private sitting room. It was just off the cavernous great hall and furnished in like style, with burgundy-velvet draperies and maroon-and-gold tapestries over the carved-oak paneling of the walls. A small wood fire had been built in the hearth, and Sir Edward had ordered a high-backed farthingale chair brought from another part of the house for Lady Compton's comfort.

He dismissed the bustling servants and prepared glasses of brandy for himself and Sir Raymond, and claret for Lady Compton. As he poured, he judged the man he hoped to make his son-in-law.

Sir Raymond had desperately tried to copy his cousin's grand style of dress, but the clothes on his thin, angular frame lacked the style they acquired when worn by Buckingham. Sir Raymond's fine brown hair, devoid of curls, just touched the shoulders of his doublet. The strands, even when they were patted in place time and again by his nervous fingers, seemed in constant disarray.

Now, as the young man stood before the fire, hands

clasped awkwardly at his back, Sir Edward could discern tight lines of worry at Sir Raymond's mouth and at the corners of his deep-set brown eyes. His glance darted from the floor to the seated figure of his imposing aunt, and Sir Edward detected nervousness in his look.

Hubbard was just under thirty, and while his thin figure left much to be desired, his face was rather handsome in a dour sort of way. But he would do, Sir Edward thought, as well as any other. "M'lady...Sir Raymond."

They accepted the glasses Coke held out, and Lady Compton turned her attention to her nephew. "Do sit down, Raymond! The fire will surely scorch your breeches before the evening ends."

Sir Raymond mumbled something in reply and awkwardly folded his long frame onto a stool near her chair. When he was settled, she turned her powdered white face and dark eyes back to Coke.

"Sir Edward, my son, the Earl of Buckingham, has spoken to His Majesty. He tells me that the king is sorely vexed at the rift between the crown and so able a subject as yourself."

"As am I, m'lady."

"My son tells me that the king would dearly love to mend this breach."

"As would I, m'lady." Sir Edward met her steady stare unflinchingly. He wouldn't glance away until the initial verbal fencing was over. "I have hopes that your son, the Earl of Buckingham, may aid me in my efforts to repair that breach."

"I'm sure he would," she replied, "were you to have the proper liaison." Here she turned to her nephew, who seemed not to be listening. He merely sat, staring morosely into the fire. "*Sir* Raymond?" she prompted sternly.

"Auntie. . . uh, oh, yes. Sir Edward."

"Sir Raymond."

The younger man's knuckles gleamed white where he clenched the stem of the goblet. He forced his eyes up to meet those of Sir Edward Coke. This tall, big-boned man of sixty-five, with his long gaunt face and riveting eyes, seemed as imposing to Sir Raymond Hubbard as his starchy, stiffly corseted aunt.

Sir Raymond had dreaded this part of the proceedings. He had never met the stunningly beautiful, raven-haired daughter of Sir Edward Coke, but he had seen her many times. Never in his wildest dreams or imaginings had he presumed that he would be asking for her hand. Her birth, her wealth and her magnificence of face and figure had always been far above his expectations.

He had often thought that he would be afraid even to speak to the lady. When he had thought of it, he had experienced a mistiness before his eyes that threatened to bring a faint. His knees had become watery, and his stomach had boded the ejection of the last meal he had put in it. Now he felt the same tremblings in the presence of her famous and forceful father.

"Sir Edward. . ." he began hesitantly.

"Sir Raymond, you have something to say?" Coke urged impatiently, his mind rushing ahead to the next step in the proceedings.

"Sir Edward, I have—have long admired your daughter, Brenna. In this, my twenty-ninth year, I feel it is time to wife. . . ." He paused.

The silence in the room was tomblike as Sir Raymond searched for the words and courage to go on. Suddenly he discovered the half-full goblet in his hands and brought it, tremblingly, to his lips.

Od's blood, Sir Edward thought, *at this rate 'twill take a year for him to consummate the match, if 'tis ever made at all!* Then Coke's eyes caught Lady Compton's. Her features mirrored his thoughts. She was lightly chewing at her lower lip. It was obviously all the lady could do to hold herself back from forming the words herself.

Sir Raymond sensed this and found renewed courage. "I can think, uh, of no better mate nor better match for the joining of our families than your daughter. I then, sir, would like to ask for the Lady Brenna's hand."

Agony accompanied his last words, and he immediately returned his concentration to the fire. The room's other two occupants sighed audibly and turned their attention to each other.

Sir Edward nodded his dark head and suppressed a grin at the young man's uneven delivery of what was obviously Lady Compton's well-prepared speech. "I accept the proposal of the match," he said, "and would deem it an honor to join the families of Villiers and Hubbard with that of Coke."

Once set on her course, the Lady Compton took the helm with a steady hand. She leaned toward Sir Edward across the low table resting between them, and spoke in a low, even voice. "'Tis needless to say, Sir Edward, that my nephew would accept such a fine jewel as your daughter were she to come to him with only her smock."

Sir Edward sat back, waiting. Lady Compton was approaching the subject of settlements head-on, without fanfare and with very little preamble. He would meet her in kind.

"But, just by way of curiosity," she continued, "we would be interested to know how much can be assured by marriage upon Brenna and her issue?"

With all the affability he could muster, Coke managed to twist his lips into a smile. "'Tis a difficult question, m'lady. As you know, my daughter and I are very close. She is easily my favorite, and I love her dearly."

"Of course," the Lady Compton said dryly. "'Tis common knowledge among the gossips of Paul's Walk. They daily gather in the gardens of St. Paul's Cathedral and often remark on how you dote on the girl." She said the lie without a blink and didn't even try to smile.

Coke took the gibe and turned it back to the lady. "I am certain that we can arrive on a settlement of dowry that will sufficiently increase Sir Raymond's income and current property holdings."

There was an audible choke from the young man near the fireplace. It was common knowledge in court circles that Sir Raymond had a very spare income—and that only on the whim of his cousins. As for property, he had none.

Lady Compton went on as if her nephew had long since exited the room. "And do you speak as well for m'Lady Hatton, Sir Edward?"

"Of course," he replied coldly.

"I see. You'll pardon the question, but there have been rumors that you and Lady Hatton don't see eye to eye on many matters of business."

"I, too, have heard those rumors," Coke bridled, "and I freely admit that there is a grain of truth in them." This was perhaps the greatest understatement of the evening thus far, since only a few weeks before, he and Elizabeth had been shouting their wrath at each other in front of the Star Chamber's full council. "But I assure you," he continued quickly, "that my wife is in full accord with my decision on this particular matter."

"Excellent. Then I think we can state the terms."

"Brenna's expectations from her mother will include the North Elmeham house and lands in Norfolk."

"And from you, Sir Edward?"

"I am prepared to augment that with this—the Stoke Poges property."

For the first time since they had sat down, the lady's thin lips curved into the semblance of a smile. She couldn't stop her eyes from flickering over the room's rich furnishings.

Then Sir Edward added, "In reversion, of course," and the smile disappeared. Sir Edward, even at sixty-five, looked hale and hearty. It might be years before his death and Sir Raymond's subsequent ownership of the Stoke Poges property.

"As for dowry, I was thinking of ten thousand pounds in agreement and one thousand a year."

Lady Compton's expression didn't change. It was obvious she thought Sir Edward's offer insufficient.

"We were thinking more of thirty thousand, and three thousand a year."

Coke's lips disappeared in the darkness of his beard, and his bushy brows met in a V over his nose. "My dear lady, let us not place the king's favor too dear."

Sir Raymond's head dropped and his eyes closed as the words echoed in the room. At last the true nature of the meeting was openly spoken. Lady Compton was bartering her son Buckingham's influence, and Coke was bargaining his daughter. The one wanted more lands and power for the Villiers family, the other the king's favor and reinstatement to his former offices.

And the pawns on the board? Himself, not altogether unwillingly, and. . . Brenna Coke.

Was Brenna willing? Did she even know this discussion was taking place? Sir Raymond doubted it. When she did learn of it, would she protest it? Would she refuse? Would she hate him before she even met him?

She probably would, he thought, his belly churning and his temples pounding.

Sir Raymond knew he wasn't the greatest match a girl as beautiful and as full of the joy of life as Brenna Coke could hope to make. But he would love her. Indeed, he would cherish her and do everything in his power to make her life with him as pleasant as possible—if she would let him.

The voices droned on behind him. He made no attempt to understand the words. It would matter little if he did, for he had no more say in the discussion than Brenna had. They were merely the instruments, the pieces being traded. It made him think of the beef auctions he had attended as a boy. He and Brenna were meat on the hoof, both sold for another's profit.

And after the sale was done? In what manner would the slaughter take place? That thought threatened to impose a fear, a sort of madness, on Sir Raymond's mind.

His aunt's words of congratulations brought him back to reality. Sir Edward stood at his side, with hand extended, and Sir Raymond rose to offer his own.

"'Tis done, lad," the older man said. "We'll post the banns within a fortnight."

That is, Sir Edward thought to himself, *if I can overcome the wrath of my shrewish wife, Elizabeth, once she learns of this day's deed!*

CHAPTER TEN

THE AIR WAS FULL OF FESTIVE LAUGHTER and chattering voices, even though a light rain had driven the guests from beneath the boxwoods of Hatton Garden into the great hall of the old house.

On the occasion of her daughter's eighteenth birthday, Lady Hatton had invited to her celebration current court favorites as well as some ladies and gallants on the fringes of nobility. It had been done to appease Brenna, for the girl cared little for the shallowness of those who did nothing but prowl the corridors of Whitehall, seeking favor and offering nothing.

Brenna preferred the company of such men and women of substance as the acerbic playwright, Ben Jonson, the actor, Richard Burbage, and the architect, Inigo Jones, who was currently absorbed in the process of designing a new manor house at Greenwich for Queen Anne.

Brenna's only disappointment was the absence of David Talbot. His letter of regret had arrived early that morning.

My dearest Brenna,
Please forgive me, but pressing business takes me to Norfolk, and from there to Ireland for a fortnight. I would be with you this day just to enjoy the exchange of barbs between us directed at the fops and

gallants your mother has surely invited. Share my regrets with those we enjoy and know that my thoughts are with you. Your loving friend, David T.

Brenna was miffed. What could be pressing in Norfolk besides cows and sheep? But, as was her nature, she accepted David's absence and was determined not to let it spoil her day.

Weeks before she had commissioned a dress for the occasion. It was of sky-blue silk, with inner pleats of a darker blue in the skirt. Soft white lace edged the low cut of the bodice, and the puffed sleeves glinted with gold thread and midnight satin in the slashed folds. Blue was the perfect color to set off her dark eyes and gleaming black hair.

"You are a vision, my darling," her mother had said when first Brenna had descended the wide stairway of Hatton House and moved into the gardens to greet their guests.

"And don't pretend that you aren't a vision as well, mother!" Brenna had quipped, taking in Elizabeth's deep rose colored satin gown.

It had been commissioned for this day's occasion from the finest dressmaker in England. The woman had spared no expense, and the folds of the gown sparkled with insets of garnets and pearls, extending in a wide V up to encase Elizabeth's mature yet still-comely bosom. Her hair was piled high and caught with a brooch of diamonds. It was a crown of auburn curls cascading down to touch lightly the creamy white skin of her shoulders.

"In fact, you look more like a sister to me!" Brenna concluded.

Elizabeth glowed. "I would always be your sister and friend, little one." Then her eyes had misted, and there was a strange, faraway look in their green depths as she glanced up at Brenna.

"Mother, what is it?"

"Nothing. It's—well, you've grown so tall, that's all. And sometimes when you hold your head to the side that way and smile you look just like. . . ."

"Yes?"

"Nothing. You—you look very beautiful, that's all. Now come, let us greet your guests!"

Within moments the threatening clouds had broken, the rain forcing the party of more than a hundred to move into the great hall, where the servants had heaped the banquet tables high with delicious food and drink.

Once the feast was finished and the servants had removed the remains, Brenna moved among the guests, cleverly discoursing on topics interesting to each of them. She fended off barely disguised propositions with aplomb and secret amusement. She flattered the older guests and carefully stayed neutral when the subject of politics—or her father—was mentioned. All in all, Brenna was utterly beguiling, with the grace and ability to charm all those around her, even those she disliked.

It was late afternoon when a sudden hush fell over the room. Brenna sensed the meaning for it at once when she saw a cloud of anger pass over her mother's face.

Sir Edward Coke had disregarded his wife's edict and had come to the party. He now stood in the opening of the garden doors, flanked by his sons Clement and John.

"How dare he?" Elizabeth sputtered.

"Mother, please. . . ."

To avert the scene she saw building in her mother's flashing green eyes, Brenna rushed across the room. "Papa," she smiled, curtsying to her father and lightly kissing him on both cheeks.

Sir Edward replied with only a nod and moved past her. Brenna embraced her half brothers and whispered in Clement's ear, "What is it?"

" 'Tis beyond me," Clement shrugged. "I was rousted from a tavern and told to follow along. Oh, happy birthday! How many is it now?"

"Eighteen, you dog," Brenna chuckled. "Come, we must get between them before the battle lines are drawn and my party spoiled!"

Brenna answered her guests' nervous stares with a gay smile as she lifted her skirts and moved as fast as she could toward her mother and father.

"You've grown," Clement whispered from behind her.

"I've been growing, you oaf. If you would pay a call now and then, you'd know!"

"Your mother—my stepmother—frightens me," he replied with a chuckle.

Brenna answered with a laugh of her own. Of her six half brothers and sisters, she only felt comfortable with Clement. He was the black sheep of the family and often rebelled against Sir Edward's tyranny. Usually it had been Clement, when Brenna was growing up, who had been a kindly buffer between her and her father.

Brenna halted abruptly before her parents. She could see that already she was too late. Elizabeth's face was contorted with fury, and Sir Edward's countenance had grown red with the attempt to hold back his own anger.

Embarrassment prickled the skin of Brenna's neck. She could imagine every eye in the room watching the little scene and every mind anxiously awaiting the explosion between the couple who had already provided London with so much gossip.

But when her mother spoke, Brenna forgot everything and everyone else. She could not remember all the rantings and battling between these two over the years, but she knew she had never heard such vitriol in her mother's voice before.

"You cur! Though I know you to be more wretched, vile and miserable than any creature living, yea, lower than the vilest toad in the world, I would never have thought you capable of such a deed!"

"Mother. . . ." Brenna gasped.

"Madam. . . 'tis done."

" 'Tis not done," Elizabeth continued in a hoarse whisper, "and will not be, for I would have us all damned perpetually in hell fire first."

Coke's fists clenched and unclenched at his sides. "I am sure that is to be *your* destiny in any event, madam."

"What is it?" Brenda hissed, suddenly grasping her mother's trembling arm.

Elizabeth whirled to face her daughter, her face white with rage. "For his own sake, this cur has sold you to the Villiers clan."

Brenna's hands came together at her breast, an unconscious pleading. "Oh, dear God, no. . . papa, *no*!"

" 'Tis true," Coke said, refusing to meet his daughter's startled eyes. "The banns are posted. You're to wed Sir Raymond Hubbard."

Brenna swayed as her knees turned to water. And just before a blackness engulfed her, she saw Clement shake his head and lower his own eyes in sadness.

CHAPTER ELEVEN
FRANCE

BENEATH THE THICK BLOND CURLS of René de Gramont's hair lay the mind of an idealist. He thought heaven on earth would be the idyll of a country life shared with his beloved Shanna in the gently rolling hills and unending vineyards of Burgundy. Had his father, King Henry IV, raised him with the rest of his bastard offspring at St. Germain-en-Laye, perhaps René would have had different aspirations.

But that hadn't been the case. Unwanted by a cloying, grasping mother, not recognized by his salacious father, René had counted himself lucky to have been raised in the tranquillity of Fontevrault and nearby Chinon.

The peacefulness of the countryside had become part of his soul, soothing the savage, unbearable ache of emptiness of his early years. That peacefulness had become a physical need for him. Almost daily he hated his life in Paris more and more. Politics and intrigue ran against the grain of his simple desires.

René was aware of the manipulations taking place around him, and he was not blind to the ambitions and faults of those doing the manipulating. He knew that Marie de Médicis was a shameless, ignorant woman who had joined with her two favorites, Concini and his wife, to squander the riches of the crown and France.

It seemed impossible to René that a common Italian gambler, and ex-croupier from the gaming tables, could rise to be Marshal of France. But indeed Concino Concini, through his wife Leonora's friendship with the Queen Mother, had done just that.

Concini had then cemented his position by becoming Marie de Médicis's lover, as well. How often René had heard the court gossip of Concini's arrogance in the affair. He would exit the Queen Mother's bedchamber and, in full view of the assembled courtiers, would button up his doublet.

And through abuse of his power, Concini had amassed vast wealth. He owned town houses in Paris, huge estates in Ancre and Lesigny. It was impossible to estimate his worth.

For all these reasons and more, Concini was hated by the French people, as well as by many of those who were in his own employ. René had often spoken of it with Rory O'Hara, his closest friend and captain of Concini's guard.

"Rory, *mon ami*, you amaze me! You complain of Concini's greed, his wife's meddling, the Queen Mother's ignorance, yet you remain allied with them!"

"Like Richelieu, I do believe a piece of bread more appetizing when buttered. You, René, may be no richer than I, but you are still a king's bastard and a Frenchman in France. I am a man with no country and no station. If I am to survive, it must be by wit and guile—and the correct friends at court."

"Then you have taken a good teacher."

"Aye, I have. For like O'Donnell, I feel that one day Richelieu, the master of deceit, will rule France. And when that day comes, I'll find a place."

And René had found Shanna was no different. Even though she hated the way the young king, Louis XIII, was kept virtually a prisoner in his own palace, she, too, was a foreigner and forced to accept what crumbs fell her way from those in power.

"Ah, René, one day you'll see. I'll again be an Irishwoman on Irish land! And on that day there will be no more bowing and scraping to a fat, ruddy-faced woman whose corpulence sags as lifeless as her brain!"

The two people he loved most in the world, and René, as a member of the king's guard, was forced to stand politically opposite from them both. The line that divided him from Shanna and Rory loomed larger the night he was summoned by his immediate superior, Nicolas de L'Hôpital, Baron de Vitry, to a secret rendezvous with the king in his own bedchamber.

The moment de Vitry gave him the news, René broke out in a cold sweat. Had the rift between Louis and his mother and her favorites deepened? Did the boy king and his own favorite, Charles d'Albert, Duc de Luynes, plan at last to overthrow the pompous Concini?

And, if so, what would this mean for Rory and Shanna?

These thoughts pounded at René's temples as he moved through the shadows of the Louvre with de Vitry and another lieutenant in the king's guard, Michel d'Ornano.

"'Tis a wart on our times," de Vitry mumbled, "when the King of France has to meet in secret with the captain and lieutenants of his own guard!"

De Vitry was a huge, gruff man, a born soldier and a known hater of the marshal, Concini. Often in the king's guardroom René had heard de Vitry openly declare Concini's wife a witch and the marshal himself a son of Satan.

As they climbed silently up the seldom-used back stairs to the king's apartments, René was increasingly certain his captain had at long last convinced Louis and the men around him to take action.

When they stood in the outer chamber, René was sure of it. Concini had erected a solid wall of his own people around Louis. But the host that met them in the chamber this night contained no man faithful to Concini.

There was the big, handsome but rather oafish favorite, de Luynes, standing between his two brothers. The Capuchin friar, Father Saint-Hilaire, who had recently spent weeks in the Bastille for openly denouncing Concini, stood just beyond de Luynes. To his right was Guichard Deageant, chief clerk in the ministry of finance, thought of as one who sold his allegiance to the highest bidder.

René soon found that the rumors about Deageant were not totally true. The man's only allegiance was to the king.

Deageant stepped forward and made himself spokesman. "*Messieurs*, His Majesty will join us shortly. In the meantime, I would like to acquaint you with the king's misgivings about the current state of the realm."

René had heard it before, most of it a reiteration of Concini's personal slights to Louis rather than a declaration on the state of France.

As an example of Concini's arrogance and contempt for King Louis, Deageant spoke of the marshal's henchmen calling their master "Your Majesty" in the king's presence. There was the occasion of a dinner at which the marshal's guests had toasted him by shouting, "The king drinks!" And, of course, much was made of Concini's scandalous affair with the Queen Mother.

Here de Luynes interrupted. "Tell me, *messieurs*, do

any of you consider this low-born maggot worthy of the title king?"

To a man, de Vitry being the most vocal, everyone voiced his distaste. Then Deageant was speaking again.

"*Messieurs*, Marshal Concini has this past fortnight planned the greatest of all insults and dangers to us and our king. He intends to have himself appointed high constable of France."

D'Ornano gasped as De Vitry exchanged a quick, glowering glance with René. As high constable, Concini would be the supreme commander of the king's army. As such, he would virtually rule both crown and country.

"*Mon Dieu,*" de Vitry cursed, "I'll have the beggar's head before that will happen!"

Deageant and de Luynes smiled as one.

The latter spoke. "The marshal will be arriving on the morrow at ten for a meeting of the royal council. At that time the king would have him arrested."

Deageant added, "We do believe the marshal capable of any treachery. But we further believe him to be, at heart, a cowardly man, one loathe to violence and fearful of it. Thusly, he can, we believe, be defeated by a combination of the two."

The inference was plain, clear as the tolling of Notre-Dame's bells on a Sunday morning. All it needed was the king's approval.

With perfect dramatic timing, Father Saint-Hilaire's voice broke the ensuing silence. "*Messieurs*, His Majesty, King Louis XIII."

As one, they turned and dropped to a knee in obeisance. From the adjoining bedchamber, the sixteen-year-old monarch walked with quick, birdlike steps into the room.

He was dressed all in fine white satin and lace, except for a purple half cape decorated with gold fleurs-de-lis draped over one frail shoulder. The king's dress alone boded a change, for usually he wore dull, drab costumes that helped him fade into the background behind his overbearing mother and his younger, more virile brother, Gaston, Duc d'Orléans.

It had been a year since René had seen the king, and his physical appearance had changed little. His head and nose were still too large for his thin body, and his eyes were filled with melancholy.

And well they might be, René thought, *for what mental tortures and fears must he daily endure.* If there had ever been any basic kindness in that long, narrow face, it had long ago disappeared when the boy realized that each day of his life in a court dominated by an uncaring mother and a scheming marshal might be his last.

Then the king spoke and René noted that, although he still stuttered slightly, there was a tone of authority and decision in his voice that had not been heard before.

"*Messieurs*, please be comfortable. I think I need not warn you that anything said in these chambers this night should not be repeated."

"We understand, Your Majesty," de Vitry replied.

"I am advised by my good counsel, de Luynes, and others here that it is time to let France know they have a true sovereign."

René's left hand had been resting lightly on the hilt of his sword. Now he gripped it tightly. Beneath his cavalier's cape, his right hand clenched nervously. No longer was Louis a fearful, nervous boy. Standing before them now was a man who would be king.

"I have an order, sire, to arrest the Marshal Concini," de Vitry said, not bothering to suppress the grin of anticipation that spread across his wide features. "Is it in the king's name?"

"It is."

"And, sire, if he resists, what would you have me do?"

Louis hesitated. His eyes darted to de Luynes who, in turn, looked to Deageant. Again the small, swarthy man stepped forward to act as spokesman.

"His Majesty, captain, would have you do whatever you must do to carry out his desires...to the fullest degree."

De Vitry's eyes fairly danced from Deageant to his king's. Louis's nod was barely perceptible, but enough.

"Your Majesty's command will be executed with the greatest of care and dispatch."

The three guardsmen bowed their way from the chamber. They turned and began to retrace their steps to the stairs when de Luynes joined them.

"Captain?"

"*Monsieur.*"

"It would perhaps be prudent to exercise the same degree of arrest on the Duc de La Mardine, Concini's right hand, and also on the captain of the marshal's Swiss guards."

"The Irishman, Rory O'Hara?"

De Luynes nodded.

"I understand," de Vitry replied, and turned to René and a smiling d'Ornano. "Haste, *messieurs*, for we have a full night of work ahead of us before dawn."

The sound of their high leather boots on the marble stairs reverberated like a funeral dirge in René's ears. He had his duty.

Rory O'Hara had his duty.

How, René thought, *can I keep the captain of Concini's bodyguard from guarding the Italian's body tomorrow morning?*

CHAPTER TWELVE

MADAME PICARD'S WAS LOCATED on the Rue Marchant, near Saint-Martin-des-Champs. The building's brown stone exterior, with its latticed ironwork, was no more or less noticeable than its neighbors. But those who passed through the high arched door of the Hôtel de Picard knew that inside was the most opulent brothel in Paris.

The main rooms were all paneled in dark rich oak and it was an ironic touch that the mantel and massive chimneypiece in the reception room were embellished with biblical scenes. Madame Picard always explained this by saying, "My religion is the basis for my heavenly soul. My house is the basis of my earthly riches. If I choose to combine the two, what thieving priest or bishop can say me nay?"

None did, for Madame Picard was known to be a large contributor to the church. Many bishops had blessed the house—from the outside only, of course.

The bedrooms were lavishly furnished with rich brocaded curtains on the wide four-poster beds, and the walls were hung with scarlet velvet. The same material cushioned the divans, and a customer's bare feet never felt the cold through thick, silk Persian rugs. Each room sported a chamber pot cleverly concealed in the base of an elaborately carved vanity. A man could hardly tell if his lady of the evening were relieving herself or freshening her makeup or both.

All was in the best of taste at Madame Picard's, in the best and most expensive of tastes. That was why, after a late evening round of drinking in several taverns, Rory was surprised when René suggested a romp at the Hôtel de Picard.

"Alas, *mon ami*," Rory had replied, "my purse won't stand such extravagance."

"Ah, but mine will, my wild Irish comrade. Come along!"

So they had arrived, weaving from side to side, their arms around each other, their voices raised in song, or loudly extolling the beauty and boudoir abilities of the ladies who awaited them.

But to René's surprise, Rory had disdained a visit to the upper floors. Instead, he had shed his sword and cape, howled for wine and thrown himself into one of Madame Picard's elaborately carved gilt chairs.

Now he lounged moodily, one leg over the chair's damask arm, the other stretched out before him. Twice *madame*'s poodles jumped into his lap, barking noisily for his attention. Gently but firmly he pushed them away.

René couldn't understand his friend's sudden change of mood, nor did he like it. Much of his plan depended on getting Rory up the stairs and ensconced in a bedroom for what was left of the night and, hopefully, most of the next morning.

Throughout the evening René had carefully poured away the contents of his own glasses while urging more and more wine upon his friend. If a normal man had consumed as much wine as Rory O'Hara had in so short a time, he would be prostrate by now.

But Rory was not a normal man. He had consumed enough for three men, yet he had been little more than bleary-eyed. And he had paid little more attention to the comely young courtesan, Monique, than he had to *madame*'s dogs.

Monique knelt now by his chair, bent slightly forward so her bodice fell away to expose the creamy fullness of her breasts. She was a jewel among jewels in the house of Picard. Her long, dark brown hair draped in thick curls down both sides of a youthful face that bespoke pouty innocence. She couldn't have been more than sixteen—seventeen at the most—but her skill in pleasing a man was legend. René knew that if Monique couldn't arouse the Irishman, no one could.

She left off running her hand through the thick mat of black hair on Rory's chest and turned a puzzled frown toward René. He motioned her to him.

"What would you have me do, *mon cher*, rape him in the chair? He is like a corpse!"

"I know," René nodded. "Fetch more wine. I will bolster his spirits."

When she was gone, he moved to where Rory sat and dropped a hand to the other man's shoulder.

"Come, *mon ami*, why such a mood? You're ruining what started as a gay evening."

"I am a coward, René."

"You? Impossible! Come, let us bed a pair of wenches and you'll regain your lost virility!"

"Nay, 'tis true. My sister would spit on me, and O'Donnell thinks me a traitor."

"Ah, 'tis Ireland again."

"Aye, 'tis Ireland, the bane of all Irishmen."

René looked down at the deep melancholy in his dear

friend's face. He saw the black eyes, usually flashing with mischief and merriment, now full of gloom and sadness.

His fingers on Rory's shoulder involuntarily tightened as he thought of the next morning. Concini would die, and those that followed him would die as well or be hounded from Paris. Armand de Richelieu, the man to whom Rory had tied his future would fall.

"Perhaps, *mon ami*, you should go back to Ireland."

"What?" Rory bolted from the chair and whirled. "How can you, of all people, say that?"

"Because I am your friend," René replied, unable to meet the other's suddenly piercing black gaze. "I envy you, in a way, for at least you have a claim."

"Bah! A claim to what? To a pile of rubble in a sad land beyond the edge of the world? Nay, René, Ireland is a treacherous mistress. I've sat as a boy at the feet of the men she's broken and listened to their sad tales. And when they died, their only reward was a ballad on the lips of a starving minstrel wandering through a land that's no longer his."

René's reply came from a choking throat. "I think, at times, *La Belle France* is no better. We have princes who would kill kings, kings who would kill ministers and civil war for a national pastime."

"Ah, perhaps," Rory hissed, reaching up and grasping his friend's shoulders. "But France will survive, and I will be a survivor with her!"

René looked down, his eyes meeting Rory's directly. "Sometimes I think that survival for men like you and me is only another kind of death."

"Then so be it," Rory growled in reply. "At least it

will come from the tip of a foreign blade and not at the hands of a brother Irishman!"

René knew the other's meaning. Shanna had regaled him with stories of Irish greed. She had told him that much of The O'Neill's and The O'Donnell's downfall in the great rebellion had been brought about by the failure of Irishmen to unite against the English. In the end it was Irish treachery against their own, in search of English favor, that had defeated them.

It was this fact that, through the years, had eaten at Rory's vitals, eroding his pride in his people and his land until he no longer wanted to call himself an Irishman.

What could René say? Very little, for his own position was akin to Rory's. He served Louis XIII not because he was the king but because that service gave René the means to survive.

"Monsieur?"

Monique stood a few paces away, holding two goblets of wine. René stepped away from Rory and moved to her. As he took the goblets, her glance darted to the one in his right hand and her head nodded. She had indeed earned the hundred crowns René had given her that afternoon.

"Come, *mon ami*, let us drown this morbid philosophy with wine and the good life. We'll settle the problems of tomorrow when it comes!"

Rory took the proffered goblet and, to René's relief, downed half its contents in one long swallow.

"You should go," Rory said, wiping his lips with the back of his free hand.

"What?"

"You should go to Ireland," Rory repeated. "You have the face of a moonstruck calf every time you look at my sister. She wants Ireland, you want her. Foreigners always fare better on Irish soil than the Irish themselves. Find a priest, make her with child and sail for Eire. Mayhap you'll find there the home you're searching for."

"Would that I could," René said softly, his eyes misting as the image of Shanna's dark features flashed before them. "Would that she would."

"Give her no choice!" Rory shouted with sudden ebullience. "Treat her as an Irishman would. Throw her over your shoulder and herd her off to bed!"

The last words were barely out of his mouth when the goblet clattered to the floor and he staggered against the mantel, holding his head in both hands.

"Od's blood. . . the night has come upon me. . . ."

René moved to catch Rory just as he pitched forward. Then, as Rory turned in his friend's arms, his head came up and their eyes met.

He knows! René thought.

For an instant he feared that the Irishman's constitution was strong enough to throw off even this powerful drug. But then, with a groan, Rory slumped and his eyes closed.

"Monique, the door!"

It was all René could manage to wrestle Rory's bulk up the stairs and into the canopied bed. Quickly they undressed him and covered his body with a linen sheet and the gaudily brocaded coverlet.

"Stay with him!" René commanded.

"I will."

"And keep the draperies tightly shut. He must not be able to tell the hour by the sun!"

The girl only nodded and, with no embarrassment, began unlacing her bodice. René gathered the guardsman's uniform they had removed from Rory and tucked it under his arm. It wouldn't do for O'Hara to be seen on the street the following day in such garb. René had already arranged with Monique for her to provide Rory with breeches, a doublet and a nondescript cape.

René paused by the bed and looked down at his friend's face. In sleep the boyishness had returned to his dark features. René hoped that one day Rory would forgive him for this night's deed.

"Sleep well, *mon ami*, and forgive me this. For whatever disgrace the morrow brings you, at least you will be alive."

CHAPTER THIRTEEN

FROM A SLIT WINDOW IN THE TOWER above the Louvre's Bourbon Gate, René's eyes flickered nervously down to the courtyard and the drawbridge beyond. De Vitry stood at another window to his right, with d'Ornano to his left.

It was a gray, overcast day filled with a dampness that fit the mood of the proceedings. A light, misty fog swirled around the other three towers of the two gates, almost obscuring the musketeers stationed on their roofs. The jagged teeth of the portcullis above the drawbridge grinned at René, as if its wood and steel were mocking him.

Word had reached them moments before that Marshal Concini, with a retinue of forty, had left the Hôtel d'Ancre. They were now making their way down the Rue d'Autriche, toward the Louvre.

Was all in readiness? Were there enough men in the courtyard? Would the split-second timing of the plan proceed as de Vitry had directed? Would the massive doors of the Bourbon Gate and the Philippe-Auguste Gate be closed at precisely the right moment to cut Concini off from his guardsmen and leave him with just a few followers on the drawbridge?

These questions and a hundred more danced through René's mind as his fingers toyed with the twin arquebus pistols in his belt.

And one question loomed above all others: was murder the only way to rid France of this man?

"If 'tis done any other way," de Vitry had roared earlier that morning, "if the son of Satan lives, if there is a trial. . . assassins will be afoot all over Paris to kill us all, including the king!"

René had only nodded and stolen away to the Louvre's upper apartments in search of Shanna. When he had found her, she had not yet finished her morning toilet and had been dressed only in a thin chemise that enhanced rather than hid the full curves and dark hollows of her delightful body.

"René—are you *mad*?" she had gasped, diving into her bed and pulling the curtains so that only her shaded features and lustrous black curls could be seen.

"*Oui*, perhaps I am," he had replied, with an unaccustomed scowl on his handsome face. "But not for the reasons you think. Shanna, I beg you, promise me you'll stay here in your rooms 'til the noon bells ring."

"What on earth for?"

"Because I say so, dammit!"

Her eyes flew open in shock. She had never heard

René speak like this, much less to her. "God's grace, the man commands me now?" she cried in mock anger.

"*Oui*. I would have your word, Shanna."

"You'll not have it!" she said, with an impudent toss of her head, which made her curls dance. "I plan on a ride this morning, rain or no."

"Damn you, woman, 'twill be more dampness afoot this morning than any rain will provide. Now, promise!"

His hands held her face in a viselike grip, and his eyes locked with hers.

"René, what's wrong? What's afoot?"

"Much good, I hope, no matter how much I deplore the way it's to be created. Now promise me—*please*!"

"I—I promise."

He then brushed her lips lightly with his and, with a whispered, "I love you, Shanna," took his leave.

From Shanna's apartments he had moved through the Louvre, locating everyone else who would be affected by the morning's business.

The king was playing billiards with de Luynes. Outwardly he was calm, but René could sense in the boy's eyes a fear of possible failure. There were rumors that Concini had received warning and was already amassing followers at his house.

René had assured the king that the rumors were false but had informed His Majesty that, just in case, a coach-and-six was ready to spirit him away should anything go awry.

Even with the king's seeming resolution, René couldn't help but wonder their fate if the plan failed and Concini did survive. "Your Majesty, many pardons, but should the marshal somehow survive and press you for the conspirators' names...."

The boy king pulled his slight body to its fullest height and spoke with apparent calm. "*Monsieur*, you can inform de Vitry and the others that I am so firmly resolved to remain silent that, were I about to die, they could not pry one word out of my mouth."

René nodded his appreciation and approval, and began to bow his way from the room.

"And, de Gramont...."

"Sire?"

"Should we all survive this day, I think you will surely have a captaincy. After all, if rumor be true, 'tis the least I can do for a half brother."

René's heart had leaped in his breast. It was the first time anyone in the royal family had ever hinted that René's claim to royal parentage was legitimate.

"I thank you, Your Majesty."

The lightness of head and heart that had accompanied him through the last of his chores had nearly overshadowed the odiousness René felt for the deed they were about to commit.

His last two stops had assured him that the Queen Mother, Marie de Médicis, was in her quarters, and that Leonora Concini was in her three-room lair directly above the queen. Leonora would very probably be at her usual pastime—counting the horde of her stolen wealth—while her husband died.

"He comes!"

De Vitry's voice was like a thunderclap in René's ears, bringing him instantly alert. His glance shot back to the yawning opening of the Bourbon Gate.

The marshal was just moving through the gate. He was dressed all in black, with satin breeches and velvet doublet and cape. The front of the doublet was heavily stitched with gold embroidery, and what little daylight there was reflected brightly off the expensive gilt and jewels of his sword.

He moved slowly, a step or two ahead of La Mardine and a bevy of obsequious courtiers. The Italian was engrossed in the contents of a sheaf of papers held in his hands.

"Damme," d'Ornano hissed. "Where's the Irishman?"

An arc of five Swiss guards had already preceded the marshal across the bridge. The rest of the troop was approaching the gate to his rear.

Rory O'Hara was nowhere to be seen.

René breathed an audible sigh of relief and gave silent thanks to the wily Monique's ingenuity.

"No matter," de Vitry grunted, moving toward the tower door. "'Tis to our advantage, for the Swiss mercenaries are loathe to fight without a proper captain. Come along!"

Taking three of the stone steps at a time, they descended to the tower's ground floor and emerged into the courtyard. A light rain had begun to fall, and in the distance rolling thunder could be heard.

René was sure it couldn't drown out the beating of his heart.

They passed the advancing Swiss guard, drawing only a nodding glance from two of them. Concini was in the middle of the bridge, still engrossed in his papers, when the huge doors of the Bourbon Gate closed with a thud behind him. Over his shoulder, René saw the doors of the Philippe-Auguste Gate blot out the backs of the Swiss.

De Vitry moved onto the bridge quickly, flanked by René and D'Ornano. They stopped just short of the marshal, and de Vitry threw up his hands, halting the entire procession.

"Concino Concini, I arrest you in the name of the king!"

The marshal looked up from his reading, his forehead furrowed in a puzzled frown. Then he quickly turned his head and saw the closed and bolted gates. The shock of realization filled his dark eyes.

"Me?" he said, stunned.

"Yes!" de Vitry shouted. "In the name of King Louis of France!"

De Vitry stepped back two paces, his hands already coming up, the fingers gripped tightly around an arquebus.

It was the signal. René pulled the two pistols from his belt. From the corner of his eye he saw d'Ornano do the same.

The papers fluttered to the bridge as the Italian turned slightly to the side, his right hand clawing for the hilt of his sword.

Pandemonium broke loose behind him. His followers fell to the bridge. A few dived from the rail into the muddy ditch below.

De Vitry fired first, with the bark of d'Ornano's pistols close behind. All three balls struck Concini at once. Mortally wounded, he fell to his knees and slumped against the chain of the drawbridge. De Vitry shoved his pistol back into his belt and stepped forward with his sword in hand. With a roar, he lunged, sending half his blade through the dead man's chest.

Momentarily stunned but now galvanized into action, René drew his own sword and, shoulder to shoulder with d'Ornano, moved in close to the Duc de La Mardine and two of his lieutenants.

La Mardine's sword was half out of its sheath when the tip of de Gramont's blade ruffled the lace at the duke's throat.

With a grunt, de Vitry pulled his blade from Concini's breast and held the bloody tip aloft.

"By order of the king! Long live the king!"

During the melee, there had been screams and shouts from passersby on the Louvre's outer walls. Now the screams turned to cheers.

D'Ornano added the tip of his blade to René's at La Mardine's throat. "Long live who?" he asked, his voice cold as ice.

The duke slid his sword back into its scabbard and removed his hand from the hilt. "Long live the king," he said, and leveled his vacant eyes on d'Ornano and de Gramont.

René's arm suddenly trembled. It was all he could do to keep himself from thrusting forward and killing the man. For in La Mardine's glazed eyes he imagined he saw his own death.

Then de Vitry was at his shoulder. "Get you to His Majesty and inform the king that the deed is done!"

René could only nod. He turned from de Vitry's scowl and headed quickly for the inner gate. The outer doors were open now, and Parisians were flooding into the courtyard to view the body.

The same phrase was on everyone's lips. "The foreigner is dead... *Vive La France... Vive le roi!*"

SHANNA HAD HEARD THE SHOUTS from her apartments, but her windows faced away from the Seine. It was impossible to know what had occurred on the opposite side of the huge palace until her two white-faced maids ran into the room.

"What is it—what has happened?" she cried.

In reply she received only whimpering and hysterical shrieks. At last she grabbed the closest of the two girls and soundly slapped her twice across the face.

"Speak, girl! What is it?"

"Monsieur le marshal. . . ."

"Concini?" The girl nodded, her eyes saucer wide with fear. "What about Concini!" Shanna urged, a slight shrillness coming into her own voice.

"He is murdered!" the girl gasped, and swooned, her body slipping down Shanna's into a crumpled heap on the floor.

"Mon Dieu!" Shanna cried, and whirled on the second maid. "Go and fetch Princess Henrietta Maria. Bring her to the Princess Christine's inner chambers and lock all the doors behind you. Do you understand?"

"I—yes, yes, I understand.

"Then hurry! Fly!"

The girl scurried from the room, with Shanna close behind her. When Shanna was sure the maid was intending to do her bidding instead of fleeing in fear, she turned and ran down the hall in the opposite direction.

The import of René's earlier warning was suddenly clear. All Shanna could think of was the safety of the princesses. If Louis had rebelled at last against his mother and Concini's tyranny, he might very well go one step further and rid himself of everyone even remotely connected with the marshal—including his sisters.

Ignoring modesty, she bunched her skirts at her hips and sprinted up the wide gallery staircase as fast as her feet would carry her. She burst through the Queen

Mother's outer rooms and entered Marie de Médicis's bedchamber.

Shanna's eyes took in the whole scene at a glance. Amid the statues, the huge gilt mirrors and the opulent Venetian tapestries of de Médicis's private boudoir, all was confusion.

The ladies of the bedchamber were moving aimlessly about, moaning and wailing their terror and grief. Some were wringing their hands and beseeching God for deliverance.

In their midst was the corpulent bulk of Marie de Médicis. The news had evidently reached her while she was being coiffed and dressed. Her huge body was barely covered by a tentlike chemise. In her ravings she had torn at her hair and her gown until the former was a mass of tangled curls and the latter was ripped open to the waist. The woman stumbled wildly from one end of the room to the other.

"I have reigned for seven years!" she screamed, her voice an ear-piercing shriek. "Am I now to look forward to nothing more than a crown in heaven? Will my deceitful son kill us all?"

This announcement brought more wails from the other women in the room. Shanna watched it all, a strange calm pervading her. She suddenly realized that she cared little for this fat obnoxious woman's safety. But she did fear for her two charges, Princess Christine and Princess Henrietta Maria. To ensure their safety, she would have to ensure the Queen Mother's.

Shouldering through the other women, Shanna made her way to Marie de Médicis's side.

"Your Majesty. . . Your Majesty!"

In reply she received only a wild-eyed stare. Dark

rivers of kohl flowed down the woman's fat cheeks from the glazed ovals of her deep-set eyes.

"Your Majesty, we must flee. The people dangerously associate you with Concini. . . ."

At the mention of the marshal's name, the Queen Mother again began to flail about. Shanna had to jump aside to avoid being cuffed.

"That fool! That greedy pig!" Suddenly the Queen Mother sank to her knees, her hands clawing at her face. Her shrieking words now issued forth in her native Italian. *"Dio mi salvi. . . Dio mi salvi."*

God save us all, Shanna thought, *if some sanity isn't brought to this confusion!*

Marie de Médicis wasn't a serving maid. Shanna couldn't slap her into reason. Instead, she gripped the woman's fleshy shoulders and began shaking with all the strength in her arms. "Your Majesty, we must leave the palace. We must to the country! The princesses—"

With a guttural wail the Queen Mother pushed Shanna down. "My babies—he's murdered his sisters in their beds!"

Shanna knew it was no use. The woman was completely incoherent and nearing insanity. Then her eye fell on Monsieur La Place, Leonora Concini's first servant, as he entered the room. Leonora had power over the Queen Mother, Shanna thought. If anyone could calm de Médicis and bring her to her senses, it was her dearest ally, Leonora.

Shanna came to her feet, meaning to intercept La Place, but she was blocked by the hysterical women.

La Place knelt before de Mécidis, carefully averting his eyes from her dishabille. "Your Majesty. . . ."

"You! What do you want here?" she shouted, recognizing the groveling man before her.

"My mistress Concini is still ignorant of this foul deed. I thought that you would want to break the news."

"Me...*me*?" de Médicis roared. "If you don't want to tell the witch that her husband's been butchered, then *sing* her the news!"

"But, Your Majesty, I thought—"

"Be gone, you slobbering fool. I have others to think about here!"

Shanna, aghast, staggered from the room, her own face white and her body shaking with revulsion. Was there no honor? Was self-preservation the only order of the day? Was the entire court of France nothing but a nest of whining thieves and murderers?

Suddenly she knew that it was—and that she somehow had to escape it.

Quickly she crossed the outer chamber and threw open one of the two tall oaken doors. A pair of stern-faced guards blocked her path with crossed muskets.

"By the king's order," one said, "no one is to enter or leave the royal quarters."

RORY O'HARA CURSED MADAME PICARD and her establishment, and sent Monique fleeing in tears. He was further incensed when his uniform could not be found and a drab broadcloth doublet and worn breeches were produced in its place.

When at last he lurched into the street, the rain and stench depressed him even more. His duty call had been for eight o'clock that morning. It was now well past midday.

As he stumbled groggily along the Seine toward the

Pont Neuf, Rory was sure that La Mardine would have his captain's epaulets at least, and perhaps his head.

Shouting, cheering voices assailed his ears from across the Seine when he reached the Rue St. Jacques. Through the drizzling mist he peered across the water toward the Ile de la Cité and the square in front of Notre-Dame. Huge crowds of men and women were dancing and chanting. Here and there Rory could see a king's musketeer, his plumed hat waving on the tip of his sword.

The chanted words had become gibberish by the time they reached Rory's ears. Even though he couldn't understand them, there was something in the frenzy of the crowd that made the soft rain feel like ice on his face.

He quickened his pace but found his progress halted by four prancing horses and a carriage. Instantly he recognized the plain black coach and the purple livery of the driver and footman.

"Your Excellency," Rory said, stepping to the door just as Armand de Richelieu's strained white face appeared between the parted curtains.

"Ah, 'tis you, O'Hara—I wasn't sure. Quickly, my son, inside!"

The tenseness in the usually calm voice alarmed Rory even more. He clambered into the coach and settled into the plush seat across from the bishop. The door had barely slammed shut when the neighing horses strained in their traces and the carriage lurched ahead.

"An excellent choice of costumes, considering the morning's events," Richelieu said, nodding at Rory's drab clothing.

Rory's face reddened. He was about to attempt an explanation when the coach careened into a turn. The clatter of the hard-rimmed wheels on rough brick told him they had started across the Pont Neuf.

"Ho there, coachman, who's your master?" came a shouted cry.

The driver brought the carriage to a stop as the bishop's hands flew to the curtain.

"Merciful Father!" Rory gasped as he gazed over Richelieu's shoulder.

There, hung by his heels from the very gallows he had erected as a warning to would-be French rebels, was the naked body of Concino Concini.

"Assassinated this morning, by the king's order and de Vitry's hand," Richelieu said, reading the look of amazement on Rory's face. "You didn't know?"

"Nay, I—"

His words were cut off when the coach door was yanked aside and a glowering face appeared in the opening.

The man's mouth yawned wide to speak, but Richelieu spoke first. "Is it the king's business that occupies you?"

"*Oui*, it is that. For we're about to quarter the traitorous Italian and spread him to the four parts of Paris!"

Richelieu's usually dark face suddenly became pale, but he managed to retain his composure. "Then on about your business and I'll do mine. God save the king! Long live Louis!"

An echoing roar went up from the peasants who had formed a threatening ring around the coach. As one, they parted.

"Pass, whoever you be," shouted the man at the coach's door. "For only Concini's henchmen—and not the king's men—will feel the wrath of Parisians this day!"

The coach moved on. Only when they had cleared the Pont Neuf and turned toward the Rue des Mauvaises-Paroles did Richelieu settle back in the cushions and fix Rory with a penetrating stare.

"Then 'tis done," Rory sighed, still not entirely comprehending the deed, his mind muddled in shock.

"*Oui*, it is, and I curse myself for a fool that I did not see it coming. Louis now has the idolatry of his people, and the conquest of complete power is his."

Rory's thoughts began to focus. Like Richelieu, he began to assess his own position in the aftermath of Concini's death.

"Your Excellency, you are still secretary."

"I'm afraid not. De Médicis is exiled to Blois until her château at Moulins can be made ready to receive her." Here the bishop's voice dropped to a bare whisper. His lips formed a taut line and the furrows in his scholarly brows deepened. "I am to accompany the Queen Mother into exile."

Suddenly Rory's thoughts were whole.

"My sister!" he exclaimed, lurching forward, only to be stopped by Richelieu's upraised hand.

"Safe. She will accompany the princesses to Saint-Germain-en-Laye. The king has decreed that the family will remain apart, to discourage de Médicis from using his sisters as a lever to insinuate herself back into favor."

Having received the knowledge of Shanna's safety, Rory's concern returned to his own situation. "I am a captain now without a command. Am I to accompany you to Blois?"

"You would be a fool if you did. Your name is on everyone's lips. I fear, Rory O'Hara, that you are the talk of the court."

"Me? How so?"

"They fear your talent as a leader and a soldier. De Vitry and the king's musketeers would have your head before you mobilize the marshal's guard and attempt to retaliate."

Rory's lips curled with distaste. "Then my only service remains with La Mardine."

"Nay, you have not even that, O'Hara. The duke thinks you are a traitor and a part of the plot because of your absence this morning. At the king's order, La Mardine has been placed in the Bastille. But he is a clever man, and like an unbreakable reed, he bends well and will, I think, be released one day soon. When that day comes, he has sworn to kill you for what he deems your perfidy."

Rory nodded and sighed. "Aye, 'tis understandable. So now all France is an enemy." He slammed the huge fist of one hand into the palm of another. "Damme, I have no choice!"

"You have one."

Rory looked up, his eyes scanning the cold, impassive expression on Armand de Richelieu's face. "I do?"

"Yes. Leave France!"

CHAPTER FOURTEEN

IT WAS A SOLEMN PROCESSION, twenty carriages long, escorted by two troops of heavily armed cavalry. Trumpets heralded their movement through Paris, but the instruments' blare was nearly drowned out by the shouting jeers of Parisians who lined the way.

The preceding days had been filled with chaos. Concini's body had finally been wrested from the masses and entombed. His wife, Leonora, had been arrested in her Louvre apartments. Many of the crown jewels and hundreds of thousands of livres had been found in a chest at the foot of her bed.

The people demanded a swift trial with a ready sentence. Leonora Concini was condemned as a sorceress. Less than a fortnight after her husband's assassination, she was beheaded in the Place de Greve, in front of thousands of gloating onlookers.

"What a lot of people," she had quipped, "to see a poor woman die."

To everyone's surprise, the king had already made a valiant attempt to rule. But within a few brief days it was obvious that, like his mother before him, Louis was doomed to be ruled by his advisors. Court wags were already saying that the proprietors might have changed, but the store was being run in the same way.

Once across the Seine, the procession veered south while three coaches left the center of the caravan and turned north. These were followed by one troop of cavalry. At their head was a smiling René de Gramont, resplendent in his newly acquired captain's uniform.

The king had given René a captaincy, but de Vitry had given René the command that would guard Princess Henrietta Maria in exile. In de Vitry's eyes, expulsion from Paris was banishment for life. For René de Gramont, it was a sentence to heaven. For, riding in the carriage beside his prancing horse, was Shanna O'Hara.

They would be many long months together at Saint-Germain-en-Laye, on the beautiful, wooded slopes above the Seine. In that time, René was sure he would attain the love of the only woman he had ever wanted.

Inside the jostling carriage, Shanna huddled with her arms around the princess. "You're not afraid, little one?"

"No, not at all, Shanna. I told you, I've talked with the king. No harm will come to myself or Christine. 'Tis my brother, Gascon, that Louis hates and will not abide at court."

Shanna had to smile at the child's composure. There was, she thought, something other than myth about royal genes. Even though kings and queens, princes and princesses, were made by the lottery of birth—and that lottery often gave a country a madman's rule—more often than not there was something extraordinary in the blood of those royal born.

"Louis says to have high hopes," the girl continued, "for Christine and I will one day wed kings."

"Of that I have no doubt, little one," Shanna replied.

Henrietta Maria chattered on about her royal future, but Shanna heard little. She was already plotting her own future. There was no one to help her now. Where was her and Rory's protector? Armand de Richelieu was in disgrace and sentenced to his own exile. And Rory was on his way to England, promising to send for her when the time was right.

But Shanna was tired of waiting for the right time, tired of waiting for others to decide her fate.

From this day on, she would determine her own fate, her own destiny. And the first step in that future was an escape from exile at Saint-Germain-en-Laye.

The elaborate *carrosse* of Marie de Médicis, with its stained-glass windows and brocaded curtains, led the southward-bound caravan. Then came three coaches and as many wagons, carrying what was left of the Queen Mother's worldly possessions.

A large contingent of the stone-faced cavalry rode beside the next carriage, for it contained the Duc and Duchesse de La Mardine. De Vitry had been adamant about La Mardine's guard, for the man still held sway over many nobles. If there was to be an attempt to overthrow King Louis, de Luynes and de Vitry were sure it would begin with la Mardine.

Only the Queen Mother herself had been able to save La Mardine from death. She had pleaded with her son and de Luynes, saying that, "There are those who would kill me in my bed. Am I to go into exile with no one to stand between my breast and a dagger from one who is supposedly my jailer?"

Though Louis had seemed icy and impassive to his mother, he could see the truth in her words. He decreed that La Mardine should accompany her into exile as her personal protector.

The duke had agreed. Even house arrest at Blois with this pompous, now powerless woman, was preferable to imprisonment in the Bastille. How he would gain more freedom once they reached Blois was now the uppermost thought in La Mardine's mind as he sat across from his pouting, weeping wife.

"Half my clothes—you would only let me take half my clothes!"

"At the château you will need but half of those," the duke replied shortly.

Carlotta, the Duchesse de la Mardine, looked more like a milkmaid than a duchess. Her long blond hair had not been coiffed for days and was tucked haphazardly under a drab brown *chaperon*. Her dress was also brown, and wrinkled.

For three nights and two days she had barricaded herself in her rooms at their Paris town house. Carlotta had refused to accompany the duke into exile. Instead, she had stubbornly insisted she would go to the château at La Mardine and await her husband there.

At last the duke, with the aid of servants, had battered down the door, dressed her in anything available and had forcibly carried her to the waiting carriage.

All across Paris she had wept, wailed and bemoaned the fact that she must be made to suffer such a fate because of her husband's loss of favor.

Since leaving the city, her discourse had turned to Blois itself. "How long? Heaven only knows how long I shall be cooped up with that boring, loathesome woman! No balls, no laughter, no one even to talk to but my maids."

And the duchess's words were only part of her thoughts. Her world was gone; she was no longer a part of the court. No more would there be handsome young guardsmen or dashing musketeers vying for her favors. How could a decently romantic affair be carried on in the close confines of Blois Castle?

"I'll die. I shall just die!" she cried, dabbing uselessly with a damp kerchief at the rivers of black eye cosmetics running down her cheeks.

"Carlotta—be still!"

She wouldn't. La Mardine closed his ears to her complaints and turned inward to his own thoughts; to the time when he would escape Blois—and France.

Years before, La Mardine had befriended a young Englishman in Paris. He had seen in the handsome youth with the well-turned leg a greed and ambition he admired. Like Richelieu, La Mardine saw much future potential in cultivating foreigners. One never knew how far they would advance after returning to their own country.

In the case of the flaxen-haired Englishman, La Mardine had chosen well.

Now he smiled. *Yes*, he thought. George Villiers, Earl of Buckingham, would prove a valuable and powerful friend once he escaped Blois and fled across the channel. Let Richelieu remain with the cow, de Médicis, and try to reap favor from de Luynes and the king by keeping them appraised of her every thought and deed.

He, La Mardine, would have the entire English court to aid him when he returned to France in triumph!

His wife's screeching voice again reached his ears and interrupted his thoughts. "You are a swine to treat me like this! De Luynes himself has said that I could stay at the château at La Mardine! I am no threat to the crown!"

"You, my dear, are a threat to everyone who comes near you."

"I have been a proper wife. . . ."

"You have been an improper whore."

"How dare you—"

La Mardine said no more, but his arm swung in a darting arc. The sound of his palm across her face was like the crack of a whip. Carlotta whimpered only once, then curled into a ball on the cushions. Her eyes, through a mist of tears, were wide with hatred as she glared at her husband.

La Mardine recognized the look, but he didn't mind. In fact, his wife's look of intense hatred brought a smile to his thin, cruel lips. For the Duc de la Mardine knew that if one was hated he was also feared, and fear was a great mover and manipulator of women as well as men.

And at that precise moment, in the coach lumbering along at the rear of Marie de Médicis's caravan, the exiled bishop, Armand de Richelieu, was writing in a journal propped across his lap. "Fear," he penned, "is like cruelty—a necessity of rule. States, like men, cannot be ruled by kindness, but rather by severity. In the right hands, this virtue of severity can forge a great nation."

He paused, set aside the quill and raised his hands to his eyes. Slowly the long, tapering fingers curled into two steady fists.

"And, God willing, these will be the right hands when the time comes!"

CHAPTER FIFTEEN
ENGLAND

THOUGH THERE WERE MANY DAYS OF SUNSHINE over Holborn in the weeks that followed Sir Edward Coke's pronouncement on his daughter's marriage, few of the warming rays penetrated Hatton House.

Inside the opulent mansion storms whirled, tempers raged, and battle lines were drawn. Lady Hatton would have her way where Brenna was concerned. Sir Edward was equally adamant. He would strengthen his place at court by using his daughter's hand, and his wife could go to the devil.

"Nay," Elizabeth had fumed, "twice my own body has been a pawn to further the ambitions of others, and by God in heaven, Brenna will not suffer the same fate!"

As the messages flew between Stoke Poges and Hatton House and her mother became more infuriated, Brenna fell more and more deeply into a state of depression.

Entire days, from dawn until late into summer's evening, were spent weeping in her rooms. When there were no tears left in her eyes to shed, she would sit at her window and stare listlessly across London toward the Thames and the Tower. Hatton House had become Brenna's tower. She felt herself a prisoner in her own rooms, with her parents as jailers. She badly needed a friend, someone to whom she could pour out her anguish and be consoled by in return.

The only person she could depend on and trust was David Talbot. It fell to Christopher, the only son of her mother's faithful servants, Honor and Charles, to carry Brenna's letters to David. Christopher and his parents were the only servants in the house she could trust. All the others—maids, cooks, stable boys, even gardeners—were in league with Sir Edward or feared him too much not to do his bidding.

But David Talbot, she learned from the letters he sent to her in return, had his own problems. Buckingham had set the crown price on the Irish property called Ballylee so high that it would take ten times David's wealth to purchase it.

Also, Brenna's father had exercised the clause in David's lease on the North Elmeham property. Because of Brenna's betrothal, David had one month to vacate. Brenna hadn't known of it before, but Talbot had been hiring Irish refugees and training them in the ways of English husbandry and agriculture. Now, he wrote, he had less than a month to find a home for fifty Irishmen and their families or lose the hard work and planning of two years' time.

Brenna didn't have the heart to add her own burden to those already on his shoulders. The light of David's Irish dream had been so bright in his eyes that the thought of his losing it only made Brenna's despair greater.

And while her daughter stumbled in the darkness of her own unhappiness, Lady Hatton became even more adamant in her quest for victory. It was no longer just the question of Brenna's marriage to Sir Raymond Hubbard. Now Elizabeth would have the complete destruction of Sir Edward Coke.

"I'll to Queen Anne or the king himself. Damme, I'll even kiss Buckingham's boots, but you'll not marry a fop, a fool or a penniless knight! And I'll not be bested one more time by a husband whose knavery and greed overshadows my rights!"

It was this statement that had suddenly shocked Brenna, making her realize that it was her mother's pride that was at stake, as much as her own future.

"Methinks, mother, that it is not so much the match you object to, but the highhandedness of my father's arranging it without your consultation!" she had stormed back. But the import of Brenna's words was completely lost on Elizabeth. The older woman was by now blind to anything beyond her personal vendetta against her husband.

As she had so many times in the past, Elizabeth again turned to Sir Francis Bacon. Almost daily she met or corresponded with the lord keeper, who was now so powerful that he answered only to the Earl of Buckingham or the king himself in affairs of the realm.

It was without question that Bacon would aid Elizabeth, not from friendship but for self-preservation. The last person he wanted back in court favor was his old archrival, Sir Edward Coke.

The letters began to fly from Bacon's quill to Buckingham in Scotland.

My very good Lord,

Out of my love for you, and in keeping with my faith toward Your Lordship, I hold this match inconvenient for your cousin and yourself. To align your family with one as unsettled and scandal ridden as the Cokes would be imprudent.

Sir Raymond would be marrying into a disgraced house which, in reason of state, is never held good. He shall be marrying into a troubled house where the man and wife have yet to live as one.

And lastly, Your Lordship would likely lose all your friends that are averse to Sir Edward Coke. That is except for myself, of course, who out of pure love for your high person shall ever be firm to you.

Your faithful and obedient servant, F. Bacon

Strong words—and rash ones—to the most powerful man in England when it was Buckingham's mother, the Lady Compton, who had arranged the match.

While word was coming from Scotland, Sir Raymond Hubbard, one of the two principals in the affair, somehow summoned the courage to take a portion of the matter into his own hands.

"What gall!" Elizabeth had cried when Sir Raymond was announced. "What unabashed, unmitigated gall. Nay, he'll not see the inside of Hatton House!"

But Brenna, having a much cooler head than her

mother, had different ideas. There might be certain advantages to the meeting. She had heard that Sir Raymond was of a different nature than his cousins, with less ambition and deceit. If Brenna spoke to him in person, perhaps she could convince him of the futility of his suit.

"Enough, mother!"

Lady Hatton gasped and took a step backward, her mouth open in surprise. Rarely had she seen anger in Brenna, and never before directed at her.

"Enough of this, I say. I would speak with him, for perhaps the two of us can settle what spiteful mothers and malicious fathers cannot!" Brenna's raven curls danced as she bounded for the stairway, speaking loudly over her shoulder to a waiting servant. "Since m'Lady Hatton refuses Sir Raymond entrance to the house, inform the gentleman that I will receive him in the garden!"

In haste she changed her attire, donning a light summery frock of apple-green lawn, bedecked with creamy satin ribbons. When she was satisfied with the color of her lips and the shade of blush she had pinched into her cheeks, she tripped lightly back down the wide stairway and walked sedately through the huge double-glassed doors into Hatton Garden.

Sir Raymond stood awkwardly by a large fountain in the center of the garden. It was from this fountain that the many graveled walks shot out like the spokes of a wheel to wind through the tall sycamores and thick leafy boxwoods, finally ending at gates in the hedgerow that encircled the three acres.

From the way he shuffled his weight from one foot to the other and darted his eyes to and fro, Brenna received the impression that he might bolt to the garden's far gate and not stop running until he reached Marston Moor.

"Sir Raymond. . .we meet at last." Brenna curtsied slightly, came back to her full height and extended her hand.

The young man started to take it with his own hand, then stopped. His brown, deep-set eyes stared unblinkingly at her face. His mouth opened as if to speak, but no words issued forth.

It was as if this flesh-and-blood creature standing before her had suddenly turned to stone, Brenna thought.

"Sir Raymond, you pale. Is something amiss?"

"No, I—I had no idea you were so very beautiful."

"Why, thank you, sir."

Brenna dropped her hand and stepped forward toward the fountain's stone bench. Her movement broke the spell and Sir Raymond seemed to regain some of his composure.

"Forgive me. It's just that I've only seen you from afar, and I—well, I—"

"It's quite all right," Brenna said, hiding the smile on her lips with a wing of her partly opened fan. "Do sit!"

He did, heavily and quickly. And just as quickly he realized that she was still standing and bounded to his feet.

Brenna could hold back her mirth no longer. She lowered the fan and allowed a bubbling, musical laugh to roll from her smiling lips. "Pray you, Sir Raymond, let us not make this situation more awkward than it already is." She sat, smoothing the folds of her voluminous skirt, then patted the bench beside her. Sit here!"

He sat, his knees spread wide, his hands worrying the wide brim of his plumed hat. Then, although a deep flush suffused his face, he managed a sheepish grin. "I must appear as an oafish dolt."

Yes, you do, Brenna thought, *but as an utterly charming and innocent dolt!*

With an appraising eye she studied this man who would have her hand. Even seated she could see that he was tall and spare, so spare that the lightly embroidered buff vest he wore seemed to swallow his thin chest. And no amount of tucks or layering in the ballooned sleeves could hide the narrowness of his rounded shoulders.

Then he turned his face full to hers. Brenna felt a tug in her breast and a lump rise in her throat. In his large, gently misted brown eyes she saw the look of a frightened deer.

Dear Lord, she thought, *he is more afraid of all this than I am!*

"Sir Raymond, I would be straight out with it." His eyes grew even wider, and once again Brenna thought that he was about to bound away. So strong was the impression that she reached out and put a hand on his shoulder. "Do you truly wish this match?"

His lower lip curled inward and whitened as he bit down upon it with his teeth. The shoulder beneath her hand began to shake.

"M'Lady Coke—"

"I would rather be called Brenna by you and feel an honesty between us."

She sensed a calm overtake him then, and he even managed a smile. But it was so sad that her heart went out to him.

"Brenna, I would never be so presumptuous as to think that a lady so wealthy, worldly and beautiful as yourself would choose me for a husband in your own right."

"Perhaps you underestimate—"

"We would be honest, remember?" he said, interrupting her.

"Aye. Go on."

"We are being bartered by our families; this we both know. I cannot say that I am against it, because wedding you would be any man's greatest desire. But I know that only I would gain, for 'tis a one-sided match."

"Sir Raymond—"

"Wait!" He paused, averting his eyes and again worrying the brim of his hat. "I pray you, let me finish lest I forget the words."

"Forgive me. Do continuc!"

"If you are bound against the match, as I feel you are, I would flee England rather than wed you against your will."

Brenna was biting her own lip now, trying vainly to stop the mist in her eyes from turning to tears. This tall, gangling, sad man was telling her in his own way that he loved her enough to ruin himself and all his expectations to save hers.

"But if there is no other way, if indeed the king, my cousin Buckingham, my aunt—and your father—have their way, I promise you that your life will be your own. If there is no consummation, I will say there was. If there is no heir, I will plead impotence on my part. And if you can never learn to love me as I love you, I will understand and respect the time when you do find someone to love."

It took a full minute for the import of his words to penetrate Brenna's mind. When it did, she gasped aloud. The man was actually giving her the license to put horns upon his head.

Clumsily he grasped her hand and brushed it with his lips. She felt a dampness there she knew to be his tears when he released it and turned to leave.

"I'll bid you good day now, for I fear my well of words has run dry."

The crunch of his boots on the graveled path was the only sound for several moments as Brenna stood, rooted in shock and dismay.

"Sir Raymond!"

He stopped, and Brenna was instantly before him, gazing up into the most wistful, sad eyes she thought she would ever see.

"Yes, m'lady."

"Methinks, Raymond Hubbard, that you are the most understanding, the most kind and gentle man I have ever met. All you have said is true; I cannot deny it. If there is any way I can retain my freedom, make my own choice of husband, I must tell you true, I will do it."

"'Tis a fair bargain, then."

"But let me say that you would make a fine man for any maid, and I dearly hope that one day you will find a woman worthy of all the kindness and love I feel you have to give."

So saying, Brenna brushed his quivering lips with her own, then fled toward Hatton House lest he see the flood of tears she could no longer contain.

CHAPTER SIXTEEN

IN THE AISLES AND ON THE WALKS before St. Paul's Cathedral, where the gossips of the court gathered, the favorite tidbit was the latest tug of war between Sir Edward Coke and Lady Elizabeth Hatton. The current scandal was even more exciting to fashionable London because those in high places were daily being drawn deeper into it.

A great roar went up and betting increased for the Coke side when the latest word came from Westminster. That morning Lady Compton, the Earl of Buckingham's mother, had appeared before council asking for a warrant to allow Sir Edward to move into Hatton House in order to maintain custody over Brenna. Over Francis Bacon's adamant objections, the warrant had been granted.

At three in the afternoon, Sir Edward Coke, his son Clement and four servants—all armed—rode into the courtyard of Hatton House.

After several moments' pounding on the locked door, with no response, Lady Hatton appeared at an upstairs balcony. "Pray you, sir, desist! You are disturbing the peace of all Holborn!"

"And I pray you, madam, to open this door, for 'tis unseasonably warm in this sun!" Coke shouted back.

"Then, sir, plant thy heated body by the garden and I shall have the spigots turned on high to relieve your condition!"

But Sir Edward wouldn't rise to his wife's verbal venom this day. He waved the papers in his hand and spoke in an almost quiet, calm tone. "I have here, madam, a warrant for access to Hatton House."

"On whose order?"

"The king's council," Coke smugly replied.

Elizabeth could fight the Villiers clan and her husband, but to defy the king's order would be foolhardy. Five minutes later, with a white-faced Brenna standing behind her in the great hall, Elizabeth read the warrant. When she was finished, she stoically replaced it in Coke's hand and turned to the waiting servants.

"Make rooms for these creatures and ready my carriage!"

Within the hour, Elizabeth sat before Sir Francis Bacon, demanding to know the reasons for such high-handedness.

Bacon's viperish eyes refused to meet the lady's, and his hands flitted nervously over the papers on the desk before him.

"Well?"

The lord keeper coughed slightly and toyed with one of the many gold rings that adorned his fingers. "My dear Elizabeth, I fear we have underestimated Lord Buckingham's interest in this matter."

"How so?"

"I think Lady Compton speaks for Buckingham, and—" Bacon paused, fumbled in his sleeve for a kerchief and with it mopped the rising beads of perspiration from his brow. "Well, Elizabeth, the truth of the matter is, I have been somewhat blind to reality."

"You? Never!"

He continued as if she hadn't spoken. "In trying to aid you, my dearest of friends, in your tempests with Sir Edward—"

"Od's blood, man, out with it!"

"And considering my only thought to be the harm that can be perpetrated to crown and country should your husband be reinstated to his offices—"

"Damn your twisted phrases, Francis! I am not a judge nor a commoner to be impressed by your exalted verbiage." By the end of her outburst, Elizabeth was standing imperiously, her hands twisted into tiny, white-knuckled fists planted on her hips.

"I fear that in my zeal I was blind to the king's desires, and therefore to m'Lord Buckingham's," Bacon hastily said.

Before she could reply a scroll of vellum was thrust into her hand. Quickly Elizabeth unrolled it and began to read.

> My dear faithful Francis,
>
> Methinks, in this business of my cousin, that you over trouble yourself. I understand from London, by some of my *friends*, that you have carried yourself with much scorn and neglect, both toward myself and my friends. If it should prove true I blame not you, dear Francis, but myself who has had such faith in you. I trust that faith will be restored, and my cousin's fortune secure, once the king and myself, his faithful Steenie, return to London.
>
> Your assured friend, G. Buckingham

The veiled sarcasm of the words were not lost on Elizabeth. Her mouth went dry and all color faded from her face as the letter fluttered from her hands to the desk.

"I am sorry, Elizabeth."

"Dear God, how can a king claim to rule justly when he does it through such fawning fools!"

"Unwise words, m'lady," Bacon said, shifting his glance to meet hers at last. "Methinks from this day hence 'tis a hard fact that the wishes of the king will follow those of the favorite."

"And yours will follow Buckingham's in turn."

"I have done—"

"You have done, Francis Bacon, what you saw fit to do to keep a better man than you from this office. Though I loathe my husband's ways I admire his mettle, for in his wisdom he doth believe that even a king can err."

"M'lady, I have stood by you. . . ."

"Yes, you have. But like the rest of the men in my life, you would sell my soul to save your skin."

Bacon's eyes glittered icily, their coldness penetrating even Lady Hatton's rage. " 'Tis done with, Elizabeth, and I advise you to do nothing rash," he warned.

"Nay, m'lord, 'tis not done! Damn you all! I'll fight the lot of you until there's not one pound left in my purse nor breath left in my body!"

CLEMENT COKE FELT TRULY SORRY for the anguish he saw in his little half sister's pretty face.

Although there was five years' difference, Clement was the closest in age to Brenna of Coke's children by his first wife, Bridget. And a kinship had grown between the two through the years.

When she had been a little girl at Stoke Poges and Holdenby, it was Clement who had been her big brother and companion. He had tumbled her across the wide, sweeping lawns, played at bowls with her, set her on her first pony and taught her to ride.

It was little Brenna, with her wise face and huge, black eyes, who had interceded with Sir Edward when Clement found himself in trouble, which had been often. And Clement, whenever possible, had done the same for her.

He was now truly saddened that he could do it no longer.

In recent years he had gained a reputation as "Clement, the fighting Coke," and it was well deserved. In the taverns and on the streets of London, as well as on the wide roads and narrow lanes of the countryside, few men would take Clement to task.

He was no foppish gentleman when it came to a fight. While he was as good as the next man with dagger and sword, and his eye with a pistol was deadly, it was the vast strength in his wide chest, broad shoulders and beefy arms that gave him his name—that, combined with a real zeal for fighting. There was nothing that would bring a smile faster to Clement's wide, open face than a chance for a hand-to-hand brawl.

But for all his wild, reckless ways and his zest for a fight, Clement Coke was a weak man. He abhorred work in any form and at every turn took the easiest way. The only man in the world Clement feared was the man he depended upon for his livelihood—his father, Sir Edward Coke.

Brenna's hands moved nervously over the pleats of her pink brocade skirt as she fixed her red-rimmed eyes on her favorite brother. "How can you do this, Clement? After our many confidences over the years, our friendship, how can you be my jailer?"

Clement, unable to face her, moved his big bulk to a window behind the settee where she sat and stared down at the carriages and riders passing by. He wished he were one of them, anything to take him out of this room and away from her sad, pleading eyes.

"'Tis not my desire to see you suffer so, Brenna. Surely you know that," he replied at last.

"Then help me!"

"I cannot."

"You can! Spirit me away. I have my jewelry—mayhap I can reach France or the Netherlands. Princess Elizabeth is there, with her Frederick. We were friends in our youth; surely she would aid me."

"You think Princess Elizabeth would defy King James, her own father, for your sake? Nay, my dear sister. And besides, would you forsake your family and friends here in England?"

"I have no friends, I see that now. And my family is forsaking me!"

Clement sighed. "Perhaps m'Lady Hatton will win out yet."

"You know that cannot be. For all her brave bluster she is still a woman—the wife. 'Tis the man, my father, who has the law on his side!"

Behind him Clement could hear his sister begin another round of sniffling. It seemed so odd. Even as a child, Brenna had rarely cried. In the past three days, she had done little else. How desolate she must be—and how helpless he was to aid her.

"Were there some way I could help you, dear sister, you know that I would."

"But you can! You can talk to Sir Edward!"

"Brenna, I have lost my seat at Gray's Inn."

"Oh, no."

"Aye. I am no longer a law student. My gambling debts have shrunk my income to nothing. I have no means of support beyond my lands, and they are now completely controlled by our father. Brenna, I am a wastrel and I admit it, but I cannot change. Therefore my only means of survival is Sir Edward and I cannot go against—"

"Damme!"

The piercing pitch of her voice made Clement whirl around. In three steps she was upon him, her fists pounding uselessly against his massive chest.

"Survival!" she screamed, tears cascading down her cheeks, her eyes wild. "Damme, is there to be nothing more to our lives than *survival*?"

CHAPTER SEVENTEEN

THE COACH ROCKED DANGEROUSLY from side to side each time its wheels hit the road's deep ruts. The four horses strained in their traces, filling the otherwise quiet night with the sound of their labored breathing and the thunder of their pounding hooves.

Inside, Lady Hatton and Brenna sat, white-faced, their hands gripping anything that would steady them on the narrow cushions.

Brenna's lips were fixed in a taut line. But the fear in her mind was of more than the danger of their headlong flight in a reeling coach. Her mother had proved true to her word after all. Just three hours before, Brenna had been awakened from a troubled sleep.

"Little darling...."

"Mother?"

"Pack a light bag, one that you can run with if need be."

"But why?"

"Because there is but one way left to us, little one. If Lady Compton and your father cannot find you, there can be no wedding. Our trusted Christopher awaits us beyond the gardens with a borrowed carriage."

"You would defy king and council?"

"Aye, I would defy God himself. Enough is enough. Now hurry!"

So they had fled into the night, and the consequences were all too clear. By committing such an act Elizabeth was giving up whatever means she had in her fights with Sir Edward. By her open defiance of the king and Buckingham, she had left the council no choice but to rule in Coke's favor in the couple's ongoing battle over monies and property.

But what was more important now in Elizabeth's mind was that she was giving up everything to keep the pledge she had made so many years ago to Brenna while standing before the burning cottage at Holdenby. "You will do the choosing, little one," she had vowed. "On that, I'll promise!"

Suddenly the coach's wheels found an especially deep rut, throwing the women inside across the carriage. Amid the curses from the driver's perch and screams from the coach's occupants, it lifted, poised on two wheels and then rolled onto its side.

Christopher frantically tugged at the coach door until at last it opened. His mistresses were in disarray, a tumble of satin skirts and velvet cloaks, but they were unhurt. One at a time he managed to lift them to the side of the carriage and from there to the ground.

The three of them stood, staring dejectedly at what was surely the end of their flight.

"I am indeed sorry, m'lady," Christopher wailed. "I

fear 'twill take an hour to unharness the horses and right the coach."

Then suddenly, from the direction they had taken on the moonlit road, they could hear the sound of a horse.

"There isn't time!" Elizabeth cried. "Already I hear my stubborn husband, and probably his rascally sons are not far behind. Loose the horses—we'll ride!"

As Christopher moved to the snorting, prancing horses a lone rider emerged from the trees at a full gallop and reined his horse to a skittish, sideways walk before them.

Elizabeth whirled. At the same time, she pulled a dag from her purse. Brenna saw the pistol and grasped her mother by the elbow. "Nay, mother, 'tis no one we know!"

"A good evening, ladies," the rider said, sweeping the wide-brimmed cavalier's hat from his head, its plume fluttering in the light breeze. "I'm fierce for the road this night, but such beauty demands my pause!"

"Pretty words won't right the coach, good sir," Elizabeth carped.

"Mother!" Brenna hissed from beside her, and shifted her eyes to the young man smiling down at them.

Even in the dim moonlight his looks gave her a start. His features were chiseled, his skin a burnished mahogany. His hair was a black mane against the sky, and his eyes were as dark as her own.

"Any aid would have our undying appreciation, sir," Brenna replied, surprised at the tremor in her voice.

Then the three of them whirled as one at the sound of more horses in the distance.

"And best it be done soon, methinks," he said with a

rumbling, throaty laugh, and slid from his horse. "M'lady?"

Brenna took the cloak from his hand as he passed her and stepped to the coach.

"Impossible," Lady Hatton murmured when it became apparent that the young man meant to right the coach without the aid of the horses.

"You there. . . ."

"Aye," Christopher replied, sensing it safe to slip his own pistol back into his belt.

"A hand here!"

Free of his cloak, Brenna could see the tremendous width of the stranger's powerful shoulders and the massive, corded muscles of his arms beneath the white linen shirt.

Together the two men strained until, slowly, the coach rose. Perspiration beaded their foreheads, and the seams of the young man's shirt seemed about to burst as his arms expanded. "A good heave now," he gasped, and suddenly the coach rocked upright.

"Damme," Christopher panted, "you've strength of ten!"

"Nay, only the will," came the reply, and again the sound of horses captured their attention.

The young man rescued his cloak from Brenna's hand and leaped into the saddle.

"A thousand thanks, sir," Brenna murmured, wanting to say more.

"Methinks you flee, m'lady. From whom and to where?"

Before Brenna could answer, her mother's voice shouted from the coach. "Hurry, girl, or we are lost!"

Astride his horse, their rescuer threw back his head and roared with laughter. "Nay, m'lady," he said.

"Methinks you have no fear. For surely those hoof-beats herald the arrival of not your pursuers, but mine!"

He leaned from his horse and took Brenna's hand. Lightly, he brushed its softness with his lips and smiled into her eyes.

"You've the face of an angel, and I'll count the days until I see it again."

Then, as quickly as he had come he was gone, thundering across a meadow.

Brenna stood, transfixed, the skin of her hand tingling still from the brief touch of his lips.

Now there, she thought, *goes a man I could love.*

And from the coach Lady Hatton saw and recognized with a start the look on her daughter's face. The look unnerved her nearly as much as the lilt in the young man's speech. For Lady Hatton had heard that same lilting cadence in another's speech many years before.

It was unmistakably Irish.

CHAPTER EIGHTEEN
ENGLAND

"YOU FOOL . . . YOU BLOODY DAMN FOOL!"

Rory O'Hara's spine stiffened and his jaw clenched in anger, a posture that had become familiar in the weeks he had known David Talbot. The man had the ability to rankle him almost to the point of drawing his sword.

Almost, but not quite. For in Talbot Rory sensed a unique mixture of qualities he had known only singly in other men. The cunning of a Richelieu, for instance, blended with the sincerity of purpose Rory had always found in The O'Donnell. And in Sir David's hooded, slate-gray eyes, Rory could see the danger and barely bridled wrath of a La Mardine.

Now those eyes were steadily boring into his, and Talbot's wrath was on the surface and boiling.

"I agree to Richelieu's insane plot, and what does he send me? A reckless adventurer!"

"'Twas unavoidable, Sir David," Rory said through clenched teeth, the powerful muscles in his arms tensing more and more with each word.

"Unavoidable be damned! Three weeks to the day you've been in England, and practically every one of those days I've warned you that this is not France. Of all King James's edicts, the one against dueling is most enforced!"

"The man was an ass. I could take his taunts no longer."

Sir David leaped from his chair and began to pace, the heels of his heavy riding boots thudding loudly on the oaken floor. "The whole Villiers clan is made up of asses, but they are powerful asses. And Sir John is Buckingham's favorite brother. How severe was his wound?"

Rory shrugged. "Slight. He will wear his sword arm in a sling for a month, no more."

"Well, there's nothing for it. Thomas Smythe must disappear, but it will take time to arrange it. Until then, you'll have to move into the stables. Try to melt into my Irishmen until I can find a way to smuggle you back into France."

Rory's face remained impassive as Talbot continued to pace. Sir David knew him only as Thomas Smythe. Richelieu had insisted on the subterfuge. As was always his way, the bishop trusted no one, not even Talbot, who had been in his employ for five years.

Richelieu had surmised that Talbot wouldn't accept a man as his substitute in England who was an Irish refugee of a rebel clan and was currently being hunted all over France. Thus, the passport papers Rory O'Hara carried when he entered England through Folkestone named him Master Thomas Smythe, merchant.

"In return for the aid I now give you, O'Hara," Richelieu had warned, "I would have your word that you will not press the suit for your Irish lands until I deem the time is right."

Rory had agreed. He had had little choice. O'Donnell, on their leave-taking, had also agreed.

"Richelieu is right, lad. Bide your time. Be the bishop's eyes and ears and one day Richelieu will return to a place of power here in France that will aid you in your quest there, in England. Mark me well on this, for I know the cunning of Armand de Richelieu!"

And now, had Rory ruined it all with his temper? The thought of his predicament, even in its gravity, brought a slight smile to his full lips. Talbot was not aware of it, but the man he knew as Thomas Smythe could no more return to France than he could remain in England.

How ironic it was that the only course of action left to Rory might very well be Ireland. The O'Hara returns to Ireland, penniless, landless, not by desire but through necessity!

"You find all this amusing, Smythe?"

"Nay, quite the opposite, Sir David. 'Tis my nature to smile at the worst of times."

David Talbot's stern features relaxed slightly. "I must admit that a few years ago I was wont to go for the sword too quickly myself."

"You have my word, Sir David. I won't be so rash again. I am in your hands."

Talbot nodded. He had to admit he liked this reckless young man with the body of a bull and the lithe step of a dancer. There was something in his manner, his quick wit and his ready smile that reminded David of himself in his own wild youth.

"Take heart, there is never a breach that is without some kind of a mend. In the meantime...."

The remainder of Sir David's words were lost in the clatter of unpadded carriage wheels on the courtyard cobblestones. Both men were instantly alert to danger.

Could the king's men or Buckingham's personal guards have sniffed out the scent, after all? Rory shook his head. "It can't be, I'm positive of it. I left them riding in circles miles from here!"

As one, they moved to the window.

"Damme, what could be afoot that they would be on the high road at this hour?" Talbot wondered aloud.

Over Sir David's shoulder, Rory saw the two women alight from the coach and felt a tug of elation in his breast when the dark-haired girl turned and the moonlight fell across her beautiful face.

For the last three hours of his ride across the English countryside that face had haunted his thoughts. It was too much to hope that he would find its owner again so soon!

Just then, the older of the two women removed her *chaperon* and shook loose a mane of flowing auburn curls. Rory had seen her earlier that evening, but the light had been dimmer, a hooded cloak had partially hidden her face, and it had been impossible even to ascertain the color of her hair under the skull-like cap.

"Who is that woman?"

"The Lady Hatton," Sir David replied, "wife of Sir Edward Coke."

"How odd."

"Odd? How so?"

When Rory spoke again, it was as if he were thinking aloud, speaking to himself. "With the light directly on her face and her hair uncovered, she is familiar. Damme, I know that woman, but I'm sure I've never met her before this night."

CHAPTER NINETEEN

In London, Sir Edward Coke brought charges against his wife before council. Now Lady Hatton was virtually without a friend at court. A writ was issued to Coke and the Lady Compton authorizing them to retrieve Brenna from North Elmeham and to place her in the care of a neutral party.

But before this could be done, a stalemate had come from the least expected quarter. Sir Raymond Hubbard had suddenly and uncharacteristically stood up to his aunt and his powerful cousin, declaring that he would not wed Brenna Coke until he had word from her lips that she desired the marriage as much as he.

This news was received with elation at North Elmeham by Lady Hatton. It was a respite she planned to use well. For Brenna, nothing changed. In her young but wise mind, she knew that the stalemate was only temporary. No one, least of all Sir Raymond, could or would hold out forever against the combined wishes of Buckingham and the king.

"'Tis useless, mother. We have merely exchanged one prison for another."

"Nay, 'tis not useless, little one. I have a plan. Search your mind for an alternate."

"A what?"

"We will make another match. *Anything* would be preferable to marriage ties with the Villiers!"

Brenna could only stare at her mother in awe, wonder and bewilderment. "Has your own life so hardened you, mother, that it is all but a game? I would choose my mate, remember? They were your own words!"

"Aye, and choose you shall. Now come, let us draw up a list! There is Henry Vere or m'Lord Drodgen, and Thomas Heywood. Aye, a good catch, Thomas Heywood, he is rich and well connected through his mother, Lady Winwood. . . ."

Brenna let her mother ramble on as she quietly left the room. There was no anger left in her heart. Her mother was trying to help in the only way she knew: counter one scheme with another.

How could Brenna explain that a list of possible suitors could be drawn up a yard long, and over them all she would probably choose Sir Raymond Hubbard, anyway. How could she make clear to this woman, her mother, who had never married for love, that there was a difference between loving and choosing? For Brenna wanted to love the man she chose, not force a love to grow after the marriage vows.

She wished with all her heart that David had remained at North Elmeham, so that she could ease her troubled mind by speaking with her dear friend. But Buckingham and the king were due back in London from Scotland, and David had gone to Whitehall to renew his suit for the purchase of Irish land.

On the night of their arrival he had barely heard Brenna's tale of woe. His own desires had become almost an obsession. Ireland was all he could hold on his mind.

How awkward it had been. Once she had related her plight, she had waited for David to take her hands in his and offer his shoulder for her tears. Instead, he had turned a deaf ear to her problems and had begun to rail against Buckingham and the power he now held over the king.

For the first time since she had known him, Brenna had wanted to hurt him. She had had the urge to reach out with both her hands and drag her nails across his intense features until he stopped his infernal complaining and listened to her.

But she had held her anger in check, somewhat ashamed of her primitive impulses, and had merely nodded until his own anger had ebbed. There was no denying the coldness that had crept between them in the two days before he had left for London, without even a farewell.

And now Brenna felt even more alone and desolate than she had at Hatton House. Without realizing it, she had wandered from the downstairs great hall to the upper floor and her own quarters in the rear of the manor.

"Will m'lady be retiring early?"

"What? Oh, no...uh, perhaps...but I will undress myself."

The girl seemed to sense her mistress's mood and slipped from the room. Being clucked over by a chattering maid was the last thing Brenna desired.

She moved to the room's only window, a tall, recessed affair that looked out over the stable's saddling yard and the endless hedgerows of North Elmeham.

Even though there was a light, misty rain she opened

the windows wide. In the distance sheep and cattle grazed, as impervious as she to the wet. Nearer, a pair of mares romped playfully with their colts.

Suddenly, the sound of a snorting horse drew her attention back to the stable yard. A groom stood, fog swirling about his knees, trying to calm a big, skittering chestnut stallion.

Then, from the stable doorway came a stocky, black-cloaked figure. Brenna could see beneath the cloak a pair of broadcloth breeches and the heavy brown hose of a workman. But there was a purpose and grace to his movements that seemed to set him apart from the other men she had noticed since her arrival at North Elmeham.

The cloaked figure said a few words to the groom and then vaulted into the saddle. The big stallion danced a few steps sideways, settled and was reined around. Both horse and rider were squarely facing Brenna's window when a gust of wind blew the dark cowl from his face.

Brenna gasped. Her hands flew to her face and she took a few quick steps back into the room. She had recognized that dark handsome face instantly. It was the same man who had righted their coach on the flight from London.

She closed her eyes, and the image of his intense eyes and flashing smile again danced behind her lids, as it had so often in the brief time since that meeting. The same chill passed over her when she remembered his lips on her hand.

She opened her eyes and moved quickly back to the window. There was no attempt to still the throbbing of her heart nor the choking feeling in her throat as she heard the horse's pounding hooves and watched his retreating back through the mist.

Even though it was foreign to her nature to think or do anything impetuous, unlike her to jump to a conclusion that had no basis in fact, Brenna could not stop herself from repeating the same thought that had crossed her mind when she had watched him ride off that first night. There was just one slight difference in the wording.

Now there goes a man I could marry!

AS THE MIST TURNED TO HEAVY RAIN, Brenna slumbered lightly in a chair by the window. Several times she was startled awake by a blinking streak of lightning or a burst of thunder. And twice during the night she sensed a maid slipping in and out of the room.

The girl probably thinks me insane, Brenna thought, *and perhaps I am. Perhaps he won't return.*

But why was a man like this, obviously a gentleman of station, quartered in the stable? And what was his connection with David? And from whom was he fleeing that night? These questions and a dozen more plagued her as she dozed off, only to awaken minutes later to stare into the darkness beyond the stables.

At last, near cockcrow, with the barest suggestion of dawn creeping over the horizon, her vigil was rewarded. The rain had slackened and the fog had again claimed the countryside as far as the eye could see.

Only her ears told her of his approach. It had to be him, she thought, as the muffled hoofbeats grew louder by the second.

And then she saw him, an eerie dark form taking shape in the fog. Nearer and larger they loomed, horse and rider, blurred into one by the mists. At last the hoofbeats had a solid sound as they struck the cobbled lane that led to the stable yard.

"No, oh, no!" she gasped aloud when the prancing horse was nearly below her window. It was no chestnut stallion, but a lathered black mare. Only when the rider's head was thrown back and she saw his face did Brenna sigh with relief.

It was he.

But why the change of horses? Had the distance he had traveled this night been so great that he had needed post horses? It was but another of the unanswered mysteries that invaded her mind and tantalized her dreams as Brenna at last tumbled into bed.

The gloom of the storm had lifted and the sun shone brightly by the time she stirred. The maid David had given her must have slipped into the room for good when Brenna herself went to bed. The girl now snored soundly in the trundle at the foot of the big, canopied four poster.

Brenna guessed it was nine of the clock, perhaps even later. The sounds of a working farm and manor house were strong outside her window. She had barely sat up before the maid was out of her own bed and about her tasks.

Brenna went absently through the routine of her morning *toilette*: a bath, two hundred strokes of comb and brush through her thick hair and the light application of cerise, rouge and scents.

It was while she applied the cosmetics that she made the decision to query Malena, her maid, about David's mysterious guest.

"Malena? It is Malena, isn't it?"

"Aye, it is!"

Brenna made a wry face. The girl was pretty enough and, heaven knew, efficient, but so surly that every morning and evening spent near her was a chore.

"Last evening I noticed a gentleman ride away in the rain." Brenna watched the girl's face in her mirror. There was no change of expression from the blank, bored stare she habitually wore. "I was wondering what a gentleman was doing quartered in the stable."

"I don't know, m'lady. I pays me no attention to the strange comings and goings of the master's friends."

"Then he is a friend of Sir David's?"

"I don't know, m'lady. I've seen 'em talk, and I helped move the gentleman's things to the stable from the big house—"

"He *was* in the big house?"

"Aye, 'til the night you arrived. Will you be wantin' or needin' anything else this mornin'?"

"No, you may go," Brenna said. In her thoughts she added. *And inform my mother, as you always do, that I am up and about!*

Brenna knew that her mother monitored every movement she made, every thought she uttered aloud. That she accomplished it by petty bribes to the servants at Hatton House and now to Sir David's people was just another fact of life that Brenna had grown to expect. She didn't really blame her mother. The Lady Hatton had been forced to match scheme for scheme for so long that she knew no other way to survive.

Ten minutes had barely passed after the maid's departure, when Elizabeth entered Brenna's apartments.

"Good morning, mother, what news has your morning courier brought from London?"

"Morning courier?" Elizabeth replied, a perplexed frown creasing her smooth forehead. "I only wish I could manufacture such a courier. Damme, I would like to know first hand what new devilment your father is creating for us at Whitehall!"

Brenna believed her. She had long ago learned to detect her mother in a lie. So the darkly handsome gentleman who hid himself away in the stables had thus far managed to escape her mother's prying eyes and curiosity.

"I was sorry to leave you so abruptly last evening, mother. I was. . . tired."

Elizabeth's glance caught her daughter's in the mirror. The smile she flashed at Brenna's reflection curled down at the corners, a tired and weary smile.

"Tired of what, little one? Your mother's constant maneuvering and scheming?"

The bluntness of the words caught Brenna unaware for only a moment before she replied, "Aye. Even though I know 'tis a necessity, I weary of it. Sir Raymond has said nay to the match unless I consent as well. This I won't do, so why won't all the combatants retire to their own portion of the field and get on with the business of living their own lives?"

Elizabeth's sad smile became even sadder as she moved to stand behind Brenna and gently place her hands on the girl's shoulders.

"How naive you still are in so many ways, little one." Here she laughed aloud, but it was a hollow laugh, devoid of any mirth. "Little one I still call you, but not because of your size. You've blossomed into a beauty, inches taller than I and more beautiful in face and figure than I ever was."

"Mother—"

"Shhh! The things I said, the suggestions I made last evening, were a necessity. I would have you make your own choice in a husband, yes. But choose you must, Brenna. . . and quickly."

"But Sir Raymond—"

"Sir Raymond Hubbard, for all his gentlemanly valor, has the spine of a reed and eventually it will be bent by those more willful and powerful than he."

Brenna whirled on the padded vanity stool and threw her arms around her mother's waist. "But I am neice and granddaughter to Cecils, the daughter of Lady Hatton! Surely I have some privilege!"

"If there be any privileges in this time in which we live," Elizabeth replied dryly, "they are surely granted to the children of the king, for James would have us believe they are the children of heaven. And those privileges, we now know, extend to the chosen favorite and his family."

Brenna's head jerked upward. "Are you then saying, marry Sir Raymond after all and have done with it?"

"Nay. I'm saying marry whom you want, but find someone quickly or you will have no choice!"

"And love? What of love, mother? Without it where have you found your happiness?"

Elizabeth entwined her fingers in her daughter's thick, ebony tresses and looked deeply into the wide, dark eyes.

"Love? Methinks love is a torrent, a swiftly moving river that passes in a rush and is hard to still. But still it does, and after a while it becomes a calm."

There were tears brimming in her mother's emerald-green eyes. Brenna saw them but refused to relent. Rarely did conversation between them wander so near Elizabeth's deeper thoughts. Brenna was determined to push on.

"You've never spoken of your marriages. Sir William

Hatton was much older—kind, you said—but you never loved him. I know you harbor no love for my father. Have you ever loved, mother?"

Elizabeth's face fell. She tried vainly to blink back her tears. "Oh, Brenna, my darling, it is our lot to be women, and we do with it the best we can. At first you think you want romance. If you are lucky, perhaps you find it. But so often it treats you ill. . . or worse, there is no satisfaction in the discovery. So then you search for kindness and some security."

Even though she knew her mother's mood to be strange and full of sadness, it was difficult for Brenna to keep an edge from her voice. "And was that enough? Kindness, some security?"

Elizabeth turned from her daughter's demanding stare and moved to the window. It was long moments before she spoke again, and when she did there was a faraway, wistful tone to her speech. "It is now, as it will be one day for you."

"No, mother," Brenna replied, surprised at the sudden calm in her own voice. "Somewhere there is a man I can love with true passion, a man who will love me the same way. And I will search until he is found."

At the window Elizabeth nodded, dabbing at her eyes with a kerchief. "Grant that your search doesn't lead you to a living hell, my darling."

"Has yours? You once said no woman is whole unless she has truly loved once in her life."

"Yes," Elizabeth nodded again, her shoulders shaking in the huge ballooned sleeves of her blouse, "I said that."

"Are you a whole woman, mother?" Brenna persisted.

The stillness in the room was like the quiet before a summer storm. Brenna felt a tenseness, a seething in the quiet, much as she had when she was a little girl standing in a meadow waiting for the rolling dark clouds above her to loose the fury of their thunder, lightning and rain.

But there was no storm. There was nothing. To Brenna's surprise, her mother squared her shoulders, turned and walked from the room without a word or a glance.

CHAPTER TWENTY

FOR THREE NIGHTS Brenna remained by the window, to no avail. And then, late in the evening of the fourth night, while the moon played a game of hide-and-seek behind rolling clouds, he again appeared in the stable yard.

She watched until he disappeared from sight, then crawled beneath the comforter. Fitfully she tossed and turned, barely closing her eyes lest she sleep through the dawn.

And then it was time. Silently she slipped from the bed and wriggled her chemise into a puddle on the floor. As quietly as possible she poured water into a pewter basin. With just her hands, she freshened her face and naked body. Then, on tiptoe, she gathered clothing and slipped into the adjoining sitting room.

"Sleep on, little Malena," she whispered to the maid as she closed the door, "for this morning you won't run to my mother to inform her that I am up and about!"

Quickly she donned underclothes, narrow petticoats

and lowheeled Spanish riding boots. Over the petticoats went a pleated riding skirt of chocolate brown cotton, with tan satin inset in every other pleat. The beige cotton of her blouse matched the skirt's pleats, and the wrists of its belled sleeves fit just under the wide turns of her gauntleted gloves. Over it all went a dark cowled cloak.

"There," she whispered, addressing herself in a mirror as she quickly ran a silver comb through her hair, "just a very proper English lady dressed for a very proper English ride!"

She padded through the rambling manor house like a thief until she had passed the servants' rooms and the stairway beyond. Gently her heels clicked on the cobbles as she flew through the courtyard to the garden and found herself beyond the stables, beside the open pens.

Starlight was a gentle dapple-gray mare that Brenna had ridden nearly every day since her arrival at North Elmeham. It was child's play to woo it from the other horses with an outstretched handful of sugar.

By the mane, Brenna led it through the gate and away from the buildings to a stand of trees. With soothing words and gentle pats to the mare's sleek neck, she slipped over its head the bridle she had fetched from the stable.

Silently, she thanked her stepbrother Clement for teaching her to ride like a tomboy, without aid of saddle and astride the horse as he did.

It was many minutes before she found a stump the right height.

"Gently, girl, gently. . . there."

With her skirt bunched brazenly about her upper legs and her knees gripping the mare's warm hide, she galloped off toward the narrow she hoped he would use.

It was the quiet of dawn just before first light, broken only by the sound of the mare's hooves in the soft earth and the gentle murmur of a stream beside the lane. Dappled, pale light sifted through the overhanging trees, guiding her to where the lane split in two. There Brenna stopped and guided the mare under some low-hanging branches to wait.

It wasn't long. Her timing had been perfect.

As the sound of a horse grew louder and louder in the distance, she hugged her arms closer to her sides. There was a chill in her body, but caused by anticipation rather than the crisp morning air. Would he recognize her? Surely he would. Hadn't he said he would find her again one day? But if that were true, why hadn't he searched her out and spoken to her while they had been practically under the same roof?

Would he think her brazen...or wanton? Probably both, but she didn't care.

And then she saw him, riding at a slow canter beneath the sprawling oaks. The cowl of his cloak was off his head, and Brenna's heart leaped in her breast at the sight of his broad, chiseled features and the thick dark hair that tumbled across his brows and down over his neck and collar.

He was all in black, save for a saffron tunic. His woolen cape was lined with satin, and the wind rippled it gently over the stallion's rump. As he neared the junction, Brenna could see the fine tooling and rich leather of his boots, and the gold and silver work on his wide belt.

Nay, she thought, prodding the mare from beneath the trees, *this is no Irish stable hand!*

He slid the big gray to a skidding halt the moment he saw his path blocked. His hand disappeared beneath the cloak as his eyes narrowed to slits. When the hand reappeared, moonlight glinted on the barrel of the pistol it held.

"Would you shoot a fellow traveler, sir, before even a word was passed?"

One dark eyebrow shot up at the sound of her voice. "A woman, is it?"

"Aye," Brenna said, reaching for her cowl.

"And what woman would be on the highroad before dawn?"

"One," she replied, dropping the cowl from her head and shaking loose her long black tresses. "One with an overriding curiosity about a man who would share her house but not her company."

"Damme, 'tis you!" he gasped, then threw back his head with a rumbling laugh.

Brenna's heart beat more wildly in her breast at the picture he made. When he laughed, his even white teeth gleamed in the darkness of his face.

He spurred the stallion and moved forward to share her patch of moonlight. Up close, Brenna discerned even more strength in the rounded jaw and the finely turned nose. The tanned skin of his cheeks bristled darkly with a day's growth of beard.

"M'Lady Coke!" he grinned, flourishing a bow with his cloak in lieu of a hat.

"You have me at a disadvantage, sir. I would know your name."

"Smythe. Master Thomas Smythe," came the reply.

"Are you a highwayman, Master Smythe?"

Again the massive head went back, and the vibrations from his laugh sent ripples over her skin. His eyes held a merry glint when they again found hers.

"Very nearly, m'lady...and if not, I'll probably soon become one. Does it frighten you?"

"No. Do you think I'm brazen?" she blurted.

"Should I?"

"I rode out here this morning just to meet you."

"I am flattered. When I become a knave in buckram, would you like to join my merry band?"

"Who are you?"

"I've told you. Master—"

"Nay. You lie, and I would know why. You have the speech, the manners and the carriage of a gentleman, yet you prefer a stable's straw mat to the soft down of a manor bed. On the night we met you were fleeing someone. Who was it, and why?"

There was a moment's pause as his dark eyes bored into hers, holding her transfixed. For Brenna, time stood still in that instant, and she felt herself being pulled ever deeper into the ebony pool of those eyes, a depth from which she would never escape. Then he spoke, jarring her back to reality.

"Let us just say that I'm not in the best graces of m'Lord Buckingham and our good king." An impish grin creased his face. "There, now you know I'm a crown fugitive. Will you turn me in?"

It was Brenna's turn to laugh. "Nay, not if you'll agree to make a fugitive out of me."

His eyebrows shot up and the surprise on his face was even more evident than when he had first recognized her. "You, fair lady? A fugitive?"

"Aye. I would rather be that than chattel to the clan of Villiers!"

In a breathless voice full of rushing words, Brenna told him everything.

"But how could I possibly help you?"

"I know not where you ride at night or why, nor do I care. If you would only aid me in a flight to France or the Netherlands—there my father couldn't reach me. And if I flee of my own accord, my mother cannot be blamed!"

Even through the shadows surrounding his face, Brenna could see the heavy brows drawn into a scowl. Anticipating a rebuff, she rushed on. "I can pay you—a great deal. I have money, some silver, and my jewelry. . . ."

They had been slowly walking the horses. Now they breasted a rise and stopped by a low stone wall. In the fields beyond, dew glistened in the first rays of the coppery morning sun.

"M'lady, if I could help you, my only payment would be a smile. . . or perhaps a kiss."

Brenna felt her cheeks flush. He was asking less than she had already been fully prepared to give when she had crawled from her bed earlier that morning. She was about to close the distance between them and offer her lips when he spoke.

"But, alas, lovely one, I fear I am not in a position to help even myself."

His words sent a chill of panic through her and made the next words tumble recklessly from her lips. "But you must! Don't you see, there is no other way! If my mother continues on this path, she will lose all. My half brother Clement cannot aid me because of our father's hold over him. David is my only friend, and he has turned from me. I must admit I cannot blame him, for my troubles seem petty, I know, beside his dream of Ireland, but—"

He had been sitting half-slouched in the saddle as she spoke. Now his head jerked up and his eyes flashed with new interest.

"Ireland?"

"Sir David would have some Irish land which Lord

Buckingham controls. To help me would jeopardize all his dreams."

"I had no idea—" His speech was interrupted by the sound of galloping horses in front of them.

Brenna's temples throbbed. Fear constricted her throat until her words were near garbled with it. "We mustn't be seen together. Be off, quickly! But promise me you will at least think upon it? Please, promise!" She held her breath as again the mahogany features creased into the smile that she had already found so boyishly appealing.

"M'lady, how can such a plea go unanswered?"

Relief flooded through her. The strength she had witnessed in that massive chest and powerful shoulders when he had lifted the carriage seemed to fill the space between them and invade her body. His dark eyes, which had seemed only to mock her before, now drew her back like a strong sea current into their depths.

Suddenly the horses were tightly side by side and she was against him. His steellike arms were around her, pulling her body hard against his. Their lips met, locking together with a hunger Brenna had never known or dreamed could be. In the instant of that kiss, with the corded muscles of his arms holding her a willing captive, Brenna knew that her search had ended.

Then she was free, and the big stallion was dancing sideways toward the trees.

"Tonight, look toward the southern hill from your window! Do you know the one?"

She nodded, gasping for breath as much from the touch of his lips as from the relief she felt that he was indeed coming to her aid.

"Pray God tonight is clear. If you see my silhouette against the sky, join me. Can you manage?"

"Aye," she whispered, and nearly swooned as he disappeared into the trees.

By the time Sir David's overseer and other men rode up, she had regained her breath and most of her composure.

"M'lady, we thought a thief had— Well, a horse was missing."

"I had but a mind to inspect the fields," Brenna stated demurely.

"The fields, m'lady?" the man replied, curiously eyeing the way she sat astride her saddleless horse.

"Aye. If one day I'm to be mistress of Elmeham, I would know what I'm to be mistress of. Now I would have a look at the outbuildings!"

"The outbuildings, m'lady?"

"Aye, and one of you hand me down. I would trade for one of your saddled horses. I think you must agree this is no way for a lady to be seen riding in daylight!"

CHAPTER TWENTY-ONE

IT WAS THREE TORTUROUS NIGHTS before a pall of fog and intermittent rain lifted enough to see even a foot beyond the immediate area around Elmeham House. In that time, Brenna realized that the man who called himself Thomas Smythe had invaded her every waking thought. Even in sleep she dreamed of being again in his arms.

When the sun shone brightly through her bedroom window on the fourth day, Brenna rejoiced and prayed that the fine weather would last through the night.

Near noon a messenger arrived from London. Lady

Hatton was commanded to appear before Star Chamber to answer Coke's charges that she had unlawfully abducted Brenna from his protection.

It was a travesty and a mere formality, but Elizabeth was forced to go. As Sir Raymond still refused to wed Brenna unless she agreed to the match, nothing could come of the appearance in the King's Council but yet another public airing of Lady Hatton's bickering with her husband.

"I shall return in a week's time," Elizabeth said to her daughter as she stepped into her coach. "Perhaps by then we can return to Hatton House and normal lives. In the meantime, beware of unescorted early-morning rides!"

A week, Brenna thought, willing the time until evening to pass faster. *Only one week.*

"Whatever you say, mother."

Brenna dined early and alone in Elmeham's great hall and then retired to her apartments at dusk. Without Lady Hatton in residence, the maid, Malena, was only too happy at Brenna's insistence to slip away to her lover.

The sun's red orb seemed to sit forever on the horizon as Brenna paced back and forth from bed to window. As darkness finally enveloped the vast fertile fields and moonlight streamed through the trees, her resolve became stronger and stronger.

She now knew that escape was not her only goal. Even more than freedom, she wanted the feel of the stranger's powerful arms around her and the touch of his lips on hers.

Be he Thomas Smythe, common merchant, or John Scallywag, highwayman, she wanted him for her own.

On and on the hours dragged, until her eyes burned

from staring out the window. Then she saw him, etched like a dark but well-defined painting against the sky.

Having dressed in the same riding skirt, cloak and blouse as she had worn at their last meeting, Brenna hurried down the servants' stairs and into the night. The fields were already damp with dew and twice she nearly slipped as she ran.

He saw her long before she reached him and spurred forward to meet her. Brenna stopped, staring, as he cantered down the hill and across the meadow to where she stood.

He rode well, his wide-shouldered, powerful body one with the horse. She noted his clothing, more elegant now. Instead of a tunic, he wore a lavender brushed-velvet doublet. The cloak was also of velvet, a deep burgundy, and his shirt was fine linen, heavily ruffled at wrist and throat. His sword hilt and his spurs glittered in the moonlight, and Brenna noticed that there was not a trace of stubble on his cheeks and jaw.

Had he dressed so scrupulously for her? She indeed hoped so. And then she realized that her own attire was dull and drab. Should she have donned something more alluring, more feminine, for this midnight meeting? Would a dress of fine silk with a low-cut bodice and tightly cinched waist have better served her purpose? What purpose? *Damme,* she thought, *Brenna Coke, you've become an overnight wanton!*

"You came," his deep voice brought her out of her thoughts.

"Of course. 'Twas I that wanted the meeting."

His dark eyes, staring down at her from his mounted height, unnerved her. They were without the humor and merriment she remembered. Now they were piercing and brooding, so much so that she took a step backward.

"You stare so."

"Aye, for I've seen you but three times, and it does amaze me that your beauty grows with each meeting."

Had such words been uttered by gallant or courtier, Brenna would have had a ready reply. But now she could only stand mute and try to mask the elation his words had caused in her breast.

"We must be off," he said, and leaned toward her from his horse.

Again she was amazed at his vast strength. She was not a tiny waif but a tall, large-boned woman. Yet with one arm he effortlessly lifted her from the ground and seated her behind him on the stallion.

"Hold close!"

And then they were riding. Brenna's cheek was pressed against the softness of his cloak and her arms were entwined around the rippling hardness of his chest.

Oh, how I wish, she thought, *we could ride on and on forever and leave everything behind!*

He skirted the village of Norfolk and turned east toward Great Yarmouth and the sea. Brenna closed her eyes and tightened the band of her arms around his chest, as if to will him to ride on to the ocean.

The horse's hooves thundered over a wooden bridge, then abruptly he veered and Brenna nearly lost her seat as they skittered and slid down an embankment until they reached a flat grassy place at the bottom.

He was on the ground, staring up at her with the same haunting expression to his eyes. His arms were outstretched toward her, and Brenna slid willingly into them.

Down, down his body she slid, feeling every inch of his muscled form with her lithe frame. At last the toes of her boots found the grass.

"It will be safe to talk here," he said, his voice deep and exciting in her ear.

She leaned her head back, her face raised toward his in open invitation. It was then that the oddest realization struck her, just as his face bent and their lips met. He was not overly tall, not nearly so huge as he seemed in the saddle. He was but inches taller than she.

His arms wound tighter as their tongues met and passion stirred deeply in Brenna's body. Her breasts spread over the softness of his doublet and she felt the rippling strength of his chest beneath.

"Yes. . . yes," she heard her own voice urge him on to yet another kiss.

With what temerity I suddenly speak, she thought. *Only a few days ago I would never have dreamed of speaking so boldly to any man!*

But there was a reason for it, she knew. She had never felt such strength in a man, never felt so secure wrapped in a pair of arms and swallowed in the darkness of a great cloak.

Their lips parted and still he stood there, her chin and cheek dwarfed in his huge hand. His heavy brows were knitted in a dark V over his eyes. The black pupils seemed to plumb the depths of her soul, asking, wondering.

"I knew," she whispered, "ever since that first night when you righted the carriage."

"And I knew your face to be the one that has haunted my dreams since childhood."

"Do you think me a wanton?" she asked, suddenly shy.

"Nay, lovely one. I think you to be a woman with a will—one who knows her own mind." Suddenly he broke free of her and strode to the edge of the stream. "There are damn few in the world."

"Then you will help me?" she pleaded.

"Flee England?"

"Aye."

He whirled and stood in a spread-legged stance with his hands at his hips, his elbows tented in the dark cloak at his sides until he seemed to loom over her like an unknown, imposing specter.

"Do you know, girl, what it means to have no home, no country to call your own?

"No, but 'tis a fate I prefer to the one I see before me."

"And you would venture all—forsake your birthright for this unknown?"

"Aye, I would."

There was a change in his voice, in his tone, that frightened her. With the moon at his back she couldn't see his shadowed face or read the look in his eyes.

Suddenly his hands worked at the gold clasp at his throat. He whirled the cloak above his head and spread it quickly and neatly on the grassy bank.

"Then lie down!" he ordered.

"What?" she gasped.

"Lie down! You mentioned payment, m'lady. 'Tis not your gold, your money nor your jewelry that I want."

The unexpected turn shocked Brenna, even though the thought had truly been in her mind since his lips had first brushed her hand. "If memory serves correct, sir, you said the only payment required was a smile and a kiss. That you've already received." She hoped her voice carried a regal and haughty tone but knew it didn't.

"I've changed my mind."

"As have I. I'll not be taken like a whore on the bank of a stream in the dead of night by a man that won't even tell me his lawful name!"

"Well said," he replied, turning his face just enough so Brenna could see his broad smile. "I only thought I detected such an invitation in the lady's lips."

She knew the flush that suffused her face was only too evident, even in the darkness. She did the only thing possible and turned from him to hide her embarrassment.

"Perhaps. . . perhaps it was," she whispered, choking back a sob. "But I thought I detected in you a gentleman instead of a rake."

There was a quick movement behind her and again his arms wound around her shoulders. His body pressed tightly to hers and his lips found her ear through the thickness of her dark curls.

"Forgive me, lovely one, for I've lived long in France where most women are wenches, no matter their station. 'Tis a place where women stalk palace halls and Paris streets in search of a man to bed and ruin!"

"I'm not so easy, and if I seemed so it was in a moment of madness."

"Was it?" he asked softly.

His warm breath at her ear made Brenna's entire body tremble against him. She replied as was her wont, truthfully and to the point, for she knew no other way. "It may sound naive and bothersome to one so worldly, but I would love a man."

He turned her in his arms and tilted her face up to his. "And I a maid. So sit!"

"What?"

"Sit! If you will not lie down, *sit* down, for we have much to discuss."

There was no foolishness in his eyes and face now, only the business at hand. Brenna sat on his cloak and, still flushed with embarrassment, gathered the folds of her riding skirt tightly around her knees.

"You were right, of course. My name is not Thomas Smythe, and I am not English nor am I French. I am Irish."

"And your rightful name?"

"I am Rory, The O'Hara, prince of the O'Hara clan and the wearer of the O'Hara mantle." He smiled when there was no change of expression on her face. "That means naught to you, does it?"

"Nay, it does not. I am sorry."

His chuckle was more like a low growl. "No matter, for 'tis a high-sounding title with no substance. There is no O'Hara clan left, as there are few O'Neills and fewer O'Donnells."

"I've heard of them. My mother has spoken of them. She called them brave and foolish men."

"Did she now! Well, your mother was right, lovely one, but that matters naught to you nor I at this point. I told you that I am a fugitive in England, wanted by the crown for engaging in a duel. In France I am wanted as well by the crown." Here he paused and knelt before her, taking her hands in his. "There is but one place left for me. I would lose myself in Ireland until exile is no longer necessary."

Brenna was suddenly struck by the irony of their situation. "How strange our lives!" she exclaimed, with a hollow laugh.

"How so?"

"David Talbot is Scottish, and he would to Ireland for his fortune. You are Irish, and you consider yourself an exile from. . . where, France?"

"Aye, it is curious, but the story would be days in the telling and we haven't time."

"But wait!" Alarm filled her dark eyes as her mind interpreted his meaning. "Would you spirit me to Ireland?"

A touch of mockery returned in the smile he flashed her. "Were Ireland to be your refuge, would you go?"

Her gaze flickered away from his and she involuntarily pulled back her hands. "I—I don't know. 'Tis said it's a heathen land, where rebellion seethes daily and no Englishwoman is safe."

"Ireland, lass, is a beautiful land full of miserable people and English lords. Methinks you would be safe from the Irish but not the English. If it was to Ireland you fled, I fear your father would have you back in a fortnight!" He rose and began pacing in the grass before her. "Nay, 'tis to France you'll go. My sister is there, and I have friends, many friends. There is an abbey at—"

"And you're for Ireland?"

He stopped. There was a plaintive tone in her voice that arrested him. "Aye, it needs must be, lovely one—for now."

Gently he tugged her to her feet. Their eyes found each other in the moonlight, and no further words were needed. Then she was in his arms, rubbing her smooth cheek against the faint bristles of his.

"Do not think me a child, or rash, Rory O'Hara, when I say that methinks I've found a man to love."

He stiffened at once and his hands loosed their hold on the small of her back. "I have known few true ladies in my time, sweet Brenna, so 'tis vexing to find one now."

"Then you, too—"

"Shhh! I am a penniless rogue, likely to stay as such. I had a patron in France, but now he is powerless. I have papers in England proving my birthright, but now I am a fugitive and they are worthless."

Brenna's mind was whirling, his nearness filling her thoughts and blocking out his words. "I lied before. As brazen as it is, I would have given—given everything for my freedom. But that was before. Now, there is more."

She moved against him, her lips searching his. Her hand found his and brought it up to cup her breast.

"I want your love, Rory O'Hara," she breathed.

For an instant, he softened. His hand kneaded the fullness of her bosom, and his body returned the longing it sensed in hers. Then, abruptly, he was like a stone, hard and unyielding, as his hand left her and he pulled away.

"No."

"What?"

" 'Tis not the time, lovely one." His words were followed by a hollow laugh. "I amaze myself! I've wenched and bedded whores, court ladies, Gypsies and jades all my life, but this I cannot do. My God, Brenna Coke, I think you would make a man of me! Come, quickly, I would have you back before dawn!"

Brenna's emotions were in turmoil as he gathered his cloak and lifted her to the stallion's back. She was happy that he respected her so much that he had not taken her brazen offer. And yet, deep in her breast, she wished he had. For she knew, as a woman knows, that she could please him beyond any woman he had ever bedded.

Now that she had found Rory O'Hara, she didn't want to lose him.

She reached down from her seat on the horse and ran her hand over the tanned mahogany of his features. "If 'twere Ireland with you, Rory O'Hara, I would go."

"Aye, I believe you would, lovely one, But 'tis to France you'll go, lass, and that's the end of it!" His voice, as he looked to the saddle's girth, was full of tension. "I've sent word to France. We should hear soon. Mark you well the way here on our ride back. 'Tis here we'll meet next."

Brenna settled into her seat on the horse's rump and spoke as if to herself while her lips curved in a smile. "Methinks I will ride on the morrow and find myself in this same spot."

"Damme, but you're a persistent wench, aren't you?"

"Aye, O'Hara, for I'm a woman who knows her mind, remember?"

CHAPTER TWENTY-TWO

THE HUGE SILVER ROWELS ON BUCKINGHAM'S SPURS jangled so loudly as he swept to and fro in the chamber that the sound threatened to overshadow his words.

Unluckily for David Talbot, they didn't. From where he stood, the earl's words reached his ears loudly and clearly.

"You must know, Sir David, that the stresses and strains of state affairs weigh heavily upon our shoulders at this time."

"I'm sure they do, m'lord."

David shifted his weight nervously from foot to foot and watched Buckingham's tall, lithe body strut and pose its way across the floor. From the corner of his eye he could see Lady Compton's hawklike stare appraise his every reaction to her son's words.

It was all Talbot could do to keep the alternating moods of anger and boredom from showing on his face.

"There is the question of the Spanish marriage, and there is this frightful business on the Continent. I do fear the king's son-in-law will overstep his rank and bring war there. These, I think you'll have to agree, are matters that a man in my position, as advisor to the king, must keep uppermost in mind."

The Earl of Buckingham now stood directly in front of Talbot. David met the man's sardonic stare blankly.

"*Do* you agree, Sir David?"

"Quite, m'lord."

David dropped his eyes to the rapier at Buckingham's side. The hilt was silver, and the hangers holding it were embossed with gold, fairer than the decorative gold on the pillars of St. Paul's Cathedral.

Idly, David fingered the plain hilt of his own blade and wondered if it would take one or two easy parries before he could thrust its point through this strutting popinjay's heart.

"Good, good, I'm glad you understand our daily cares." An imperial wave barely missed David's cheek, and the king's favorite resumed his pacing. "I know you to be a soldier and a man of cards and dice, Talbot, not truly of the gentry but risen through your own skill and wit. I like that."

"I thank you, m'lord," David replied through a tightly clenched jaw. But his mind was railing. *On with it, man! Damme, the next thing he'll bring up is his latest bedchamber romp with the king!*

"In these days in order to gain wealth in London one

must run an ale house, a tobacco house or a whore house. You have managed well with none of these. It bodes well for your intelligence."

David bridled at the earl's careless slurs but remained outwardly calm. It had taken weeks to manage this audience and he wanted nothing to spoil it now.

"Thusly I think we can speak on the same plane. 'Tis vexing that I must handle such trivial matters myself, but sometimes necessary." Again the man lounged before him, the nostrils of his long thin nose narrowed, his lips pursed. "But then, this matter of Irish property is probably not small to you, is it, Talbot?"

"Indeed it is not, m'lord."

"Good, good." Here the flaxen head dipped and the lips curled upward into more of a sneer than a smile. "And I think you'll agree that this smear on my family name by the Coke wench is also no small matter."

"Smear, m'lord? I've heard 'tis your cousin, Sir Raymond Hubbard, who would have none of the match."

A quick, red flush crept up from the duke's cravat until it had nearly suffused his whole face. "The wench has bewitched my cousin's mind! He has some grand delusion of chivalry from days long dead! To be sure, I will soon convince him of his error but, in the meantime...."

David felt his heart sink to his stomach and his breath catch in his throat. "In...the meantime, m'lord?"

"Your offer to the crown for Ballylee is really quite acceptable, you know. I think were you to—"

"Steenie...Steenie...."

The doors at the far end of the room flew open and two pikemen stepped through them. "His Majesty the King!"

David immediately dropped to one knee as Lady

Compton rose from her chair by the fireplace and curtsied low.

Buckingham stood at his ease, dabbing lightly at his lips with a kerchief.

How ironic, David thought, that the king should refer to the Earl of Buckingham as "his little dog," when, in fact, it was the earl himself who was the master!

King James waddled through the door balanced precariously on his spindly legs, and with bleary, red-rimmed eyes searched the room.

"Here, Your Majesty," Buckingham murmured, stepping forward and lightly brushing the king's lips and each cheek with his own.

David chanced a glance upward and barely managed to suppress an audible gasp. It had been years since he had seen the king. Indeed, it had been nearly as long since the monarch had ventured into public from his apartments.

James, who had never been a handsome or healthy man, was now nothing but a ravaged shell. His eyes were as wildly unsteady as his legs. From the odor permeating the air around him, David deduced the reason. The king was drunk.

His appearance was far from kingly. His doublet was stained with food and drink. Where it gaped open, the white linen shirt beneath was filthy. The beard, where it covered the now gaunt face, was matted and badly in need of a trim.

David shuddered. *And this,* he thought, *rules our lives!*

"Steenie, come quickly!" James cried. "The court is dry, and 'tis a perfect afternoon for tennis! 'Twill be a fine match—you, my darling Steenie, and my beloved Charles!"

"Of course, Your Majesty."

"And you will play only in breeches and hose. It is so good to see the sun on my Steenie's bare chest!" As he spoke, the King of England lovingly stroked the Earl of Buckingham's chest and shoulders.

"Of course, Your Majesty."

Buckingham preceded the shambling king from the room. At the doorway, he spoke over his shoulder to Lady Compton. "See to it, mother!"

When they were gone and the pikemen had closed the doors, she rose from her curtsy and regained her seat by the fireplace. "The king hasn't been well," she offered.

" 'Tis a pity, m'lady," David replied, barely stopping the bile that threatened to rise to his throat.

"We are told that you have some influence over the young lady, Brenna Coke."

"We have been friends."

"I have talked to Sir Edward, and he has agreed to extend your lease at Elmeham House until all your Irish workers can be moved to Ballylee."

"Does that mean—"

"It means, Sir David, that we are assured of your sway over the young lady."

CHAPTER TWENTY-THREE

BRENNA RODE THE NEXT AFTERNOON to the same secluded grassy spot and waited. She waited until dusk, but he never came. She nibbled on the lunch she had prepared and alternated between cursing herself for her girlish foolishness and decrying Rory O'Hara for not meeting her.

All she could think was that he had changed his mind, that he had been merely toying with her hopes, her emotions and her affections.

But if that were true, why had he not taken her when she had so brazenly and willingly offered herself?

By dusk, when she reluctantly mounted Starlight and rode back to Elmeham House, she was thoroughly confused. She was almost frightened enough by the thought that she wouldn't see him again, that he had already fled, that she felt an urge to storm the stable quarters, find where he slept and face him with her questions.

But the prudent part of her mind held her in check. Instead, as night wore on, she took up her vigil by the window in case that dark silhouette again appeared on the horizon.

Little could Brenna know the turmoil she had caused in Rory O'Hara. He was actually fearful of venturing forth from his tiny stable room lest he should meet her on Elmeham grounds.

For the first time in his life, Rory felt that he wasn't in command with a woman. He feared he couldn't control his actions. How stupid it would be—and how dangerous—to pull her lovely body against his and devour her lips in front of Elmeham's servants and field hands. Yet he felt if he saw her again, that is exactly what might happen, so strong was his desire.

For hours at a stretch he lay on a straw pallet, his hands beneath his head, staring upward at the barn's rough-hewn beams and roof.

But it was Brenna's face and form he beheld, taking shape, fading and jarringly taking shape again as if to haunt him. He saw the slightly almond eyes as darkly lustrous as her raven hair. He licked his own lips as he discovered the pouting beauty of hers, cerised just enough to give them a rubylike inviting glow.

He imagined her dressed in a tight-bodiced ebony satin dress. The firmly rounded swells of her breasts above the deep, square-cut neckline made his palms tingle and his groin stir to life.

He could remember no other woman with a waist so small, a hip so smooth or a leg so perfectly formed. She was a bewitching creature, and Rory O'Hara knew she had bewitched him. But how could it have happened in such a short time and under such appalling circumstances?

He had known from the instant he set eyes upon her that it was the face of his dreams. He had known that face since boyhood, but he had never thought of it as more than a dream. Now the dream was a reality. Rory O'Hara had no doubts that he loved Brenna Coke.

His sister Shanna's oft-said phrase came rushing to him. "'Twill only be a fine woman who will tame your wild soul, dear brother. Pray God I see the day it happens, for then and only then will you be a man!"

Well, he thought, it had happened, and little good it would do. His immediate fate was to hide away in an Irish booley house until he could again sell himself as a mercenary in Spain or France. What life would that be for a lady as grand as Brenna Coke, riding after her husband into battle like a camp follower?

The thought not only saddened him, it sickened him enough to make him roll over on the pallet and blot her face from his mind. And as sleep claimed him, O'Donnell's words, uttered so often so many years before, echoed in his ears. "To be unfulfilled and unhappy in love and war is an Irish curse."

It was a warning Rory had heeded all his life, but even

as he thought of it, he knew he would ride out to meet her the next afternoon.

NO ONE WOULD KNOW THE FEAR IN HER BREAST from the look of fierce determination on Brenna's face as she rode across the narrow wooden bridge and guided her horse through the trees down to the stream. Starlight whinnied as she alighted, but there was no answering neigh from the great stallion.

No matter, Brenna thought, *he will come. I know he will come!*

She spread her cloak near the stream, retrieved a small basket of food she had tied to the saddle and sat. "I know my mind and I know my heart," she said aloud. "And I know I can't be wrong in what I do."

Shadows lengthened as the sun reached its peak and began its downward slide. The shrill cries of crows and blackbirds faded until all was calm and quiet, awaiting the thrush's evening song.

"He will come," she whispered to the gently moving stream. "Dusk is safer. That is when he will come."

As if the rippling water were a sorcerer answering her wish, the sound of a galloping horse shattered the still air. Across the bridge the hooves clattered and then the big gray stallion was snorting its way down the embankment.

Brenna was on her feet, fingers pressed tightly to her lips, her eyes wide.

It was a moment that seemed an eternity. He sat astride the dancing stallion, his dark eyes locked on hers. When he spoke, the lilt of the Irish accent she could now detect seemed more marked.

"'Tis a daft thing we do, lass."

"Aye."

"You're sure."

"As sure of this as anything I've ever done or ever will do," she whispered, and raised her arms toward him.

He unclasped his cloak as he slid from the saddle. It trailed to the ground as they rushed into each other's arms. Beneath the mahogany-colored tan, his face was transformed by passion as he bent his head to hers. "You're a witch that has stolen my soul, Brenna Coke."

"Nay, Rory O'Hara. I'm a maid who would give you my heart."

Slowly, their lips parting for only an instant, they slid into the tall grass at their feet. He lay, stretching his limbs beside hers as he hooked a finger under his cravat and tore open his shirt to the navel.

Again they kissed, and Brenna thrilled to the touch of his broad, bare chest beneath her hand. She sensed an undercurrent of animallike desire in the insistent way their bodies met, yet his hands as they worked at the laces of her bodice were skillful and gentle.

The moan that escaped his lips was full of awe and love when at last her chemise was raised and her breasts bared to his gaze. Lightly he brushed the taut nipples with his warm lips before covering her face with kisses.

There was an odor of sweat and horse on his body and clothes, but Brenna cared little. She reveled in it, in the pure masculinity that emanated from him, so different from the heavily perfumed fops and gallants in London who had plagued her with their veiled and empty propositions.

"The cloak," he murmured, suddenly realizing where they had fallen.

"Nay, my love, it matters not."

His hands were almost hesitant, as if he were still not sure of her acceptance. To urge him on and calm her own vague fears, Brenna encircled his neck with her arms and pulled his face forcefully to hers. Between parted lips her tongue sought his, and her body arched to meet his exploring hands.

"I would love you as no man has ever loved a woman," he said huskily, as he broke from their kiss at last, his dark features as pleading as they were demanding. He had never felt such need in his loins for a woman, such desire in his soul to give as well as take.

"Rory, my O'Hara, my Irishman, my man!" she murmured. Brenna wanted nothing more than to dissolve beneath this exciting Irishman's powerful body and be devoured by his love.

"Can you truly love me, Brenna Coke?"

"I know it," she sighed, "as surely as there is night and day."

Slowly and with more gentleness than Brenna had thought possible he claimed her, his throbbing manhood entering her and filling her mind and body completely with its demanding passion. Then there was nothing but the aching sweetness of their love. The stream nearby that had been so quiet was now a roaring torrent in her ears as they consummated a desire that would not be denied.

She thought she heard his voice murmuring words of love and endearment, but all her being was focused on their union. They were clasped tightly, desperately together, moving as one.

What pain she felt was unbearably sweet, and then even that was gone in the explosion of fulfillment.

Finally they lay, his tremendous arms wrapped protectively around her, both breathing heavily for many moments. Slowly Brenna's mind swam up from the depths of exhausted relief and her eyelids parted.

He was looking down at her, his eyes full of adoration. He smoothed the damp hairs from her temples and stroked her face and neck.

"Do you feel loved?" he smiled.

"More than I ever dreamed possible," she murmured, running her fingers over the rippling smoothness of his powerful back.

He rolled to his side. It was then, for the first time, that Brenna realized they were both naked. It surprised her, since she couldn't remember how it had been accomplished. Giddily her mind filled with all the intricacies of love. . . of man, of woman, and their joining.

She allowed her eyes to move downward, drinking in the manly perfection of his powerful frame. His body was godlike in its olive-skinned beauty. She was fascinated by the rippling movement of his muscles under the smooth skin.

It amazed her that she had barely noticed or felt the tremendous weight of his body when it had covered hers. She couldn't resist running her fingers over the hardness of his belly, gathering the fine drops of perspiration she found there. With joy and delight she found herself totally unembarrassed.

"You are so beautiful," she said.

"As are you," he smiled, filling his nostrils with the sweet scent of her hair.

Brenna looked down at her own nude body. It, too, was covered with a light sheen of perspiration, and it seemed to glow in the rays of the sun muted by the leafy trees.

Suddenly she burst into laughter. It was a gay laugh, like the bells on a passing tinker's cart.

"You must forgive me," she said, in response to his questioning gaze. "This is all so new and strange, yet so wonderful. I wish. . . ."

"Yes?" His voice was muffled in the side of her throat while his hand gently caressed her.

"Is it a perversion to wish that there was a mirror here beside us? The thought has just struck me that we make a beautiful couple. I would truly love to see us together!"

His rumbling laugh filled the glen as he wrapped his powerful arms and legs around her and began to roll over and over in the grass.

"Damme, if you aren't a miracle!" he roared. "How can one so innocent be such a wanton wench?"

"By loving you, Rory O'Hara. By loving you!"

IN THE DAYS THAT FOLLOWED the lovers stole away from Elmeham House at every opportunity. Rather than receding, the tide of their need and desire for each other grew with each meeting, each touch, each kiss. They were like children, whether they were gamboling in dew-damp grass or lying naked, side by side, in a vacant shepherd's hut.

Brenna felt full of lighthearted gaiety and happiness, as though she were riding on a gilt-edged cloud. She soon realized that she had not laughed much in her young life, having always been caught in the middle of the struggle between her bickering parents. Being with Rory O'Hara seemed to sweep all that away.

The tiniest thing—a word, a smile, a gentle touch—communicated volumes between them.

"Do you know, O'Hara, that you have a regal head, and you hold it well...at times. And then at other times, you bow it as though in defeat."

"Ah, my wise philosopher—look to yourself!"

"How so?"

"Because you do the same," he chuckled.

She paused, and then studied his face through narrow eyes. "Have you realized how alike we are—our appearance, I mean?" she asked Rory one evening as he lay gazing at the twinkling stars. "We could well be twins rather than lovers!" she giggled.

"An appalling thought," he laughingly replied.

"Indeed it is," she said, "but 'tis true. Sometimes I look at you and I feel I've known you all my life."

A strange cloud passed over his face before he replied. "I know. 'Tis indeed odd, but often I feel the same about you."

Brenna's lovely forehead wrinkled in a frown. "Do you suppose it to be a bad omen?"

"I believe not in omens, lass!" Suddenly he reached up and tousled her hair. "Od's blood, what maudlin talk. Come, a midnight swim will cool your fears!"

"But not my passion!" Brenna laughed, as she romped before him to the stream and dove in to let the cold water rush over her naked body.

They lolled in the water, touching, caressing, and then he carried her back to the grassy bank and made tender, sweet, beautiful love to her.

But always, in the quiet stillness of the aftermath, they would realize that they were adults and time was short. It was then that Brenna learned much about the handsome Irishman with the rakish smile who had so captured her heart. She was glad that it seemed he had always been in her life, this burly, reckless man with the powerful body and the gentlest of hands. She learned of his days in Rome and then Paris, drinking, wenching and living by his wits. He told her of his boyhood in Ireland and described his warlike father, Shane.

"Perhaps that is part of my fear of Ireland and of being Irish. I fear I am my father's son. Deep down here, in my breast, is a devil. Shane, my father, had it and his father before him. 'Tis the will and lust for war."

Then, in whispered words with a voice more like a poet's than a soldier's, he told her the terrible, beautiful story of Deirdre of the Sorrows, an ancient Irish tale his own mother, Deirdre, had related to him as a child. It was a story of star-crossed lovers and strangely echoed the fate of his own parents.

"And my mother, Deirdre, so loved my father, Shane, that she killed him herself rather than let the English defile his death."

"I think, Rory O'Hara, that I love you as much," Brenna responded, her voice tremulous with deep emotion.

And just as quickly his mercurial mood would change. He would damn Ireland and all the Irish.

"They love a good fight, and methinks they almost love to lose. Perhaps because they're so accustomed to it!"

But underneath his sarcasm Brenna detected a deep attachment to the land of his birth. She sensed that he was afraid to bare his heart and admit that, like his sister, Shanna, he also dreamed of one day reclaiming the land. It was during one of these moments, when he spoke quietly, with nostalgic reverence, that Brenna received the first premonition that all might not fare smoothly in their relationship.

"Odd things come to my mind at times, lass, of those days so long ago. I remember lazy afternoons on the heath with my sister, my mother and a girl called Annie who cared for us like a saint. I remember a traveling harper who could pluck his strings to make the sounds of a rippling sea as he sang sad laments to long-dead heroes. There were many good times before the bad ones at Ballylee."

Brenna felt an arrow of fear suddenly strike through her heart. "Oh, dear God!" she gasped, sitting bolt upright beside him.

"What is it, lass? You're as white as a sheet."

"You said. . . Ballylee?"

"Aye, 'tis the land of the clan O'Hara, in the west between Donegal and Connaught. You know of it?"

Brenna swayed where she sat. A hand seemed to be grasping her throat as if to cut off her breathing. "Is this the land you spoke of, the land you have papers of ownership for?"

"Aye," Rory replied, alarmed now, for huge tears had welled up in her eyes and he thought she would surely faint. "Damme, girl, you look as if you've seen a ghost. What is it?"

"You mean, you don't know? The Irish workmen at Elmeham House? Sir David's plans. . . ?"

"Nay, as I told you, we speak little. Sir David doesn't even know my true name."

Suddenly she leaped up and ran to the stream, there to crouch, huddled into a ball. Rory sensed a strange agony in her that he couldn't fathom, and waited for her shoulders to stop quaking and the sound of her sobs to cease before he approached.

"What is it, lass, about the rubble of Ballylee Castle and the untilled, wasted lands of my father that so unnerves you?"

She told him of her conversation with David Talbot in the Inn of the Three Ravens. In a halting voice, she described the look in David's eyes when he spoke of Ballylee, and the dream he had to better the lot of his Irish kerns, as well as to become an Irishman of landed gentry himself.

For many moments Rory crouched beside her in silence. Brenna couldn't turn, couldn't face what she was sure would be a thundercloud of anger on his face.

What toys we are in the hands of fate, she thought. *My lover and my only true friend vying for the same plot of earth!* And for both of them, admit it or not, this land of Ballylee could change their lives, could truly give meaning to those lives!

And then other thoughts crept into her mind. Would the issue of the land cause a duel between them? She knew Rory to be a soldier, probably skilled with pistol and sword, and fearless. But she also knew the reputation of David Talbot. No man, no matter how accomplished, had ever survived a duel with Sir David.

"Rory, you must—"

She was brought up short when she turned, and instead of scowling anger, she was met with a wide, jaunty smile.

" 'Tis indeed odd, this life we lead."

"Then you're not angry?"

"Angry? How can I be angry, lass. Talbot has his dream. Methinks it more worthwhile than mine, in fact. And he has the funds to give it life."

"But Ballylee is *yours*—by the king's own hand! You've said so."

"Aye, but what would I have in the end? 'Twould still be rubble! Nay, it sounds as though David Talbot's idea of plantationing is far more akin to the dream of an Irishman than it is to his Scots brothers or English cousins. If 'tis true, I may even help him get his Ballylee!"

CHAPTER TWENTY-FOUR

"PREPOSTEROUS! RIDICULOUS!" ELIZABETH HISSED, her hand shaking violently as she raised a glass of wine to her lips.

"Is it, madam?" David Talbot replied, moving slightly in his chair, his spurred and booted feet thrown casually over a padded footstool. "Do you think the resolution so preposterous...or is the thought of having me as a son-in-law so ridiculous?"

Elizabeth moved to his side and stared down into his watery eyes. They had arrived at North Elmeham from London two hours before. Since then, David had been drinking heavily. *Amazing,* she thought. *By now he should be immobile or in a stupor!* Immobile she was sure he was, but his speech was still clear and his mind seemed little affected by the many goblets of brandy he had poured down his throat.

"I admire you, David, you know that. I admire you as I admire all survivors. You have a wit and a will. You have ambition, and God knows you are true to yourself as a man, even if you appear the wastrel."

David answered with a low chuckle, "It sounds as though the mother would prefer me for herself."

"I'm ten years your senior!" Elizabeth retorted.

"Touché," he grinned, letting just the touch of a slur enter his voice. "And I am fifteen years Brenna's. But this leads us to nothing. I—"

The clatter of hoofbeats in the courtyard interrupted him. Lady Hatton was at the window in an instant. David twice attempted to pull himself from the chair, gave it up and slumped back to sip more brandy.

"'Tis Brenna! And riding in a misty rain—the girl will catch her death!"

"Good—I mean, that she's here. She can decide for herself."

A moment later Brenna rushed breathlessly into the room, shaking the dampness from her dark curls.

"Mama...David...." Talbot saluted Brenna's curtsy with a smile and with a wave of the brandy goblet in his right hand. With his left he reached for the half-full decanter. "Mama, you've returned a day early...?"

"The council has voted in your father's favor—"

"Oh, no!" Brenna gasped, and rushed to the window. Carefully her eyes scanned the tiny window above the stable. Could they run now?

"Tell her the rest," David growled from his chair.

Brenna's spine stiffened and her breath caught in her throat. "Sir Raymond has relented?" she whispered.

"Nay, not yet," Elizabeth said. "But I fear he will soon have no choice in the matter nor voice to speak his will. 'Tis the king who speaks now."

"The king?" Brenna gasped, whirling to face her mother.

Elizabeth's face was composed, but beneath the facade of calm Brenna could see her mother crumbling as she spoke. "The king's own command has come down from Falkland to that puppy Bacon and Archbishop Abbott. I have been commanded to restore you to Sir Edward and not entice you away again. And you shall not be contracted to anyone without the assent of your father."

"And if you refuse?"

David coughed and answered for Elizabeth. "If the

Lady Hatton refuses, your lovely mother will be thrown into Fleet Prison at the king's pleasure. 'Tis the type of rule we now live under!"

"Then all *is* lost!" Brenna moaned.

"Nay, not a bit." David lurched to his feet. Unsteadily, decanter in one hand and goblet in the other, he weaved his way across the room. "There is a simple solution. We must have you carted off and wed. Without your mother's knowledge or consent, of course!"

Brenna's eyes flickered toward the stable and her jaw set in a determined line. She was about to speak, to tell them both of Rory O'Hara, when David continued.

"I had my audience with the king's dog, his Steenie, and his hatchet-faced mother. What a pair they are, those two. With all the poison in the realm, 'tis a pity I can't bribe one of their tasters. I'm sure all of England would canonize me and dance on Buckingham's grave!"

Here, he paused to drain the goblet he held.

"Forgive me, where was I? Ah, yes, my audience. I was informed that my offer for Ballylee was quite acceptable—under certain terms."

Brenna blinked and furrowed her brow in bewilderment. "Terms?"

"Aye. The old bitch and her whelp are well acquainted with the fast friendship between us. I was informed, in clear terms, that should I be able to convince you of the advantages of this match with Sir Raymond, I could start moving my Irishmen to Ballylee."

"Oh, David!" Brenna cried out, biting her lower lip and thrusting her hands out as if to grasp his tunic.

"I must admit, lass, that for a moment—just the barest of moments, mind you—I entertained the thought of being a traitor to your friendship." He laughed aloud now, almost hysterically, and refilled his goblet. "But my stupendous sense of loyalty, my unswerving devotion to the rights of my fairest damsel, my— Are you believing all this *merde*?"

The incongruity, the sheer lunacy of it all suddenly struck her. Though tears filled her eyes and choking sobs racked her chest, she could not hold back a bubbling laugh. For here was the old David, the friend she knew who could make her laugh, make her forget her own cares.

"But I digress. Actually, my sweet Brenna, I decided that Ballylee would be hell if I attained it in such a manner. Also, Ireland is still under English rule, and England is under James's rule. And that drunken lecher is under the foot of Buckingham and that matronly crone he calls mother. I fully believe that England under the leadership of these nincompoops will fade into the sea and take Scotland and Ireland with her. Therefore, I'll to France and save you as well as myself?"

"Me?"

"Aye," Talbot replied as he dropped to one knee. "I would wive you, Brenna Coke!"

"David, 'tis a joke—"

"What say you, woman? *Joke?* You thrust at my pride and honor!"

Again he had brought a laugh to her lips. But just as quickly it died when she saw his face cloud with an expression of sober solemnity.

"Nay, Brenna, 'tis no joke. Naught can they do if I steal you off. And, at the same time, 'twould strike a blow at Buckingham! Your betrothal is no great matter of state, I grant, but someone must defy that popinjay in some way—even in a small manner—or all our lives will one day be forfeit."

Brenna looked up at her mother. Elizabeth's eyes were blank, staring into nothingness. It shocked Brenna. Never had she seen her mother at a loss for words or action. Now she seemed as a ghost, adrift in a maze with no end.

Her concentration was drawn back to David as he struggled to his feet and stared at her through red-rimmed eyes. Never had she seen him look so pathetic. Had all this at last combined to break him?

"You would give up your dream, your Ballylee, for me, David?"

"Aye, lass, for methinks it was ever just a dream, no more. And I give you my word I'll wive you in name only. We'll to France and when the stir dies, for surely it will, we'll divorce and you can return on your own terms."

His generosity was too much to bear and far too much to ask. One of the men she cared most for in the world was willing to give up everything for her.

"David, I think you should hie to the stables."

"Aye, we should both hie to the stables and then to France, while there's still time."

"Aye, soon," she said. "But first talk to your boarder."

The lopsided smile on David's face disappeared and a flash of sobriety entered his eyes. "Smythe? What know you of him?"

"Methinks more than you, David. His name is O'Hara, not Smythe. He is The O'Hara, of the clan O'Hara."

"Damme," David growled, suddenly sober. "Of Ballylee!"

"Aye. And 'tis O'Hara I would wed. We leave tonight for France and the protection of his godfather, one Rory O'Donnell."

There was an audible gasp from behind David, then Lady Hatton crumpled to the floor.

RORY O'HARA CHUCKLED TO HIMSELF as he surveyed the fine clothes strewn about the room. Their tailor had been purchased with Armand de Richelieu's money. They were meant to be the finery that would allow him entrance into London society.

Now they were excess baggage, and it was just as well. In the weeks since he had been in England, Rory had discovered that he had no taste for subterfuge. He would never make a spy, even one whose only duty was to watch and report to Richelieu the daily life of Londoners and what he could learn of the court at Westminster and Whitehall.

No, he thought, where he was bound he would not need fine clothes and polished boots. It would be to France, but only long enough to deposit Brenna with The O'Donnell and Sister Anna. Then it would be on to Ireland to do his own spying, in his own way.

A half hour before, Brenna had rushed into the room. Breathlessly she had recounted the scene in the big house: Sir David Talbot's chivalrous but drunken proposal and her mother's strange swoon.

"Ready yourself," Rory had told her, "and take very little, for we will have to ride for speed. There will be no time for a coach."

She had rushed away, and as Rory had watched her running across the courtyard, her skirts to her knees, her shining black hair flying behind her, his heart had swelled. He knew as sure as life itself that he had found his woman to love, his reason to be.

And now he was tying leather thongs around a narrow saddle roll. In it was The O'Hara mantle and a single change of shirt and breeches, as well as a leather tunic to replace the finely embroidered doublet he now wore and would wear until he left France to wait in Ireland for a commission in the French king's musketeers.

It was nearly done when David Talbot burst into the room.

"Tom Smythe, hey?"

"'Twas Richelieu's conception, Sir David. He thought it best."

"Aye, he would. But no matter the deception now."

Talbot stood, weaving slightly as he stared strangely at the younger man. Then he was lurching toward Rory, his arms outstretched. "O'Hara! O'Hara of Ballylee!" he cried in a strangled voice.

For the briefest of moments Rory backed away, his glance alighting on the sheathed rapier that hung on a peg near his head. Then something in the other man's contorted features, some ironic twist to his parted lips or, perhaps, the insanity in Talbot's wild, bloodshot eyes held his hand.

"Aye, Sir David. I am indeed Rory, The O'Hara of Ballylee, as Brenna has told you."

"She told me that and more." Suddenly Talbot's arms came forward and seized him by the shoulders. Rory was amazed at the strength in the much slighter man's grip. "Is it true? Do ye really have papers proving you are The O'Hara and rightful heir to the lands of Ballylee?"

"I do," Rory nodded, "and Haskins House and lands here in England as well, though they will do me little good on that score."

Talbot's eyes rolled. The low, guttural laugh he forced out was almost satanic. "We shall see about that, O'Hara of Ballylee!"

"'Tis Ballylee I would speak to you of before we leave, Sir David—"

"And I to you, lad, but first these golden papers," Talbot roared, lurching backward and releasing Rory. "I would see them!"

Rory smiled to himself as he crossed the narrow room and retrieved the papers from an inner pocket of his cloak. "There, Sir David. I give you the ten thousand acres and the rubble that is Ballylee."

David Talbot caught the sheaf of papers with more agility than his tipsy state would seem to allow. He paid no attention to Rory's words nor to their veiled implication as he tore the binding from the thin package. Raptly, he dropped to his knees and read.

"Signed by King James himself, they are," he murmured, and read on. "And, damme, look at this phrase, '. . . and such heir or heirs shall not be forced to institute a suit in order to obtain their rightful possession of lands should said lands and houses pass back into the hands of the crown.' And all witnessed by Sir Robert Cecil." Here, Talbot turned his hooded, slate-gray eyes upward and a tight grin slashed across his haggard face. "Lad, 'tis indeed a legal document. Ballylee can well be yours without suing for your livery. The king has enough trouble with the courts and Parliament without denying a writ of law laid down by his own hand."

The look of sheer joy on David Talbot's face amazed O'Hara. It was just as Brenna had described. Rory envied him, for here knelt a man who had his dream in his hands.

But then, hadn't he, Rory O'Hara, found his own

dream? He had—and he was determined to pursue it at all costs.

"You would to Ireland before you would breathe, wouldn't you, Talbot?"

"Aye, lad, I would, for I love the spirit of the people and the look of the land. Had I been other than but a few years of age during O'Neill and O'Donnell's days of war, methinks I would have been a gallowglass mercenary and taken a piece of Ireland as reward for my services."

"'Tis yours there, Talbot, and without lifting a sword."

"What say you? Are you mad?"

"Nay, 'tis just that I have no taste for the land. I would to France with Brenna and plead justice before King Louis. I have some friends there. I think with their help I can raise a post in the king's musketeers."

With a roar, Talbot came to his feet. His eyes were narrowed to slits as he stomped the room, whirling on Rory and away again as he ranted.

"Damn me for an idealist and you, O'Hara, for an Irish fool! *I'll* to France with Brenna and care for her in your stead. You stay and fester in Buckingham's skin like a bad boil with your rights. If they would try you before council, then bargain your sentence with the Haskins claim and settle for Ballylee. You'll win, lad! Mark me, I know Buckingham's greed. It takes the place of justice—even the king's justice!"

Rory shook his head. How like The O'Donnell himself Talbot now sounded. "Nay, Sir David. Your words are true, but their end is false. If I would win today, I would but lose tomorrow."

"How can you speak thus?" Talbot replied, his eyes full of fury. "Od's blood man, do you realize who you are? You are The O'Hara! You are the family, the name, you have the blood. Zounds, but I do envy you that, and here you are, wallowing in self-pity for what is lost, not living for what can be gained!"

"It was lost before I was born, and it will not be gained back in my lifetime," Rory said, taking the rapier from the wall in preparation for his departure. "I've wanted or needed little in my life, Talbot, 'til now."

"The girl...."

"Aye, and I'll not have her the wife of a penniless Irishman sitting on land that only waits the grabbing of an English taxman." Talbot opened his mouth to speak, but Rory stopped him with an upraised hand. "Hold! Each day more land is seized from the native Irish. 'Tis done on the pretext of a defective title. Aye, now I have a valid title, but the day will come—and you know it, David Talbot—when Buckingham or the king or, if James dies, his son, will find a way to deny my right. And if 'tis none of them who does me in, then it will be some petty lord who has the law on his side. 'Tis the way of the English. You have the will, the funds and the men, Sir David, to rebuild Ballylee. And you are a Scot. Hard put they would be to put you off the land once it was yours."

"Nay, I cannot," Talbot replied. "Not now, not when I know of this!"

Now it was Rory's turn to grab the smaller man by the shoulders. "You can! Those papers can be even more fodder to force Buckingham and the crown to sell you Ballylee. Don't you see? They would rather settle in such a manner with you and take the gold you would put in their coffers than chance dealing with a rightful heir and receiving nothing!"

David Talbot's eyes grew wide as he saw the saneness, the logic, of O'Hara's words. With the papers he now held he could practically force Buckingham's hand.

"I would ask you but one thing, Sir David—that you share your good fortune with my sister, Shanna. Of the O'Hara brood, 'tis she who has the dream of Ireland in her blood."

Talbot shook his head as he gazed into the other man's eyes. "'Tis hard to believe, O'Hara, that you would give up what so many others hold so dear." He moved across the room and paused, staring with brooding eyes through the narrow window. "I do not understand you."

"'Tis enough that my sister has her piece of the old sod, and I'll be thankful for it," Rory said softly. "For myself, 'tis Brenna I want, and peace where I can find it."

"'Tis tempting," Talbot groaned, more to himself than to the room's other occupant. "Had I the choice, I would have been born to Ballylee as you have been. Damme, O'Hara, I dreamed of one day being Baron of Ballylee!"

"And you will! Send your men to Ireland. Settle your claim with the crown. I will oversee the land there until you have settled your problems here and can join me. By then, my friend René de Gramont will have interceded with King Louis for me and, I hope, have paved my way back to France."

At the window Talbot was in his own world. "Baron of Ballylee," he whispered. 'Twould indeed be a dream realized. But I fear 'tis a false mantle I would wear and I would know it."

Suddenly he turned, and the David Talbot who faced Rory now was again the man he had first met weeks before. The shoulders were squared, the spine straight and the gray eyes steely sober.

"'Tis you, Rory O'Hara, on whose shoulders the O'Hara velvet belongs, but damme if I won't take your bargain!"

O'Hara was across the room in an instant. The two men embraced and stood back, holding one another by the shoulders.

"But mark me, Rory O'Hara, 'tis in fourths we and our heirs will share Ballylee. And you as well as your sister will share alike!"

"In fourths?" Rory replied with a puzzled frown.

"Yes, you and your sister, myself and my daughter, Aileen," David answered. Rory raised his eyebrows in question again, surprised that David had a daughter somewhere, but before Talbot could answer him, a crashing sound assaulted their ears from the gatehouse at the end of the long avenue leading to Elmeham's manor.

Both men whirled at once. It was David who read the situation first and spoke. "Od's blood, lad, it looks as though our bargain might be dissolved before it's begun!"

"What the devil—"

"I wager 'tis the fool, Coke. He would take the king at his word and the matter into his own hands!"

Even as David spoke the huge iron gates splintered beneath the onslaught of a dozen or more men wielding a huge log. The gates had barely hit the ground when a second dozen men on horseback streamed down the avenue toward the manor house. At their head, brandishing an old-style broadsword of Elizabethan vintage, was Sir Edward Coke.

They rode directly to the main entrance, where Coke

alighted and, waving the sword toward the upper windows, demanded entrance. When he received no reply, he motioned the men with the felled tree to the huge oaken doors and shouted again.

"Madam, I know you are there! I demand my daughter in the name of King James and I warn you, should you and yours see fit to deny me my paternal rights we have a warrant in the king's name for her return. And, madam, be further warned. If we should kill any of your people, it would be justifiable homicide; but if any of you should kill one of us, it would surely be murder."

At Rory's elbow at the stable window, David Talbot guffawed loudly. "And that from the greatest barrister in all England and the former chief justice of the king's bench. Come along!"

"To what end?" Rory asked, counting the milling men at the front of the house.

"Why, lad, to save the day!" Talbot replied with a laugh. "If you would aid me in my dream of becoming landed gentry, the least I can do is aid you in rescuing your lady!"

"Sir David, there are two dozen at least—"

"Aye, good odds," Talbot replied, already heading for the door. "Two fighting Irishmen against a dozen English. Let's to it, lad, and mind you, try only to wound them!"

CHAPTER TWENTY-FIVE

ELIZABETH LAY ATOP THE SATIN COVERLET, staring through a break in the curtains that hung from the great canopy. The curtained sides of the huge four-poster gave the illusion of a tiny room inside a larger one and imparted a sense of serenity and safety. But she knew that feeling was false when she saw her beloved Brenna standing at one of the room's tall, recessed windows. The girl was wringing her hands and staring unblinkingly down into the courtyard.

Was he down there, already saddling horses for their flight, Elizabeth wondered. She narrowed her eyes to slits and focused all the attention she could muster on the image of her daughter. Brenna was dressed to ride, and it was as a peasant or milkmaid rather than a titled lady. Elizabeth noted sadly the coarse gray woolen riding skirt, the plain brown blouse with the laced bodice, the unfinished leather of cheap, low-heeled black boots.

If she goes with the Irishman, Elizabeth mused, *it will be her garb for the rest of her life. Is it what I've raised her to, fought for, perhaps sacrificed all I own, so as to give her a life without the struggles and unhappiness that I have had? Is this to be the end of it?* The thought made bile rise to the woman's throat.

Brenna was speaking, but Elizabeth paid little attention. At last she broke in on her daughter's words with thoughts of her own. "'Tis folly, you know!"

"Aye, it has all been folly, 'til now," Brenna replied with a trace of bitterness in her voice.

"I mean, it is folly this thing your father does to us,

but 'tis a greater folly, my darling, to do what you would do with this Irishman!"

"Nay, mother, 'twould be folly not to go, for I know now that to love is to live."

Tears welled in Elizabeth's eyes at Brenna's unknowing reproach, but she managed to hold back the sobs that threatened to rack her.

"But your place, your wealth, the Hatton wealth that I've schemed to guard for you all these years.... Would you turn your back on that?"

Brenna turned to face her mother. Elizabeth could barely see the girl's features from where she lay, but she sensed their sternness. "I don't mean to hurt you, mother, please believe that, but aye, I would. 'Tis a curse I say, this Hatton money. It has brought you unhappiness all your life. Would you have it bring me a loveless marriage?"

Then Brenna was standing over her, the tears in the girl's eyes matching Elizabeth's. But in Brenna's eyes Elizabeth saw no doubt, no fear, only flashing determination. There was a resolute line to her delicate jaw and her voice, when she spoke again, was firm and full of conviction.

"For too many nights I have cried myself to sleep, only to awaken in the morning with more misery than that which accompanied me to my bed the previous night."

Brenna grasped one of her mother's hands and clamped it tightly to her bosom. "Do you feel that, mother? Do you know why my heart pounds so? 'Tis because of this Irishman. Aye, he probably is the rogue you say he is, and his destiny is probably all the sadness that you say it will be. But you must understand. I don't care. He is my Irishman and my man, and I will have him!"

"Brenna, I—"

"You could never know how it is to have those strong arms around you, that deep voice at your ear whispering the words 'I love you,' until it seems like thunder in your brain. Every moment I am not at his side, seeing him, touching him, is a wasted moment in my life. I don't blame you for not knowing how I feel—"

With a tiny gasp of pain, Elizabeth pulled her hand away and rolled to the opposite side of the bed, more than anything to remove her tortured features from Brenna's gaze.

Know? Oh, dear God, little one, how well I know of what you speak...and how all of it has rushed back over me like the driving waves of an ocean at the mere mention of his name. Love? You think that I have never known love? Oh, child, I've had the greatest love a woman can have—and you are the product of it!

All thoughts of Brenna were swept away as Elizabeth's mind swirled back in time and she relived the wondrous moments of her own tempestuous affair with the young and dashing Rory O'Donnell.

So many years it had been, and yet she could still feel his kisses on her lips and body, still see him starkly outlined against the flashing lightning in the sky above Corfe Castle. And she still heard his voice as he wrapped her in his arms. "Elizabeth, my love, my only love!"

Then he was gone, back to his Ireland and his wars. And Elizabeth had tried to push his memory from her brain in the same way she had pushed Coke from her bed.

But it had been impossible. How many nights when a huge crescent moon had sat on the trees outside her window, had Elizabeth looked across Hatton Garden to what had once been Haskins House and seen his handsome, smiling face?

What had happened? Where had the fault lain? With her uncle, Robert Cecil, for putting them together and then forcing them apart? Or had it been Elizabeth herself who had made the final choice?

"Come with me, lass," he had cried so often, "and be my queen. We will rule Ireland together!"

An empty dream, and they had both known it. But he had had to leave her, for he loved his Ireland. It was in his blood to save his land as much as it was in Elizabeth's to follow the dictum of her birth. She was a daughter and granddaughter of Cecils and a Hatton by marriage. She had wealth, position and power in her own land, England. Her choice had been to keep it.

Oh yes, little one, I had my love—the very love you now think you have—and I chose to give it up!

Suddenly, as if the tides had changed, Elizabeth grew calm. She opened her eyes and they were clear. The beating in her breast had stilled, and the bed, the room, as well as her whole life, was in focus.

She rolled back and came to a sitting position, her face on a level with Brenna's.

I had my love.

"And you shall have and keep yours," she gasped.

"What?"

"Go, little one!" Elizabeth said. "Run with your Irishman! Ride to the ends of the earth with him if you must, and never look back!"

"Oh, dear God, thank you," Brenna cried, and fell into her mother's outstretched arms.

The embrace was brief but complete. Each of them kissed the other's tear-stained cheeks, and then Brenna walked to the door. Once there, she paused and turned.

"I love you, Lady Hatton. Know that I always will,

for beneath it all it is the grit you gave me as a child that lets me do what I do this night."

And then she was gone toward her freedom and her love, her booted feet echoing hollowly down the hallway.

For many moments Elizabeth sat, staring at the arched doorway where her daughter had been standing. If all went well, Brenna would soon be in France with Rory O'Hara. And the child would see The O'Donnell, and he her. Would Brenna recognize in his aged and war-ravaged face enough of her own features to know?

The thought was as alarming as it was depressing. How often in her wars with Coke, when her frustration and disgust had overreached all limits, had Elizabeth entertained the thought of telling Brenna the truth, if for no other reason than to spite her hateful husband. But always she had held back, for Elizabeth knew that the truth would hurt Brenna more than it would Sir Edward.

She slid from the bed and crossed to the armoire that held more than a dozen of her finest dresses. She opened the ornately carved doors and adjusted them so that she could peruse every angle of her face and figure in their mounted mirrors.

Would O'Donnell recognize her now? Yes, she was sure he would, for age had been kind to Elizabeth Hatton. There was little change in her since that last night at Corfe Castle, just before he rode away into the mists and out of her life forever.

"Do you doubt my love, Rory O'Donnell?" she had cried that night.

"Nay, not a whit, and I hope you do not doubt mine. But beyond our love there is, I fear, very little understanding. Perhaps we have both been spoiled by so much love."

He had then wheeled and spurred his mount into a canter. At the gatehouse he had looked back once more. It was then, with the swirling mists dancing snakelike around the darkness of his face and raven hair and his lithe body so tall and straight in the saddle, that the full brunt of his parting had struck Elizabeth like an arrow in her chest.

How would he look upon her now? Did he still remember that ancient love, or had he long ago pushed it from his mind? What would they say? Would the gulf between them be too wide to bridge?

Foolish, she thought. *How girlish and childish it is even to entertain the thought.* He was already aged, beaten and bowed that last time she had seen him in the garden at Holdenby, when Brenna was still a child. Then, she had disdained meeting him, speaking with him, preferring to remember him as he had been.

What would he be like now?

Suddenly she didn't care. Whatever he looked like, no matter how ravaged his face or body, he was still Rory, The O'Donnell . . . the love of her life.

She began rifling through the clothes, when suddenly a scream from the bowels of the house chilled her bones. Shouts of anger and the sound of splintering wood drew her to the window.

"Damme!" she cried at the spectacle she saw. "God, what brand of fool have you become, Sir Edward Coke?"

IMPATIENT WITH THE PROCESS of battering down the stout doors, Coke had led half his followers around the manor until he had found a first-floor window low enough to gain entrance.

Rory and David had entered the house through the

servants' wing in the rear. They had paused just long enough for Talbot to issue commands to his Irishmen not to interfere in the melee that was sure to ensue.

" 'Tis enough that half of them are in England illegally as it is," he had murmured to Rory.

Now they crouched in a hallway adjoining the house's great hall, watching Coke and the others stream through the window.

"Go you, O'Hara," Sir David whispered, "and find the lass. Ride for Boar's Head, by the Yarmouth road. 'Tis there I'll meet you both."

"I'll not leave a friend with these odds," Rory replied.

"What odds, lad?" Talbot chuckled. "There's not a swordsman in the lot, and I'll fell the first man who draws a pistol with a ball of my own. Mark me, once one falls there will be no more of that. Now go!"

Reluctantly, Rory moved down the hall.

Sir David waited until the last man had dropped from the window to the floor, then stepped into the room. Gently he closed the door behind him, turned the key in the lock and pulled it from the slot. As he moved forward, he jammed the key into the dirt beneath a potted plant and drew his sword.

"An entrance most unbecoming a gentleman, Sir Edward," he said. "But then, you have rarely been accused of being of that status, have you?"

Coke had been marshaling his servants and dependents. At the sound of Sir David's voice he whirled, his eyes narrowed to pierce the darkness near the door.

Talbot stepped forward and moonlight from the windows bathed his face. One of the younger men to Coke's right reached for a pistol in his belt.

Talbot swung the dag in his left hand up until the light

shone on its barrel. "Nay, lad, a foolish move, for I'll make your wife a widow or your mother mourn your passing as sure as you stand."

White of face, the boy dropped his hand to his side and took several paces backward.

"Stand aside, Talbot, for I'm here on the king's business!" Coke thundered.

"Nay, that I cannot do, Sir Edward, for I'm bound to protect this house for its rightful owner, the Lady Hatton, until I return its keys to her hand."

"Damn you, man," Coke sputtered, "if 'tis a fight you want, 'tis one you'll get!"

"Then *en garde*, Sir Edward, and beware you do not cut yourself with that ancient blade in the process!"

THE FRONT DOORS SPLINTERED just as Rory passed them. He had already searched for Brenna in every room on the ground floor. Now he sprinted toward the rear of the house and the servants' stairs.

The sound of heavy boots on oaken floors echoed throughout the house by the time he reached the second floor. Several doors were open. A single glance into each room told him they were empty.

Where, his mind screamed, *where can she be?*

He was about to chance shouting her name when Brenna's voice reached his ears from outside the house. He darted into a room, rushed to the windows and threw them open.

There, in the garden below, stood a giant of a man inches taller than Rory and equally as broad in chest and shoulder. In one hand he held the reins of his horse and in the other arm, Brenna. Rory could hear her curses as she tried to reach his face with her nails. It appeared that the man was pleading with her to mount the horse as much as he was forcing her.

The man had his back toward the house and the balcony where Rory stood. Without a thought, O'Hara rolled one leg and then the other over the balcony's rail. There he stood on the edge for a brief moment, gauging the distance, then jumped. Like a rock he dropped until his booted feet thudded against the man's shoulders. Both of them fell but jumped instantly to their feet. Rory clawed for the pistol in his belt and found only air. It had slipped free, somehow.

Like a wounded bear, his adversary charged. Rory sidestepped the onslaught, drawing sword and dagger in the same move. "I'd like not to kill you, friend," Rory growled.

The words were barely out of his mouth before the man charged again. Rory brought the dagger up in his left hand. But before its point found flesh, his wrist was locked in a vise of steel.

So surprised was he that he lost his grip and the shorter blade fell to the ground. Then with an unexpected swiftness Rory's wrist was released and the fist that had held it found his jaw with a crashing blow.

He reeled back, and for a moment the sky above him was devoid of moonlight, totally black. Before he recovered, the rapier had also been wrenched from his grasp.

"Now, laddie," the giant roared, breaking the blade between his hands as if it were a twig, "we'll fight like men!"

Rory evaded the other's churning arms and buried his fist, wrist deep, in the man's midsection. Then his hammering blows moved upward until he was pounding the round, fleshy face.

The ferocity of Rory's attack drove the other man backward until a tree stopped his retreat. Then a telling blow directly to the point of his chin brought him to his knees.

Rory could hardly believe it. The man should have been unconscious. Instead, he shook his head and, displaying a bloody grin, looked upward.

"By God, you fight well, laddie!"

"And an adversary you are. Tell me, why do you steal young ladies in the middle of the night?"

"Call it a son's duty, or the fact that a man must live. You are. . . ?"

"I am called Rory, The O'Hara."

"Damme," the other cried with a roaring laugh, "a bloody Irishman! No wonder you fight so well!"

"And you?" Rory asked, warily moving to the side as the man started to rise.

"They call me the fighting Coke, Clement." He was on his feet now and advancing. "Well, let's get on with it, O'Hara."

"Nay, Clement!"

Both men turned at the sound of Brenna's voice. She stood, feet wide apart, her arms raised. Looking huge and menacing in her small hands was the arquebus that had slipped from Rory's belt.

"Make your next step toward the house, Clement, or I swear, brother or not, I'll put this ball in your belly!"

Clement's jaw dropped. "Damme, girl, I don't think you jest."

"Mark me, Clement, I've not time to dally. Back away!"

Clement grudgingly obeyed Brenna's command, in awkward backward steps. Rory was instantly at her side, lifting the pistol from her hands.

"My regrets, Coke. 'Tis a pity you are English born—you fight like a man."

"Another time, Irishman!"

"A pleasure!" Rory replied, shouting over his shoulder as he and Brenna sprinted across the gardens toward the stables.

They bolted through an opening in the hedgerow and Rory pulled her up short. He turned her to face him and his eyes were riveting. "All is still not lost to you, lass. Tomorrow could be far more a curse than a blessing. France may not have us. Are you sure of this commitment you make?"

"I am sure. Whether it be France or Ireland or Cathay, I am sure."

"Would that you were Irish, lass," Rory replied. "For then you would be like me, with nothing to lose and everything to gain. But you're not. You're born to the English, and 'tis a pity, because you've got the spark of Irish fire in your eyes."

"Then I'll make myself Irish!"

At this he laughed. "The Irish are born, not made. But 'tis your choice alone now."

"And I've made it, O'Hara. For I would rather be an Irish wench, bare before God, stomping your grain, than be gentlewoman to an English fool."

"Words my mother must have said when she married my father. Then come along, lass, for we're bound for somewhere other than here!"

Hand in hand, they raced along the graveled path to the rear of the stable and streaked into the open meadow beyond, where Rory and David had left tethered horses before joining the fight.

"They're gone!" Rory hissed as they burst into the clearing.

"Nay, lad, here!" From the shadows of a giant oak stepped a smiling David Talbot, leading three mounts. "What kept you?"

Rory was about to reply, when a fourth horse and rider emerged from the shadows.

"Mother!" Brenna gasped. What—"

"Shhh! Mount your horse, girl, for we've a long ride. I've already sent Christopher ahead to warn his parents, Honor and Charles, that we might need a night's lodging and hiding on our journey."

"You mean—"

"Aye, little one. I'm going with you."

CHAPTER TWENTY-SIX

LADY COMPTON CONSIDERED HERSELF TO BE a very managing woman. She had managed well the inherited rewards gleaned from three husbands. She had been instrumental in placing one son in a high seat of power and in maneuvering her other sons and family members into positions of wealth.

Now the only thorn in the side of complete success was her recalcitrant nephew, Sir Raymond Hubbard. Even with the threat of the Tower hanging over the young fool he remained adamant.

"I am, auntie, disgusted with the whole sordid affair. The main reason being that I admire and have truly fallen in love with the lady, and want only her good will and love in return. For us both, I would like peace. And I would like to escape your and m'Lord Buckingham's domination, for I fear it threatens to ruin my sanity," he had said with uncustomary firmness.

Lady Compton agreed with the last point. In her opinion, Sir Raymond had never been completely stable, for he refused to recognize what she considered the realities of the times. "Dear boy, we live in an age of plunder and greed. 'Tis a perfectly normal vice, even in churchmen. And so I beg you, do not disdain to build up your treasures, for one never knows when they will be needed!"

But still he had refused to bow to her will, forcing his aunt into yet another series of maneuvers that took up every moment of her day and many hours of her nights.

When Frances Carr, Countess of Somerset, requested a meeting with Lady Compton it was particularly vexing. She had little time to waste listening to the pleas of a convicted murderess and so had ignored the first missive from Cheswick House, where the disgraced Frances was being held under house arrest.

Then the fool Coke had ruined everything by storming Elmeham House and forcing his wife's hand. Now the little raven-haired bird of prey, Brenna, had flown to France and no amount of pleading with the French court could get her back. Indeed, King Louis was reveling in the embarrassment her flight had caused Lady Compton's son, the Earl of Buckingham.

When the second missive came from Frances Carr, Lady Compton paid more heed to it.

My dear Lady Compton,

I have anxiously awaited a reply to my last letter. I know of the stress of your days. It is perhaps for that reason that my letter has been overlooked. I beg you, pay more heed to the one you now hold.

Even secluded from court as I am, a prisoner in this wretched house, I do hear news from the outside world. If my interpretation of the news I hear is correct you have been thwarted in your desire for a Coke-Hubbard match.

Hear me out, m'lady, for I think I have a way to break the stalemate which I am sure is so vexing to your person and those nearest you. If you would desire knowledge that could be a blade held to the rebellious Lady Hatton's throat, I urge you to call upon me at your earliest convenience.

Your obedient servant, Frances Carr

Lady Compton knew Frances Carr to be of such a nature that she would do anything to gain her own ends. For this reason she did indeed accept the lady's invitation. Under the cover of a dark moonless night, with only a trusted driver and footman, she set out for Cheswick House.

She was met by Frances herself, and ushered into the gardens by a little-used gate. At Lady Compton's request, the woman had dismissed all the servants in her wing from their duties for the night. In a tiny, dimly lit salon the two women, one at the height of her power, the other in total disgrace and under house arrest, sat down over wine and appraised each other.

Neither spoke for many moments. Lady Compton took her time, examining the state of the Countess of Somerset's dishabille. The woman had aged radically since the trial. Tiny wrinkles creased the puffy skin around her eyes, and the mouth had become a pinched line marked by ill-applied cerise. Frances's dress was disordered, badly in need of a press, and her hair looked as though it had lacked the use of a brush or comb for days.

"You're looking quite well, Frances," she said at last.

"Your snide remarks I accept, m'Lady Compton, for I'm accustomed to them. I receive the same daily from my servants. But that is to be expected, since they are all spies in the employ of your son."

"I will mention it to the Earl of Buckingham. Methinks 'tis a useless expense to spy on you."

"I would appreciate it," Frances replied, nervously twisting a vellum scroll in her hands. "And I would appreciate some degree of liberty."

"I fear that is impossible, Frances. The king—"

"Damn the king for a doddering fool. It is your son who is my absentee jailer, and I would have you intercede for me. I ask only permission to leave this wretched hovel once a week."

"I fear you ask a great boon," Lady Compton replied, her eye falling to the scroll Frances held, wondering if it held the key to her vexing problem.

" 'Tis a boon that you could grant, m'lady. Your son has nothing to fear from the former favorite, my husband. Robert Carr is a broken man, a mere shell. As for myself, I have naught to do with him. He has his wing of this prison and I have mine. The boon I ask does not extend to him."

Lady Compton shrugged, eyeing Frances over the rim of her wineglass as she sipped. *How ironic it is,* she thought. Frances went to the ultimate ends to capture Carr. Now she discards him as she would so much excess baggage.

"There may be a way. But then, why would I take such steps to free you, Frances?"

"Because the match you propose between your

nephew and Lady Hatton's daughter has become a scandal," Frances replied calmly. "Nothing can fully represent these proceedings except to call them a comedy."

Lady Compton stood, bridling at the other woman's words. "I did not come here to have—"

"Sit down, m'lady, for I know we are birds of the same feather, and for that reason tact is useless between us. All London is ridiculing you, your son and the court for applying more worry and care to this frivolous marriage than to the state of the crown, the country and the government."

Lady Compton sat down.

"I think, m'lady, that here is the solution to your problem."

Frances Carr passed the scroll over, and Lady Compton could barely conceal her glee as she read it. At last she looked up.

"You would swear to this before king's council?"

"I would."

"And freedom once a week is all you ask?"

"Aye," Frances said. "I will accept your word."

"You have it," Lady Compton replied, smoothing the document on the table between them. "Sign."

Frances Carr signed with a flourish, and Lady Compton quickly took her leave. In the coach she clutched the document closely to her breast as she rode back to London. Her mind quickly formulated a plan for its use. She looked to France, and beyond.

Once Sir Raymond was married to Brenna Coke, Lady Compton was sure she would be able to control the considerable dowry that came with the girl. And with the hold over Lady Hatton she now held, she was equally sure she could dip even farther into the Hatton pie controlled by Coke and his wife.

And once the marriage was fact, Lady Compton vowed to herself that she would find some way to clip Sir Raymond's wings, both for his stupidity in the matter and for the fact that he had had the audacity to block the wishes of her herself and her son, the Earl of Buckingham.

CHAPTER TWENTY-SEVEN

IT WAS A WILD RIDE, made by night over unfrequented and circuitous routes. Just before dawn they reached the tiny farm of Elizabeth's former servants, Honor and Charles. The couple owed all they had to the Lady Hatton, so it was without a qualm that they agreed to hide the fleeing party through the day.

It was only as they wearily dismounted that David Talbot's wound was discovered. A random shot had pierced the elbow of his right arm as he had fled through the window of the great room. Honor and Elizabeth managed to pry the ball free, but the wound it left was ugly and inflamed.

Rory urged the man to remain, but Talbot would not hear of it. "Nay, lad, I'm a hung man, or as sure of Fleet Prison as you are if we're caught on English soil now!"

Rory had to agree. Anywhere on Irish, English or Scottish soil they rested too long would give Buckingham's men time to find them. And knowing the earl, there was no guarantee they would be returned to London alive after their arrest.

That night they rode on, until at last they made the coast. The boat Rory had secured on one of his many midnight rides was waiting. By morning they were in France. Using a portion of the money Brenna had brought with her, Rory hired a litter and they continued on to the abbey at Fontevrault.

Because of David Talbot's weakened condition, the trip took three days. During the journey, Elizabeth realized that Benna's choice had been correct. This young giant, Rory O'Hara, never took his eyes from the girl, nor she from him. A blind person could sense the love that flowed between the two of them, and it gladdened Elizabeth's heart.

And with each mile they rode, her heart pounded faster for another reason; it was a mile closer to O'Donnell.

They were within ten miles of the abbey when O'Hara spurred ahead to pave the way for their arrival. A place would be needed for Talbot's recuperaton, and Rory himself might be forced to hide or ride on immediately.

When he reached the abbey, he went at once to Sister Anna and was elated when he found his sister, Shanna, with her. But the elation was quickly diminished when he saw the looks of sadness on their faces.

The O'Donnell was dying. It was only a matter of time.

"I would see him at once," Rory said, and told them of Talbot's wound and the imminent arrival of the others, mentioning Lady Elizabeth Hatton and Brenna Coke by name.

"Oh, dear God," Sister Anna gasped in a tone of voice Shanna and Rory hadn't heard from her lips in years.

"What is it?" Rory asked, pausing halfway across the room and staring quizzically back at her ashen face.

"'Tis nothing," Sister Anna replied. "Go! Go to him! I will see to their quarters."

O'Donnell was terribly thin and pale. The cough that had wracked his chest for months was now an almost constant irritation. But his eyes and ears were alert as O'Hara filled in the wide gaps of information that had not been given in his written messages.

When he finished, O'Donnell sighed and weakly grasped his godson's hand. "Perhaps it is indeed written in a ledger somewhere that we are not meant to regain our land."

"'Tis a great debt I owe this man, Talbot. Perhaps, in time and with his aid, Shanna can bear the O'Hara name back to Ballylee."

The thought that O'Hara's words were but wishful thinking was mirrored in O'Donnell's eyes. "But, in the meantime, it's back to France for you after all?"

"Aye, there's naught for it, if Louis will have me. If not, it's Spain or the Netherlands—and I've no taste for that."

O'Donnell nodded wearily. He loosed Rory's hand and grasped his chest as another wracking cough surged through him. When it had subsided, he managed to speak again.

"And this Englishwoman—you would wive her?"

"Aye, as soon as I can be as safe in France as she."

Again O'Donnell nodded, and a strange smile creased his wrinkled lips. "'Tis an odd thing, lad, what these English wenches do to our minds. Is she of family?"

"Aye. A Coke—Brenna, by name."

THE REST OF THE PARTY ARRIVED at the abbey and David Talbot was immediately transferred from the litter to a room where he could be tended. While this was being done, Sister Anna managed to maneuver Elizabeth out of the sight and hearing of the others.

"M'lady, the years have been kind to you."

"Annie. . . ."

The two women embraced, tears wetting their cheeks as the past silently washed over them. When they could speak again it was Sister Anna who abruptly changed the mood.

"Does the girl know?"

"Nay, not a word has been said." Elizabeth paused, gazing around the abbey gardens, assembling her thoughts. "It was my choice to come here. Perhaps it was wrong, but at the last minute I couldn't resist."

" 'Tis The O'Hara and she, isn't it?"

Elizabeth twisted her body on the stone bench on which she sat and faced the other woman. "Aye. What irony after all these years that they should meet and be drawn together."

"And you approve?"

"I didn't...at first. But then I remembered what agonies I've gone through since...." She couldn't continue.

"M'lady, O'Donnell is dying." Elizabeth's head shot up and her eyes widened as the nun spoke. "Perhaps this is God's will. He has never forgotten you and daily speaks your name."

"I would see him at once, please!"

Sister Anna averted her eyes, her brows knitted in thought.

Elizabeth rushed on, the words and phrases tumbling from her lips. As briefly as possible she spanned the years of her life since their last meeting. She told of how she had pushed O'Donnell from her mind and heart and admitted that she had many times vowed never to see him again or even think of him.

But the last few weeks' events had changed her, made her want this one last meeting. She would have to go back to England, she knew, to one day return and face her husband and the crown's wrath. But if she could see O'Donnell just once, she felt she could return with a calm heart and a feeling of peace at last.

With a gentle squeeze of Elizabeth's hand, Sister Anna rose. "I'll see to it!"

"And, Annie. . . ."

"Aye?"

"You remember Honor, my maid?"

"Aye."

"'Twas her duty for years, and now her son Christopher's, to each week place flowers on Ned Bull's grave. We could not forget the highwayman who so nobly aided my O'Donnell—and who was your lover. But forgive me, that was another lifetime."

Annie's back was turned, but Elizabeth saw her shoulders sag slightly and then go straight again.

"Bless you, m'lady," she said softly, before her heavy black skirts rustled as she hurried off through the garden.

BRENNA SAT, STUNNED, IN THE TINY ALCOVE adjacent to where David Talbot lay. With the help of two nuns and one of the abbey workmen they had managed to put him into a bed and a doctor had been summoned from the village of Chinon. The doctor's diagnosis had been instant upon seeing David's wound. The right arm would have to be amputated.

Brenna had fled the room at the pronouncement, but now she sat, listening in agony to the preparations for surgery.

And agony it was. One of the few things her dear friend David Talbot had counted on for survival was his magical ability as a swordsman. The loss of his right arm would be akin to cutting out his heart. What would happen when he awoke and discovered what they had done?

"It must be," the doctor had said. "Else the man will be dead in a day's time."

Brenna dropped her head into her hands and kneaded her feverish temples with her fingers as an agonizing moan came from the room. But the firm hand of Shanna, Rory's sister, at her shoulder brought her upright in an instant.

"They will do better without us. Come!"

The look in the girl's beautiful face, the tone of authority in her voice, made Brenna rise. At the litter, Shanna had taken command at once, applying a sure hand and a quick wit to the situation. Brenna remembered this and allowed herself to be led away.

They moved through the stone corridors and down long flights of stairs until Brenna found herself in an airy courtyard surrounded by trees and high stone walls.

"Sit. We should talk."

Too distraught to do anything but obey, Brenna sat and absently sensed the other woman settle beside her.

"The letters from my brother spoke constantly of you, but never by name."

"Coke. I am Brenna Coke."

"I know that now, and your mother is the Lady Elizabeth Hatton."

Brenna nodded dumbly, staring down at the hands folded in her lap.

"And the wounded man?"

"Sir David Talbot, a friend. A very dear friend."

The hands began to move, to twist and wring against each other in Brenna's lap. Shanna, sensing the other's emotions, put her arm around Brenna's shoulders.

"Your friend will live," she said, her voice calm.

"Now tell me what my brother has not told me. Tell me everything."

Brenna spoke, slowly at first, and then sensing a kindred soul in Shanna, she began pouring out the last year's events.

As she spoke Shanna listened and nodded, her eyes intent on Brenna's features as they reflected the girl's words. Long before the story was finished, Shanna had discovered what Rory had missed, unearthing what had remained dormant in her brother's memory.

Shanna had instantly recognized the Lady Hatton as the woman in the locket that constantly hung around The O'Donnell's neck. Now, as Brenna spoke and Shanna observed the toss of her head, the fine line of her jaw and the dark depths of her eyes, Shanna was almost positive she had identified the other face in the locket's miniature portraits.

IT WAS AT THE DOORWAY OF O'DONNELL'S ROOM, with Sister Anna standing aside to let her enter, that Elizabeth realized her state. She still wore her riding clothes, and they, like her hair, were in total disarray. She was sure that she still had smudges of dust and mud from the rutted French roads upon her face and body. She was equally sure that her clothes reeked with the smell of horse. And for the first time in her life that she could remember, she didn't care.

Her darting, nervous gaze met the calm, steady stare of the woman she remembered as Annie Carey. *How much,* their eyes said to each other, *we have all been through.*

Beneath the doorway's rounded arch Annie gave Elizabeth's arm a friendly squeeze of confidence. Then Elizabeth, the Lady Hatton, stepped into the room to meet the only man she had ever truly loved—the man who was the father of her child, the man whom she hadn't seen for eleven years nor spoken to in fifteen.

Curtains were drawn across the narrow abbey windows, blocking any sunlight that was left to the fading day outside. The only light inside came from a four-candle sconce embedded high in one stone wall.

The room itself was much as Elizabeth would imagine a monk's cell. Only one wall was hung with a threadbare tapestry and the room's furnishings were sparse, with a nightstand, a second stand for a wash basin and a pallet-like bed.

"Elizabeth...is it truly you?"

Elizabeth narrowed her eyes, peering into the dimness toward the bed from whence the voice had come. She placed a hand against the wall's cold stones to steady her quivering legs.

"You're but a blur," the voice said. "Come nearer!"

For several seconds she was unable to move, positive that once her hand left the wall her legs would no longer hold her.

And there was another fear, one that had plagued her from the moment she had decided to join Brenna and Rory's flight across the Channel. Was this all a foolish whim? By seeing him again, after all these years, would they only realize how fruitless their love had been from the start?

"Elizabeth."

She managed to find the courage to take a step, and then two. Then she was around the bed and moving up its length. She couldn't hold back the tiny gasp that escaped her lips as the white-robed figure on the bed took on face and form.

The candles' dancing shadows illuminated a head of

gleaming white hair over a seamed, leathery face. The dark, ebony eyes were sunken and the cheeks were hollow. But beneath the neatly trimmed beard and mustache, as white as the hair on his head, Elizabeth could see the firm line of O'Donnell's jaw.

Then his lips parted, and memories flowed over her like a welcome fog. For the smile that had charmed her in her youth could still cause her breath to quicken.

She remembered the first kiss he had stolen in a carriage, and how breathless it had left her. She lived again the first time he had held her in his arms. It had been in a shepherd's hut, and she could still feel the hardness of his young, muscular body pressed against her.

"Rory O'Donnell," she breathed.

"My God, girl, you haven't aged a day."

Suddenly the face blurred before her eyes. The hair returned to its original, satin-black sheen, and the wrinkles became merely creases in the always-laughing face. The chuckle was a robust guffaw challenging the world, and the raised hand was strong and steady.

Elizabeth knew that her thoughts at that moment were reflected in her eyes. She also knew, from the way he returned her gaze, that he could read them.

Oh, God, how much in love we were. How we did make time stop and the world stand still when we were one!

Elizabeth took the proffered hand in hers and let it draw her down to the bed. She brushed the furrowed forehead with her lips and felt his face in the tangled mane of her hair.

As if it were but a day before and he was again recovering from his wounds in her private Holdenby cottage, Elizabeth cradled him in her arms.

"Elizabeth, my love, my only love."

"Rory, my dashing rogue of the night...."

FOR THREE DAYS AND NIGHTS David Talbot lay in a state near death. Shanna and Brenna took turns nursing him, spelled now and then by Rory O'Hara. Most of the time the man was unconscious, and when awake his ravings were near hysteria.

On two occasions, however, he became coherent and there was a strange, intense, almost haunted look in his eyes. Both these times he demanded that O'Hara be brought to him.

The first time Rory wrote down patiently, with pen in hand, Talbot's words of instructions as to a last will. In it were described David's many holdings, the placement of his cash and how O'Hara coud lay claim to it all should Talbot die. Then, with a trembling hand partially guided by Rory's, the wounded man signed the will.

"Od's blood, Talbot, you are indeed a rich man," Rory chuckled, scanning the paper.

"Aye," David replied, managing a weak smile. "All ill-gotten gains, I assure you. But spendable!"

Soon after Rory had left the room, sure that his friend would not last the night. Near dawn Talbot awoke, coherent again and evidently surmising the same. Again he demanded to see O'Hara.

Shanna, who had barely said two words to Talbot in the time she had nursed him, argued with him to rest instead.

"Who are you?"

"The O'Hara's sister, Shanna."

"Then, Shanna O'Hara, hie ye to your brother, and be quick! 'Tis a curse on you 'twill be to deny the last wish of a dying man!"

Moments later, Rory arrived and seated himself beside the bed. Talbot was about to speak when he noticed that Shanna had seated herself on the opposite side of the bed.

"You, leave us alone!"

"I'll not," Shanna replied. "You need rest. 'Tis my responsibility to see that you get it."

"I'll rest enough in hell."

Shanna was about to refuse further, when her brother's dark eyes flashed a warning. Loudly she stomped from the room.

"Your sister is not like you, lad," Talbot growled. "She's belligerent."

"Aye, but she's right. You do need rest. We'll talk come morning."

"Nay, now, for there might be no dawn for me!"

Rory settled back in the high-backed chair.

The tale that spun from David Talbot's lips in the next hour was not unexpected. Rory had already surmised that a man of Talbot's background and reputation had more than the welfare of Irish workmen or the saving of an Irish estate in mind in his pursuit of Ballylee.

"So you see, O'Hara, I promised myself that I would do for the lass what I was never able to do for the mother. I would return her to her mother's native land. 'Twas all she ever spoke of."

"Methinks, Talbot, that what you ask is unfair. The girl. . . Aileen, you say?"

"Aye."

"How can I return her to Ireland when I can't return myself?"

"Ah, laddie, methinks you don't know your own heart. But no matter. All I ask is that you watch over the girl if I go. And if 'tis indeed one day Ireland for you and your lady, then take her with you."

"'Tis fair enough. You have my word on it."

"Good. Now go away and send your sister back in. She has the look of an angel. Much better to die with the memory of her face than yours."

Rory took his leave and went to find his sister.

Shanna returned to Talbot's side just as he dozed off. Carefully she dampened a towel and cooled the fever from his face and chest. Then she inspected the bandaged stump where his arm had been and carefully tucked the covers around his body.

She must have dozed off, because she was suddenly jolted upright by an intense pressure on her hand. In his sleep, David Talbot had reached out and found her hand. Without removing her hand from his, she quietly moved her chair closer to the bed.

Once more before drifting into a half sleep, she felt the pressure of his fingers and returned it.

BY THE END OF A WEEK AFTER THEIR ARRIVAL, the pall that had hung like a gray cloud over the abbey had descended lower. Sister Anna and the Lady Hatton ministered to O'Donnell day and night, much the same as Brenna and Shanna attended to Talbot. But as Talbot's condition improved, O'Donnell's worsened.

Rory O'Hara spent only fleeting moments with Brenna, and these were used to declare their love for each other no matter how much a mystery their future together remained.

He spent even less time with his sister. But Shanna, in their brief contacts, had told him of the change in their mutual friend, René de Gramont. René's mood at Saint-

Germain-en-Laye had grown more surly with each passing day during their exile.

No matter how Shanna had tried to stay close to their childhood friend, it had become impossible. His love for her had become an obsession until he saw its culmination as a conquest rather than a romance.

Angry words and threatening arguments became more frequent between them. His mood had been so ugly at times that Shanna had been afraid of him.

"It was a reprieve of sorts when word of papa's illness came, and little Henrietta Maria freed me from my duties to return here to be at his side," Shanna confessed.

Rory's only comment was "Poor René," as he kissed his sister's cheek and moved away. "I fear now I will receive no help from that quarter with my suit to Louis."

His words trailed behind him to sting Shanna's flesh and bite into her troubled mind.

"Nay, brother," she murmured to herself. "There will never be more aid from our old childhood friend, and I fear in its place will be much mischief."

How odd it is, she thought, *how our lives do change, and in such strange ways.* René, who for years had professed love and friendship, now brooded with hate. Rory, whose roguish ways had gained him a reputation as a rounder and wastrel, now seemed so much the man and in command of his life.

For hours after that conversation with Rory, Shanna had walked in the chilly garden air, debating whether she should tell her brother the truth.

She decided against it, for he might very well not believe her. And if he did, Shanna shuddered at the thought of what might happen, for she knew only too well her brother's fiery temper. That part of him had not changed. Nay, should she tell Rory the true facts, Shanna was sure he would kill René and forever ruin his chances at the French court.

René de Gramont's action had been nearly unbelievable to Shanna herself, though the signs had been there for weeks. Her dear friend René's love had turned to hate, and that hate had turned him into a madman. So much so that he had returned from an evening of brooding and drinking and invaded her apartments. Like a wild animal he had hurled outlandish accusations at her and with his powerful hands had torn her gown to shreds.

It was only later, after her screams had alerted his own guard and they had pulled him by the heels like the animal he had become from her rooms, that Shanna fully realized that he had intended to rape her.

On the following day Shanna had made up her mind to leave Saint-Germain-en-Laye. Then she had met René in a courtyard.

"You have disgraced me, you bitch!"

"I you?" she had replied, hurt to the core of her being by his words.

But it was more than just René's words that had chilled her. It was the look of hatred in his now sober eyes. It was the same look they had held the previous night when he had been mad with drink and lust.

That very afternoon Shanna had gone to the princess, Henrietta Maria, to ask for a discharge from her duties. Even though so young the girl had known fear and could recognize it instantly in her friend and tutor. For that reason, the princess had accepted without question Shanna's then-fabricated story about O'Donnell. It was only upon her arrival at Fontevrault that Shanna had learned the irony of its truthfulness.

And now, she mused, making her way back through the gardens to relieve Brenna at her bedside vigil, *how odd it is that I find myself attracted to this strange man, David Talbot.*

CHAPTER TWENTY-EIGHT

IT WAS NEAR MIDNIGHT when word flew through the abbey that Father Joseph had been summoned to The O'Donnell's room. Rory O'Hara arrived at the bedroom door just as the father emerged carrying the tiny bronze burner of annointing oils used to administer the last rites.

Beyond the priest's shoulder, Rory could see Sister Anna motioning to him to enter. He did, following and then passing her as she knelt at the foot of the bed.

O'Donnell's breathing was a grating rasp as he took the younger man's outstretched hand. But his eyes were bright and his grasp firm. While they talked, Sister Anna prayed silently.

"She prays," O'Donnell said, "in four languages I wager, when I would have only Gaelic strike God's ears."

Usually Rory could muster a smile at the good-natured gibes The O'Donnell would throw at his old friend. But now it was impossible.

"Would you have anything of me beyond what I already know?" Rory asked.

O'Donnell answered him in kind, his voice and features taking on the same solemnity as O'Hara's. "Just this, lad. I pass on to you the promise I made to The O'Neill. Return us one day to the old sod, but not until the day our graves can be trod and tended by Irishmen."

Rory promised, and said further that he would pass the promise along to his sons, should God grant him any.

O'Donnell's last request of his godson was to be wrapped in the velvet of the O'Donnell clan's mantle. This, with Sister Anna's help, Rory did. Then he leaned forward and kissed the old man's forehead. "Goodbye, papa," he whispered in Gaelic, and hurriedly quit the room.

After a few moments, Sister Anna spoke. "Shanna is waiting."

"Aye."

"Do you want me to fetch the Lady Elizabeth?"

O'Donnell's wan lips creased into a faint smile. "Nay, there is no need for goodbyes between us. We've said too many already. But, Annie. . . bring the girl."

Annie's eyes went wide in surprise. Till now, The O'Donnell had refused to see Brenna. He read the look, and his smile grew.

" 'Tis time I saw her, Annie, and she me."

"Will you tell her?"

"Nay, never, you should know that. But I would pass on to her a thought or two. Now fetch her—and best you hurry for I feel the mists."

Shanna brushed past Sister Anna the instant the door was open and rushed to O'Donnell's bedside, covering his frail hands with kisses as the tears spilled down her cheeks.

Sister Anna quickly covered the distance to David

Talbot's bedroom. He was sleeping soundly as she tugged Brenna from her chair.

"What is it?"

"He would see you now!"

"Who?"

"The O'Donnell. Come quickly!"

Brenna knew of the old Irishman upstairs and knew he was dying. But other than noticing her mother's strange reaction whenever his name had been mentioned, she had thought little of his existence. She had been far too busy tending Talbot, making friends with Shanna and trying to fathom her life with Rory O'Hara.

Now she suddenly found herself standing beside a bed staring down at a gray-haired man whose eyes, as dark as her own, studied her face as though he were an artist about to paint her portrait.

"You're a fine buxom lass," he smiled, taking her hand in his.

Brenna flushed, her eyes glancing up to Shanna's for an instant. The other girl's face was expressionless. In one hand she worried a golden locket. Her other was clasped tightly by the man on the bed, much the same as he held Brenna's.

"Do you know me at all, Brenna?"

"I know of you. You are Rory O'Donnell, the Irish rebel."

"Aye," came a croaking laugh. "Do ye hear that, Annie? That's how I'll be remembered, thank God!"

Then the regal head lay back on the pillow, and again a chill went up Brenna's spine as those deep black eyes found hers.

"We met but once before, a long time ago in an

English garden. You were a tiny lass, but even then I could see the woman you would grow to be."

Brenna narrowed her eyes and furrowed her brow in concentration. But no matter how hard she searched her memory, she couldn't remember the meeting.

He saw her expression and gripped her hand tighter. "'Tis no matter, don't trouble yourself. 'Twas but a short meeting, but I remember it well. 'Tis a bit sad that our second meeting must be as short."

There was a soft quality to his voice that strangely touched Brenna and made her grasp his hand with both of hers.

"You're to be an O'Hara," he whispered.

"God willing," she nodded.

"Good, you'll make a fine one, I know. I—I've something that must be passed along to you both. I say it to you as if you were my own sons—or daughters. A long time ago, when my father was breathing his last on the wilds above Donegal Bay, he posed these same words to his sons: 'All on earth that is worth a man living his life is the love he has for a woman and the love he has for the land. And the land is all a man has to pass on to his sons. Don't ever forget the land because, if the land is not yours to give then your sons, your grandsons and your great-grandsons will naught have reason to stay.'"

Suddenly the hand gripping hers was like a vise, but the pain faded as Brenna found herself embraced by and becoming one with the light in O'Donnell's piercing eyes. She was frightened yet warmed by their glow.

"And my soul, lass, will burn in misery, whether it reside in heaven or hell, if there comes a time when there is no O'Donnell in Erin. Remember that. . . even if it is all you remember of me."

"HE'S RESTING."

"I would sit with him," Elizabeth said.

"But—"

"Annie."

The white face in the black cowl seemed to blur and fade. Then Sister Anna stepped aside and Elizabeth entered the room. She moved to the chair with a swish of skirts and seated herself where she had so many times before in these last few days.

"Who. . . ?"

"'Tis me, O'Donnell."

The lids fluttered and O'Donnell's eyes flickered open at last, focused and found her face. "Have we not had enough goodbyes, dear Elizabeth?"

Her lip turned white where she curled it between her teeth. She would not cry; on this she was determined. Gently she took his hand in both of hers and tugged it into her lap.

"There were so many years when I could close my eyes and see you so clearly but never touch you. Don't deny me these few moments of touching now, to make up for them."

His mouth twitched into the barest hint of a smile, and the nod from his gray head was barely perceptible.

"Ah, lass, but when we did touch, the sparks flew."

"Aye," she said, unable to stop a single tear from finding its way down her cheek. "And the thunder rolled and the heavens roared."

And then they were silent for many long moments, each with their own thoughts and memories. But when their eyes met again, they both knew that their thoughts were the same, of each other and the brief but wonderful times when they had been together. Elizabeth relived every kiss, every caress of his powerful hands, every joining of their bodies.

For an hour they sat in silence, his hand in hers. Now and then there was a faint squeeze from his fingers, which Elizabeth would return.

Suddenly his fingers curled, gripping her hands like a vise.

"Thank you, Elizabeth—"

"My darling...."

"—for letting me love you."

The dark eyes gleamed like ebony coals and then began to dim. Elizabeth swayed in the chair as if those eyes, for one more moment, consumed her in their inky depths.

And then his hand relaxed.

She knew but for several moments denied it. Then, as she leaned forward, she could no longer hold back the tears.

Tenderly she ran her fingers down over his eyes and then placed her lips on each of the lids.

"Goodbye, my Irishman. Dream still of me wherever you are."

BRENNA SAT LIKE A STATUE IN THE ABBEY GARDENS with Rory and Shanna. Hours before she had been led from The O'Donnell's room as if in a trance, his words still humming in her ears, jumbling her brain.

They drank a strong amber liquid that burned her throat as she swallowed but did nothing to remove the memory of O'Donnell's eyes when they had riveted on hers.

"'Tis uisquebaugh," Rory had said. "Irish whiskey fit for a wake."

They waited for what seemed an eternity, and then the huge bells above the abbey's two chapels began to toll.

A look passed between brother and sister.

Like The O'Neil and before him his father, Black Hugh, The O'Donnell, Rory O'Donnell had exited life the Irish way—in the last hour before dawn.

First light was breaking when Sister Anna stepped into the garden and walked toward them. She stopped directly before Rory.

"O'Hara?"

"Aye."

"The O'Donnell is gone."

For some reason she couldn't understand, Brenna still sat stunned, unable to move. Shanna burst into wailing tears. Rory merely nodded and rose. Then he took the abbess of Fontevrault into his arms.

"The last warrior has fallen, Annie. Ready him. We'll to Rome in two days' time. Brenna. . . ."

"What?" Brenna replied, somewhat dazed.

"Ready yourself as well, lass, for we'll be wed in Rome!"

THE NEXT TWO DAYS were hectic ones at the abbey, with each person assigned to see to the various plans and arrangements that needed to be made. The O'Donnell's body was prepared in the ancient way, his arms crossed over his sword laid the length of his body, and the whole wrapped in the O'Donnell mantle. The countryside was scoured for horses, a stout wagon and a four-hitch coach. Preparations were made for Lady Hatton's trip to Paris. There she would beg an audience with King Louis and his favorite, de Luynes, in hopes that they would intercede for her with Buckingham and thereby allow her a safe return to London.

A messenger was sent to Rome to notify the many exiled Irishmen there of The O'Donnell's death. They were also told that as soon as the prescribed time had passed after the old warrior's wake and entombment there would be a wedding.

There was a moment of fear when a detachment of the king's musketeers arrived at the abbey with an arrest order for Rory O'Hara. Through Father Joseph's intervention and with Rory's written rejection of all his former posts with Concini, O'Hara was allowed to retain his freedom, on the condition that he would present himself at the court immediately after his return from Rome.

Brenna was elated when Shanna appeared with samples of material, furs and ribbons.

"As the bride of The O'Hara, I plan on dressing you to look like a princess!" Shanna laughed.

Brenna knew that helping to choose material for her wedding dress and designing its cut helped take Shanna's mind off The O'Donnell's death. It also brought them closer together as women, close enough for Shanna to pry information about Sir David Talbot from her brother's bride-to-be.

Brenna gladly told her new friend all she knew of David, for she had begun to sense some special spark between the two, one that might well flare into love. She mentioned as much to Rory.

His reply was a laugh. "I doubt it, lass. Have you not seen them in the garden? I think they merely take the air together so they have more room for their railing!"

It was true that David and Shanna seemed constantly to be at each other's throats. But Brenna sensed in their mocking and bickering an underlying admiration that seemed to deepen almost hourly.

True to his word, O'Hara had made all the necessary preparations by the evening of the second day.

"We'll leave in the morning, lass, early. That is, if you haven't changed your mind?"

"Never!" Brenna cried, brushing her lips against his.

"Then you're mine," he whispered, and bid her a good night's sleep.

"I would sleep better in your arms," she teased.

Rory chuckled and squeezed her tenderly. "Nay, lass, we've chanced enough already. I'll not have you with a full belly before we're wed. 'Tis my way of breaking with Irish tradition. And besides, waiting will make it sweeter!"

He left her then, and Brenna made her way down the abbey halls to the rooms assigned her mother.

To Brenna's surprise, she found Elizabeth on her knees in prayer. Elizabeth had never been an overly religious woman, so it was with some embarrassment that Brenna began backing from the room the moment she entered.

"I'm sorry, I should have knocked."

"Nay, come in, little one. We should say our real goodbyes this night, for the morning's parting will be early."

The sight of her mother, there on her knees before the room's altar, with her face alight from the candle's glow, gave Brenna another start. There was a calmness and serenity in her face and a glow from her dark green eyes that Brenna had never witnessed before.

"What's the matter, darling?"

"I think that I have never seen you so beautiful," Brenna whispered.

A slight flush appeared in Elizabeth's cheeks, but her gaze never left her daughter's eyes.

"'Tis because of you, little one. . . because of your happiness."

Elizabeth stood and Brenna rushed to embrace her. "Then you don't fear for me?"

"Nay," Elizabeth replied, "not a whit—and don't you for me."

"But I do," Brenna said.

"Don't! I'm more than a match for them, and I'm sure they tire of the scandal, anyway. No, little one, I'll still have to barter with Sir Edward for what is ours in the days to come, but I'm sure King James and the earl have given it up. If there is anything Buckingham despises, it's ridicule. And if he pursued your match with Sir Raymond now, his efforts would cause as much laughter here as it already has in England."

"How can I ever thank you, dear mother, for what you have done. . . for what you have given up for me?"

Elizabeth's spine stiffened and her chin came up in the old haughty, regal way Brenna remembered so well. "By giving me grandsons and granddaughters by your handsome Irishman and by teaching them to live their lives in such an independent way that it will make me proud to say they are mine!"

"M'lady. . . ."

They turned as one. Sister Anna stood white-faced in the open door, a puzzled frown creasing her forehead.

"Aye, Annie, what is it?"

"There is a coach at the gate. An Englishwoman would speak to Brenna."

"To me?"

"Aye. She said *only* to you."

BRENNA FELT SICK AND DIZZY ENOUGH TO SWOON, but she forced herself to read through the Countess of Somerset's indictment of her mother one more time.

"This cannot be!" she said at last, looking up from the papers into Lady Compton's stolid, coarse face.

"But it is. And Frances Carr, if need be, will present the original of that document and herself before the king and council to attest to it."

Again Brenna's eyes lowered and from the paper she held certain phrases leaped up to thunder in her brain and tear at her heart: "...that the Lady Hatton did falsely attest to my virginity at Lambeth Palace and thereby free me from marriage to Lord Essex...that the Lady Hatton did carry to me from Mistress Turner, the necromancer, certain wine jellies wherein was contained the poison with which I eventually murdered...."

Brenna could read no more. Her eyes had so misted that the paper was a blur. "Oh, dear God, what a horrid woman she must be! How can she accuse my mother?"

"Because she, like us all, would use whatever is at one's hands to gain the ends one desires. 'Tis sound advice, girl, and you should heed it."

For the first time in her life, as she looked across the table at this stern, ugly woman, Brenna felt true hatred for another human being.

"What would you have of me?"

"I would have you in that coach yet this night, bound for England."

"Never!"

"And I would have your signature on this, to deter those at the abbey from following us."

With quivering fingers, Brenna took the second paper and laid it out on the table before her.

> To all those concerned with my recent mental lapse, whereby I foolishly fled England and my rightful betrothed, I address the following statement: I vow before God and take the Almighty to witness that I, Brenna Coke, youngest daughter of Sir Edward Coke, former Lord Chief Justice of England, do give myself absolutely to wife to Sir Raymond Hubbard. It is to him that I do plight my faith and inviolate vows, to keep myself till death do us part.
>
> And even if I break the least of these vows, I pray God to damn my body and soul to hell fire in the world to come. And in this world I humbly beseech God that the earth may open and swallow me up should I not be honest in the fact that my one true love in this world has been and always will be Sir Raymond Hubbard.

As she read this phrase, Rory O'Hara's darkly handsome and laughing face danced in front of Brenna's eyes, obscuring the papers. With a kerchief she dabbed at her tears until once more she could see the words.

> In witness whereof, I have written all this in my own hand with full knowledge of my recent behavior, and do hereby reject any and all that has passed before this signing that would lead me astray from my only rightful betrothed, Sir Raymond Hubbard.

"You would have me sign this?"

"I would," Lady Compton replied, her thin lips creasing into a smile that Brenna was sure was inspired by Satan. "Because if you don't, girl, Lady Hatton will lose everything but her empty title and rot the rest of her days in Fleet Prison. Mark me on it!"

Brenna gasped and found her feet. Blindly she stumbled to a window and threw the shutters wide, but the chill night air did little to ease the heat of her fevered brow.

So close to happiness, she thought, *and now so far!*

What had been her words such a short time ago? "How can I ever thank you, dear mother, for what you have done, what you have given up for me?"

Were they empty words? Was she now meant to be the daughter who let her mother rot in a filthy prison cell? Brenna shuddered when she remembered peering from a carriage window and seeing the emaciated and tortured faces peer back at her from Fleet Prison's barred windows. Could she let her own mother become one of those lost souls? Did the hateful woman who now sat staring at Brenna's back with her dark, beady eyes have such power?

Brenna knew she did.

For over an hour she stood, immobile, her brain whirling with images of her O'Hara, of Shanna, even of the old warlord, The O'Donnell, and the strange spell his dark eyes had cast over her as he stared up from his death bed.

As time wore on another face flashed before her, that of Sir Raymond Hubbard, and his words came back to echo in her ears. ". . . but if there is no other way, if indeed the king, my cousin, my aunt—and your father—have their way, I promise you that your life will be your own. If there is no consummation, I will say there was. If there is no heir, I will plead impotence on my part. And if you can never learn to love me as I love you, I will understand and respect the time when you do find someone to love."

Brenna's misted gaze drifted across the thatched

roofs of Chinon's cottages and returned to where candlelight blinked in the other abbey windows.

It will not be forever, Rory, my love. And you will ever be in my mind and heart until the day I can again feel the warmth of your chest pressed to my breasts and the strength of your arms about my body!

She willed the gentle wind outside the window to carry those thoughts to her lover. Then she clenched her jaw, straightened her shoulders, and turned to face the Earl of Buckingham's mother.

"I will sign. But I would have something in addition to my mother's freedom."

"You're not in a position for bargaining, girl—"

"Am I not?"

The Lady Compton took pause. There were no tears in the girl's eyes now. And the set of her jaw told the woman that, should she push too hard, the game might yet be lost.

"What is it?

"It has to do with a part of Ireland called Ballylee and one Rory O'Hara's claim to it. . . ."

Part II

CHAPTER TWENTY-NINE
IRELAND

Rory O'Hara guided his mount through knee-high bushes of golden furze and emerged in a clearing carpeted with lush green grass still damp from a morning rain. The air was sweet with the scent of whitethorn, and the breeze that cooled his face had the unmistakable scent of salt, telling him that the ocean, and the end of his journey, was near.

He reined in the horse and adjusted his ride-weary body in the stirrupless saddle. It was an Irish saddle, no more than a padded strip behind the horse's withers, designed so that its rider could guide the horse with only knee and spur, leaving the arms and hands free to fight.

Rory chuckled to himself at the thought. He had done no fighting in the three years since his return to Ireland, and it looked as though he would do precious little in the future.

How strange it was, a peaceful Ireland. Would it remain peaceful? It would seem so. Englishmen and Scotsmen were still swarming over the land, stealing it or taking it from the native Irish with shady legal maneuvers. But acceptance rather than rebellion seemed to be the rule now.

Rory had spent three years on the land at Ballylee and while they hadn't been boring years, there was still something lacking, an itchiness in this spirit that he couldn't deny. And so, three months before, he had arisen from his bed and announced that he was off to see the rest of his Ireland.

"I'm glad you're at last calling the land yours, lad," David Talbot had said in reply. "Be off with you then, and be the saints willin', maybe a fine buxom colleen will be ridin' pillion behind your saddle when you return."

They both knew that there was little chance of that. No matter how hard he had tried to forget her, Brenna's face, her voice, even her scent, haunted him. Roistering, drink, hard work—nothing could remove her from his mind and heart. How often he wondered if it were the same with her. Many letters he had sent her since that evening at the abbey in France, when she had fled into the night without a word to him or to anyone. None of his letters had been returned or answered.

All he wanted to know, *had* to know was...why? Why had she so radically changed her mind? And why so quickly? They had been so in love, had planned such a full and exciting future together. She had given Rory a new joy and purpose in life, a reason for being. They had been so much a part of each other he couldn't imagine life without her.

And then, suddenly she was gone, vanished from his life.

He thought that somehow she had been forced into her decision that night. He could feel it, sense it. But he could do nothing about it. While still in France, he had tried to follow her, to find her and demand some reason for her actions. But every trail had led to a dead end, and no one seemed able or willing to help him.

And so he had remained in limbo, rejecting the advances, the coyly lowered eyes of any woman he met. There had been women, a few, generally after a night of wild drinking with the tenant lads. But not once on the following mornings could he even remember their faces. Now, after three months of travel, there was no fair colleen behind Rory's saddle. He had seen none that could compare with Brenna Coke.

But he had seen his Ireland, and now he had to admit he had found another love. Not one to take Brenna's place, but one he wished he could share with her.

He had ridden the wilds of Connaught in the west between the ocean and the River Shannon. He had stood on soaring, jagged cliffs and traced their sheer faces downward to the ocean hundreds of feet below. His ears still rang with the curlew's mournful cry and the violent explosion of wind and wave as they pounded the rocky shore.

In Connaught he had met the hardier Gaels who still lived in the clannish ways of their ancestors. Moving among them he could sense their pride in being Irish. It was in these strong men of Connaught that he had found the undercurrents of rebellion still boiling. And it was here that men whispered his name in reverence. They told tales of his martyred warlord father, Shane, and his mother, the Lady Deirdre.

Unknowingly, a seed had been planted in Rory O'Hara that in the next three months would grow and blossom.

He rode on south and east through Munster where the earth rose up like jagged fangs to meet the mountain mists. Traveling the narrow lanes and vast fertile fields, he discovered that the ravages of war and rebellion had almost disappeared. Now the Anglo-Irish, those professing their undying loyalty to King James, and the new English settlers had moved in and taken over the lands. Their houses could have been built in England and moved whole to Ireland.

These new landlords settled in with the surety that they were born to rule and that the Irish were born to be herdsmen and water carriers. Rebellion was a thing of the past. It was now time to reap the rewards of being English in a conquered land. O'Neill, O'Donnell and O'Hara were not legends; they were merely names associated with bygone troubles.

But in the booleys and peasant cottages where he spent his nights, even in the inns when he stopped to eat, Rory found that the Irishmen of Munster remembered the O'Hara name in the same way as their Connaught brethren.

"Aye, I'd know you in a second, lad, for you've got your father's look. Praise the saints that an O'Hara has come back to the land!"

By the time he had passed through the golden vale of Tipperary and ridden up into the massive, heather-covered granite domes of the Wicklow mountains, Rory O'Hara's chest was swollen with pride. For every ballad he heard sung of brave rebels like O'Neill, O'Donnell and Macquire, there was always a harper who could add one about Shane, The O'Hara.

And the pride in his name that Rory O'Hara had found among the Wicklows' shillelagh oaks had not faded as he had ridden on through Leinster and Ulster. Now he was back in the rolling green pastures of home, Ballylee.

Home, he thought, How strange to call it thus after so long away and so short a stay after his return. But home it was, and for the first time in his life, he was glad of it.

He was about to put spur to horse when the silence of the mists was broken by bleating sheep. A shepherd materialized at the head of his herd, his hand raised in welcome.

Rory returned the salute and the man moved forward. He was a tall fellow, aged, but with squared shoulders and a robust figure. He sported a red mustache that curled clear to his cheekbones in a ruddy, weathered face.

His clothes were those of a workingman or peasant: a leather tunic, brown breeches and rawhide brogans. Beneath a shaggy mane of red hair his face wore a puzzled frown until he came to stand at the horse's flank. Then his eyes grew wide and his seamed face creased in a wide, toothy smile.

"Ye be Rory, son of The O'Hara."

"Aye."

"I be O'Higgin, once yer father's kern, now his son's tenant."

The man lifted a goatskin from his cross belt and offered it. Rory tipped and gulped two swallows of the harsh liquid before returning it. The man did the same, slipped it back into his belt and spoke.

"'Tis a fine thing you and yer Scot do with the land."

"My thanks. Is your treatment as a tenant fair?"

"Aye, as it was from yer father and better. Do ye trust the Scot?"

"Like a brother he is," Rory replied.

"Then I'll gladly pay my rents to the family O'Hara."

"And may we all prosper in peace," Rory said, and spurred his horse.

"M'Lord O'Hara. . . ."

The now-familiar title stopped Rory. Again he reined in and turned his mount to face the man called O'Higgin. "Aye?"

"You were but a lad before the flight, when The O'Donnell, O'Neill, Macquire and the others left Ireland to find their graves in Rome."

"Aye, I was."

"Then ye can't remember how bad the troubles were. I've seen the time when we were brought to such wretchedness that we were forced to crawl from every corner of the woods and glens on our hands and knees, for our legs would not bear our weight. For want of food we looked like death and spoke like ghosts already crying from our graves. We would eat anything we could find, and 'twas a feast when we came on an unburned plot of cresses or shamrocks that could sustain us for one more hour or day."

"But now there's peace and your belly's full, old man."

"Aye, I've a belly full of food. But I'm an Irishman, and I'd rather fight than eat when my belly's just as full of English law. In Ireland, English laws make tyranny legal. There's peace in the land now, aye. But 'tis only because the sassenachs have their way with us. They have the land—or most of it. Methinks they won't stop till they have it all."

"Nay, old man, for there's still a few Irishmen left. And as for Ballylee. . .if needs be, I'll make an Irish island out of it in a sea of English landlords."

The man smiled briefly and nodded.

"Then have sons, O'Hara. Mark me. If ye don't, the bloody English will find a way to make Ballylee theirs again!"

Without a reply, Rory reined around and rode on. *Have sons,* he thought. *Would that I could forget the one woman I want, so another who would make O'Hara sons could take her place.*

He rode for another two hours, with the scent of sea air becoming stronger and stronger in his nostrils. Then, near midday, he topped a rise. There below him across a wide heath covered in heather, lay Ballylee.

In an instant he relived the moment when he, Shanna and David Talbot had stood on the same spot nearly three years before.

"You've made good your vow," Shanna had said, her eyes misting as she lightly brushed his cheek with her lips. "You've taken me back to Ballylee."

Rory had only nodded solemnly as he gazed down at the rubble of the once proud and mighty castle. In those first few seconds he had thought of turning his mount around and riding away, anywhere, just to escape what he saw. In his stomach he had the empty, sinking feeling that he knew he would have upon seeing his ancestral home again.

Ballylee, like an Irish Ireland, was no more. 'Twas foolish to try to ressurect the dead. In their ride from Dublin, he had seen scores of people who had been thrown off their land. They wandered aimlessly, living off the kindness that others could give them. Many had taken to the mountains to become reparees, the Irish counterpart to the English highwayman.

Many of the dispossessed gentry, who had not been as lucky as Rory and Talbot in their suit for land, had become reparee leaders rather than accept exile or servitude under their new English masters.

How could the three of them, even with what appeared to be a solid claim, hope to build their heritage back to what it once was?

And if they did, could they keep it?

As if David Talbot had read Rory's thoughts, he spoke from where he stood next to Shanna. "We'll rebuild it, my friend. We'll make Ballylee as strong and as grand as it once was."

"Stronger and even more grand!" Shanna had cried, throwing her arms around her new husband.

And David Talbot had been as good as his word. The man had boundless energy and talents that neither Shanna nor Rory had ever dreamed he possessed. Even with one arm Talbot could still outwork most men. His mind, formerly often besotted with drink, had cleared in the air of Ireland.

He had begun with the land, using the Irishmen he had trained in England. No more was plowing done by tying the tails of six or eight horses to a cumbersome swing plow. Talbot had devised a harness and a handled plow so that six times the work could be done in the same amount of time.

Timber was needed for everything, but under Talbot's careful eye a tree was planted for every one cut down. Kerry cattle were purchased and lovingly cared for, until the booley trails were dark with their ebony hides and at night the barns echoed with their lowing.

And to Talbot, the Irishman himself was a product to be cultivated. No man, woman or child on Ballylee received less than their fair share of the land and its yield.

It didn't take long for Rory and Shanna, as well as the tenants, to realize that David Talbot had planned on being a different kind of gentry. He didn't believe that a landowner, rich or poor, should sit in the big house and hear from his overseers reports on his land, crops and cattle. Every day before dawn, Talbot was in the saddle, riding from one end of Ballylee to the other.

He had a kind word, a gentle suggestion or a helping hand for the fullers, the cobblers, the smiths, the shepherds, even the chimney sweeps.

And life inside the big house was the same.

"In the old days when a king sat at the table, his minstrels and servants would sit with him and share his cup and plate. 'Twas, methinks, a praiseworthy custom where everything was in common but their bed. I want no more than to be known as a country gentleman of the old school, fond of the bottle and generous with it to others!" Talbot had declared.

He was, and the people had grown to love him for it.

When he was finally satisfied with the land, he had set out to redesign and rebuild Ballylee itself.

He had retained what was left of the barbicans, the great towers, and the twelve-foot-thick walls that connected them. Then to the defensible castle he had added a three-story manor house built over cellars.

Crenellated parapets decorated the roofs, from which also rose many chimneys. Around the whole structure wide courtyards and lavish gardens were built, complete with orchards of May Dale cherries, Bellegarde peaches and so many other fruit trees Rory couldn't remember them all.

Such elements of defense as protective twenty-foot-thick walls were reconstructed with shooting towers and a walkway around the whole. Firing holes were cut into the blocks around the doors and windows.

But, above all, David Talbot had designed the new Ballylee for gracious living.

"You'll never have to fear, Shanna mine, that when I'm done with this rubble, you won't be shamed to invite your little Princess Henrietta Maria herself to visit O'Hara's part of Ireland!"

Nowhere were his efforts more apparent than inside the big house. Venetian glass was everywhere, as well as handsomely crafted objects in brass, pewter and silver. Richly embroidered cushions graced the massive chairs and couches, and everyone slept in feather beds shipped from France.

Talbot was partial to everything being large in size,

considering bigness to be worthy, impressive and beautiful. So he had imported even more artisans to design and build the furnishings. So huge they were that they had to be built and carved inside the rooms.

"On purpose," he had chuckled. "For if the outside ever goes again, I want the inside to go with it. They would have to hoist a cannon into the hallways to blow the doors wide enough to get our furniture out!"

The rest of the interior had been richly decorated with tapestries from Venice, plasterwork friezes, handsome paneling and everywhere the carved O'Hara crest.

Two wide, handhewn-oak stairways branched from the high-ceilinged great room into the upper stories of the house's two wings. The railings carved by artisans from Brussels.

"If there ever be a true king of Ireland crowned," Talbot had said in defense of his extravagance, "I'll tell him there's no better place for it than O'Hara's Ballylee!"

And there was no doubt that Ballylee was pure O'Hara. The family crest, a rampant lion holding between his paws a chaplet of oak leaves with the motto By Virtue and High Repute, was emblazoned above all twenty-three hearths in the house.

When Rory had objected, saying that it was all as much or more Talbot than O'Hara, David had protested even more.

"Don't ever say that, lad—not ever, do you hear?" Storm clouds were in the gray eyes as he spoke, and his voice had the husky grit in it that must have sent many a chill up the spine of an opponent in years gone by. "Religion I care not for. I can be a Presbyterian Scot, an Irish Catholic, an English Protestant.... I care not beneath what banner I talk to my God in order to keep the land. What name a man prays under means nothing. 'Tis the name he lives under and the family that carries it on that matters. 'Tis pedigree that is important, lad—the blood, the family, the name. 'Tis that that keeps the land and makes the world. You have it; your blessed sister has it; I lack it. Mark me: were it possible I would have my sons and daughters take the name. For by Shanna they are O'Haras, and O'Haras I would have them be."

Rory had protested no more. Indeed, he envied David Talbot his pride in something, even if it was his wife's family name. And so the building of the O'Hara family fortune and Ballylee went on.

The huge kitchen of the old castle was rebuilt and enlarged. Talbot devised a way to divert a nearby stream to flow directly through the kitchen and constructed a runway to hold it. Thus a continuous flow of fresh water was always available, without time wasted in carrying, and uneaten food was transported to the stock without manpower.

New winding staircases, four of them, led from the kitchen up to the great hall and a smaller dining room. These were wide from necessity. Quarters of beef and full-sized lambs were boiled or roasted whole and carried up those stairs.

Ballylee's second floor consisted of the great hall, which for supper could seat more than a hundred guests. Off the hall was a smaller dining room, two damask rooms, two drawing rooms, a billiards room and six lounging rooms for guests to rest or freshen themselves from a long ride.

On up the wide stairways were the two bedroom wings and the servants' garrets. All of the third-story rooms were large and well lit in the new French style, with high wide windows paned in glass.

Each wing contained suites with dressing room, parlor, parlor closet, bedroom and a study. Between the two wings were nursery rooms, ten in all.

"You would breed and raise your own Irish army!" Rory had chided Talbot a year before.

"Aye, I would—or enough wombs to conceive an army, seeing as how our whole litter thus far is female!"

And he didn't stop with the land and house. David Talbot had a dream of wealth, wealth so great that the Talbots and the O'Haras of the future could control their own destiny.

In answer to the growing demand for iron, smelting furnaces had been built. What sheep and cattle couldn't be sold in Ireland or used on Ballylee itself, Talbot had sold abroad in England and France. So successful were the new methods of tillage that huge surpluses of corn and other crops were also available for sale.

Through brokers in France, Ballylee's profits on its crops had tripled, and with those profits more land had been added to Ballylee.

Rory smiled at the perfection Talbot had wrought. Not that he, O'Hara, hadn't done his part. But it was Talbot's taste and genius that had conceived the beauty that now was Ballylee.

He compared what he saw now before him to other strong houses he had seen in his three months of travel. There was the great turreted mansion of the hated lord deputy, in Dublin, the Rathfarnham Castle, Coppinger's Court with its two huge towers, and O'Donnell's castle in Donegal, now being reconstructed under the eye of its new owner, Sir Basil Brooke.

All beautiful and costly, Rory thought, but none could compare with Ballylee. But then, perhaps it was the land it sat on or the fact that it was his.

And as he spurred his horse down the hill, another thought struck him.

I am The O'Hara, and all that I see is mine. Would that Brenna were here to see and share it with me!

CHAPTER THIRTY
ENGLAND

IF BEFORE HER MARRIAGE Brenna's life had been in the hands of her father and mother, after the marriage it was in the hands of Buckingham and the Lady Compton.

From the day of the wedding at Hampton Court Palace, in the presence of the king, the queen and all the court hangers-on, Brenna knew that her hopes and dreams were doomed. The one thing that had saved her sanity was the knowledge that her beloved Rory and her dearest friend, David Talbot, had their dreams.

Thoughts of them were uppermost in her mind as she mounted the steps and entered the King's Chapel. Sunlight danced through the diamond-shaped panes of the mullioned windows, but it failed to erase the gloom in her heart.

Words were said, vows were exchanged, but through it all Brenna saw and heard nothing. Only when the ring was slipped on her finger, making everything final, did she blink and awaken to reality.

She looked down at her hand and struggled to hold back the tears at what she saw. The ring was gold and fashioned like two hands clasping a diamond heart.

In a daze she went through the ritual of holding up the wedding gifts and commenting on their splendor. Indeed, many of them were splendid. There was a rapier for Sir Raymond, its hilt encrusted with gems. There were slippers and rich gloves embroidered in gold and silver. There were gold and silver-wrought candlesticks that she could barely lift.

Sir Edward Coke, being true to his nature as an economical man, had given his daughter on what was supposed to be the most glorious day of her life a basin and ewer of silver gilt.

Because the king had sanctioned the marriage and the bridegroom was his favorite's cousin, no expense had been spared for the banquet following the ceremony. It was held outdoors beneath spreading beeches on the grassy slopes behind Hampton Court.

Her new husband, looking as confused as Brenna was sad, sat on one side of her. Charles, the Prince of Wales, sat on the other.

"'Tis right this thing you do, for our elders are also our betters and have more wisdom in these affairs than we," he said to Brenna.

"Then, Your Highness, when it comes time for you to take a bride, you would give up the choosing?"

"Aye, I will, unless I am king when that time comes. If 'tis so, I will do the choosing, for as king I cannot but make the right choice. The king, like God, does not err."

Preserve us, Brenna thought, *for we will surely have more of the father in the son on James's passing. And pass he must soon do,* she mused, watching the sunken-eyed, sallow-cheeked monarch being carried from table to table in a litter. A child of five could see that James's years of overindulgence had begun to take their toll. He was a weakened man in a sick condition, but he continued to imbibe prodigious quantities of wine.

Everything Brenna had heard whispered behind tilted

fans about His Royal Majesty, James Stuart, King of England, Scotland, Ireland and Wales, had proved true. The contents of glass after glass of frontinac, canary, and Scottish ale passed his lips. The king cared little what kind of wine he imbibed; he only roared when there was not plenty of it at hand.

"The British Solomon," he called himself. Brenna thought he looked more like a misshapen Cheapside tavern keeper. His wide, protruding eyes rolled when he drank, and a great deal of the wine found its way onto his already stained doublet and breeches instead of down his throat.

When his chin wasn't nodding on his chest, he was shouting for Buckingham. "Steenie! Where is my darling Steenie!"

"Here, Your Majesty."

"Come, Steenie, give your wife and dad a kiss!"

And this, Brenna thought, *is the ruler to whom I must give my fealty and obey for all my days?*

Somehow she endured it all, even the sloppy kisses of the king and the snide congratulations of the now Duke of Buckingham and his brothers. At the conclusion of the masque following the banquet, she threw her stocking rolled in her garter, as was expected, ensuring a speedy marriage to the one who caught it. The king requested that the couple lay abed till noon the following day, for he would visit them and hear details of the wedding night.

"He is a lecher, warped in his own sex and expecting the same of others," Sir Raymond whispered as they were ushered to the bridal quarters assigned to them.

Brenna stood like a statue, frozen in time and space, while maids readied her for the marriage bed. Then candles were extinguished, and everyone else was gone.

Sir Raymond slipped silently into the chamber. Brenna squeezed her eyes so tightly shut she was sure the pain it caused would bring blindness. She felt the huge feather mattress shift with his weight and heard the rustle of his nightshirt as he moved across the bed to where she lay.

Her mind flew back to Elmeham, to the soft grassy slope in the glen beside a meandering stream. She could feel Rory O'Hara's powerful body between her willing thighs. She could taste his kisses and thrill to the gentleness of his hands exploring the wonders of her body.

Then Sir Raymond's trembling voice filled her ears, spilling across her thoughts, scattering them like smoke.

"My dearest Brenna, you are the most beautiful bride any man could dream of bedding. But I know that this marriage is a sham and travesty of love."

Brenna opened her eyes and looked up at this strange, gentle man who had become her husband. Her heart went out to the plea in his soft brown eyes, but her body wouldn't move, nor would her lips make words.

"This Irishman, O'Hara, do you love him?"

Brenna nodded.

"And does he love you?"

Again her head bobbed.

"Then know, sweet sad lady, that you have two men worshipping at your shrine. Know you this as well: I can't return you to him, but I'll not take what you consider rightfully his. For I think the laws of God are not one with the laws of kings. I would obey the rule God has over your heart before I would obey a besotted monarch's rule over your body. Good night, and try to sleep well."

It took Brenna several seconds to realize the full import of what had happened. He had lightly brushed her lips with his own and had then rolled to the far side of the bed.

Tears welled in her eyes at the deed, at the sacrifice he was making. It was then that she dared to believe Sir Raymond meant to keep the vow that he had made to her that day in Hatton Garden.

As the tears pooled and spilled from her eyes to flow down across her cheeks, Brenna let her hand creep across the bed. At last she found and clasped his.

And like that, with their hands clasped across the gulf that separated them, Sir Raymond and Lady Hubbard passed their wedding night together.

TIME PASSED FOR BRENNA, often without her realizing it. Indeed, weeks, sometimes months, went by in what seemed like the blink of an eye. Events whirled around her with little meaning.

Her mother's old ally and her father's bitter enemy, Sir Francis Bacon, rose to the height he so long had coveted. In 1618 he became Baron Verulam and then two years later, Viscount St. Albans. But so corrupt was his office that, even in a corrupt court he was charged with twenty-three counts of bribery and banished from court and Parliament.

Sir Walter Raleigh's grand search for El Dorado had ended in disaster. In 1618 he had paid with his head, and Buckingham at last had rid James's court of all the gallant heroes of Queen Elizabeth's reign.

Summer brought plague and winter produced famine. War raged in Europe, and the trickle of immigration to the New World had begun to swell. In 1620 one ship, a merchant vessel called the Mayflower, alone had transported 102 desperate souls to a place called Plymouth.

Sir Raymond Hubbard was made Master of the Robes in the household of Prince Charles. He and Brenna moved into Somerset House, the prince's London residence on the south side of the Strand.

By all rights a young bride should have been happy in the huge mansion with its vast courtyards, manicured gardens and stately rooms. Brenna tried to be, if for nothing else than her husband's sake. For not once had Sir Raymond broken his vow, and she knew the agony of it was telling on his mind and body.

As much as she could, Brenna took part in the life of the court. She tried to emulate the other women, including her mother, in manners and dress. She tried to cultivate an interest in falconry and masqueing which, being forthright and honest, she had always heretofore abhorred. She dressed in the outmoded styles still adopted by the queen: heavy velvet with hot satin linings and many foldings of weighty, gold-encrusted material.

Buckingham dictated opulence in the court, while the poor died in the streets of starvation.

Brenna learned everything well, except acceptance. Beneath the sparkling trappings of the woman who came to be known for her ability to wear diamonds in the morning, there was still a raging sadness and a dormant seed of rebellion.

She longed to be free of the lewdness and the fakery around her. And she longed for love. Not the puppylike adoration of Sir Raymond that she could never return but the wild, uninhibited passion of Rory O'Hara, for whom her body ached.

But it was not to be. There was little doubt as time passed that her thoughts that night at Chinon would never come true. There would be no brief span of marriage and then annulment. There would be no escape or flight to France or Ireland and a life with Rory O'Hara.

Hers was a marriage made and blessed by the king himself. If she objected any further to it they would all be ruined. When, through France, Rory O'Hara's letters from Ireland arrived in England, Brenna didn't even break their seals. She was too fearful of the words of love she knew they would contain and the demands they would put on her for explanations. She knew that if she read them their contents might shatter her will. So into the compartment at the bottom of her jewel box they went, unopened and unread.

Lady Hatton had become more bitter than ever after the wedding, which she had refused to attend. For months she had begged Brenna for the truth. Why had she changed her mind? Brenna saw no reason to muddy the waters of their lives further, especially after she realized that what was done, was done for good.

"'Tis finished, mother, and there is naught we can do to change that which King James hath wrought in God's name. I beg you, leave off with it. Let us both, nay, let us all, get on with the business of living or, in my case, existing."

Lady Hatton had begrudgingly agreed but not without tendering a vow that, Brenna somehow knew, her strong-willed mother would one day find a way to fulfill. "Aye, 'tis done then. But I vow this—one day I will right this grievance, for 'tis not true that kings cannot fall!"

As much of Lady Hatton's anger was directed toward Sir Edward Coke as it was toward the king. To James she could do nothing, but against her husband this iron-willed woman could direct a great deal of wrath.

"By God in heaven, since I've had to yield in this, I will have all the honor and thanks in it, and so defeat my husband's purpose. He will gain none! 'Tis unfortunate that all this has been the means of injuring the daughter I love, but it is fortunate that it might yet be the means of injuring the husband that I truly do hate!" Elizabeth cried out.

Greed, wealth, hatred, ambition—all of it meant little to Brenna now. Let them play their games. She would no longer be a pawn.

Squabbles between her parents over income and property hadn't been settled with Brenna's marriage. By law Lady Hatton could not dispose of her estate without the permission and agreement of her husband. Thus she had to buy Coke's permission to sell her own lands in order to meet her daily living obligations. Back to the council table they went.

Fearful that they might lose the Hatton fortune that could come to them through Sir Raymond, Buckingham and Lady Compton urged a ceasefire in the couple's long-standing marital war. Even the king himself, during a gala dinner Elizabeth gave in his honor at Hatton House—without Coke's presence—suggested a reconciliation between the feuding couple. To this, Lady Hatton had the effrontery to reply, "Your Majesty, should he come in at one door, I would be pleased to go out the other."

Once again it was common scandal that the Lady Hatton would go so far as to ruin herself if she could savor the joy of overthrowing her husband.

The results of Sir Edward and Lady Hatton's last round of wrangling gave a full week's gossip to the wagging tongues on St. Paul's Walk. Coke had sacrificed his daughter on the chance of gratifying his ambition. Elizabeth had met the dowry demands of Lady Compton in an attempt to regain her position at court.

They had both lost.

Sir Edward was not returned to his office of lord chief justice but was instead made an at-large member of the Privy Council with no pay and no power. He retired to Stoke Poges to lick his wounds and nurse his bitterness over a false king and a favorite whose word was as solid as smoke on a windy day.

At court Elizabeth Hatton refused to fall prey to Buckingham and his mother's devious attempts to pry loose more of her fortune. She retired to Hatton House to live with her memories and write long letters beseeching Brenna to use what influence her new husband had with his family to intercede for her when the need arose.

Brenna cared little for any of it. She withdrew into herself, walking through her days without thought and tumbling into an empty bed at night to toss in the throes of dreams that could never be.

But as sad as Brenna was, she felt even more compassion for her husband. She would catch him in offhand moments staring at her so intensely that a chill would ripple up her spine. The look in his deep-set eyes was a mixture of pure love and haunted desperation.

"Will you ever love me, Brenna? Perhaps not as I love you, but enough to bring some meaning to this sham we call marriage or this madness we call living?" he had asked.

"I do love you, Raymond, as the dear friend you have become. Dear Lord, I wish it could be more, but I don't know how to make it so."

When they would touch, by accident or when Brenna could not resist running a reassuring finger down the line of his jaw, his eyes would turn on her.

The question was always there.

"Time, dear sweet, gentle husband. . . give me time, I

beg of you. For I have no desire to be the ruin of your life, and I know you would be the making of mine if you could. Time, just. . . time."

But the look in those eyes didn't change, and gradually it became more haunted. There were moments when she sensed a creeping madness in the looks he gave her. It frightened and repelled her even more, but she never spoke of it. She felt she owed the man that much.

To give some meaning to his life, Sir Raymond threw himself into the duties of the office created for him by his cousin Buckingham. But he was woefully ill-equipped to be first Master of the Robes and then Master of the Horse to young Charles, Prince of Wales. That he became a joke to the court burned his soul.

More and more, those around him noted a creeping strangeness in Sir Raymond's words and manners. It was rumored that he sought solace in the company of a Jesuit priest. Some thought that he might even embrace the Catholic religion. If any act committed in the Protestant England of King James could be construed as an act of madness, it was a man's conversion to the popish faith.

Only Brenna knew the real reason for her husband's seeming madness, and she was powerless to do anything about it. So far in her lifetime, two men had truly loved her, but only one had received her love in return. And, because she was sure that man was out of her life forever, she was unable to take seriously the business of being a wife to the other.

But the problems of the Coke family mattered little to the Duke of Buckingham or Lady Compton. They had but one objective in mind: more wealth and more power through the installation of family members in offices of prestige.

Lady Compton was able to obtain a large estate, Poole House, in Dorset on the sea. It stood across the bay from the Isle of Purbeck and the Lady Hatton's Corfe Castle. Once this was accomplished, it was a simple matter for the Duke of Buckingham to petition the king for his cousin, Sir Raymond Hubbard's peerage.

To pay for this peerage and the use of Poole House, Lady Compton set about the sale of Elmeham House, part of Brenna's dowry.

When word reached Lady Hatton, she was livid. She wrote letter after letter to her daughter, and her son-in-law as well, warning them that what little wealth they had was about to be lost.

My dearest Brenna,

I do now agree with Sir Edward on at least one fact: there is nothing in this world more foolish than a subject's belief in the divine right of kings. I disapprove as strongly of this as I disapproved of forcing my daughter into a loveless marriage. But since I cannot fight the former and was unable to prevent the latter, I have determined to make the best terms I can for both myself and you.

My darling little girl, you must be protected not only from the viciousness of the Villiers clan but from yourself. There are rumors that Sir Raymond grows mad. If this is true, mark me, no good will come to you, for he is the only one now who stands between us and Lady Compton's wrath at not obtaining more of my fortune and your dowry than she has already.

Because of this, I feel I must venture forth from the solitude of Hatton House and petition the queen, for she alone seems to be an island of sanity and righteousness at court in a sea of madness and dissolution. I pray you to venture forth from what has become your nunlike existence and plead this case at my side.

Your loving mother, Eliza. Hatton

Brenna paid no attention.

Sir Raymond brooded, lost in the morass of his family's dealings and unable to cope with their overbearing personalities. He could think only of the wife he had in name but could not possess in fact.

But before Elizabeth could do any petitioning, Queen Anne took to her bed. The self-willed, pleasure-loving queen who had endured so much in her lifetime from an unloving husband soon breathed her last. And with Queen Anne's death, so, too, died Elizabeth Hatton's last hope of saving what fortune her daughter had.

Thus, Sir Raymond and Brenna became Viscount and Viscountess Poole, and their indebtedness to Lady Compton increased. Elmeham House was sold.

Before moving from London to Poole House, Brenna made one last trip to the little glen where she had been so happy in Rory O'Hara's arms. She sat for hours beneath the huge oaks and leafy beech trees, staring at the rippling stream where they had loved, oblivious to the world. She talked to the soft breeze, wishing it could carry her words as thoughts across the Irish Sea.

Had he married? Was he happy? Were there children? And what of David? Had the light of love she had seen in Shanna's eyes borne fruit?

There was such a swelling in her breast that Brenna thought surely she would burst. It wasn't fair! The three of them were probably so happy living on their Ballylee.

And she, who had made their happiness possible, was so miserable.

"The Viscount and Viscountess Poole," droned the liveried footman as they descended the stairs and entered the great room of Somerset House for what Brenna hoped was the last time.

The occasion was a ball given in their honor by young Charles, Prince of Wales. The next morning Raymond and Brenna would leave for Poole House. All the glittering court was there bedecked in their excess of finery.

The question was constantly asked, "Oh, my dear, how can you leave London and all this? Dorset is so drab! The sea—dear Lord, however will you control your hair? And the court. . . . However can you leave the court at the height of the season?"

Brenna only smiled, wishing it would all end quickly. How could she truthfully reply that she and the viscount had practically been ordered to Poole House. Hubbard's fits of melancholy had begun to cause his cousin and Lady Compton embarrassment.

And how could Brenna admit that this court that she had tried to be a part of now disgusted her. Buckingham had filled Whitehall with licentious gallants and ladies who matched them in dissipation and libertine behavior. It was common gossip on the streets of London and along St. Paul's Walk that no one was in so great favor with the Duke of Buckingham than bawds, parasites and others who humored him in his unchaste pleasures.

There was doubt in no one's mind now that the handsome and supposedly harmless favorite had merged his personality with the monarch. He had become insolent, cruel, a monster not to be endured and, worst of all, dangerous to the very existence of England.

Brenna was glad to be free of it all, and at the end of the evening she told her husband so.

"As am I," he replied. "Perhaps in the seclusion and tranquillity of Poole House you will find a way. . . and we can find each other."

CHAPTER THIRTY-ONE
IRELAND

THE MORNING OF ALL HALLOWS' EVE DAWNED in the midst of a fierce, teeming rain accompanied by a howling southwest wind. Later it had abated to a heavy gray overcast. Uninterrupted clouds chased one another lazily through the sky as every hand on Ballylee turned to the holiday preparations.

That afternoon there would be dining, dancing and drinking as the tenants came from the far corners of the estate to the great house. That day the ancient feast of Samhain, the feast of the dead, would be celebrated, and the day after that, All Saint's Day would be observed.

The first of November marked the end of autumn and the beginning of winter. Spring and summer crops were in, stockpiled against the hard winter to come. Kerry cattle and sheep had been moved from the mountain pastures to fields nearer the big house. Milk cows had been herded into the byre, where they would be hand fed with stored fodder until spring came.

Thatched-roof tenant cottages had been well stocked with turf and wood for the winter fires. The great house was amply supplied with sweet-smelling bog-deal, the choicest clear-burning roots of ancient pine trees.

For Shanna it was a time to leave off the chores of supervising the women of Ballylee in their spinning, weaving and dyeing of the family clothes. And it was a brief rest from overseeing the daily round of cleaning, baking and the hundred tasks that fell to her in the constant reconstruction of the great house.

"I swear," she had cried a few days before, "David Talbot will never be done with it!"

"Nay," Rory had replied. "And well he shouldn't, for once the dream is completed, there's little glory left in it—I know."

It was Rory who had become Shanna's one big worry amid the peace and happiness she had found at Ballylee. For her brother wasn't happy, and it showed in his eyes more each day.

Since his return from the three months' ride through the land, Ireland was constantly on his lips. But Shanna knew, as only a woman can know, that it was Brenna who really occupied his mind.

"You'd best forget her, dear brother," she'd chided.

"Aye, I know."

"She's wed by now and probably borne twice the children I have."

"Aye, I know."

"But you still love her."

"Aye."

"'Tis foolishness! Find yourself an Irish lass and breed some Irish sons! She's lost to you, Rory. 'Tis three years—time the mourning period be over."

"Should Talbot bid the bye, is that what you would do?"

"Aye, I would, for it takes a man to hold the land."

Shanna could only hope that the coming holiday and

the threat of a new uneasiness in the land would revive Rory's will to live and make him see that the past and past loves were over.

By midafternoon, all the tenants and laborers of Ballylee had gathered in the two great courtyards between the big house and the outer wall. Children ran among the tables and played blind man's bluff, shuffle and brogue or four-corner fool, while their elders sang, talked and lifted glass after glass to each other in good cheer. Tall tales were told, politics were discussed, weddings were planned, and wakes that had taken place for friends, relatives and neighbors that year were remembered.

Through it all, Shanna, swollen with her second child, moved with a gleam of pride in her eye. Her brother and her husband had performed a miracle. Behind her loomed one of the grandest houses in the land. And before her, shining, happy faces mirrored her own content.

They are as proud to be on Ballylee, she thought, *as I am to be mistress of it!*

"Sure an' it's not a fit day fer a birthing, m'lady. Best you sit and let the serving girls do the rest!" Dick, the shepherd, said to her as she passed.

"Nay, for the whelp barely kicks, and I've a month to term, anyway," Shanna replied in the man's own dialect. In answer he flashed her an adoring smile, and she returned it.

She was the lady of the manor, yes, the woman who commanded respect of every man, woman and child who set foot on the vast acres of Ballylee. But she was also a revered and idolized friend. They knew that she had been convent raised and was graced with an education that they and probably their sons and daughters would never have. But it didn't matter, and Shanna made sure of it. She was always the first on a tenant farmer's doorstep when his child was ill or his woman was screaming in the first throes of labor with yet another wee one.

"To yer health, m'Lady O'Hara!" an old man roared, raising his tankard of mead as she passed. "Never was there a holiday time so glorious!"

"On with you, Casey, and watch your tongue, or my husband will box your ears with his one good arm! For I'm the Lady Talbot, and don't ye forget it!"

"Aye, that ye are, but yer still an O'Hara on Ballylee, as is yer brother, and by the saints I never thought I'd see the day come again by the time the last troubles was over."

"Bless you, Casey," Shanna said in a whisper, and leaned forward to kiss the top of his balding pate. "And watch your drink, for you know what befell you last Hallow E'en."

The farmers and herdsmen near them whooped with laughter and among themselves retold the tale of what had befallen Shamus Casey Hallow E'en the year before.

'Twas the night when the fairies, the hobgoblins and evil spirits held their high revels. 'Twas the night when the dreaded Puca, the black pig, was abroad in company with the horrible headless apparition, the Dallachan. 'Twas said that on Hallow E'en night a family could awaken from their sleep and find their dead kin returned and sitting around the kitchen hearth.

Foolish was the unwary traveler who returned from the evening's revels alone. The previous Hallow E'en, Shamus Casey had been such a foolish traveler setting out with his horse and two-wheeled cart. For besides fairies and hobgoblins on the road that night, there had been—as there always were on Hallow E'en night—boys setting out to do mischief.

Casey, having had more to drink than was needed to induce sleep, had nodded off halfway through his journey. When he awoke he had found his coat, his breeches, his shirt—and even his hands and face—painted many colors. As if that weren't enough, his horse had been unharnessed, the shafts of his cart thrust through a fence and then the animal re-harnessed on the other side.

"And what did ye do, Shamus Casey?" Shanna asked at that point in the narrative.

"What could he do?" another man said, roaring with laughter. "He went back to sleep 'til morning. He was too drunk to unharness the horse and right the mischief!"

More laughter followed, and Shanna moved on. Beneath a gateway leading off the courtyard into one of the terraced gardens she saw Aileen. Beside her, little Maura Talbot, near two now, toddled along clasping the older girl's skirts.

Shanna stopped for a moment to stare. Though they were only half sisters, they looked like two peas from the same pod. At fourteen, Aileen Talbot was tall and slender, with fair skin and wide blue eyes. Her hair was the color of golden wheat and long, with just enough natural curl. Maura, like her older half sister, was fair-skinned, and her hair was an even lighter gold.

"Come, little one!" Shanna called, and the child rocked forward on her short pudgy legs. After three steps she was saved from a fall by Shanna sweeping her up in her arms.

"'Tis a grand day," Aileen smiled, her English marked with a strong French accent.

"Aye, that it is. Peace brings prosperity, and prosperity happiness."

Together they watched the milling crowds. Nearby some children had placed on the ground a half barrel filled with water. Coins had been thrown into the water by their parents, and apples bobbed on the water's surface. Boys, their hands tied behind them, gleefully tried to rescue the apples with their teeth. The more daring ones submerged their heads and shoulders completely in the water in an attempt to retrieve the coins.

Another group had hung from a gateway rafter two pointed sticks in the shape of a T. An apple and a lighted candle were stuck on the ends of the T and then sent spinning. Wild whoops of laughter rang out when a boy or girl would miss the apple and get a mouthful of tallow instead.

"You don't join in the games," Shanna said to her stepdaughter.

"Nay, they're for children," Aileen replied.

Shanna only nodded and held her tiny daughter more tightly to her breasts. It was true, Aileen was no longer a child. Indeed, she had seemed old for her years when they had first met at Luçon three years before.

How afraid Shanna had been before that first meeting. The love between herself and David Talbot had sprouted and blossomed so swiftly that there had been little time for Aileen to become accustomed to the idea of her father's remarriage.

But Shanna's fears were put to rest at once. They had liked each other immediately, and their friendship had deepened during the crossing. By the end of their first year at Ballylee, Shanna and Aileen Talbot were more like sisters than stepdaughter and stepmother.

And even though Aileen had been born and raised in France, there was no doubt of her Irishness. Between the refugee priests at Luçon and her father, David, they had instilled a sense of heritage in the girl that had amazed Shanna. Aileen had taken to the land and the people at once. Now only her accent was all that remained of her time in France.

From the corner of her eye Shanna studied this blossoming woman who, while not a product of her own womb, was as dear to her as the child she held in her arms. Like Shanna, Aileen wore a long cotton leine that came to her ankles. Over it was a plain yellow sleeveless dress with a high, laced bodice. On purpose they had chosen plain colors and clothes to wear this day, for it was also the dress of the tenants' wives.

But for wear on the morrow, for the Feast of All Saints, when other planters and what was left of Irish gentry in the west would travel to Ballylee to celebrate, velvet, silks and satins had been brought out from long storage and lovingly aired and pressed.

"I hope you'll take a greater part in the festivities on the morrow," Shanna said playfully.

Aileen turned her head slightly until their eyes met. A hint of a smile played at the corner of her lips. "Would you be counting on me to entice a lad?"

Shanna gave a low chuckle. "Of course I would. There's no need for you to wait as I did. You're fourteen, near fifteen; 'tis time you thought of such things."

Aileen turned away to stare across the courtyard. "Oh, I think of such things lately. . . often." The smile broadened as her lips parted over even white teeth and her hand slipped into the tiny pocket of her smock.

How truly Irish I've become, she thought, her fingers idly toying with the ivy leaves in the pocket. *So Irish that I've taken to using charms and spells, just like other Irish lasses, to divine my love and future husband!*

She carefully went over in her mind what the servant girls had told her. Later that night she would save the first and last spoonful of colcannon, or barley meal, from the supper dish. This she would put in her left stocking, along with the nine ivy leaves. Then she would tie the stocking with her right garter and place it under the head of her bed. And just before sleep came she would chant the words:

> Nine ivy leaves I place under my head
> to dream of the living and not of the dead,
> To dream of the man I am going to wed,
> And to see him tonight at the foot of my bed!

While standing beside Aileen, Shanna wondered at the intensity in the girl's face and then followed her gaze, across the courtyard to the steps of the big house's main entrance.

There, dressed in a green velvet mantle trimmed at the hood and hem with beaver, stood her brother, Rory, The O'Hara.

"COME, LAD!" TALBOT SAID, throwing his good arm around Rory's shoulder. "We'd best speak now before this mountain of food is set before them, or they'll not hear a word that is said!"

Rory nodded and followed David to the stairs that led to the walkway around the courtyard. Once there they were joined by a priest and a herdsman with his horn.

"A blast, if you would," Talbot directed.

The herdsman raised his horn and its mournful wail rolled across the courtyard, bringing an instant hush to the throng below. Talbot stepped to the walkway's edge and raised his arm in welcome as he leaned out over the low retaining wall.

"Tenants, farmers, herdsmen and servants, I welcome you all this day to Ballylee!" Talbot, tankard in hand, raised his arm higher. "God save Ireland!"

"God save Ireland!" came the answering cry of five hundred voices.

"God save Ballylee!" Talbot cried.

The crowd roared its answer and the toast was completed. Talbot set his tankard on the wall and again leaned out over the crowd.

There was a hushed tenseness in the air, and narrowed eyes in the upturned faces. For even though David Talbot had proved to be a just landlord and an honest man, he was still a Scot, and if he professed a religion, they suspected it would have to be the religion of his forebears—Presbyterianism.

These facts were enough to make the Irish distrust him, no matter his accomplishments. For this reason, to reassure the men of Ballylee that there would be a tomorrow under David Talbot's guidance, speeches were to be made this day.

The silence was tomblike as Rory stepped forward.

"We've come far together, and we'll go farther. But I know that in your hearts you remember the past and fear the future, for peace in Ireland is as fragile as a newborn babe," he began.

"I stand before you, forbidden by English law to wear this green of the O'Hara mantle. But I wear it proudly and defiantly. Why? Because I stood here, years before, on these battlements, and watched Ballylee crumble at my feet. I vowed to return one day, but along the way I forgot that vow. I lost the desire to be an Irishman.

"This man you look upon as a Scot has given me back my Irishness. . . and Ballylee. And now that the land is mine again, I would keep it.

"Good men of Ballylee, I fear we would hide our heads and hope that the troubles are over. They are not. I've ridden Ireland and I've smelled the smells of war in the air and heard the sounds of rebellion in the land. I've talked to men like Phelim O'Neill and Rory O'More. Brave men they are, but not happy with their lot. Why should men endeavor to get estates, they tell me, when their ownership is never agreed upon by Dublin or Whitehall. Why should great houses like Ballylee be built, when English tricks and words can destroy natural rights and property at the touch of pen to paper?

"The hills are full of men turned to crime through English greed. Our shores abound with Irish pirates, and those that have not the taste for danger wander the land destitute.

"And what of the Irish left on the land, those not as prosperous as we on our little island of Ballylee? Should we turn aside from them if the troubles come again? I think we'll not be able to.

"An Irishman has no wealth but his flocks and herds. He has no trade but pasture. Many are unlearned men. They have no arms now, but I sense them so active in mind and body that it is dangerous to drive them from their ancestral seats. They have no weapons, but are in a temper to fight with nails and heels, yea, even their teeth, if need be.

"Not again will we see a flight such as that of the earls of years past. An Irishman now would rather starve upon husks at home than fare sumptuously elsewhere. They will fight for their altars and hearths. They would rather seek a bloody death near the sepulchers of their fathers than be buried as exiles in unknown earth.

"Even now the greed of the English thieves in Dublin outdoes king and council in England. I would have us a voice in Dublin's parliament. Little good it will do, but a voice is a voice. And I would have that voice be Sir David Talbot's!"

There were a few grumblings from the crowd as Rory stepped back, but for the most part they stayed silent, waiting to see what Talbot had to say.

" 'Tis said, mostly by Englishmen, that idleness is Ireland's national disease. The Irishman's answer?" Talbot asked in a strong, clear voice. "Why, damme, 'tis not idleness but a love of living some of a man's life rather than working it all away. Why should all of a man's time be spent at work when we have potatoes? Isn't it true that with this glorious food the Englishman, Raleigh, has given us, the work of one man can feed forty? Mayhap this is the real reason King James had Sir Walter's head removed from his body. He gave Irishmen a food to use for survival!"

A roar of laughter greeted these words, and Talbot joined in with the rest before continuing.

"And isn't it true that one cow will give enough meat and drink for three men? And can't a strong man, when he's of a mind, put up four walls and a thatch roof in three days? Of course he can.

"Nay, 'tis not base idleness that gives us cause for sloth. 'Tis perhaps more the fear that what we gain the bloody British will carry off!

"Methinks 'tis a major problem—the English just don't understand the Irish! There are times when an

Irishman prefers good drinking to good eating, just as there are times when he would rather have his freedom than all the gold in the world."

Another roar greeted his words. Standing just behind Talbot, Rory eyed the crowd and suppressed a smile. Here was a new wrinkle, a new facet to his friend and brother-in-law's character. He was a speaker, a spellbinder. Rory could feel the tenseness leave the crowd, could sense them sway more and more to Talbot's way, hanging on his every word.

When the noise died down David spoke again. No longer was there a lightness of tone in his voice. His words came out almost like a growl, which seemed to be directed at every man, woman and child in his audience.

"We till the land, we breed our sheep and cattle, and we make and raise our children now in peace. But hear you this: unrest and rebellion still boils in many hearts even though it seems to be dead.

"James's schemes for Ulster come true more so every day. English towns rise up where Irish castles used to be. There are walled towns now called Belfast, Enniskillen, Coleraine, Omagh, Cavan and a dozen more. And from these English towns, Ireland is being ruled. So be it.

"But what of the Irishman in these towns who couldn't flee, as many of you have done, to Ballylee? What is his plight in his own Ulster land? 'Tis poverty and depression. 'Tis working for a pittance the land that he once owned, and seeing no better for his children.

"A man can remain wretched and treated as a slave in his own house only so long.

"They say the Irish are doomed to be nothing but hewers of wood and water carriers. . . servants because they follow the Pope instead of King James. 'Tis because a man is Catholic, says the Englishman, that he makes of himself a landless servant.

"Don't believe it! I've been to London, where the English Catholic is persecuted. But ask the Englishman who is a Catholic, and he'll say the same about the Irish as does his Protestant countrymen.

"A man will tell you that he hates the Catholic because he is a Protestant. And the Catholic man will say he hates the Protestant because of religion. Believe not a word of it.

"They hate each other because they are Irish and English and they both want the land. Using the worship of God is only an excuse for one man to take from another what is rightfully his!"

Talbot paused, scowling down at the many faces, letting his words sink in.

"Mark me, people of Ballylee, should those wretched souls in northern Ulster spark a fire, its flames will spread over all of Ireland just as quickly as it has in the past.

"In all the woods of Ireland there are the lairs of wolves. As the English rape the woods, the wolves have fewer lairs. When they have no lairs left, the wolves will come out into the open. But this time, methinks things will be different. This time it will be the Irish on one side and the English on the other. The day of the clans is over, and the bloody English will rue its passing."

Total silence met Talbot's last words as he stepped back. Rory was about to move forward, when a husky voice rose from the crowd.

"Yer pardon, Sir David. . . ."

"Aye?"

"No offense to you, Sir David Talbot, but 'tis Scottish pipes that fill the glens of Antrim and move south. The towns you speak of are Scottish towns. Where the O'Neill stone once stood, Scottish sheep chew alongside those of the English. Should we ever hear those war pipes above the hills of Ballylee, where would your fealty lie?"

Talbot exchanged a quick glance with Rory and then, smiling broadly, faced the crowd again.

"'Tis true I wasn't birthed on Erin's shores. But methinks a man from anywhere can feel quite at home in Ireland, provided he can ride a horse tolerable well, doesn't shy away from a gargantuan meal, can at least make himself understood in the Gaelic tongue and is prepared to drink and gamble at any hour of the day or night."

A ripple of laughter flowed through the crowd, and Talbot held up his hand, palm outward, to stem it.

"And look you there at my wife's full belly. I'll tell you this, and before God I make this vow. If the child proves to be a boy, I'll call him Patrick, for Scot I was born, but it's Irish I breathe!"

A MOUNTAIN OF FOOD WAS CONSUMED, and then the tables were cleared. It was time to observe the tradition of settling debts. Checkers and counters took their places, and before long name after name was ringing across the courtyard. The workmen and servants of Ballylee were paid their wages. Tenants were paid their rents. And all were given their fair share of the profits from the investments Talbot had made for them.

Among themselves they settled their debts and agreed on the parceling of pastureland and acres for crops in the coming year.

Mead, good Irish whiskey and even fine wines flowed like a snow-melted mountain stream. And above it all, Rory O'Hara stood at a high window, morosely looking down. One hand held a goblet of brandy. With the fingers of his other hand he tapped a paper resting on the table at his side.

A door opened behind him and David Talbot's voice broke the room's stillness. "'Tis a good day and a fine conversation with the people." Talbot moved briskly toward him and laid his hand on Rory's shoulder. "And 'tis just the beginning. This idea of using lime on the grassland for a better yield is spreading. We'll build more kilns to burn it in, for mark me—there will be a demand and we'll fill it!"

Suddenly Talbot realized Rory's mood. "What is it, lad? 'Tis not yet dusk; the ghosts don't arrive 'til then. Yet you look as though you've seen one."

"A letter," Rory replied shortly.

"Aye?"

"A peddlar brought it from Dublin. Aileen has just given it to me."

"From England?"

"Nay. From France," Rory replied, handing the paper to Talbot. "From Richelieu."

Talbot took the paper from Rory's hand and moved closer to the window for more light.

My dear O'Hara,

Many thanks for the gift of such an exquisite animal. I am told that the Irish wolfhound is indeed prized all over the Continent, and I relish being the owner of such a beast. I have named him *Diable* because he terrorizes my cats and, like his namesake, never leaves my side. I often think that all men should have such a reminder of Satan, to keep their thoughts on an unswerving path.

Your news that Ireland once again seethes is of no surprise. I have word that the people of England seethe as well under the favorite Buckingham's thumb. 'Tis said he is now king of England in all but name.

He and the Prince of Wales's foolish mission to Spain was a disaster, as I'm sure you have heard. Phillip had no intention of allowing his sister, the infanta, to marry Charles. But, as usual, Buckingham heeds no words of wisdom from a Catholic Cardinal.

Ah yes, my Irishman, the heights we talked of so often so long ago have at last been realized. The Bishop of Luçon is now Cardinal Richelieu, and methinks soon to be minister of France!

After de Luynes's death at the siege of Montauban, our good King Louis chose a succession of inept ministers, among them the Duc de La Mardine. One by one they have fallen from grace through their own greed and stupidity. I daily expect the king's summons to Paris. Which brings me to your request.

I do believe that it could be arranged. Even though you gave your word to remain outside of England, as a representative of France, Buckingham and King James would have little room for objection to your presence at the English court.

There is rumor that I think will soon prove fact. 'Tis said that Lord Kensington will soon cross the Channel to sue for the hand of Princess Henrietta Maria, in the Prince of Wales's stead. Should this happen, I would think it a wise move to have a strong arm, even an Irish arm, as captain of the princess's guard were she to become the Princess of Wales, and one day Queen of England.

Your faithful friend in God,
Armand du Plessis, Cardinal de Richelieu

David Talbot wadded the paper in his fist and whirled to face Rory. "The man only wants to use you as he has tried to before—and as he did use me for five years!"

Rory nodded and moved back to the window. "I know that, David. I know it only too well."

"And what you said out there, less than an hour ago. Damme, man, I do all I can, and now we've the people behind us. But 'tis you that matters in their eyes. 'Tis you who is The O'Hara of Ballylee!"

"I know. Oh, God, man, do you think I don't know? But it would be a chance to see her... to know for sure. I—"

The rest of the words choked in Rory's throat. He raised his arms and placed his huge hands on the sides of the window, as if he would push the whole casement into the courtyard below. Then he hunched his broad shoulders and lowered his head.

David Talbot was about to protest further but stopped when he saw the set of his friend's body. Rory O'Hara was in enough turmoil; there was suffering enough in the depths of his soul. Gently he laid his hand on Rory's shoulder and looked down through the opened window at the people below.

" 'Tis a hard thing you must decide, my brother—this choice between the love for a woman you may never have for your own, and this love of the land you've found."

Below them, the carding and dicing had ended. Babes

slept in mothers' arms as candlelight danced on their serene faces. Men lazily sipped on a last tankard. In the center of the throng a piper put his reed to his lips and the air was filled with its wailing cry. Sounds of the melodic, softer tones of the harp joined in, and then the harper's voice was heard.

Alas for Sweet Erin, that day long ago
The lovely they fled, and the valiant were low
Erin's rocks looked won from their cloudland of
 air
To see shadows, destruction and naught but
 despair.

No voice greets the bard from his desolate glen,
No music or mirth or the murmur of men,
No voice but the eagle's that screams o'er the slain,
Or the sheepdog that moans for his master in vain.

Of O'Donnell, O'Neill, the bards they do sigh,
How strange is the grave where these warriors now
 lie.
Ye sleep not, my kinsmen, the sleep of the brave—
The warrior fills not the warrior's grave.

Ye died not, my friends, as your forefathers died,
The sword in your grasp, and the friend by your
 side.
The sword was in sheath, and the bow on the wall,
And silence and slumber in every clan hall.

"I'll be off tomorrow," Rory whispered.

Talbot shivered, and his own head dropped to his chest. "For France and England?"

"Nay, for the Wicklow Mountains. . .O'Byrne's land. Have some men build a crypt in the chapel and ready a monument."

"To whom?"

"To The O'Hara, Shane, and his lady, Deirdre. I'm off to bring their bones back to Ballylee."

SHANNA SAT, HUMMING AS SHE RAN A SILVER BRUSH again and again through the thickness of her dark hair. Her only dress was a thin chemise with gold piping at the arms and bodice.

From where he sat David Talbot could see the arching slope of her full breasts through the sheer material.

In the mirror her gaze caught his. "You have lust in your eyes."

"Aye, what man wouldn't, with such a picture before him," David said softly.

Shanna smiled at his reflection and continued brushing her hair.

How extraordinarily happy I am, she thought. *I have a beautiful daughter, another who is like a sister to me and new life growing in my belly. I have Ballylee and a husband who loves me more than any woman deserves.*

And that was what saddened her. She had so much now, and her brother had so little. She would never have dreamed, just a few years before, that Rory was capable of such an enduring love. It was hard to believe that after such a period of separation from Brenna—more than three years—he wouldn't find another.

Shanna's eyes dropped to the opened jewel box before her. There in its center, nestled in soft blue velvet, was the locket The O'Donnell had always worn and had given her just before he died. Should she urge Rory to return to England? Should she even give him a reason to return? Would it make any difference if Brenna did know the truth?

Shanna believed that there was an innate rebelliousness in the Irish blood, an overwhelming passion and need for the land. But did Brenna have it? Aileen had it. The girl had been born in France, but in three years' time on Irish soil, her Irish soul had wiped France from her memory.

David's voice broke into her thoughts. "I lust for you," he murmured, "and from your stare and furrowed forehead I'd say you were counting the rents."

"Nay," Shanna replied, tossing her head and letting her hair fall in a perfect sweep around her face to her shoulders.

"Then what is troubling you?"

"Aileen—" she blurted, and then thought better of saying any more.

David wouldn't understand. If she told him of finding the girl weeping in her room, earlier that evening and the cause of it, he would merely think it a young girl's infatuation with an older man. But Shanna was a woman and Aileen was swiftly becoming one. As a woman, Shanna could see the depth of Aileen's feelings in the girl's eyes when she looked at O'Hara and spoke of him.

Perhaps it would be best if Rory did go to England, if he found out the truth once and for all.

"What about Aileen?" David asked again.

"What? Oh, nothing... woman things."

David stood just behind her chair. So absorbed had she been in her own thoughts that she hadn't heard him move.

"Whatever is troubling the lass, she'll get over it."

"I hope so, but—"

Suddenly David's face was in her hair, his lips pressed against the back of her neck. His hand moved around her body and cupped her breast through the chemise's thin material.

Her nipple responded immediately, and a thrill of instant anticipation quivered through Shanna's body, driving from her mind all thoughts of anything beyond David, beyond her man.

She stood and turned to him, melding her body to his. "Dear Lord, but you are a wanton man," she smiled.

"Nay," he chuckled. "I am a satyr who loves you as well as lusts after you!"

His kiss was as sweet now as the first one had been so long ago. His one hand caressed the slope of her back, drawing her as close to him as possible.

"Be careful, David—the child."

"Am I not always careful?" he said, drawing her across the room to the huge canopied bed.

"Yes, my darling, always."

He deftly lifted the chemise over her head. Awkwardly, because of the swell of her belly, Shanna rolled onto the bed and he quickly joined her, his flesh like a burning brand along the length of her body.

"How can you possibly desire me when I am like this?"

"How can I possibly not?" he chuckled, and began the ritual he always followed with his lips, his tongue and his whole body.

Because of her love for him and the passion in her body, the ritual was rarely needed. But Shanna looked forward to it, enjoyed it and appreciated it from this man who never failed to lift her desire to a higher peak each time he loved her.

Yes, she thought, as the first spasm of fulfillment surged through her, *I am truly a lucky woman!*

CHAPTER THIRTY-TWO

IT TOOK A FORTNIGHT FOR RORY O'HARA and the twenty kerns accompanying him to reach O'Byrne country, around Glendalough in the Wicklows. When they arrived they found that word of their intent had already reached Dublin. English messengers awaited them, forbidding them to remove from O'Byrne ground the bodies of Shane and Deirdre O'Hara.

After much haggling and even threats the Dublin men backed down and turned tail, returning from whence they had come. The final resting place of an Irish rebel's bones wasn't worth their own lives.

Finally the cortege was mounted, with the double coffin draped in black velvet. The four horses were harnessed by polished black leather studded with silver. The horses were caparisoned with elaborate trappings, and huge black plumes danced on their heads. The roofless coach's sides were blazoned with the armorial crest of the clan O'Hara, so all who saw its passing would know its burden.

On bad roads—and most of the time on no roads at all—they wound their way over mountains, through valleys and glens and across icy streams. And everywhere they passed there were scores of people lining the way, kneeling and making the sign of the cross.

At night the coffin was unloaded and moved inside an

inn, if one were available. If not, it was placed under the widest oak that could be found, on a makeshift bier draped in O'Hara green. But no matter where it was placed, by morning it was surrounded by burning tapers placed there during the night.

Rory was awed and deeply touched by the hordes of men and women who passed reverently by the bier to pay their respects. Many had traveled for miles to intercept the cortege on its way north and west.

Once again the O'Hara legend filled him with pride, as it had months before when he had listened to the bards and harpers sing of it on his trek through Ireland. In many ways it confused him, as well. He soon realized that these people were not only paying their respects to a dead warrior, a martyr to the Irish cause, but they were also paying homage to the love between that warrior and his lady. It had been a love of such depth that it now kept them together in death as it had in life.

The legend of the one coffin was even murmured by the lips of children. Those nights, standing watch around a fire or in the great room of an inn, Rory heard the tale of Deirdre, who had died for love, told over and over again. Each time it brought tears to his eyes, much the same as it had that first time years before when he had heard it from his mother's lips.

Little had he known then, when but a stripling lad at his mother's knee while she suckled the baby, Shanna, that Deirdre was preparing her son for his parents' death.

There were old men who remembered that day on Dublin Castle's gallows green. They had been there and seen the battered and tortured Shane O'Hara mount the scaffold and spit in the traitor McTeague O'Byrne's face.

They recalled with awe and wonder how Lady Deirdre O'Hara had mounted the scaffold, thrown back the cowl that hid her face and pointed a pistol at her husband's heart.

"For love, Shane!" she had cried as she fired the fatal ball.

Lady Deirdre could have accepted O'Hara's death in battle. She could even have accepted his death at the end of a noose. But the degradation beyond the hanging—the knife and the quartering by four horses—her love for him would not let her accept that. Such a death was not fit for a chieftain of Ireland.

Revenge was hers as well that day. With a second ball she had killed McTeague O'Byrne, the sod who had been the cause of O'Hara's capture.

A British soldier had ended her own life seconds later as she had sprawled over O'Hara's body, murmuring the words, "Dig the grave both deep and wide."

So now they had come home to Ballylee at last, just as she had wished, placed side by side in a single wide coffin.

Talbot had done Rory's bidding well and with haste. The crypt in the small chapel near Ballylee's outer wall was ready when the cortege arrived.

The wake was held, subdued as Irish wakes go, but Shanna wanted it that way. There was no need to hire professional keeners. Many women with deep, wailing voices came from the far corners of Ballylee to put the lovers finally to rest in their own home ground.

THUNDER BOOMED AND LIGHTNING FILLED THE SKY, sending dancing white light through the chapel windows. In one of the deep-set portals just off the nave, Rory O'Hara's bulk loomed in front of the completed crypt.

For one month now the crypt had been filled in with cement and stone. Over this the tablet had been laid. Burning tapers twinkled like eerie fireflies in the gloom, illuminating the inscription.

> Here lies THE O'HARA, SHANE
> Together with his LADY DEIRDRE
> Who so loved him that she chose death for them both before degradation.

And in smaller letters beneath it, Deirdre's Lament:

> The lion of the hill is gone
> And I won't be left to weep alone.
> Without my love I can't abide,
> So dig the grave both deep and wide.

"Methinks," Shanna said, standing in the darkness of the aisle near her brother, "'tis time we let them rest in peace."

"Aye," Rory nodded slightly, his shaggy black hair moving in the candles' flickering light. "It is that, but they won't let me."

Shanna bit her lip and twisted the gleaming object in her hand. Feeling in her own breast her brother's grief, she could barely hold back the tears, for she knew that the melancholy that had overtaken him and daily grew worse was not grief for the dead. It was grief for the living, for himself and for the part of his heart that had been ripped out and now rested somewhere on a foreign shore.

Standing there watching him, as she had so many nights before, Shanna could feel the turmoil that gave him no respite.

They had spoken of it, and Rory had finally repeated in desperation what The O'Donnell had said to him. "Methinks 'tis a curse on the O'Hara men, this loving of English women!"

She now knew her brother's moods as well as what caused them. He was torn. Half of him was Shane, the Irish warrior, the man of duty. The other half was Deirdre, who could love so deeply.

Slowly Shanna moved forward until she, too, was bathed in the tapers' flickering light. "Dear brother, methinks you will never be satisfied or at peace until you know."

"There is nothing to know," he replied. "It is but as a death that I can't forget. Were she an Irishwoman, or had reason to be one, there might be a way. Too much, too many things, have happened since. David depends upon my presence to hold Ballylee together. I sense enough unrest in the air that one day we may see war again. If that should happen, this is where I must be."

"So be it," Shanna said urgently. "If that should happen, drop all and flee back to us here, to Ballylee. But in the meantime—*go*! For if you do not, I sense that the agony of wondering 'what if' will send you to an early grave!"

Rory turned his dark, brooding eyes on his sister and curled his lips into a cynical smile. "She fled from me once. Even if I should find out why, even if it was a decision not of her own making, what right do I have in asking her to give up her land in favor of my own troubled one?"

"Dear God, I thought you had aged. I thought some brains had grown between your ears! Go to England and find out if there's still a love between you. You think if you steal her away, your Brenna won't be able to stand the rigors of this, our Irish life?"

"I think we have both found that Irish men and women are born, not made. Even she, Deirdre, was not entirely English." He nodded his dark head toward the tablet before them. "As to the daughter of Rose of Ballyhara, half her soul was always in Ireland."

Shanna looked down at the shining locket she held in her hands. "Never to hurt," O'Donnell had said, in passing it to her. "Neither of them must ever know, unless it would be a way of keeping them together should anyone try to pry them apart." Suddenly, twisting chain and locket into a ball, Shanna thrust it into her brother's hand.

"Go! Go to her as you should! And if she has doubts—this will wash them away. Bring home your Irish woman, Rory O'Hara!"

She whirled and flew to the chapel door. Leaving a single blast of cold wind and driving rain behind her, the door slammed and she was gone.

Rory fumbled with the locket for a moment, found the catch and sprung it open. Many times he had seen it around O'Donnell's neck, but never had he seen its contents.

Now he gasped as the candlelight revealed the miniatures it held. Now he knew why he had felt that he had known the Lady Hatton before. She was younger, of course, but there was no mistaking the strong, perfect features, the wide, emerald-green eyes and the flowering auburn hair.

And there was no mistaking the beautiful, raven-haired child pictured with her.

"Dear God," he cried as, all at once, so many things

came into focus, so many memories flooded into his tortured mind.

He ran to the door and pulled it open. Rain battered his face as he stepped out of the tiny chapel. In a flash of lightning he saw the courtyard and the path leading up to the big house. Shanna was nowhere to be seen. But it didn't matter, for now he knew.

He leaned his back against the cold, wet stone wall and turned his face to the sky. He closed his eyes to the jagged shafts of lightning, deafened his ears to the pealing thunder and let his mind go back in time.

He saw a garden and a little dark-haired girl on a bench. Over her stood The O'Donnell, with both joy and sadness in his eyes. How much alike they looked.

And later, in a carriage, he had seen the same miniature he now held. The words that had been spoken then came back to him now.

She's a very pretty child.

Aye, she is. Her name is Brenna. . . Brenna Coke.

He remembered the look on Lady Hatton's face those last days at Fontevrault each time she had entered and left The O'Donnell's room. So blinded with love had Rory himself been that he had not recognized that look in another.

Brenna.

Elizabeth, the Lady Hatton.

The O'Donnell, Rory.

She's a very pretty child.

Aye, she is. Her name is Brenna. . . Brenna Coke.

Rory O'Hara opened his eyes and welcomed the stinging rain that washed away the blindness. The roar of laughter that left his throat threatened to drown out the thunder in the midnight sky.

"Aye, Brenna Coke it is," he shouted. "But O'Donnell it should have been!"

He kissed the locket and carefully pulled its chain over his head as he made for the big house, France and then on to England.

CHAPTER THIRTY-THREE
ENGLAND

UPON THEIR ARRIVAL AT POOLE HOUSE both Brenna and Raymond had been shocked and dismayed. They found the old manor more like a dank and drafty barn than a home. Much of the house had risen from the remnants of an ancient Norman castle. Many of the rooms in the older wing were eerie and solemn, enjoying minimum light through slitted windows.

Though they did allow the entrance of daylight, even the mullioned and glass-paned windows in the newer wing whistled year round with wind from the sea. The casements had sagging shutters and wide cracks.

Repair was out of the question. There was no money, or at least so decreed Lady Compton in her weekly letters from London. There was little money for staff as well, so Brenna had to make do with as few servants as possible.

She really didn't mind. The fewer servants underfoot, the greater the solitude. And it was solitude that Brenna craved above all else.

A good room-by-room cleaning had improved the old house somewhat, and together Raymond and Brenna had agreed to make the best of what had been allotted to them.

One saving grace was the forest and the green sweep

of pasture and farmland around the old estate. If the interior of Poole House was less than befitted a viscount and his lady, the surrounding countryside was majestic and perfectly fit both their moods.

Almost daily they took long walks down narrow tree-lined lanes that led to the sea. The salt air was laced with the scent of blooming roses and larkspur. Nearly always there was a stillness in the air, broken only by the light tread of their own footsteps, the lowing of cattle in distant pastures or the neighing of a mare summoning her new-born colt back to her side.

For the first few months, Brenna and Sir Raymond seemed to draw closer together. There was no whim or desire voiced by Brenna that, if it were at all possible, wasn't carried out instantly. Evenings were spent by a warm hearth. Some were solemn, as Brenna silently dwelled upon the past and Raymond brooded on the present and the seeming lack of any future.

But more often than not talk between them became gayer, lighter. They were even able at times to make jest of their strange situation and those who had caused it.

"They say your father's stay in the Tower has given him an ague," Raymond had bantered.

"Oh? Where?" Brenna had inquired.

"In the fingers that hold his pen. This will make him use his voice all the louder in Commons against the king and my sweet cousin!"

Elected to Parliament as a member from Liskeard in Cornwall, Edward Coke had roared back into London bent on judicial righteousness and revenge on Buckingham. His tirades in the Commons against first the proposed Spanish marriage and then the wastefulness of the king and his favorite soon became quoted across the land. So much so that he found himself in the Tower.

From his dank, lightless and airless cell, Coke wrote his sons and daughters for aid. Since the Viscountess Poole was the most highly placed of all of them, Brenna received twice the number of letters as her half brothers and sisters. Even though the treatment she had received at her father's hand had been ill, to say the least, it was not in Brenna's nature to hold a grudge against her own kin, least of all her father.

She implored her husband to intercede, which he did. Sir Edward was released, only to return to public life with a louder voice and to go so far as to suggest impeachment proceedings against Buckingham.

Thus, Brenna's father was driving an even larger wedge between the families which, in turn, made the gulf between the viscount and viscountess loom larger.

Lady Compton's constant demands of Lady Hatton for a larger yearly stipend to support Poole House didn't help. Particularly when Elizabeth announced to all of London that she would give every last crown to the poor before she would let it filter into the Villierses' coffers. The two women were like battling felines, complete with raised backs and unsheathed claws.

Rumors circulated through the court that Lady Hatton was causing yet a new scandal by cuckolding the husband she wouldn't allow under her roof. Elizabeth was linked with everyone from the handsome and single lords at court to her footman. Because, even at fifty, she was still a beautiful, witty and vivacious woman, there were a few who heeded the scandal. More often it was considered preposterous and doubly more so when it was quickly guessed from whence the rumors had sprouted.

When Brenna heard of it, it brought tears of laughter to her eyes. Would that these rumors were true, she thought. Perhaps then her mother would leave off trying to untangle the web of her daughter's life.

Lady Compton summoned her nephew almost weekly to London. Each time, she urged Raymond to force his wife to beg her mother for more money.

To combat this pressure, Lady Hatton planned lavish parties at Hatton House to show unity of strength in her cause, for all the invited guests were people who were outspoken against Buckingham and his family. They became weekly galas, with much feasting, music, elaborate masques and dancing. Hatton House rang with the music of galliards and corantos.

Naturally, Lady Hatton wanted Viscount and Viscountess Poole at her parties. By their mere attendance they would be taking Elizabeth's side in the fray. But Brenna saw through it all and declined to attend. While her mother waged war among London's fashionables, playing hostess amid the blazing fires and splendid furnishings of Hatton House, Brenna chose to stay in the south, amid the castoff relics of a bygone time at Poole House by the sea.

Brenna's own will, her calm acceptance of the inevitable became the armor that shielded her from the storm clouds in London. She did all she could to make her husband a home. With what meager funds she was allowed from Lady Compton, she stocked the larder with the best food possible. Poole House was in the midst of a large park and so she had it stocked with deer and hired a gamekeeper to add fox, hare and badger. Then she gifted Raymond with fine sport hounds for the hunt, and spaniels and terriers to lie near his feet at the end of the day.

All was to no avail.

"His Grace, the Duke of Buckingham, requests the

company of his sweet cousin, the Viscount Poole, for the month at Bath. M'lord the duke hopes that the spa waters will aid in bringing to an end the dour melancholy that so afflicts the duke's sweet cousin."

The letter came from Whitehall just at the time when the calmness of resolution had begun to pervade their relationship. Raymond had begun to smile, even laugh at times, as had Brenna. His gentleness and his sudden good humor had begun to break down her barriers.

"Dear God in heaven, why can't they—all of them—just leave us alone?" Brenna had cried.

"Aye, why can't they, sweet wife. But they won't, and I fear they never will," Raymond replied gloomily.

Had they, the loveless couple might have found a way to love, but it was not to be.

It was only once in a great while now that Brenna thought of Rory O'Hara. Fewer and further apart came the daydreams where she saw herself in the handsome Irishman's arms, her own arms moving impulsively to encircle his neck. Rare were the times now when she could fully recall the memory of their lips in kisses that had once made her ache with a longing to melt into him.

And as those memories receded, she began to look deeper and deeper into the sadness of her husband's eyes and feel a kinship building.

If only they could have kept their independence, their solitude together, a few months longer.

"M'Lord Buckingham would have you take the waters with him, but methinks Lady Compton would woo you away, back to the family fold and away from me," Brenna said to her husband.

"Aye, I know that."

"And yet you will go, anyway."

"Aye. Do I have a choice? Have I *ever* had a choice?"

"But you are a peer, a viscount!" Brenna protested.

"You know, I know—damme, all London knows that peerages are no longer obtained by merit. They are gotten by connections, and as such are empty. My dear cousin in his greed has even gone beyond the family to bestow his favors on anyone, as long as the bribe he or my aunt obtains is large enough."

"But you," Brenna repeated, "are a viscount."

"And he, dear Brenna, is a duke. And for all that, he might as well be king!"

The month of Sir Raymond's stay at Bath stretched into two, then three and four. Brenna became alarmed. She wrote Buckingham and Lady Compton. There was no reply.

Those days alone at Poole House should have been bliss. In the beginning they were. But the longer Raymond remained away the more fearful she became, until that fear turned to terror.

She began to realize the far-reaching import behind the duke and his mother's schemes. Should they find some way to incapacitate Raymond and keep him away from her, she would have no income. For the duke and his mother, as the Viscount Poole's administrators, held control over his and Brenna's property holdings.

She was about to resort to the one thing she didn't want to do—flee to her mother for aid—when Raymond finally returned. Wild-eyed, on a lathered horse, he rode into the courtyard of Poole House like an apparition from hell. He was hatless, his clothes were torn and in disarray, and filthy bandages covered his bleeding hands and arms.

THEY SAT IN THE PARLOR, Brenna in a window seat, her husband in a frayed cushion chair beside a low table. It was a large, long room and the only one in the house properly furnished.

Now and then Brenna's eyes strayed from the forested park outside the window and moved to take in Raymond's slouched form.

How far down he has come, she thought, *and 'tis as much my fault as theirs.*

"They think me mad. . . and perhaps I am."

His voice in the tomblike silence of the room startled her. Her legs had been curled beneath her. Now she swung around on the window seat and stood up.

How he had changed in the months of his absence. Raymond's narrow pointed beard had always been neatly trimmed, as had the delicately curved mustache on his upper lip. Now both were grown shaggy and many days of bristly beard adorned his hollow cheeks.

He had always kept his clothes, no matter what his state of despair, in immaculate order. Now his breeches were torn and the leather of his boots was badly scuffed and muddy. The heavy lace cuffs of his cambric shirt showed dust from the road and spots of blood from his bandaged hands.

"Your hands are bleeding again. Let me change—"

"No matter." With both hands he painfully lifted a brandy goblet from the table before him and drank. He emptied the goblet, replaced it and squinted into the light from the window haloed around his wife's figure. "You stayed here like a nun in your abbey, so it was easy for them to have their way with me."

"Do you blame it all on me?" Brenna asked softly.

"Nay, damn little of it," Raymond chuckled mirthlessly. "The ceremony performed in God's own house was one of sacrifice, not holy union. Mayhap now we pay for it in the eyes of the Lord."

"We pay," Brenna suddenly cried, making fists of her hands and letting the tears she had been holding back burst forth. "They—'tis they, your family, who would evilly trod over anyone in their path to satisfy their all-consuming need for power and wealth!"

"Aye, but in the next life 'tis you and I who will be forgiven for what we endure, and 'tis they who will burn."

"That is naught but Raymond the new Catholic speaking," she said, trying to hide the disgust in her voice.

"Aye, it is. But with this new faith I am able to survive, to wait. Perhaps you, too, should seek conversion."

"So I can smile with forgiveness as they rape our means and leave us penniless? Nay, I'll stay an Anglican. And if all this gets much worse, I may give that up, too!"

Raymond's voice was barely a whisper when he spoke again. "The only reason I was to marry you at all was the connections of your friends and family, your yearly expectations, and the fifty thousand pounds in your dowry. Indeed, practically everything I have, you have brought me."

Here he paused, until Brenna was forced to look up from her wringing hands and meet his eyes.

"They never believed me when they forced us into this marriage. They never believed me when I told them that I truly loved you. 'Tis that which has been the true thorn in their side."

Through her tears, she saw him suddenly smile.

"Maybe," he said, his voice gaining strength,

"maybe we should just give it all to them. . . for we now know they will go to any lengths to obtain it."

Brenna shuddered and covered her face with her hands. For the last hour she had sat in stunned silence as he had related the events of the past four months.

At Bath, Buckingham had implored Raymond to finish with his marriage. It would be an easy matter for him to petition the king, the duke had said.

"She has bewitched you, my cousin! 'Tis plain to see that these fits of madness you endure are caused by your wife. Leave off this marriage and return to the bosom of your family. And have no fear, for I feel sure that, because of your wife's inability to bear a child, coupled with the fact that she doth drive you mad with her witchery, the king would grant you all her lands and monies upon your leave-taking!"

At the mere suggestion of this banditry, Raymond had flown into a rage. In front of many witnesses, he had thrown himself upon Buckingham and would have throttled him had not others pulled him away.

But in his anger, his despair and his frustration, he could mouth nothing but gibberish.

This played right into Buckingham's hands. The duke went directly to the king. "I fear, Your Majesty, that my dear sweet cousin has indeed contracted the malady of madness. I pray you, sir, that you suffer some course that he may be conveyed into the country, that he may be restrained from doing himself harm. Need I say further, Your Majesty, that the actions of my cousin, the Viscount Poole, will surely reflect one day, should they continue thusly, on his most noble king!"

All this had been said and done in front of an entire room of courtiers, so the tale would be told that Buckingham was only trying to protect his kinsman.

The chief object of the duke's fervor was not lost on the king. It was best to put the Viscount Poole away before his behavior might cause gossip or scandal that would reflect on His Majesty's dearest servant, Buckingham.

The weak James readily gave his approval, and Sir Raymond had been shut up at Wallingford House until arrangements could be made to pack him off to Scotland.

But Raymond had had none of it. In a rage he had overpowered the man assigned as his keeper and had sought escape. In so doing, he had added fuel to the rumors of his madness by demolishing several rooms of furniture on his way out of the house.

Once having found a room by the street, he had broken out the window glass with his shoulders and bare fists. Bloody, haggard, clothing torn, he had dropped to the street and had sought a horse from the first man he met. Two days later he had appeared in the courtyard of Poole House.

"And so I was just freeing myself from being held a prisoner against my will," he concluded the sorry tale.

Brenna lifted her face and stared. Raymond still sat, sprawled across from her in the chair, his long legs thrust awkwardly before him. In front of his face he held his bloodied, bandaged hands.

"But now 'twill be easier for them to fuel the fire of their lies. All of London will now surely think me a distraught madman running amok!"

RAYMOND KNEW THEY WOULD COME FOR HIM. In less than a month's time they did. The Earl of Middlesex was accompanied by twenty of Buckingham's personal guard.

The Viscount Poole had elected to return with them quietly this time. "Acceptance, my darling Brenna, is our only course now, for the people know what befalls us. That will keep you safe and cared for until the time comes when I can appeal our just cause to a new king."

Brenna, for the time being, agreed with her husband's advice. James was a tottering king. Almost daily another illness was added to the score he already endured. Raymond, though ineffectual in his service to the Prince of Wales, had nevertheless garnered Charles's friendship. Should Charles ascend the throne, there was a chance that Raymond could right James's wrongs against the embattled couple.

In the meantime, acquiescence and acceptance seemed the only way. To fight had quickly proved useless.

But neither Brenna nor Raymond suspected the now unrestrained rapaciousness of the duke and his mother. Little did they dream, as they stood like waiting victims in the great room of Poole House, to what lengths of audacity Buckingham would go.

They heard the ear-shattering clatter of shod horses in the cobbled courtyard and seconds later Middlesex marched through the door. Behind him came the armed pikemen in helmets and breastplates.

"M'Lord Viscount Poole, by the order of the king you are commanded to London!"

"Aye," Raymond nodded, and stepped forward.

Flanked by four of the guard, he was marched into the courtyard. The little party had barely cleared the door when the rest of the men spread through the house. All too late Brenna saw their intent.

They stopped at nothing. They began dismantling what furnishings he had acquired for Poole House. Men descended the stairs with trunks of her apparel and her jewel boxes. Costly tapestries from Hatton House, a gift from her mother, were ripped from the walls. Buckingham meant to not only take charge of his cousin's person but of his estate as well.

"How dare you!" she cried. "By what right?"

"By the king's order."

Middlesex drew a scroll from his sash, with a flourish dropped it open and read:

> Be it hereby known that due to the mental incapacity of Viscount Poole, we hereby warrant his beloved aunt, Lady Compton, to hold all powers over goods, monies, household properties and land. Be it further decreed that Viscount Poole is much deranged, that he is unable in mind to live with his wife, that the witchcraft practiced upon her husband by the viscountess, coupled with her unkindness to this poor man, is the cause of his distemper.
>
> James R.

Brenna's face clouded with rage. She flew at Middlesex, snatching the paper from his hand and tearing it in half. Like a tigress, both her hands ripped across his face, leaving eight even red lines on his cheeks.

"Damme, you witch!" Middlesex bellowed, darting out of range as Brenna clawed at him a second time.

Two guards grabbed her by the shoulders, but she wrestled free. She ran to the wide doors and down the stairs only to find herself in the center of milling, frightened horses.

"Raymond, they would rape us, leave us penniless! Raymond!"

But he was gone, atop a far hill, out of earshot in the center of four helmeted riders.

Brenna whirled around to return to the house and found herself pinned between two snorting, rearing stallions. Suddenly one of them spun his hindquarters toward her and kicked.

The two iron-shod hooves hit her directly in the belly, knocking all the air from her lungs. She felt her body lift into the air. She fell with a dull thud on the cobble, and then there was darkness.

CHAPTER THIRTY-FOUR

LADY ELIZABETH HATTON SAT in a high-backed chair like a wrathful empress upon her throne. Her dress was stiff white satin pleated with black. The tight bodice was trimmed in black lace and disguised at the low, square neck with a line of black fur. It was as if she had purposely chosen mourning colors to listen to her daughter's tale of woe.

"They took everything. . . but I thought they would at least leave the roof over my head! A week later, all my servants save a caretaker were dismissed. Then workmen came and began to close up the house. I do believe, mother, if I had not fled here to Hatton House, they would have boarded up Poole House with me inside it!"

Lady Hatton listened and fumed. As she grew angrier, the flush crept up her throat to her cheeks. "And the wretch Buckingham refuses even to give you some provision to live—some income from your own means?" she said at last.

"He refuses," Brenna replied. "He contends that my

conduct makes it impossible for us to live together, even if Raymond were not mad."

"Conduct?" Elizabeth cried. "Good Lord in heaven, what conduct? What conduct can you pursue except that of a woman forced to marry a man she does not love?"

Brenna merely shook her head. It would do no good to tell her mother that Raymond's supposed madness stemmed from not sharing her bed. Such a matter should only be settled between a husband and wife.

"'Tis monstrous! Who can dare remove a husband from his wife by force?"

"Dukes and kings, mother. Dukes and kings."

"Thieves!" Elizabeth hissed. "Robbed by a crowd of despicable creatures whose power stems from the whims of a drunken, lecherous despot!"

Her mother went on, but Brenna heard little of what was said. She was defeated. She had returned to Hatton House and her mother's charity, worse off than when she had left it to marry Sir Raymond Hubbard. She was now Viscountess Poole, but without estate, a titled woman without means.

THE DAYS STRETCHED INTO WEEKS. Brenna wandered the elegant rooms and gardens of Hatton House, listless and fretful by turns. Upon her shoulders and mind was a burden that wore away at her very soul and wearied her with its weight.

Then one evening she was summoned to the far gate in the garden wall. There she was handed a letter by a black-cloaked figure who said nothing. His mission completed, he slipped away into the darkness, but not before Brenna had one brief glance beneath his cowl.

She recognized Father Fisher, the Jesuit priest who

had been the means of Raymond's conversion to the Catholic faith.

With a wildly beating heart, Brenna rushed to her rooms and tore open the missive.

My dearest Brenna,

Heavy is my heart and the hand that writes this letter. I fear, sweet wife, that through me you have been brought to depths that no woman should endure. It grieves me that I am not man enough to stand up to my family, with sword if necessary, to deflect the wounds they would inflict upon you, so gracious and grand a lady. But, alas, it cannot be.

Middlesex is to be my keeper, and I daresay that this time there will be no leeway for my escape. They would bundle me off to Scotland and anonymity. My mood is one of grief and, at times, I must admit, relief, for I feel that perhaps I have gone mad and would be better off sheltered from the world.

They say you have bewitched me, darling girl, and indeed it is true. You have bewitched me with your wit, your beauty, your grace and your charm. You have addled my brain with your wonderful capacity to love. I would give all, including my life, if but for one moment I could claim that love, as he has all these years.

With love, R.

That night Brenna wept into her pillow for hours before exhaustion brought sleep at last. For the first time in her marriage, her heart truly went out to Raymond Hubbard, and she ached to be at his side.

CHAPTER THIRTY-FIVE
FRANCE

THE SIGHTS, SOUNDS AND SMELLS were completely foreign to Rory from the moment he set foot on French soil. It was as if he had never been raised in this country nor served in its military.

No longer were soldiers in suits of steel. They now looked more like colorful plumed birds. At an earlier age, Rory would have gloried in the costume of a shorter cape draped from one shoulder at an elegant angle and the mountains of lace at collar and cuff. He would have been the first to learn the elegant bow that began with the right foot placed forward in the first position of the dance and ended with a ground-dusting flourish of the cavalier's wide-brimmed, many-plumed hat. Now he could only smile with amusement at the antic bravado he saw.

Women's fashion, too, had changed and for the better. Gone was the clumsy farthingale. Full, flowing skirts now flattered a woman's figure and low-cut, jewel-encrusted bodices made an appealing bosom swell rather than flatten.

He made a one-day detour to the abbey at Fontevrault to pay his respects to Sister Anna and to thank her in person for her many letters keeping him informed of events in France. The major topic of conversation among those travelers he met along the way concerned the hated and feared minister of France, the tyrant Richelieu.

From Fontevrault it was on to Paris. Within an hour of his arrival, he made his way to the Rue des

Mauvaises-Paroles and announced himself at Richelieu's door. The woman who greeted and ushered him into the downstairs parlor was dressed all in black, with a nunlike cowl that concealed all her hair.

"I am Marie-Madeleine de Combalet, the cardinal's niece," she said, correctly interpreting Rory's quizzical look. Never in the past had Richelieu retained women servants in his household. "If you will wait but a moment. My uncle is most anxious to see you." She glided soundlessly from the room, as if beneath her voluminous skirts her feet were unshod.

O'Hara assayed the room's furnishings and muttered to himself. All had been redone in exquisite taste and, apparent even to a layman's eye, executed with no thought given to cost.

Monsieur le Cardinal, Rory thought, *is already reaping his rewards on earth as a prince of the church of heaven!*

"The cardinal will see you now."

Rory followed the woman up a wide, sweeping staircase and into a book-lined study. She was barely gone when Richelieu emerged from a tiny alcove chapel.

Rory was startled. It was the same Richelieu, yet different. The man's almost melancholy eyes still assaulted his senses with their dark intensity. Even in the flowing robes, the bearing of the lithe, wiry body was still upright and military, making him as much soldier as churchman. He still wore his mustache with the curled, upswept dash of the musketeer, and the pointed *beard royale* had the same jaunty flair Rory remembered from years past.

Then Rory realized that the difference was in the robes—they were long, flowed regally with every movement and were deep crimson in color. They added just the right touch to the man and made him exude the one thing Richelieu longed to stand for: power.

"My son," the cardinal intoned, extending his hand to be kissed. "Welcome to a new France."

"AND THERE YOU HAVE IT, the three accomplishments absolutely essential to continued prosperity and sovereign rule in France. The rebel nobles and the independent Huguenots must be brought under royal control. Hapsburg power must be diminished in the German states. If not, and if they are victorious in this war, I think they might turn their eyes on the frontiers of France. And lastly, I would have closer relations with England to prevent English alignment with Spain."

Rory lounged on a chaise across from Richelieu, who sat behind a huge dark mahogany desk, the contents atop it in scrupulously neat piles.

Diable lolled at Rory's side. The wolfhound, only a pup when sent from Ireland, was now a huge white beast with black splotches on his silky fur. Idly, Rory scratched the dog's immense head as he digested Richelieu's words.

"You are the first person besides myself he has allowed to touch him. Even my niece won't go near him. She says he is indeed the devil."

Rory looked up, then down at the contented hound and chuckled. "'Tis because he smells the Irish in me. We have a distinctive scent."

"And have you truly become an Irishman?"

Rory met the other man's eyes in a level stare and didn't blink or look away as he would have years before. "Aye, I have, to the core of my being and the marrow of my bones."

"Good," Richelieu nodded, and stood. He adjusted

the gold sash at his middle and moved to stand at the window, his hands clasped behind him in contemplation. "Being Irish makes you basically neutral and, if not quite that, anti-English."

"All of that," Rory chuckled. "So again you would send me into the teeth of the Villiers tigers as your eyes and ears?"

"If I can."

Rory left off scratching the wolfhound and sat bolt upright on the chaise. "But your letter said—"

"Let me explain. Monsieur le Duc de la Mardine had become a powerful man, in his deviousness an ally to the king and an enemy of mine. While the Queen Mother was in exile in Blois, La Mardine played a double role. He professed fealty to Marie de Médicis, while reporting each of her schemes in detail to de Luynes and Louis. Upon de Luynes's death, La Mardine was summoned to court and a high post. He botched it, of course, and I stepped in."

"Then the power is yours."

"The power is the king's. Our Louis is a weak man, but he is no fool. He would keep La Mardine in favor and power so mine does not become too great."

Here the red-robed figure moved from the window to stand near Rory.

"La Mardine would dearly love to head the Princess Henrietta Maria's retinue, should she go to England as queen. He has been for years now in league with that fool Buckingham. Were he allowed to do this, I would have not one word of truth from the English court. In times to come that could be a disaster."

"That might come to be even if 'tis I that am your messenger, Your Excellency. I have my own business in

England. Once that is done, I would be gone, back to Ireland and Ballylee."

"The woman?"

"Aye."

Richelieu shook his head and folded himself back into the chair behind his desk. "Women. Let me tell you, my son, as men employ their abilities for good, so women use them for evil. They are strange animals. Sometimes they seem incapable of doing harm because they can do no good. I maintain in all good faith that there is nothing more capable than a woman of ruining a kingdom!"

"Pardon, Your Excellency," Rory replied with a smile. "But I think were my good sister Shanna to hear your words, red robes or not, she would claw out your eyes."

"And your Englishwoman—what would she do?"

"Very likely pray for your heavenly soul, Your Excellency."

Richelieu leaned back in the chair and the room was filled with his high-pitched laugh. "Then you would be wise in forgetting her and searching out a woman more like your sister. It is that kind of mate you'll need one day soon in your Ireland!"

"Mayhap. But I fear I've changed since my youth. Now I do believe that women are to be loved, not used."

"And there you have it," Richelieu hissed, leaning forward and slapping the desk with both hands. "La Mardine would use all at his command to gain his ends. When Lord Kensington arrived at the Louvre to negotiate the marriage proposal, he was first received into the boudoir of La Mardine's wife, Carlotta."

Rory couldn't suppress an impish grin in remembrance of that night when he had dropped from the duchess's window and skittered across the roof to safety. How things—some things—and people did change and others, not a whit.

"So Carlotta hasn't changed."

"Quite true. Her lovers are legion, and all to the same end—advancement. The duke has harnessed the power of his wife's body and made of her an instrument, an instrument that is wielded well. It is because of that, O'Hara, and his lack of principles in all else, that I must use anything and anyone at my command to bring him down."

Something in the man's eyes, in the grating tone of his voice, planted a question in Rory's mind. "Down, Your Excellency? As far down as death, perhaps?"

Richelieu nodded. "If needs be."

"A rather unsaintly desire, sir, coming from a prince of the church."

There was no laugh now, only a tight-lipped grimace that brought a chill to Rory's spine.

"I agree with the Italian, Machiavelli. The ethics of Christ cannot be safely followed in the ruling of a nation!"

Quarters were acquired for Rory on the Rue des Bourdonnais, near Richelieu. For two weeks O'Hara idled the time away by gazing out his window at Paris and absorbing news of the marriage negotiations for the Princess Henrietta Maria's hand that arrived daily from the cardinal.

The French were asking for a great deal, but there was a good chance they would get it. News from England was that King James was close to death. Buckingham was wooing Parliament for funds to wage war against

Spain and to do this, he needed an alliance with France.

Richelieu's price was high. In all places where Henrietta Maria resided, she was to have her own chapel. To perform religious functions in these places of Catholic worship, she was to have twenty-eight priests, almoners and chaplains. The complement of her domestic staff was to be a hundred, including a personal guard of fifty under the captaincy of an officer chosen by King Louis. At all times, her priests would be allowed to wear their vestments, as would the guard be allowed their armor and weapons. As it was also stipulated that they would have complete freedom in court and country, Richelieu's intentions were all too clear. He planned to install a small army of spies in every part of England and to do it with the approval of the English court.

Rory was skeptical that the demands would be met, but he waited patiently. He knew from past experience not to underestimate the cunning, the ruthlessness and the deviousness of Armand de Richelieu, particularly since the man was now the head of the Catholic church in France, as well as minister of the king's government.

As the weeks wore on, Rory emerged more and more frequently from his cramped quarters but always at night, for he had no desire for a chance meeting with La Mardine. The cardinal had also sent him a warning concerning the current temperament of young Parisian gallants.

"Though I have passed edict after edict against it, the plumed dandies who strut our streets still treat dueling as their most popular sport and pastime. Carry yourself well, my son, for it takes merely a miscast look, the brush of a shoulder or a shun in passing to bring a glove across the face and crossed swords in a deserted park or field."

Rory heeded the warning, for he knew that his skills with rapier and dagger had rusted mightily while he was in Ireland. Thus he took long evening strolls in the Marais quarter, near the Place Royale. His boots echoed hollowly on the cobblestones of the Rue de la Ferronerie, near the place where Louis's father, Henry IV, had been stabbed by the fanatic, Ravillac.

All around him he could see Paris growing. Through his architect, Lemercier, King Louis XIII was refashioning the Louvre. In the center of the Seine, the Ile Notre-Dame and the Ile de Vaches had been joined together to form the Ile St.-Louis. New churches were being built, and the old boundaries of the city were expanded by wide boulevards and row after row of stately new homes.

Paris was becoming a beautiful city. Years before, when he had been a student and soldier here, Rory would have welcomed and reveled in this beautification, for it meant that the city would be an exciting place to live. Now he felt lost, alone and homesick for the vast green fields of Ballylee. He realized he much preferred the bark of hounds, the lowing of cows and the cock's crow to the clatter of carriages and the hawking cries of an army of street vendors.

And his mind was troubled with doubts. Would his departure from Ballylee prove fruitless after all? Even if the marriage between Princess Henrietta Maria and Prince Charles became fact and he found his way to England, would Brenna see him? If he did see her, talk to her, what good would it do?

And even if the riddle of why she had suddenly returned to England that night from Chinon were solved, what rest would that give the burning ache he felt?

But still the waiting was agony, for no matter the

doubts, he knew somewhere he would find a way to reach England and Brenna one last time.

Then a summons came from Richelieu—but not for the reasons Rory had hoped for.

"THE FOOLS!" Richelieu said, turning a goblet of brandy between his long, tapered fingers. "They should know by now that I have ears in every corner of Paris. It would be impossible that I wouldn't hear of an assassination plot, no matter how well hidden!"

Rory sat, unable to move, digesting the news he had just received. Gaston, King Louis's younger brother, had been lured by La Mardine and his duchess into a plot to assassinate Richelieu. If the cardinal were gone, La Mardine would then have an open road to England and be able to set himself up as the master of the alliance between France and England in the eyes of the people. Also, Louis was childless and ailing. Should he die, Gaston would inherit the throne and rule, without the impediment of his worst enemy, Richelieu.

"They would butcher me like a hog at my very table! And indeed they might have been successful had the instrument they chose been of heartier mettle," the cardinal railed.

Rory closed his eyes and groaned. He could easily see the imperious, red-robed figure rising from his table and squarely facing the assassin's dagger. He could almost hear the steellike tone in the cardinal's words as he verbally assaulted his would-be killer and brought him to his knees and a confession.

"What will you do with them?" Rory sighed.

"With Gaston, what can I do? He is a prince of the blood. He will be slapped on the hand by Louis and will return to revel with his loose women in taverns and gambling houses. La Mardine and his whorish wife I can exile from court for a time but not much else."

"And the poor fool who would have wielded the dagger?"

Richelieu shrugged his crimson-covered shoulders and stretched his arms wide. "Someone must be made to pay—a lesson must be learned from all this foolishness. I will have his head."

O'Hara felt ill at the pronouncement. He couldn't prevent his mind from returning to the roistering good times of earlier years in the taverns and brothels of Paris. He remembered the fateful day of Concini's death, when he had been saved from certain death himself by his youthful friend's intervention.

"I didn't know René de Gramont had aligned himself with La Mardine," he said dully.

"I fear your old friend is not the man he once was. He would now align himself with anyone who would pay his bills and keep his cup filled to the brim. And like most men, de Gramont falls easily under the duchess's spell."

Rory pulled his powerful frame from the chair and leaned across the desk toward Richelieu. "I must see him."

"It will do no good."

"I'll need permission to enter the Bastille."

Richelieu's always-cold eyes became more like ice as they stared at O'Hara while he weighed the request. "They say that his is an old sickness, one of the heart, and it has turned into madness. His jailers tell me that at times he is coherent, even cunning. But at other times he raves like a wild man, froths at the mouth and grovels like a dog."

"Your Excellency—"

"I would have La Mardine's head if I could, but in lieu of his. . . de Gramont's will have to do."

"Your Excellency. . .a pass," Rory spoke, his voice half pleading, half demanding.

Richelieu again shrugged and placed pen to paper. He kept his face bent low over the desk so that Rory couldn't see the smile spreading across his thin lips.

FLANKED BY TWO PIKEMEN, Rory followed a warden across a walled courtyard beyond the main gate. A heavy door swung open, and they left the sunshine and stillness of the courtyard behind. Dank, fetid odors assaulted his nostrils, and from the torchlit gloom came the agonized sounds of prisoners and the constant clanking of their chains.

"This way!"

Rory's wide shoulders brushed the damp walls as they descended narrow stone steps that spiraled ever deeper into the bowels of the Bastille. The air was even closer on the lower levels. The cells were tiny rooms, stone on three sides and faced with a slotted steel door. They stopped at one and the warden unhooked a huge ring from his belt. Deftly he found the right key, and the door swung open.

Rory was relieved of his dagger, his sword and both his pistols before entering. Then a candle was placed in his hand and he was waved inside.

"Bang on the door with your boot when you've a mind to leave."

He nodded, and the heavy door slammed behind him. For several seconds he stood, eyes narrowed, peering through the gloom with the candle high above his head. It was a moment before he realized that the bundle of rags in a corner had human shape.

"René. . . René de Gramont," he called.

There was no answer or movement. Rory leaned forward and gently grasped a shoulder. "René. . . ."

The rags moved, shook and slowly took form: the back of a head, shoulders, arms and torso. Then it turned over, and Rory gasped. He knew it to be René de Gramont, but only one once close enough to the man to have been his brother could have recognized him.

Beneath many days' growth of beard, the face was nearly skull-like, with jutting cheekbones and gray hollows for eyes. The once proud mane of blond hair was tangled and matted with filth. Beneath the rags that had once been a waistcoat and cambric shirt, the pale skin of the man's sunken chest glowed unhealthily white in the candlelight.

"René, 'tis I—O'Hara. Rory O'Hara."

"O'Hara?" the voice croaked between swollen lips.

"Aye. . . Rory O'Hara. Do ye not remember me, man?"

Rory moved the candle closer to his own face and dropped to his knees. Slowly, he saw realization come to the once blue eyes now misted to a cloudy gray.

"Rory O'Hara."

"Aye." Rory set the candle on the stone floor between them and brought a small loaf and a bottle of wine from beneath his cloak. "Here—eat, my friend."

At the word "friend," René shrank back against the wall, his eyes wild with a look of madness.

"What manner of greeting is this? Eat," Rory urged. "You look starved, man. Here!"

Slowly a bony hand came forward and then, like a ferret, snatched the loaf from Rory's fingers. The man tore at the bread like an animal, stuffing chunks into his mouth until he could hold no more. When he drank, the wine overflowed his lips and ran from the corners of his mouth in maroon streams.

Unable to watch, Rory turned away and leaned against the cell door until the ravenous sounds abated.

Then he turned back, and the two old friends faced each other in the candle's dancing glow.

Richelieu had been right. There was indeed madness in the red-rimmed, darting eyes, Rory thought.

René licked crumbs from his fingers and tugged slowly at his lower lip, appearing to have forgotten O'Hara's presence.

"René—" Rory tried once more.

"Go 'way." De Gramont's voice was more growl than human speech.

He had begun to roll his emaciated body back into a ball when Rory grasped him by the shoulders. As he tried to turn him, René lashed out. The back of his hand struck Rory a solid, stunning blow that sent him sprawling. There was more shock than pain. It seemed impossible that the wretchedly shriveled body could deliver a blow of such strength.

Rory came up on his haunches in a crouch, only to find René in the same position, his arms at the ready as if to battle. His cracked lips were pulled back from feral teeth, and his voice was a snarl.

"Go 'way!"

Cautiously and slowly, Rory rose to his feet. "I came as a friend. I would only help you. So much has passed between us in the years gone by, I cannot bear to see you like this."

Rory continued to talk, keeping his voice low and soothing. He reminisced about the nights of revelry in Paris taverns. He chuckled over their youthful debaucheries in the brothel of Madame Picard.

Moments passed, and René seemed to grow calmer. Some life other than that of a haunted animal seeped back into his eyes.

"O'Hara," he said at last with some recognition.

"Yes, René, the Irishman, O'Hara."

The lips quivered and then he spoke. "I'm to die, you know."

"Yes, I know."

"Madmen don't go to hell, do they, O'Hara? They soar with the angels."

"René, dear friend. . . why?"

"Why what? Why am I like this? Because 'tis my due."

"Your due for what?"

"For being a fool. For loving a woman."

"Carlotta?"

Rory took a step backward as the cell suddenly reverberated with a hysterical, high-pitched laugh. On and on it went, and during it René's eyes grew brighter with that same look of wildness. At last the eerie laughter ended in a choking cough.

"Carlotta? No man loves La Duchesse, he only beds her!"

"Who, then?"

"Who? Dear God, you fool, who else but your sister!"

"You mean after all this time—"

"This time? What time? The time since she left is but the blink of an eye compared to a lifetime, O'Hara. And that's how long I've lived with this witch, your sister, tearing at my vitals!"

"Old friend—"

"Friend? Nay, not friends, O'Hara, for I can no more call you friend than I can call your sister wife. Had

I a dagger this moment, I would drive it through your heart. Had I strength I would squeeze your neck until you were a lifeless doll in my hands."

As René spoke, his voice slowly rose again to a hysterical screech. "When Shanna left St. Germain-en-Laye, I swore I would go after her, bring her back. And if she would not return, I would kill her—and then myself!"

"You are mad."

"Mad?" René shouted, trying to roll to his feet but only reaching his knees. "Aye, I am mad, O'Hara. I know it as only a true madman can know it. I know that I am mad as truly as you are sane. Why else would I agree to assassinate Richelieu like a man and then grovel at his feet like a whimpering dog? 'Tis because I am no longer a man, O'Hara."

"You will be again, René, I swear it." Rory thrust his hand forward as if to clutch René's and pull him to his feet. "Somehow I'll free—" His speech stopped as his hand was slapped aside.

"Leave off, O'Hara, and let me be. Leave me to my fate. At least the ax is an honorable death and better than a Paris gutter with the rain washing my face and the dogs gnawing my bones."

"She has found love, René. His name is David Talbot."

"I know!" the madman replied with a cackle. "I've followed her every move, even in your heathen land."

Rory sensed something chilling in the calculated way René spoke now. There was still madness in his eyes, but they seemed clearer, more intent.

"She loved you as a friend, René."

"What kind of love is that? 'Tis all in jest! And what do you, the cavalier O'Hara, know of love, anyway?"

René's pitifully haggard face came up and the eyes, when they found Rory's, seemed almost sane for a moment.

"What do you know of love, O'Hara? You'll never know what it's like to have the one woman for you on earth, and then lose her. You'll never know what it is like to love a woman so much that not having her can weaken your mind, drive you to such despair that you prefer death to life. I know. I have known thirteen years of a love that is hell."

The speech seemed to drain all life from his body, and René curled his emaciated form away from Rory to face the wall.

With an aching heart Rory replied, "Ah, my friend, but I do know. I will pay this all back to you, somehow. But first you must be freed from here."

Rory pounded his boot on the door. When it was opened and he was about to step into the corridor, René spoke one last time.

"Don't, O'Hara. Let me die—and in peace, or one day you'll regret your interference."

IN THE DAYS THAT FOLLOWED, Rory pleaded again and again for René's life. He used every argument he could think of: René's kinship to the king, even though it was illegitimate and not recognized; his former loyalty to the crown in the matter of the Concini plot; his friendship to Rory in years past. He even pleaded the man's apparent madness.

Richelieu was adamant—strangely so, Rory began to think. In his present state, René could hardly be an effective example to other would-be assassins. But as the days dwindled and René's execution date approached, Richelieu became even more resolute.

"Someone must pay. 'Tis sad that it is this fool, de Gramont, but who else is there?"

Rory was in turmoil. There was no escaping from the Bastille, and even if there had been, helping René to freedom meant risking Richelieu's favor and possibly losing his chance to see Brenna.

Two nights before the execution was to take place, while Rory was taking supper in a tavern, an urchin girl came by his table. For a second she paused, whispering, *"Monsieur le Gael?"*

"Oui."

A folded note was thrust into his hand, and the girl vanished. Rory discreetly unfolded the paper and read:

> Allo, my wild Irishman! Only recently have I learned of your arrival in Paris. His Excellency, the cardinal, does well moving his pawns in darkness. I would have us meet for the reason agreed upon these many years ago, but I fear business of more import is at hand. Whatever you may have heard of me, O'Hara, since your return to Paris, let me say that I am a slave to my husband's desires and schemes, helpless before his wrath. For this reason I would aid you in your quest for de Gramont's freedom. There is a way to accomplish such a deed.
>
> If you wish my aid in this matter, meet me at high moon, nearer to the first hour than to midnight, in the fields beyond Notre-Dame-de-Bonne-Nouvelle, near the Porte St.-Denis. Enter from the eastern side. You will see a stand of stately oaks, more than a dozen in number. I will be on a horse beneath them.
>
> With fondest regards and even fonder memories,
>
> Carlotta

Rory O'Hara touched a candle to the letter as he considered the dangers of associating with Richelieu's enemies. Then he thought of his old friendship for René and he knew he would go.

CHAPTER THIRTY-SIX

IT WAS A CLEAR MOONLIT NIGHT, with few strollers or riders on the winding lanes around Porte St.-Denis. Much of the land was marshy, forcing Rory to ride slowly for safety as well as stealth. Now and then small animals, startled by the horse's tread, skittered across his path. In the distance, the bells of Notre-Dame-de-Bonne-Nouvelle tolled the half hour. Over the trees he saw the spires of the recently completed church looming taller as he drew nearer.

Moments later he drew his mount up at the edge of a vast field. Spring flowers filled the night air with sweetness, and ankle-high grass waved gently in a soft breeze. Slowly and carefully his eyes surveyed the terrain. Tall poplars and beech trees grew randomly around the well-trod paths of the field. Near at hand was a small stand of oaks, and a hundred yards farther on he detected the gnarled limbs and heavy trunks of what had to be the grove he sought. Then his horse snorted and received a whinny in reply.

Still holding his mount to a walk, he approached the grove. Most of the oaks were large of trunk and tightly packed. Two of the largest stood apart from their peers and were arranged like gate towers before the others. Between these two, a horse and black-cloaked rider sat in the shadows.

Rory tensed in the saddle for a moment and then relaxed when he was close enough to see that the rider was mounted side-saddle. He rode forward until the horses were flank to flank. Only then did the figure move. A black-gloved hand came up, and the cowl fell away.

Carlotta shook her head and the mane of her long blond hair came free to spill around her shoulders and down her back. She hadn't changed, hadn't aged a day. The complexion of her fine-featured face was still clear and youthful, and under the long lashes the same fire danced in her dark eyes. O'Hara couldn't stop a tiny smile from curling his lips.

"*Eh bien*, my fine-figured Irishman, you are as handsome as ever."

"And you, Carlotta, are as bewitching and, from hearsay, just as deadly."

"Oh, *mon cher*," she cooed, her heavily rouged lips pursing in a perfect pout. "This is no way for a gallant to greet a lady he has been so intimate with in days gone by!"

"Days gone by long enough, Carlotta, are often forgotten," he replied sternly, anxious to bring the conversation to the business at hand.

But Carlotta eased her horse forward until she was right at his side. "This, *mon cher*, is the way to greet an old lover!"

Before he could stop her, she had entwined her arms around his neck. Using her weight, she tugged him forward until their lips met in a grinding kiss. Her tongue forced its way between his lips and Rory could feel the fullness of her breasts against his side.

"Ah, she is truly the most artful of courtesans, don't you think, Irishman?"

Rory pulled his lips from Carlotta's and wrenched his

head around. There, bareheaded and cloakless, was the Duc de La Mardine. He had maneuvered his mount soundlessly behind Rory while Carlotta had occupied his mind with her lips and body. Now he sat, his sword unsheathed, its steel blade glinting blue in the moonlight. On his thin lips Rory saw the cruel sneer he remembered so well.

Furiously, he fought to untangle himself from the arms of the duchess. At last he did, but not before she had managed to slide her hand down his baldric until she grasped the hilt of his sword.

"So sorry, *mon cher,*" she smiled, and Rory's blade whistled from its scabbard. Before he could retrieve it, she had put spurs to her horse and was yards away.

This, Rory thought, *was not meant to be a gentlemanly duel.* La Mardine was taking no chances that Rory might have improved on his skills as a swordsman since leaving Paris. A duel it was not—more like murder.

"*Monsieur,* I have killed seventy-two men with my blade. Yet, I must admit, not one moan of agony nor the sight of a single drop of blood has brought as much joy to my heart as will skewering you this night!" the duke said.

Rory barely had time to draw his dagger and meet the charge. The clash of steel, of long sword against shorter blade, rang clear. The point of La Mardine's blade was barely deflected from Rory's throat. Steel ground against steel until the hilts met, and then they were past each other, whirling their horses.

"Time, Irishman, 'tis only a matter of time. I toy with you until death!" La Mardine taunted.

Again they met, but this time Rory was ready. Their blades licked at each other and, by sheer will, Rory deflected La Mardine's blade before it found his flesh. He leaned back in the saddle, letting the other man's momentum carry his body forward.

Then, in passing, at the last moment, Rory recoiled. He went under La Mardine's sword, and with all the superior strength of his powerful physique, Rory drove his shoulder into the duke's middle.

La Mardine lost his seat and tumbled to the ground, with O'Hara close behind. Too late—Rory had underestimated the man's resilience. La Mardine rolled to his knees with his own dagger unsheathed. O'Hara barely had time to bring his right arm up as the duke lunged.

The dagger pierced his forearm to the hilt. La Mardine struggled to free it, but with a cry of pain Rory managed to lurch free of his grasp. He fell to his knees. Frantically he searched for his own fallen weapon to parry another attack.

None came. The duke had scrambled to his feet and dove for the reins of his horse. For a brief second O'Hara thought the man meant to flee. Then his eyes fell on the brace of pistols attached to the saddle.

Suddenly, as he watched the duke's hand move down the horse's neck, all movement slowed and time stood still for Rory. Eerily, he was a youth again, sitting at the feet of his tutor, The O'Donnell. The old warrior's words rang in his ears.

In war, 'tis survival that matters, lad. Anything less than victory is death. No quarter should be taken nor any given!

La Mardine's hand found one pistol's butt and tugged it from its sheath.

Rory's mind was suddenly calm, his body in control. There was no pain in his arm nor failing in his legs, no faltering as he stood and smoothly drew a pistol from his own belt. Using the hilt of La Mardine's dagger as a crutch, where it still protruded from his arm, he steadied the barrel and fired.

The ball hit the duke squarely in the center of his chest. He stopped, eyes wide with shock, as he stared in disbelief at the widening circle of red staining his immaculate white shirt.

By the time he looked back up and began to lurch forward, O'Hara had already drawn his second pistol. The ball struck La Mardine to the left of the first. He died before he fell to the ground at Rory's feet.

Still dazed, his movements stiff, as if under the control of someone other than himself, O'Hara pulled the dagger from his arm and dropped it by the duke's body. He turned, blinking the mist from his eyes as he searched for his horse.

Carlotta stood directly in front of him. Daintily, she stepped over her husband's body and threw her arms around Rory's chest. Her lips were parted and her dark eyes smoldered as she turned her face up to his.

"To the victor goes the spoils," she whispered.

Rory struck her across the face with all the power left in his wounded right arm.

Then the pain came, crumpling him to his knees as his voice filled the quiet field with a groan of agony.

BECAUSE CHARLES, the Prince of Wales, was Protestant, his marriage to Henrietta Maria, even performed by proxy with the groom still in England, couldn't take place inside the walls of a Catholic church.

So, accompanied by the blare of a hundred trumpets, the long nuptial procession wound its way between thronged galleries from the archbishop's palace to the west door of Notre-Dame. There the long line of courtiers, all adorned in regal splendor, stopped on the steps where the ceremony itself would take place.

Heading the procession was the princess's guard, led by Richelieu's choice for its captain, Rory O'Hara. There were gasps of wonder and admiration as the guard passed in their red, full-sleeved tunics trimmed in silver, with a cross in silver thread emblazoned on their chests. White plumes danced in the bright sunlight above the rakish, upswept brims of their cavalier's hats. The baldrics holding the long swords were gold, as were the cupped hand guards on the hilts.

Behind the princess's guard came two hundred of the king's musketeers, their open helmets and silver breastplates dazzling the onlookers' eyes. The musketeers marched in perfect time to the trumpets' blare, their muskets and pikes aligned in geometrical harmony.

The ladies-in-waiting surrounding the future Princess of Wales and Queen of England seemed to be a moving sea of black and purple velvet cloaks and scarlet and gold dresses cleverly cut to reveal dazzling blue petticoats of satin.

In the midst of her ladies and walking between her two brothers, King Louis XIII and Gaston, Duc d'Orleans, was the tiny, dark-skinned Henrietta Maria. Her bridal gown was fashioned of priceless cloth of silver and gold, liberally laced with golden fleurs-de-lis and trimmed in diamonds.

Rory O'Hara proudly led his guards to the steps of Notre-Dame, where they separated into two rows. Silently he watched King Louis pass his sister's hand to the aging Duke of Chevreause, who would act as proxy for Prince Charles of England.

Rory remembered the sighs of relief that had gone

through court when it was learned that the Duke of Buckingham would not be able to fulfill this duty. Because of his manner and deportment in Paris during the last days of the marriage negotiations, no one wanted a return visit from that Englishman.

He had arrived at a ball wearing a full-length cloak stitched in pearls. The thread holding the pearls was so fine that it broke as he entered the room. Courtiers dove to retrieve over a hundred thousand pounds' worth of gems, and Buckingham had stood in the middle of the floor and laughed. He was heard to whisper to an aide that courtiers in England had wealth enough that there was no need to grovel on the floors of Whitehall for baubles.

In two weeks' time, Buckingham had antagonized the entire French court and, most of all, its king. At the duke's first meeting with Queen Anne he did his best to dazzle her with his charms. Because Louis paid little attention to his queen, the poor woman was indeed dazzled by such lavish attention. Too much so.

Buckingham, sensing a conquest, went too far. After a garden party at Amiens given in his honor, the duke had had the audacity to steal into the queen's private rooms.

Though the king cared little for his wife, his sense of royalty was offended when someone else did and particularly in so open a manner. Through Richelieu, Buckingham was asked to leave the country and never to return.

And this, Rory thought, as he heard the vows exchanged, *is the situation I face in England!*

King James was dead, but little would be altered by his son becoming King Charles I. Buckingham was as much the favorite of the son as he had been "Steenie" to the father.

Rory's gaze roamed past the figure of the petite bride

where she knelt before Cardinal Rochefoucault as he pronounced the nuptial benediction and came to rest upon the most influential and chief among Henrietta Maria's appointed ladies-in-waiting, the Duchess de La Mardine.

Bile stirred in his throat as he thought of that night nearly two months before in the fields beyond the other Notre-Dame. And his mood grew worse when he thought of their subsequent meeting a few nights later.

He had been summoned to Richelieu's apartments to receive his captaincy. At the same time the cardinal, who had seemed pleased beyond belief at the death of La Mardine, had signed the clemency order for René de Gramont.

"Thank you, Your Excellency," Rory had bowed low with a flourish.

"Do not thank me," Richelieu had replied. "It was not my doing that another's head took the fool's place."

There was no doubt in Rory's mind to whose head Richelieu was referring. Then Carlotta had stepped from the tiny alcove chapel, not in weeds of mourning but gaudily adorned in crimson satin.

"*Madame la duchesse* will accompany the wedding party to England as head of the new queen's household," the cardinal had pronounced smoothly.

It had taken neither the look on Richelieu's face nor the smile of triumph on Carlotta's to tell Rory the truth.

"Your Excellency, what would you have done had I taken the fatal ball instead of La Mardine?" Rory had inquired, the sarcasm in his voice barely veiled.

Richelieu had merely shrugged. "There was time. There would have been someone else. The road to power, my Irish friend, is often paved with old ties."

Before him the wedding party turned, snapping his mind back to the present. All but the English Protestants attending the ceremony began moving into the cathedral to hear the nuptial mass. Suddenly Carlotta was directly in front of him, awaiting her entrance in the procession. "Ah, my handsome Irishman," she whispered, leaning her lips near his ear, "what fine times we'll have together across the sea!"

Part III

CHAPTER THIRTY-SEVEN
ENGLAND

BRENNA WROTE LETTER AFTER LETTER to anyone at court she thought might listen and plead her case. She knew that more than one peer's heart went out to her, but no one wanted to stand up to the wrath of Buckingham or be forced to outmaneuver his wily mother.

When it was obvious that mere letters would not produce any results, Brenna went to Whitehall in person, only to be subjected to the greatest indignity she had borne thus far. She was denied admittance to the council chamber. In front of bawds, whores and untitled gallants of even less means than herself, the Viscountess Poole, wife of a peer of the realm, was spurned, not by the king or even the duke, but by a page. She was rebuffed as if she were no higher in station than a street urchin.

Her mood, as she trudged the length of the Strand and up the hill to Holborn, was no longer one of desperation but abject despair. A viscountess who had been wed with a dowry of fifty thousand pounds and a stipend of three thousand a year, and she hadn't the funds to hire a coach, all of it now controlled by the Villiers clan.

The streets of the city reflected her despair. No longer did they ring with the cries of hawking vendors. Had Brenna been able to afford a hackney, it would have been hard to find one.

It had been a strange year already, this year of 1625, and many felt in their bones that it would prove even more eventful. January had been mild, at times warm, even hot. February had been unseasonably cold, with tides that boded evil signs. One high tide had washed over Thames Street, ruining many houses; another had flooded Westminster Hall three feet deep in water.

March was already bitterly cold, with seemingly endless rain. Mist hung like a pall over the houses and streets. There was no room left in the ground for water, so it was impossible to avoid the pools and puddles with her slippered feet. On every fifth door Brenna passed she saw a scribbled red cross. Already, even this early in the year, the plague and its German cousin, spotted fever, was making its yearly visit to London.

By the time she reached Hatton House, her clothes and shoes were soaked and she was chilled to the bone. Elizabeth whisked her to bed at once and insisted on Brenna drinking quantities of hot mutton broth.

It was all too clear from her dejected state what had occurred. Slowly, word by word, Lady Hatton extracted from her daughter the story of her humiliating experience.

"It is the way of our world now," Elizabeth sighed at last. "That is why, almost daily I agree more and more with Sir Edward and the Parliament. 'Tis they who should rule and not the king!"

Brenna sat propped against a mountain of pillows, her jaw clenched tightly, her lips drawn into a thin line. " 'Tis not the king who rules, 'tis m'Lord Buckingham. And this is why I am so confused. The man has all of England. Why should he take my meager means and still want yours as well?"

"My dear girl, when will you learn? They hate us.

They will always hate us. 'Tis the nature of the beast born low and raised high, to hate and devour those born higher but now under his power!"

"Is that all there is to be?" Brenna cried. "Hate, distrust, greed, ambition? Is that all we are—all we will ever be?"

"Yes, that is all," Elizabeth calmly replied. "If we are to survive."

For two days Brenna tossed restlessly on her bed, racked with a fevered cough. On the morning of the third she awoke well. Her fever was gone, the sun shone brightly, and church bells tolled from London to Westminster. Elizabeth entered Brenna's apartment, trailed by a servant with a breakfast tray.

"It is a marvelous, glorious morning!" Elizabeth said, her face beaming as she threw the draperies wide and opened the windows.

"It is," Brenna replied, her spirits bolstered by her mother's mood.

"Our good King James has been rewarded for his glorious rule."

"How so?"

"He is dead."

Brenna was unable to eat the food placed before her. It was not because of the king's death. Rather it was because of the beatific look of sheer joy on her mother's face when she had announced it.

THE PLAGUE GREW WORSE. London was evacuating. People poured into the country in any conveyance possible, and if nothing was available they took to the roads on foot. Now there was not a single coach rattling across the cobbles and the Thames was empty of boats for hire.

From her window Brenna could see mourners following the carts carrying their dead kinsmen's coffins. To ward off the plague they had stuffed rue and wormwood into their ears and nostrils.

Now, rather than every fifth house, entire streets were marked with the scrawled red cross of plague. The court scurried north to escape, and Lady Hatton made preparations to depart for Bristol and Corfe Castle. She urged Brenna to join her.

"Nay, mother. I've lived off your generosity for too long already. At least I can stay here and play the caretaker of Hatton House while you are gone. Besides, at Corfe, on clear days I would be able to look across the bay and see Poole House, and those memories I would rather lose."

Elizabeth was adamant. "No person of quality is staying in this plague-infested place. Now, pack!"

But Brenna was just as unswerving. "I vouchsafe you are right, mother. No person of title or quality remains anywhere near London. Now be off and have a safe journey!"

A staff of three was left with Brenna. The rest of the servants departed with Lady Hatton.

Brenna spent her days walking in the gardens, and her evenings sitting at her window gazing across the rooftops toward the Thames. The stillness of London was shocking, broken only by the rumbling wheels of the dead carts and the cry of their black-robed drivers.

"Dead, ha' ye dead!"

"Heave out yer dead!"

There was an unending stream of them on Holborn Road heading toward Tyburn Hill and burial.

From a servant girl Brenna learned that no longer were the dead being buried in individual graves. There was no one left to dig them. Communal pits became the last resting place for London's poor. Few of the wealthier class were dying for they had all fled.

It became a strange consolation for Brenna. For the first time since her youth, she felt a kinship and it was toward those poor souls who huddled behind the doors, illuminated by the bright light of the plague fires. She, like them, had become a part of the London poor.

SHE WAS IN THE MIDST OF WRITING yet another letter to Raymond that he would never see when the nausea struck. At first she paid it little mind, but it grew worse. When her body became heated and a temple-throbbing headache refused to go away, she took to her bed.

The servants cared for her, thinking that this was only a recurrence of her former fever or a result of her constant depression. But as she complained of rheumatic pains and a stiffness in her muscles, the servants grew fearful. When she became slightly delirious and dark spots appeared on her body, they were thrown into a panic.

Leaving the city now was difficult. Sending a message south to Lady Hatton was well-nigh impossible. All three of the servants left behind had been in the service of Lady Hatton but a short time. But in that time they had learned of the towering animosity between Lady Hatton and Sir Edward Coke. Elizabeth had given directions that her husband was never to be allowed to step foot inside Hatton House.

But who else could they call upon? And even then, would Sir Edward come? His scandalous treatment of his daughter in the past was common knowledge.

Two more days passed, during which garlands of green waddy were hung on the walls of Brenna's room to sweeten the air. For the same reason, pomanders were hung around her bed and bunches of crushed sage above it. The hearth fire that burned day and night was heavy with the scent of dried mint, thyme and rue. Soon the odor of these ancient remedies so permeated the air of Brenna's room that it was difficult to breathe.

The sweats and fever increased, and her delirium turned to hysteria. A servant was dispatched to Sergeant's Inn to summon Sir Edward. To the servants' great surprise, he arrived within the hour.

"Aye, 'tis the German fever, you fools," the old man railed, after only seconds at Brenna's side. "Clear this garbage from the room and open the windows for air!"

The old barrister took command in the sick room as he had so often taken command in the House of Commons. Orders were barked in his harsh voice, and the servants leaped to carry them out.

The bed Brenna had slept in and any other linen that had come near her was stripped and taken to the courtyard. There it was boiled in huge vats. While that was being done, vinegar sponges were used to scrub the patient and everything else in her room. By nightfall Brenna slept in a clean robe on spotless linen. The room itself was also spotless, and cold packs had been placed around her body to lessen the fever.

Sir Edward had done all he could. Now he tugged a chair near the side of the bed and wearily sat down to wait. Near midnight her dark eyes fluttered open.

"Father?"

"Aye. Rest, girl. I've not been by your side often, but I'm here now."

Even though Sir Edward was ill himself from gout and that disease that no one can avoid, age, he never left Brenna's side in the days that followed.

It was a shock when he discovered that the three servants had fled, but he took it in stride. He brought kitchen utensils up to the room adjoining Brenna's. There, on a pot suspended over the hearth fire, he made a broth and boiled the meager supply of meat that had been left in the larder.

Day and night he tended and nursed her. There were moments when she would awaken and be almost coherent, and she would see his gray head bobbing on his chest. She would reach out and gently touch the back of his wrinkled hand. His eyes would immediately pop open.

"Aye, aye, girl. . . what is it?"

"Nothing, I—nothing. Sleep, you look so tired."

Other times her eyes would open but they would be sightless. Her body, frail and emaciated now, would quiver beneath the sheets like a drawn bowstring.

During one of these incoherent spells of wakefulness, she cried out for pen and paper. She would write her husband and beg his forgiveness for the hell she had caused him during their wedded life. By the time Sir Edward had scoured the house for the writing materials and returned, she was again in a deep troubled sleep.

But even in sleep she babbled, and that was how Sir Edward learned of her love for the Irishman, Rory O'Hara. Red-faced, he sat and listened to the most intimate details of their affair and the reason for its conclusion.

He learned of the hellish life she had shared with her husband. When she began praying for her soul's forgiveness because she had never allowed her marriage to be consummated, Sir Edward could listen no more.

With tears streaming down his cheeks, he left the room, sadly whispering to himself, "'Tis not the lass's fault, for she is her mother's daughter. It is as if history repeats itself."

Brenna improved, but in fits and starts. It was on the second day after her fever finally broke that the spots began appearing on Sir Edward's face and the backs of his hands.

That was how Sir Raymond Hubbard found them; Brenna, awake but without strength to raise a hand, and her father nodding in a cold sweat at her bedside.

He moved around the bed and grasped the old man under the arms. Sir Edward shook himself into wakefulness and turned his fever-hot eyes on the intruder.

"You would kill yourself to save what you have sold so freely, old man?" Raymond murmured.

Coke bristled, but he hadn't the strength to break free of the younger man's grasp. "Had I known I was pledging her to a madman, I would have thought better of the sale!"

"There is a madness, Sir Edward, in all of us. 'Tis a fact that not everyone, like you, has the mettle always to hold it in check. Now, where is another bed?"

Sir Edward had no strength to argue. He pointed the way.

Raymond undressed him and did for the father much the same as Sir Edward had done for Brenna. He was about to return to her when Sir Edward spoke.

"You'll care for her?"

"Aye, just as you have done. . . this time."

He turned away and then, in the doorway, paused. "Let us hope, Sir Edward, that she forgives us both our weaknesses. Perhaps, together, we can make her live."

RAYMOND WAS OVERJOYED. The color had begun to creep back into Brenna's face, and the dark hollows around her eyes had diminished. She now had enough strength to feed herself and carry on short conversations.

"How is it," she joked, "that you have so mastered the art of cooking?"

"By being a bachelor longer than a husband."

Her face reddened, but she took his retort in stride and begged him for news.

"Upon James's death it would have been unseemly for my cousin to keep me harnessed any longer. Besides, my old friendship with Charles remains somewhat intact."

"The king is buried?"

"Aye, I was in attendance. And, like so many others, methinks it was more from curiosity than purposes of mourning. Indeed, I saw not a wet eye in the procession."

"But still it was a funeral befitting a king, I hope?"

"Aye, I suppose. Some say it cost Charles fifty thousand pounds to put his father away. The eulogy was by the lord keeper, Bishop Williams. He went on for hours, speaking of the wisdom of Solomon and the wisdom of King James. No matter his eloquence, I don't believe there was a single soul there who thought James the greater Solomon of the two!"

"I hate to feel happiness over a dead man's bones," Brenna declared, reaching out and grasping Raymond's hand. "But at least now, under the new king, perhaps we will be able to lead a more normal life."

A cloud passed over Raymond's face. Brenna saw it at once.

"What is it?"

"I fear, Brenna, that already our Charles the First, like his father, has more power than sense."

EVEN WITH THE HINDRANCE OF HIS ADVANCED AGE, Sir Edward's fever broke quickly. It was as much due to his iron will and constitution as it was to the quick cure administered by Raymond, the Viscount Poole.

By the time he was well enough to be moved by hired litter-bearers the few blocks back to his lodgings at Sergeant's Inn, he was as crotchety and irascible as ever.

"I have sent for Doctor Weymouth," Raymond told him, handing him into the litter. "He should be in your quarters when you arrive."

"And I shall promptly send him away!" Coke retorted. "I have not been bled nor physicked since I was born and will not begin now. 'Tis all a doctor could do for me, since they are all quacks, anyway. 'Twas not a doctor who cured Brenna, 'twas me. 'Twas not a doctor who cured me, 'twas you. Doctors are naught but necromancers with little black bags!"

"But, Sir Edward—"

"Lad, hear me! Not all the drugs of Asia, the gold in Africa or all the doctors in Europe can cure the one disease that will eventually kill me—old age!"

Raymond shrugged and good-naturedly stepped back from the litter.

"Tote on!" Coke cried. "And, damme, move at a pace, for I've been too long away from my books!"

Recovery for Brenna was much slower, but as the days wore on she regained her strength. Her face and body fleshed out, and the light of life returned to her eyes.

Then one evening Raymond entered the room and found that she had risen from her bed. He stopped abruptly when he saw her at the window, dressed in chemise and robe, taking in deep draughts of fresh air.

"The plague fires burn low," she said, without turning. "And the wind carries the smoke away."

"Aye," Raymond replied, feeling the familiar ache of need in his loins as his eyes followed the smooth line of her body beneath the gown.

" 'Tis a relief to have air not heavy and tainted with death."

"Aye, 'tis, but beware of too much bravery. You think you have regained more strength than you actually have."

She turned then, and he nearly dropped the supper tray he held. In his absence, Brenna had lightly blushed her cheeks, added cerise to her lips and shadowed her eyes. She had also attended to her hair. It was combed and brushed to a raven sheen and then pulled back from her forehead and clasped so that it fell in twin cascades to frame her face like a perfect portrait in stark black and white.

It was the look of Brenna's face that struck him now, submerging the erotic passion of a moment before and replacing it with awe and adoration. He thought she had never been so beautiful. *It is the bones,* he mused, *they are perfect behind the skin that is again radiant.* Brenna had the smoothly contoured face that would be beautiful until the day she died. It would never age, no matter the hardships imposed upon it.

"Is the result so ghastly?" she asked, avoiding his eyes.

"Nay, quite the opposite. You have never been more beautiful."

Suddenly the scene was awkward for them. They stood for several moments, he holding the tray and she nervously twisting the band of gold on her left hand.

"Come...eat," he said finally, placing the tray, "and I'll regale you with the current grisly tales of the town."

Brenna made a wry face as she sat and folded a napkin over her lap. Then she noticed the food.

"Where on earth, Raymond...?"

"I rode into the country this morning," he said proudly, lifting the covers off dish after dish, and then seating himself opposite her. "Veal, vegetables, cheese, strawberries and...wine!"

"Fit for a queen!" she giggled.

"At least a viscountess," he replied, pouring the wine.

They dined in silence for some time, both surprised at the extent of their hunger.

"Mmm, it's delicious!" Brenna exclaimed, daintily licking her lips between bites. "Thank you, m'lord!"

"You're welcome, m'lady," Raymond grinned.

When they reached the strawberries and cream, Brenna felt a sudden pang of guilt. "Raymond?"

"Yes?"

"Are there many dead?"

He paused, a huge berry halfway to his lips. "Many," he nodded. "'Tis said well into the thousands, and the toll still climbing."

"Every year it comes, and every year hundreds, even thousands, die. Methinks 'tis indeed God's way of punishing us for our sins."

Impulsively, Raymond reached across the table and grasped her hand. "Then we must be innocents, you and I, for we have survived."

Their eyes met, but only for a moment. Raymond's glance would not hold, and Brenna was sure she saw a flush of embarrassment redden his cheeks as he withdrew his hand.

"Odd," she said impulsively.

"Odd?" he croaked. "What is odd... how odd?"

"You've shaved your beard and mustache."

"Aye," he said, his head bowed.

"Why?"

"I—I—" His cheeks grew redder.

"Raymond!"

"When I was a lad...."

He began to stammer, grope for words. This time it was Brenna who reached across the table and found his hand.

"When—when I was a lad, my older sister once took my hand and ran it across her cheek."

"Yes?" Brenna said, puzzled.

"She said to me, 'Raymond,' she said, 'D'ye see how smooth is a lady's cheek?' Aye, I said. And then she told me that if I ever wanted to be a great gallant with the ladies, I'd best see to the smoothness of my cheek as well... for smooth-cheeked ladies don't take kindly to bristly men."

Brenna hid a smile behind the back of her hand. "And so you've shaved."

"Aye," he coughed, and lurched to his feet. "Now 'tis time you were back to bed and rest. I'll play the maid here!"

As he busied himself with clearing the dishes from the table and placing them in neat stacks on the tray, Brenna moved to the bed. He was nearly to the door with the laden tray when her voice stopped him.

"Raymond."

"Aye?"

"When you are finished downstairs. . . will you come back up to bid me good-night?"

"I—aye, I will," he stammered, and went quickly out the door.

Brenna moved to the window, the sheer gauze of her gown wafting behind her from the soft breeze. As she looked out across the moonlit rooftops of London town she felt her heart fill with a calm peace and happiness she had not felt in a very long time. So much had happened in her short life, most of it difficult to bear. But now she was well, and her father, thank God, was well, and even Raymond seemed to be fully recovered from the debilitating melancholy that had consumed him as the plague had consumed others.

She breathed deeply of the exhilarating night air and whispered a silent oath to herself that, to the best of her ability, the rest of her life would be filled with love and happiness.

There was a tentative knock on the bedroom door.

"Come in, Raymond."

Brenna turned from the window as her husband entered the room. The moonlight sifted through her sheer gown, outlining the perfection of her body, and the flickering light from the candle cast an alabaster glow over the soft curves of her face.

Slowly, she raised her arms and shrugged out of the chemise, letting it softly crumple to the floor.

Raymond's breath caught in his throat as he gazed at his wife's naked loveliness.

There were no words between them, and none were needed. His eyes devoured every movement of her body, every ripple beneath the smooth skin as she walked toward the bed.

Once there, she lifted the candle until the flickering light danced across her breasts. There was a brief puff of air from her pursed lips and the hue of her skin turned from shadowed fire to an eerie moonlight blue.

He stood, rooted to the spot, as she slid into the bed, not bothering to cover her naked loveliness with the sheet.

"Come, Raymond," she whispered, patting the bed beside her, "lie with me awhile."

"Brenna. . .I—"

Her arms extended toward him. Slowly, with halting steps, he moved until their fingers touched and entwined.

"Raymond. . .are you afraid of me. . .of us?"

"I—aye, damme, I think I am," he blurted.

"Good. So am I."

She took his face in her hand and brought his lips to hers. Slowly, sweetly, she kissed him until she felt his body relax.

"Oh, Brenna. . .my beautiful, darling Brenna," he murmured.

Ages later Brenna lay, her dark head cradled in the crook of Raymond's arm.

Now, she thought, *I've been truly loved by two men. At long last the marriage of the Viscount and Viscountess Poole has been consummated.*

CHAPTER THIRTY-EIGHT
FRANCE

THE PROCESSION OF THE NEW QUEEN OF ENGLAND left Paris on a sunny May morning. The roadway was thronged with cheering people. With her guard before her and her retinue at her heels, the queen bounced along in a red velvet litter borne by two mules. The archers, guilds and trumpeters of Paris joined the pageantry of the passing parade, adding to the color and glitter. Even the mules were draped in crimson cloth embroidered with aigrettes.

At St. Denis, the Parisian contingent returned to the city and Henrietta Maria transferred from the litter to a magnificent coach-and-four. The royal party then wound through the French countryside toward Boulogne by way of Amiens. In every town and village there were pageants, parades, fireworks and plays that would be attended. It would be over a fortnight before they touched English soil and, at best, a week more before they reached London.

At the head of the column rode Rory O'Hara, resplendent in his high, top-rolled boots, in his gaily plumed cavalier's hat and jaunty cape that trailed over the rump of his horse. But his face was grim and his thoughts were far from the winding French lane he rode.

The time had come. He was on his way to England and he longed to get on with it. Any delay nettled him.

But delays there would be, and Rory knew it. Many peasants and farmers had never set eyes on a member of the royal family. To have all in the same train the Queen of France, Anne, the Queen Mother, Marie de Médicis, the new Queen of England, and the heir apparent, Gaston, Duc d'Orléans, was a once-in-a-lifetime treat that could not be denied the people.

The royal assemblage halted the first night at Chantilly, where the castle of the Duc de Chatelet had been prepared.

A pageant on the great lawn accompanied the evening meal, followed by a huge display of fireworks. Because of his station, O'Hara, as captain of the Queen's guard, was obliged to stand directly behind his mistress through the entire ordeal. He was tired, but the pity he felt for the little dark-haired queen overcame his own weariness. She sat, benumbed by the past month's balls, galas and other festivities leading up to the proxy wedding.

When he saw her eyes close and her head sag, he was immediately at her side. "Your Majesty."

"Yes, yes?" Henrietta Maria said, her eyes popping open, the lids blinking furiously as she tried to orient her thoughts.

"Your Majesty," Rory said, just low enough for the local officials seated around her to hear. "Your pet, the poodle Pepé, howls mournfully. I fear he has been taken with a malady from his evening meal."

"Oh, dear, I must to him at once! Pray excuse me all."

There were no sour faces nor objections. All present knew how much the young queen doted on her four poodles.

Walking on O'Hara's arm toward her quarters and trailed by her ladies-in-waiting, Henrietta Maria's dark eyes rolled upward and met his.

"I trust, captain, that by the time I arrive, Pepé will have made a remarkable recovery?"

"Aye, I do believe he has already, Your Majesty."

"Thank you, captain. Every day I respect *monsieur le cardinal*'s choice in leaders more and more."

It wasn't only for his mistress that Rory had extricated them from the nighttime display. He was bone-tired and brain-weary himself. In his own quarters he shucked hat, cape and sword at once and called for his aide-de-camp and valet.

"André...André, my boots, dammit. I would to bed."

He poured a goblet of brandy, lolled back in a wide, comfortable chair and let his eyes flutter shut.

He felt one leg being raised and a boot removed. Just as the second boot left his foot, a scent of strong perfume filled his nostrils. His eyes flew open.

"Carlotta! How—"

"It seems your André has lusted after my maid, Isabelle, for weeks."

"The fool," Rory hissed, and jumped to his feet.

He had barely taken one step toward the door when she blocked his way, her hands raised, cradling his face.

"I have never forgotten that night so long ago, O'Hara."

"I have."

The smile on her red lips only widened at his retort. She moved closer to him until the softness of her breasts grazed his chest. Again the intoxicating scent from her blond hair filled his nostrils. No matter how he tried, he couldn't stop his eyes from dropping down to the dark hollow between her breasts.

Carlotta caught the look and brazenly inhaled to swell her bosom's roundness upward from the lace of her bodice. "Then 'tis time your memory was jogged. Are you still like a bull, Irishman?"

Her arms tugged his head downward until their lips met. Rory's head swam as her lithe, angular body with its inviting swells and hollows writhed against him. His own arms curled around her and his hands cupped the full firmness of her buttocks as her serpentine tongue found its way between his lips.

The kiss is sweet, he thought, *like honey—or as the*

nectar of the apple must have been when Adam took the first bite.

Deftly he swooped her into his arms.

"Yes, lover, yes!" Carlotta whispered, her teeth nibbling at his ear. "Take me like the animal I remember you to be!"

Suddenly she found herself standing in the hall outside his door.

"The animal, *madame la duchesse,* has been tamed."

"You fool...you peasant...you, you...Irishman! You'll regret—"

Rory slammed the door and locked it, effectively cutting off her protests.

Yes, he thought, stripping his quaking body and falling across the bed, *I probably will regret it.*

"In fact," he said aloud with a chuckle, holding his shaking hands in front of his eyes, "in a way I already do, Carlotta. But not for the reasons you think!"

THE FOLLOWING MORNING there were two sour, anger-filled faces on the road: Carlotta's headed for Amiens, and André's, Rory's page, returning in the opposite direction to Paris.

More pageantry, parades and accepting of well-wishes and gifts plagued the entourage as they passed through even the tiniest of villages. At last, five days from Paris, they reached Amiens. Awaiting them in the courtyard were the lords Holland and Carlisle, who would accompany the party to Boulogne and across the channel to England.

The royal ladies alighted. Amenities were exchanged, bows were made, hands were kissed, and then a sudden hush fell over the whole assemblage. O'Hara followed the others' gaze to the top of the château's wide front stairs, and an involuntary gasp escaped his throat.

There, dressed like a king, in a white doublet studded with pearls in gold thread and a flowing cape of royal ermine, stood George Villiers, Duke of Buckingham.

The fool, Rory thought. The treaty arising from the marriage alliance was already in danger; Buckingham could scuttle it completely by defying Louis's edict to not set foot in France again.

The duke's tall body glided regally down the steps. The sensuous and cruel lips belied the charm on his handsome face as, one by one, he greeted the royal women.

As he knelt before Queen Anne of France, holding both her hands in his, his eyes held hers as if they were magnets. There was little doubt in Rory's mind as to what they were conveying, and he was sure none in the others present. In Buckingham's look they could all see raw, lustful desire.

Rory turned away, only to find Carlotta's eyes coolly appraising him with a look that said, *Touché, monsieur l'irlandais!*

It was then he remembered seeing Carlotta and Queen Anne together, hour after hour in their carriage, their heads bent close in rapt conversation. Carlotta had obviously been the funnel through which messages had been passed between Queen Anne and Buckingham. It was the duchess who had paved the way for Buckingham's arrival.

Beware, Carlotta, Rory thought. *In your desire for royal favor, you will one day intrigue too far!*

THE QUEEN MOTHER, MARIE DE MEDICIS, complained of aches in her rotund body from the jolting carriage. She convinced Henrietta Maria to postpone continuing the journey on to Boulogne for two days. This pleased no one more than the Duke of Buckingham, and it created chaos for Rory O'Hara.

The royal party, each and every one of them, was his responsibility. He knew Queen Anne's weakness. It was like a beacon every time she cast her eye on a handsome courtier. Even Rory himself had more than once been the recipient of a flirtatious glance from those smoldering eyes so full of frustration.

Damn Louis for a fool, he thought. *Why doesn't he bed his wife, or if not, keep her under lock and key?*

The gaiety and abandon of the court swelled now that they were away from Paris. The moment it was announced that there would be a four-day delay in Amiens, a general mood of frivolity set in. Within hours, liaisons were formed. Even discipline among the junior officers and guard broke down. The men searched the village for willing peasant girls.

The second evening, the court became even more lighthearted. A feast was laid out in the château's great room, and the sounds of revelry filled the night air. Rory had posted a guard around the château and the surrounding gardens. He could do little more. Royalty would do what royalty wished when they wished to do it.

He had drafted a letter to Richelieu that morning, complaining of the Duchesse de La Mardine and notifying the cardinal of Buckingham's arrival. Then he had torn it up. It would do little good. It would take three days for an answer to reach him from Paris. By then they would be gone.

And if he did get an answer—or order—he wasn't sure he would want it. King Louis's anger would know no bounds. Rory had no taste for escorting the Duke of

Buckingham to Boulogne under arrest. Then he would reach England's shores as an enemy of that country's most powerful man.

Footmen reported to him every few minutes on the progress of the evening's meal. The Queen Mother had retired, as had Henrietta Maria. Both had graciously given their ladies permission to continue their revelries.

Rory cursed.

Gaston, the Dauphin, with two of his courtiers had retired to his quarters and demanded that whores be brought to them.

The English lords had made obvious conquests among the French ladies. It was only a matter of time before they would disappear into the château's upstairs bedrooms.

Madame Saint-Georges had suggested dancing. Buckingham then suggested the entire party adjourn to the gardens for a breath of night air. The Duchesse de La Mardine and Queen Anne had both concurred.

Moments later, they streamed in couples from the wide oak and glass doors of the château's great room. High hedges created a maze throughout the enormous gardens. Torches blazed above each archway, but many of the pebbled pathways and stone benches in tiny alcoves still lay in secluded shadows.

The garden was filled with whispering voices and the swishing sound of silk and satin. As O'Hara watched the bejeweled women and the gallants beside them stroll away in every direction, he suddenly felt dejected.

What care I, he thought, *if this woman cares so little for her honor, or the honor of her adopted nation, that she would cuckold its king?*

But he knew he did care. He cared because his reaching England depended upon his being here. If Queen

Anne succumbed to the English favorite's charms, Rory would be blamed. It was the way the minds of kings worked.

He bolted from the veranda and moved down one of the wider, main paths of the garden. Faster and louder his boots crunched the pebbles as his eyes searched the couples for Queen Anne's green cloak and tiara-topped dark coif.

"Come, Irishman, walk with me! I am unescorted!" Carlotta materialized by his side, slipping her arm through his.

"Does nothing cool your ardor, Carlotta?" he hissed, trying with no success to free himself.

"Nothing, and I forgive you. Come along."

He gave up and matched her steps, his eyes still scanning the strolling couples.

"Methinks you've already picked a wench, the way your eyes dart about, searching."

"Aye," he smiled, "I have."

He could feel the duchess's body stiffen beside him, but still she continued to guide him, chattering at the same time.

"What sort of milkmaid or other slovenly peasant wench is my rival tonight?"

"Your maid, Isabelle, perhaps. André did tell me before he left that she was indeed a wild wench beneath the sheets."

"Good," Carlotta said in a tight voice. "Tell me if you have any trouble in your arrangements. Perhaps I can aid you. The slut does my bidding in all matters."

Rory noticed that they had returned twice to a fountain. Each time he had swerved to the right, only to be tugged left by Carlotta. This time he wrenched his arm free and moved toward the archway to the right.

"You fool," Carlotta hissed after him. "Don't go in there!"

Rory halted abruptly. She was right, of course. He was damned if he did and damned if he didn't. What right did a mere captain of the guard, and an Irishman at that, have to interfere with the business of a French queen?

He was about to rejoin the duchess when a feminine gasp of pain reached his ears from the other side of the hedge. Quickly it was followed by a half-muffled voice.

"*Monsieur*, my arm—how dare you. I command you—"

The voice was stilled, but Rory recognized it. He was through the archway in three strides. One glance gave him the entire story. The queen's flirtatious replies to Buckingham's overtures had gotten out of hand.

Her bare shoulders were pressed against the rough back of a walnut tree. The tiara had fallen from her hair and lay at her feet, along with the green cloak she had been wearing.

One side of her bodice had been pulled down until a breast was fully bared. There was a look of pain and stark humiliation on Anne's face as she struggled to free herself from Buckingham's grasp.

The duke held her flailing arms by the wrists, and his face was buried between her heaving breasts.

"Good evening, Your Majesty," Rory said loudly. "I believe you wanted an escort to your quarters."

Buckingham's saturnine face turned. His eyes took in Rory's uniform, and without releasing the queen, he sneered, "Be off, you fool."

O'Hara could hardly believe the man's gall and

audacity. He spoke the words and then calmly turned his face back to the queen's breast.

"By your leave, Your Grace," Rory replied, "but I believe Her Majesty would have you be off." He glanced quickly at the queen and breathed a quick sigh of relief when her eyes told him he had guessed correctly.

The duke's usually calm features grew red with fury. So much so that his perfectly trimmed and pointed *beard royale* seemed to quiver. He loosed Anne's wrists and stepped toward Rory.

"Did you not hear me, swine? I said be off! Do you know to whom you speak?"

"Begging your leave again, Your Grace, but I know full well to whom I speak. I also know that the man to whom I speak has been pawing the Queen of France."

Buckingham's hand moved like a whip as he pulled a pair of gauntlet gloves from his sash. Just as quickly, he whipped them across Rory's face in a stinging blow.

"My compliments on your taste, Your Grace," Rory grated from between clenched teeth. "Your gloves are of the softest leather."

The gloves were dropped as Buckingham's hand went to his sword. His fingers had barely touched the jeweled hilt when Rory's blade hissed free of its scabbard and the point danced in the torchlight before the duke's eyes.

"You are a bloody fool. You would draw your blade on *me*?"

"Your Grace, as you can see. . . I already have."

Buckingham growled like a wounded animal and tugged frantically at his sword hilt. The point of Rory's blade whistled as it slashed five, six, seven times across the front of the duke's satin doublet.

"I think the madness caused by Queen Anne's beauty

is only momentary in Your Grace. . . isn't it?" Rory insisted.

Buckingham's face paled as he looked down at the tattered remnants of his doublet. When he looked back up, Rory was sure he had never seen such hatred in a man's eyes.

"Who are you?" the duke demanded.

"O'Hara, m'lord, Rory O'Hara, captain of the queen's guard."

Buckingham's eyes narrowed, and his forehead furrowed in concentration. Then he smiled, and Rory knew that he remembered.

"Captain of *which* queen's guard?"

"Henrietta Maria," Rory replied, with a sinking feeling in the pit of his belly.

The smile became a leer. "Good. That means you will soon be in England." The leer faded and the duke's face became as darkly brooding as a storm cloud as he turned and stalked through the archway.

Rory turned his attention to Queen Anne. She had repaired her décolletage and replaced the tiara in her hair. Rory retrieved the green cloak and draped it around her shoulders.

When he stepped back, her hands were clasped tightly in front of her and her eyes held steadily to the ground. O'Hara's heart went out to her, this poor woman who had been brought from Spain when only a child, to marry another child. She could not truly be held at fault for wanting love, when the child she had married had grown into such an unloving man.

"Your Majesty," he said softly.

"Yes?"

"I think this entire evening has been but a dream, and when you awaken you'll remember it as such."

"And—and you, captain?" came the tiny voice from the tree's shadows.

"I never dream, Your Majesty. 'Tis impossible to remember what never was."

Her face came up and in the flickering torchlight Rory could see two dark lines of tears down her cheeks.

"A foolish woman thanks you, Captain Rory O'Hara, and wishes to tell you that if the bad dream is forgotten, she will never forget the one who swept it away."

Rory bowed slightly from the waist as her slippered feet moved lightly toward the arch. Beneath the leafy boughs, she paused.

"Captain?"

"Your Majesty."

"Would you—would you have. . . ?"

"Most assuredly, Your Majesty. Like a pig on a spit."

He heard her gasp, saw her shoulders quake beneath the cloak, and then she was gone.

He waited a few moments and then stepped through the archway. A step on the pathway to his rear brought him spinning around. It was Carlotta, idly tapping the tip of her nose with an open fan in a white-gloved hand. The fan lowered slowly to reveal the smile of Circe on her darkly crimsoned lips.

"It would seem, Irishman, that I have made a friend in England. . . and you have made an enemy."

CHAPTER THIRTY-NINE
ENGLAND

RAYMOND SECURED COMFORTABLE QUARTERS for them on the south side of the Thames, near Lambeth Palace. In defiance of Buckingham's order that they should live apart, he and Brenna moved in to live once more as man and wife.

Raymond vowed that upon Buckingham's return from France, he would go back to court, regain his position and the control of their lands.

"For the first time," he told her, "I have something in my grasp that will bolster me into standing up to my cousin!"

Brenna smiled encouragement at his words, but in her heart she knew differently. Raymond was a good, kind and gentle man, but he was weak and easily cowed. For that reason she accompanied her husband when he was summoned to York House and an audience with his fire-breathing old aunt, Lady Compton.

"It will be but a moment," a liveried footman said, motioning them to seats in an alcove just outside the enormous parlor where Lady Compton held court at York House.

Behind the massive, hand-carved doors they could hear voices raised in bitter argument. One they could recognize as Lady Compton's; the other was more like a growling bear than a man's.

Suddenly the doors burst wide and a tall, lank man in the uniform of a lieutenant in Buckingham's guard burst from the room.

"Sir, do you realize to whom you speak?" came Lady Compton's voice from behind him.

"Aye, I do, m'lady," the man replied, thrusting his left arm into the air, revealing a crippled, withered hand. "I know well I speak to the mother of the son who would deny me the king's justice!"

"Be gone!"

"'Twas because of yer son I took the wound that caused this," he shouted, waving his hand in the air. "And now ye would deny me the captaincy he promised me because of it!"

Lady Compton appeared in the center of the doorway. She was bent now and gray, hobbling on two canes, but she was still her domineering self as she shouted the man down.

"Be off from here, you creature! And best you be off from London as well before the duke returns, lest you also lose the use of your other hand!"

"Aye, I'll be gone," he replied, his voice again dropping to a menacing growl. "But, mark me, you've not heard the last of John Felton."

Then he whirled. For the briefest of moments his wild, protruding eyes locked on Brenna's, sending a ripple of fear up her spine. His eyes were huge but the pupils were tiny, almost minute, and coal black. They were like the haunted eyes of a cornered animal. Then his heavy boots were clomping across the oaken floor and he was gone.

Lady Compton stared at them for a moment, and then spoke. "Come in—you, not her." She turned and tap, tap, tapped her way out of sight.

Brenna and Raymond exchanged looks.

"No, Raymond," she said, rising and taking his arm.

Together they walked into an oak-paneled room with a high-beamed ceiling and walls lined with art. From the Titians on the walls to the huge Persian rug on the floor, the room was a monument to the Villierses' ability to buy and accumulate.

Lady Compton had seated herself on a damask-and-velvet chaise that looked more like a throne on its raised dais. She was as regally dressed as always, in yards of black satin that covered all of her but her blue-veined hands and her harsh, wrinkled and unsmiling face.

"I told you—"

Raymond grasped one of her hands and quickly brought it to his lips. "Madam, she is my wife."

"She is the woman who has bewitched you, who denies you children because all those in league with the devil have in them barren wombs!"

"M'lady, I beg you—"

"You would beg for a witch?"

"She is not a witch. She is a sinned-against woman, driven by you and your son—my cousin—from pillar to post, from degradation to shame, from—"

"Silence!" cried the old woman, pounding her canes on the dais.

Raymond lurched backward as if he had been struck. There was the merest chance that, if it were his cousin rather than his steel-spined aunt facing him now, Raymond might have the mettle to stand up to his family.

But it wasn't, and Brenna knew this day's battle could better be waged woman to woman. She stepped forward and looped her arm through her husband's. Tightly she grasped his elbow and turned him toward the door. "Come, Raymond."

"But Brenna, if we are to ever—"

"Shhh!"

Behind them, Lady Compton's gleeful laugh was almost a cackle. "Aye, be off, both of you!"

Brenna opened the door and gave her husband a gentle shove into the outer room. "Wait, Raymond."

Raymond realized her intention, but before he could stop her Brenna had resoundingly slammed the heavy door behind him. She turned the key, removed it and, as she turned back to face her enemy, dropped it down the front of her bodice.

"How dare you!" Lady Compton cried, standing and pounding one of her two canes on the floor.

There was no hatred in Brenna's expression, only calm determination as she put one slippered foot on the dais and leaned toward the woman. Both her hands came forward, grasped the canes and yanked them from Lady Compton's white-knuckled fists.

"Ayeee, the witch would kill me!" the old crone bellowed. She steadied herself against the chaise and then, having no choice, sat back down with a thump. "It will be the Fleet for you! Give me back—"

The canes skittered across the carpet and clattered against a far wall. Lady Compton gasped, fear in her eyes now as her hands clasped one another tightly and came up between her breasts.

"Quiet, you greedy, spiteful, hateful old woman!" Brenna hissed, her face inches away from her adversary's.

Lady Compton went pale. It had gone beyond a mere affront now. She was being challenged, and all the power of her position couldn't help her at that moment.

"You would slay me!"

"I don't have to," Brenna replied, "for the evil bile of hate that has built up in you all these years will be your winding sheet soon enough. But in the meantime, I would have you recognize the duty I owe a husband and the affection I bear him."

"I would remind you, madam—"

"Nay," Brenna cried, holding up a silencing hand, "I would tell *you*! You have dispensed with the laws of God to keep Raymond and me apart, and aggravate his melancholy further by denying us our means. I came no beggar to this marriage, yet you would add ills to ills and make me one. I give you fair warning, old woman, for your own honor and conscience' sake. Take some course to give me satisfaction, to tie my tongue from crying to the world for vengeance for the dealing I have received!"

Brenna took a deep breath and stood to her full height, staring intently at the black-clad figure before her.

"If you don't, I will drape my sash of title over rags and go begging in the streets of London. I will tell all who would lend an ear of the deprivation you have caused. I will rail at pauper, thief and peasant alike that it is no wonder they lack bread on their table when a peer of the court under Lord Buckingham hasn't the means to fill her belly."

The old woman's shrewd eyes narrowed now, calculating Brenna's words. Her son was hated and she knew it. The ills of the country rested on Buckingham's doorstep. Soon Charles would be crowned, and it behooved the Villiers family to convince the people to believe the fairy tale that there would be changes with the new king.

"You would do that? . . . Take to the streets?" Lady Compton asked haltingly.

"Aye, and more. I would tell the world how I was brought to this marriage that night in Chinon. All of London would love to know how the murderess, Frances Howard, gained the freedom to ride through the streets while those she conspired with, those men and women of lower station, were hanged."

Lady Compton settled against an arm of the chaise. Her breath came in great rattling gasps. "What would you have of me?"

"Naught but the means that are lawfully due us and the right to live in peace without harrassment from you and your sons."

Lady Compton's eyes fluttered and her lips trembled. She was beaten, and she knew it. But only for the time being. "You have it. Now leave me!"

"Gladly," Brenna said, moving to the door. "And should you change your mind, m'lady, I beg you to remember I have a dress and cloak of rags constantly at hand."

THE NEW QUEEN OF ENGLAND had landed at Dover, where she had spent her first night on English soil. King Charles had met the party at Canterbury the following day. Rumor had it that, unlike his father, Charles could not wait until the second wedding had taken place in London. The marriage had been consummated that very night.

Now King Charles and Queen Henrietta Maria were arriving in London. Even though the plague had not completely abated and the rain came down in blinding sheets, thousands lined the Thames to watch the approach of the royal barge. Hundreds more cheered the royal couple from houses along the river or from boats that followed along, darting back and forth in the barge's wake. Cannon boomed from the Tower as well as from the ships of the royal navy, and the air was filled with the clanging of church bells.

Beneath a hastily erected pavilion in the gardens of Somerset House more than two hundred peers of the realm awaited the royal barge. Among them stood Viscount and Viscountess Poole.

Brenna was smiling, more sure of herself and her future than she had been in years.

Her husband was handsomely attired in a crisp new blue doublet of the finest silk. His hose, boots and breeches were also new, as was the wide-brimmed hat that sat jauntily on his head.

The viscountess had arrayed herself in the finest costume she could find. She was also dressed in blue, a summery, sky-blue voile blouse beneath a wesket of navy satin and a flowing skirt to match. In place of a stomacher, she wore a wide pink sash that matched the ribbons in her hair. Her feet and ankles were encased in silk hose and low-cut white slippers embroidered in blue-and-gold thread.

Not all, but most of the allowance due them from her dowry had been reinstated by Lady Compton.

A great cheer erupted from those standing at the head of the waterstairs, and hats sailed into the air. The royal barge had appeared and there stood Charles and his new bride. They were both dressed in green from head to toe and smiling broadly as they waved to the crowds.

The lumbering barge left midstream and minutes later rocked against the bumpers at the foot of the stairs of Somerset House. A glowering Duke of Buckingham was the first to set foot on land, closely followed by the lords Holland and Carlisle.

The crowd surged forward, carrying Brenna and Raymond with them. She saw colorfully dressed soldiers, crosses emblazoned on their chests. Beautifully dressed and coiffed women were helped from the barge. Then there were two flashes of royal green, and the massed bodies came together in front of her, blocking Brenna's view.

A receiving line was quickly formed once the king and queen had entered the garden proper. One by one, by order of their rank, the gentlemen of the court and their ladies stepped forward to greet the new queen and congratulate the king.

"She is lovely," Raymond whispered.

"She is," Brenna agreed, "but she is so young, and she looks so tiny and fragile!"

How difficult her life will be, Brenna thought, looking at the young girl who had been thrust into this marriage of state. She would be a Catholic emissary in a Protestant country. Laws had been enacted against her faith, and there was already talk that the new Parliament would demand that her husband, the king, enact stronger enforcements of those laws.

And if religion did not become a stumbling block in her marriage then surely the tall, flaxen-haired man standing a few paces behind her would. For it was already said in court circles that the Duke of Buckingham would brook no interference from the new queen in matters of state or religion. No one, even his queen, would have more influence over Charles than the duke himself.

Brenna shuddered when she thought of the struggle for power that would soon come.

"The Viscount and Viscountess Poole," said the steward, hitting the ground three times with his gold-headed staff.

Brenna and Raymond stepped forward. The viscount bent to one knee before his monarch. Brenna curtsied, and together they murmured, "Your Majesty."

Charles cast a puzzled look toward Buckingham and then turned back to the couple. "Our eyes are made glad by the reuniting of your family, Lord Poole."

"I thank you, Your Majesty," Raymond mumbled, and kissed first the king's hand and then the queen's.

Queen Henrietta Maria's gloved hand trembled like the wing of a captured dove in Brenna's. Brenna kissed it, and looked up to meet the queen's frightened stare.

"I do hope, Your Majesty," Brenna began in perfect French, "that you find our land and ways not too harsh, and any sadness in leaving your own court will quickly be lost when you learn of your new subjects' love."

The queen's dark eyes grew wide and Brenna was sure she detected relief in their gaze. "Your French, madam, is impeccable...as if it were your native tongue. Please call on us here at our new home...uh—"

"Somerset House," Brenna offered.

"Yes, here, just as soon as we are settled."

"It will give me the greatest of pleasure, Your Majesty."

Brenna and Raymond moved away from the royal couple as the steward again banged his staff. "Sir Roland and Lady Jane Newport!"

"What did you say to her that elated her so?" Raymond whispered, linking his arm through Brenna's.

"'Twas not what I said, but how I said it. Her Majesty will need some English women in her court. Those that speak French will have the greater chance for invitation."

Raymond smiled. "I do believe you've caught some of your mother's flair."

They moved arm in arm down the path to make room for those in the rear of the packed crowd to move closer to the king and queen. At last they reached the steps leading up to the porticoed rear entrance to Somerset House. Guardsmen lined the steps, from the ground upward to wide glass and oak-paneled doors.

They were halfway up the steps when Brenna stopped with a gasp. Her arm tightened on Raymond's and her body swayed against him.

"Brenna, my dear, what is it?"

She said nothing. Her gloved hand gripped his arm like a vise. Her lower lip had curled between her even white teeth, and her whole face was drained of color.

Raymond followed her gaze upward. The object of his wife's attention and sudden fright was a man slightly shorter than himself but nearly twice as full in the chest and wide in the shoulder. Unruly dark hair flowed from beneath his wide-brimmed hat and captain's epaulets gleamed on the shoulders of his red-and-silver tunic.

What would so unnerve her, Raymond wondered, about a French captain in the queen's guard? And then he saw the dark, square-jawed face and the intensity in the black eyes as they returned Brenna's stare.

Raymond's heart sank as he looked back at Brenna. He knew. There was no mistaking the shocked look in her eyes.

The knowledge was confirmed when a beautiful blond woman in a flowing white dress passed them and spoke to the officer.

"Captain O'Hara, are you ill? You look as if you've seen a ghost."

CHAPTER FORTY
ENGLAND

IT WAS ONLY A MATTER OF DAYS before Rory O'Hara heard the complete tale of the Viscount and Viscountess Poole's stormy marriage. The story changed depending on the teller, but it wasn't difficult for Rory to ascertain the rocky path Brenna had trod in the years since he had last seen her.

There was no doubt in O'Hara's mind that he still loved her as much or more than before. He had known it the instant he had laid eyes upon her. The years had melted away, and he had barely been able to hold himself in check. His impulse had been to step forward, throw his arms around her and cover her face with his kisses. And he was certain that he had detected the same light of love in her eyes.

But moments earlier, before she had seen him, she had looked radiantly happy on her husband's arm. Did he dare to usurp that happiness?

Could he?

Had Brenna made this choice from her own free will? Was Hubbard, after all, the man that she loved? Had that been the reason for her decision to flee France that night and return to England?

O'Hara's quandary, rather than nearing a solution, was compounded tenfold. For the time being he resolved to wait, to see if she would contact him. It was the easy course, made easier by the burden of his duties at court.

The Duke of Buckingham had lost no time since his return to setting forward a plan to discredit Rory. He had started with the queen. When Henrietta Maria refused to listen, the duke went before king and council, pleading O'Hara's agreement of years before that he would remain in Ireland and outside politics.

Wearily, Charles sent a message to his new brother-in-law, Louis XIII of France, requesting the Irishman's recall. Rory was sure the denial to the request had come from Richelieu as much as King Louis.

O'Hara wrote to Shanna and Talbot, stating his misgivings and what he had discovered about Brenna. The reply was swift.

My dearest and only brother,

It was with a sad heart that I received your letter, but isn't it as I have said it would be? She has been torn from you, and you from her. Though beneath the ashes the embers may still glow, I fear the fire is gone.

Give it up, dear brother, and return to the bosom of your own family and your own land. Little Maura calls out often for her Uncle Rory. Patrick already has his legs and grows into a fine Irish lad. And you would blink in disbelief to see Aileen now. She is beautiful and far from the child you think her to be.

They miss you, dear brother. We all miss you and wish you would return to those who truly love you.

Your loving sister, Shanna

Rory began to write yet another letter, its gist being that he would return soon, but ripped the paper in half and discarded it.

For hours he would sit looking at the miniature in the golden locket and wondering. He worried constantly about meeting Brenna again and whether he would be able to hold his peace until she broke the silence.

And there were other worries, most of all the unhappiness of the young queen.

The English court was vastly different from the court of her brother in France. It lacked the pomp and pageantry she had grown up with. Compared to Louis's court, Charles's was austere for the reason that, unlike the French king, Charles was dependent on a tight-fisted Parliament for funds.

At court the presence of the queen's priests in their clerical robes angered the Puritans, and the presence of armed French cavaliers on English soil angered the populace. This in turn had so angered Henrietta Maria that she had refused to learn English and even disdained attending her husband's coronation.

Buckingham added coals to the fire constantly by being rude to the queen, ordering her about and even attempting to dictate her manner of dress. He also insisted that the queen take his mother and sister into her most intimate circle at court.

Henrietta Maria adamantly refused and retaliated by excluding all Englishwomen from her private circle except the one woman whom Buckingham hated above all others: the Lady Brenna Hubbard, Viscountess Poole.

RAYMOND'S FACE GLOWED FROM THE CRISP AUTUMN AIR as he walked into the sitting room. Two maids bustled about, packing large trunks under Brenna's direction. The somber look on Raymond's face turned into a scowl as he watched the dresses and petticoats disappear into the trunks.

"A good ride?" Brenna asked, bussing him on the cheek and returning her attention to the maids. "No, Mary, not the pink. The queen can't stand the color around her."

Raymond poured a glass of brandy and walked to the window. There, with his back to the activity, he sipped the stinging liquid and slapped the quirt he held against his thigh.

Brenna paid no attention to the sound for several moments. Then, when it became a steady, rhythmic tapping that unnerved the maids she could ignore it no longer.

"Raymond, must you do that?"

"Aye, I must," he replied in a harsh, rasping voice, shifting the riding whip to the window seat before him.

Brenna motioned in dismissal at the maids. When the door closed behind them, she joined her husband at the window. "Must we start the day as we ended the last—bickering?"

" 'Tis not bickering, 'tis discussion."

"Raymond." She grasped his arm in an effort to turn him toward her.

He shook her hand away and began tapping again on the window seat with his quirt. Brenna sighed, rubbing the tips of her fingers over her temples. Her head ached and her body was weary from lack of sleep. What had started out as a sane discussion the previous evening had ended near dawn in a shouting argument.

The king had dissolved Parliament when Sir Edward Coke had risen to demand a better explanation from Buckingham about the money he requested for the Spanish war and other foreign affairs. When no explanation came, Coke convinced Commons to deny the funds.

Charles had angrily told them all to go home and had announced a trip to the hunting preserve at New Forest. As a gentleman of the chamber, Raymond was obliged to go along.

The queen, having no taste for the hunt, had announced that she would spend the month at the Earl of Southampton's Titchfield Estates. As a lady-in-waiting to the queen, Brenna was obliged to accompany her.

"'Tis Buckingham's way of keeping us apart again!" Raymond insisted.

"It isn't!" Brenna countered. "'Tis the way of the court, and there is naught we can do about it."

"We can plead illness and stay here in London."

Brenna sighed. "Raymond, we have come so far. Nearly all our means have been returned to us. We live again as man and wife, without the shadow of your aunt hanging over us. We are in court favor, you with the king, I with the queen. Would you spoil all that now?"

"I? *I*? 'Tis not I who puts our favor in jeopardy, 'tis your father! 'Tis he who would write his new Magna Carta and dilute the king's power. 'Tis your mother who would refuse the king's request for the lease of Hatton House. Od's blood, woman, can't you speak some sense to the two of them before they ruin us all?"

Brenna exhaled another long sigh. It was true. Both Sir Edward and Lady Hatton were making Brenna's and Raymond's presence at court difficult. It was also true that neither of them would relent an inch at Brenna's request.

But this was not what was deeply troubling Raymond, what had taken away his usually calm and docile demeanor. She had seen the beginnings of his jealousy and its growth each day at court. She had seen it reflected on his face every time Rory O'Hara appeared. On the evening of any day the three of them had been in the same room, supper with Raymond became a hellish struggle.

"This Irishman, your O'Hara—"

"Raymond, he is not my O'Hara."

"The bastard has the face of a god, doesn't he? And the body to go with it. I would warrant he has the strength of ten. Have you noticed his hands? I would warrant he could crush a normal man with the grip of just one of those hands! They say this O'Hara is the lover of the blond Frenchwoman, the Duchesse de La Mardine."

Brenna ate in silence.

"It is rumored that it was O'Hara who brought my cousin, Buckingham, to heel in France. Few men would have the courage to draw a blade against the duke."

"Raymond, why do you torture yourself?"

"I? Is it I who am being tortured?"

The first few times Brenna had run from the room in tears. Eventually her good common sense had told her that it would one day end.

But it didn't. It went on and grew like a cancer in her husband's brain. Now Raymond's nightmare was coming true. For a whole month, his wife would be under the same roof with her lover while her husband was miles away.

Again Brenna put her hand on his arm, this time forcibly turning him to face her. "Raymond, let us bandy words no more and be out with it!"

There was no gentle softness nor pleading tenderness now in his large brown eyes as they stared down at her. "Aye, let us do that."

"I have barely glanced at him and not spoken to him in the months since he arrived. And, unless I am forced to do so through my duties to the queen, I won't in the future."

Raymond's lips curled into a mirthless, bloodless smile, and again the quirt began tapping at his thigh. "Then 'tis truly over? You have no memories, no thoughts at all of him?"

"I. . . ."

Her brief hesitation was enough to throw him into a fury. He whirled, the quirt like an extension of his arm. In a single motion he cleared goblets, decanters and glasses from the sideboard. Glass shattered against wall and floor, and before the pieces fell he was at the door.

"Raymond, I would be truthful. No one can totally forget the past. It returns to haunt us all. Raymond, I beg—"

The thudding slam of the door cut off her last words.

She sank to the window seat, groaning and holding her arms tightly to her sides. "Oh, dear God," she whispered. "I did not tell the truth, for I dare not."

Tearfully she stared out the window, across the Thames, at Somerset House. "Why did you come back, Rory O'Hara? Why did you come back into my life to remind me how shallow it is and has been without you?"

RICHELIEU'S INSTRUCTIONS WERE PLAIN, clear and precise. As head of the queen's household in England, O'Hara was expected to exercise his duties as Louis's emissary as well as the queen's keeper.

"And in so doing," Richelieu wrote, "you will do all in your power to maintain the French-English alliance as set forth in the marriage contract. You will do all in your power to create an aura of comfort about the queen to retain her happiness. And you will stress to

Buckingham and Charles that the King of France expects compliance with the promises the King of England has made, to suspend the religious laws against the Catholic faith in his country!"

All easier commanded than carried out.

Neither the English people nor Parliament knew of the secret agreements concerning religion that Charles had ceded in the marriage alliance. The king was forced to bow to the people and banish all priests except those in his queen's immediate retinue.

Rory knew that Richelieu actually meant, "keep England at war with Spain," in his comments about the French-English alliance. This was near impossible due to Parliament's lack of confidence in Buckingham. They would vote no money for the war.

O'Hara became a diplomat without portfolio and an advisor to whom no one would listen.

Frothing horses carried Rory from Titchfield to New Forest and back at the king's command.

"Captain, I would have you inform your mistress that her king and husband is in dire distress that she is not acquainting herself with the people!"

"Yes, Your Majesty."

"I would further have her informed that her sullen manner to myself and my court must come to an end, on pain of making the lady more unhappy than she would seem to be!"

The threat was implicit, and Rory took it as such.

"And one other thing, captain. . . ."

"Your Majesty."

"You are an Irishman. As such, you are a subject of the English crown. How is it that you are in the service of the French king?"

"By your leave, Your Majesty, but I am in the service of an English queen."

For a moment Charles was nonplussed. Then Buckingham whispered in his ear. "It has been brought to our attention that you still hold large grants of land in Ireland—a place called Ballylee."

"With all due respect, Your Majesty, I do not. The land you speak of is held by Sir David Talbot, a Scot. It was lawfully deeded to him by your father and His Grace, the Duke of Buckingham."

Rory knew that to avoid the maze of legal tangles neither the king nor the duke would pursue the matter of Ballylee. But the implied threat was there. Indeed, O'Hara was being threatened on all sides. Every other waking moment brought back the desire to give up his quest and flee.

But always in the next moment he would see her face, would remember the quick, darting glances from those dark eyes.

Was it love he saw in those glances? He couldn't be sure, but he couldn't give up until he knew.

In private audiences with the queen, Rory urged her to relent, to soften her attitude toward the people, the king's court and the king himself.

But Henrietta Maria the girl, had become Henrietta Maria the queen—petulant and commanding.

Rory suspected that much of her manner and attitude came from the tutelage of the duchess, but there was little he could do about it except offer more and more unheeded advice.

Ah, he thought often, *there is no man, least of all myself, who can ever completely understand the ways of women and kings!*

There was one avenue left open to the queen, but

O'Hara refused to take it. The Viscountess Poole was as close to Henrietta Maria as La Mardine was; perhaps closer. If Rory could convince Brenna to sway the queen to heed his words, the road for all of them might be smoother.

But that would mean private meetings and shared secrets with Brenna, perhaps against her will and desire. This Rory was not yet ready to do.

The fuse that set off the final explosion was a minor occurrence, but its detonation was heard all over England. On an otherwise calm and sunny Sunday morning, Buckingham's sister, the Countess of Denbigh, arranged for a Protestant service to be held in the great hall of Titchfield House.

O'Hara wasn't informed. Had he been, he would have been able to stop it or have it moved. As it was, he had been summoned yet again to New Forest by Buckingham. The matter was trivial, and after it had been dealt with Rory begged to be excused. But much to his surprise, Buckingham begged him to stay the day.

"Come, Irishman, I would test your skill at the hunt. Then perhaps we can talk out our differences over a good wine!"

At the end of the hunt, there was no wine and no talk. Rory was dismissed. When he reached Titchfield the following afternoon, he found out why.

The Countess of Denbigh had not only neglected to obtain Rory's permission for her Protestant services, she had also neglected to obtain the queen's.

Taking the affront to heart, Henrietta Maria had retaliated. At least ten times the queen had led her ladies and her four barking poodles through the middle of the Protestant services. Each time their laughter and chattering had grown louder, eventually bringing the service to an end.

By Monday evening the news had spread of the queen's slight to the English religion. The populace was outraged. The Archbishop of Canterbury demanded an apology. The king was livid, and both houses of Parliament together demanded that the queen's French retinue be sent packing, back to France. Through it all, the Duke of Buckingham remained silent.

And at the eye of the storm was Rory O'Hara. He had no choice left. Through a trusted aide, he sent a message to the Viscountess Poole.

THE LIGHT RAIN HAD TURNED TO SLEET by the time Brenna reached the outer perimeter of the gardens. She shivered as blast after blast of the stinging pellets hit her face.

She was thankful that she had worn heavy velvet riding clothes and, at the last minute, donned a velvet cloak lined with fur. But the chill persisted as she ran toward the distant gatehouse, reminding her that not all of it was caused by the winter storm.

Insane, she thought. *What you are doing is insane!*

She had ignored the first two messages from Rory, but the tone and plea of the last one couldn't be ignored.

> I beg you, nay, plead with you, dear lady, to meet with me as soon as possible. I, France and even England may depend on the outcome of such a meeting. You and only you may be able to reason in this matter with our queen.
>
> If it is because of the past, our past, that you

refuse to meet with me alone and in secret, I beg you to put your fears to rest. My reasons for this request are in no way personal, I assure you.

There was more, but Brenna had needed no further urging. From the receipt of the first message she had wanted to meet him. Only fear of discovery—and what it would do to Raymond's mind—had deterred her. But now O'Hara had placed it on a level she couldn't ignore.

She passed into the inky darkness beneath the gatehouse and paused to let her eyes adjust.

"M'lady—here!"

"Who is it?" she called. "Your name?"

"Phillipe, m'lady."

Brenna prayed that it was indeed the Phillipe of O'Hara's instructions and stepped from beneath the gatehouse arch. She cupped her hands over her eyes to shield them and saw him standing beside a tall bay. The horse stomped its forefeet in the cold and snorted steam from its expanded nostrils.

"Begging your pardon, m'lady, but it would have been improvident to saddle the mare with a side mount."

"No matter. I ride well and can handle her with one stirrup. A leg, quickly!"

The man called Phillipe took her hand and knelt on one knee. Brenna placed her booted foot on his other knee and slid into the saddle, her foot deftly finding the stirrup. The mare danced sideways, her head bouncing, mouth tearing at the bit.

"Easy. . . easy, girl," Brenna whispered, gentling the horse with a few tugs on the reins. "Where?" she asked, when the mare stood calmly.

"Follow the stream, there, about a mile. You'll come to a stand of beeches. Just beyond them is a lane. Go left another mile. To your right you'll see a cattle lean-to atop a low hill. 'Tis there the captain will be waiting."

Brenna nodded and reined the mare around. Once she was sure the path was solid and without rocks, she broke the bay into a trot and then a slow canter.

The icy pellets stung her face bitterly now, but she welcomed them. The pain they brought took her mind off the beating of her heart as she drew nearer and nearer to Rory O'Hara.

True to Phillipe's word, the path became a wide cart lane at the stand of beeches. Even though she could only see a few feet in front of her Brenna trusted the animal and gave her the rein.

Minutes later the slanted roof of the lean-to loomed on her right. She veered from the path and reined up just short of the roof's edge. Suddenly a hand came out of the darkness and grasped the mare's bridle.

In answer to Brenna's gasp of surprise, O'Hara spoke. "Don't be afraid—'tis me."

She dipped her head as the mare walked forward under the roof. She could hear the gentle lowing of the cattle farther away in the darkness and could smell the straw and dung.

Then his hands were at her waist.

"No, I—"

But her boots had already touched the ground. The skin beneath her clothes rippled where his hands had held her, and Brenna was glad he could not see her face in the darkness.

"There is a mound of straw over here. We can sit."

"No—no, I'll stand."

"As you wish," he replied. She couldn't tell if there was a hint of mockery in his voice or not. "I'm sorry, but likely there are shepherds about. We dare not light a candle."

"That's all right," she blurted. She heard him ease his own body to the straw. There was a rattle as he adjusted the baldric holding his sword and the sound of a sigh escaping his lips. "Your message was cryptic," she began. "I would know—"

There was another quick intake of breath and then his voice cut the darkness like a dagger. "Brenna, how goes the queen's mind about an apology to the archbishop?"

"She says that she will apologize for nothing, least of all to the head of a heathen religion."

"Damn her for the childish little fool she has become."

"Rory—"

"'Tis true. Listen, you—and most of England—do not know of secret terms in the marriage treaty. It is enough to say that Charles is ignoring them, but not always of his own mind."

"Buckingham?" Brenna whispered.

"Aye, the man would have favor and power any way he can, even at the expense of his own country. He would also take revenge upon me for a certain slight."

"I have heard," Brenna said, not masking in her voice the disgust she felt for the duke. "You should have killed him."

"Aye, I should have. But I didn't. And now he finds devious means to goad the queen in her childish ways and keep her and the king apart. Both Charles and Henrietta Maria play into Buckingham's hands, for the duke would have glory in the eyes of the people by becoming the savior of the French Protestants!"

"He would push us to war with France?"

"Aye, if he can."

"What can I do?" Brenna asked, trying to keep her mind on his words rather than the deep rumbling sound of his voice, which threatened to turn her knees to jelly.

"The queen admires you, Brenna. She respects your opinions. You are the one English link in her court."

"Aye."

"Use your influence with her. Make her see that such an apology is necessary. Convince her to learn English, and most of all, convince her to be more civil to the king!"

"I can try."

"Nay, you must do more than try. You must succeed."

She longed to move closer to him, to feel the strength of his presence. Instead she gripped the bay's bridle as if the horse would pull her back should she bend toward temptation.

"Why is it that an Irishman has become so involved in English and French affairs, Rory O'Hara?"

The answer was slow in coming. Across the void between them, Brenna felt that he was contriving a reason to give her rather than replying in truth.

"Trade with England, France and Spain is important to Ireland...and to Ballylee," he replied at last. "I would meddle in these politics to keep peace."

Brenna's heart fell. Then she had nothing to do with his return. But why should that sadden her? Had not she cursed his return not so very long ago?

She managed to keep a level tone in her voice when she spoke again. "And how is Ballylee?"

"Beautiful...prosperous."

"And David?"

"He and Shanna are married. They have two children. They are very happy."

Brenna slumped against the mare. She bit her lip to hold back her sobs, but she couldn't stop the tears that swelled from her eyes and ran down her cheeks.

"I must be back," she gasped.

"Are you happy, Brenna?" He had moved to her. His voice rumbled at her ear, and suddenly his hands rested on her shoulders. "Are you?"

She didn't struggle as he turned her into his arms. And then, when his lips brushed at the tears on her cheeks and eventually found hers, bells of warning went off in her brain.

"No...no," she mumbled against his lips as they became more insistent. "Please."

He kissed her harder. She felt her body begin to betray her, melting against his. He moaned her name and a hand crept beneath her cloak to cup her breast.

"By all that is right, I beg you, Rory O'Hara, go no farther!" she cried.

It was like a slap in the face. He took his arms from around her body and stepped back. Both could still feel the tension in the other's body and hear it emphasized in gasps for air.

"Forgive me. 'Twas my fault, but just your scent was enough to make me see your face, feel your softness, even in the dark and from a distance."

"Oh, dear God," she moaned, sobbing openly now. "It was almost over...so close. Why, why *did* you come back?"

"I lied before. 'Twas you, Brenna. My mind these years has been filled with naught but you. I must know why you did flee that night. The way of it threatened to unseat my mind if I stayed away much longer."

Again Brenna sagged against the bay. She daren't tell him the truth, for then he would surely guess, if he hadn't already, that the fire of her love for him had never dimmed.

Then there would never be an end to it.

"I returned to England because I came to my senses that night. I realized that our love was merely the foolishness and rebellion of youth."

"Brenna—"

"I realized that I am an Englishwoman, of English stock—born, bred and raised in English ways. I could never be an Irish farmer's wife in a heathen land."

"I don't believe you," Rory said, a rasping choke in his throat.

"Don't you now?" she replied, a little too loudly, grasping the mare's saddle for support.

"The way you returned my kiss just now—"

"Come now, Rory O'Hara, are you still so naive? I am a woman with some weakness and you are a handsome, virile devil, you must admit."

"Brenna, don't—"

"And if you need further proof, Irishman, take stock of me now and my position! I am a viscountess, wife of a peer. Could you have made me a viscountess in your troubled land?"

"I see."

The steellike new tone in his voice struck her heart like the point of a sharp spear, but she refused to relent.

"For the good of my king and country I will aid you, but I would have your word that what happened here tonight will never happen again."

"Indeed, m'lady. You have my word on it. A knee?"

"Thank you."

She vaulted quickly into the saddle so she would receive no more of his touch than was absolutely necessary.

"I will send word through my maid to your Phillipe when I can meet you again with news."

"Good," Rory said, stepping back from her horse's side. "And a word of caution. The Duchesse de La Mardine is a female Buckingham. She would flaunt the commands of her own king in order to gain favor and influence. Do not trust her."

"I know well the woman's contrivances and would avoid them. Good night."

The mare bolted from beneath the lean-to roof at a kick from Brenna's boot. She kept control over her body and nerves until she reached the stand of beeches. There she brought the mare to a walk and fell across her mount's neck, racked by anguished sobs.

CHAPTER FORTY-ONE
ENGLAND

FOR RAYMOND THE SCENE WAS REMINISCENT of another much like it that had taken place years before. He sat before the fire, staring into its flickering glow, thinking of Brenna, knowing that she did not love him.

Behind him sat his aunt, just as she had during the bargaining for Brenna's hand with Coke at Stoke Poges. But instead of Sir Edward as the room's third occupant, his cousin, Buckingham, stood a few paces to Raymond's left, warming his backside at the fire.

And instead of bargaining for Brenna's hand in marriage, they intended to bargain for her dowry once they had convinced Raymond that he should sue for divorce.

Buckingham spoke in a flinty voice. "What say you, cousin?"

"'Tis hard to believe. She gave me her word."

"The word of a witch!" Lady Compton hissed, but clamped shut her lips at a warning look from the duke.

"Come, come, Raymond," Buckingham pressed, "hasn't she admitted her former affair with the Irishman to you?"

"Aye, but—"

"I have told you of their meetings...their lying together on a bed of filthy straw in a lean-to—"

Raymond bolted from the chair and began pacing the room, his fingertips grinding at his temples as sweat popped out in beads on his forehead. "I cannot believe on the word of a mere maid—"

"More, cousin. The Duchesse de La Mardine has given you the dates and times of their meetings. She watched your wife ride back nightly from her debaucheries."

"Stop, stop!"

"One night they were even discovered by a herdsman!"

"How much proof do you need, nephew, to see that she has made a cuckold of you?" Lady Compton raged. "Must you feel the horns rising from your forehead?"

Proof, Raymond thought, the blood pounding in his fevered temples and the word roaring in his ears like shod hooves pounding on hard cobbles. At court he had seen the looks pass between Brenna and Rory.

"I have hurt you enough in the past, husband," Brenna had said. "I vow not to do it in the future."

How could she not hurt me, his mind screamed, *meeting like lovers in secret!*

Raymond wanted to believe in her with all his heart,

but the seeds of doubt had been planted the day her old lover had landed on English soil. Slowly, instead of frustration bringing on a kind of madness, causing a fever in his boiling brain, it was now jealousy and doubt.

"Proof!" he suddenly shouted, whirling on the smug faces of his aunt and cousin. "I would have proof rather than the whispered words of backbiting women behind fluttering fans!"

Buckingham exchanged a long look with his mother before giving her an imperceptible nod.

The old woman pulled herself to a standing position and hobbled to a massive oak chest. From her bodice she withdrew a key on a golden chain. When she turned back again, she held in her hand a thick packet tied with blue ribbon.

Raymond moved to his aunt and gingerly lifted the packet from her hand. "What—what is it?"

"Proof," she said. "Letters of love."

Breathing heavily, Raymond sank to his knees. As if he were touching a coiled snake, he carefully untied the ribbon.

Above him, Buckingham and Lady Compton smiled in satisfaction at each other. Days before, they had carefully sifted through the letters from the bottom of Brenna's jewel box, deleting those that were dated. They had also taken out any letters that alluded to France.

Raymond would never know that the letters hadn't been written within the last few months.

UPON THE COURT'S RETURN TO LONDON, Brenna felt buoyant for one moment and pitched into despair the next.

The diminutive queen had listened to her logic and

reasoning. At Hampton Court, Henrietta Maria was all smiles when she met her husband. Her words had been conciliating and boded for Charles a new attitude of obedience.

"I would beg my husband, the king, to forgive his wife, the queen, and forget the offense she has done to give him hurt," she had said.

A private apology was made to the archbishop concerning her affront to the English religion, and she vowed that in the future she would pay as much attention to her husband's advisors as she did her own.

Brenna was elated at the contribution she had made, but it was tempered by her husband's sullen moods. Her moments of despair came when Raymond would spend days away from her.

When he was under the same roof, he was a stranger. Long evenings were spent sitting in front of the hearth, brandy bottle in hand. No longer were there suggestions from him that they retire early. And not once since their return to London had there been a late-night tap on her door accompanied by Raymond's whispering voice.

No matter how hard she tried, Brenna was unable to penetrate the wall of silence he had built up around himself. He began to let the affairs concerning their lands go unattended. His actions at court took on a well-remembered strangeness, enough to revive the gossip that Viscount Poole had once again gone mad.

But this time Brenna herself began looking oddly at her husband. Indeed, there was a wildness about his eyes and a nervous tic to his lips that had never been there before.

And then she learned where Raymond had been spending his time while away from her. Half of it had been with his cousin, the duke, even though Raymond still professed a dislike for the man. The rest of the time, Brenna learned from her mother, he had spent with the bishop at Ely House.

On his short and infrequent forays back into her world, Brenna soon began to realize he was pulling further and further away from her.

Much of the time, in his conversation, he would ramble as if he were speaking to himself. When he would speak directly to her, his tone was curt.

"Tell me, wife—"

"Brenna, Raymond. Though they may now abound in England, we are not of the Puritan faith. . . yet."

"Aye, we are not, thank God."

"Raymond, what is it that is troubling you so?"

"Do you know that in the eyes of the church we are not married?"

"In the eyes of the Church of England, we are."

" 'Tis not the true faith. If you would join with me in the true faith, absolution could be yours through confession—"

"Confession? Raymond—"

"We eat and drink to our own damnation if we do not confess our immoralities along with our other sins."

"I have nothing to confess," Brenna had declared flatly, and left the room.

As the weeks passed, long days were spent wandering her quarters alone. When she would venture out, it seemed as though the specter of Rory O'Hara was everywhere: at court, riding in St. James Park, on the streets, even in a passing boat on the Thames.

And always she sensed the question in his eyes. *Why?*

In their subsequent meetings in the little lean-to, Brenna had done her best to hide her true feelings. But it had been nearly impossible, and eventually she knew that much of her brave speech that first night had been washed from his mind.

Every time she was near him and saw that crooked grin and the tousled black locks of his hair tumble over his handsome face, she felt her resolve weaken more and more.

There would come a time, and soon, when she would have to tell him she would no longer be able to meet him.

Rory was heavy on her mind the evening Raymond brought up the matter of religion again. They had been sitting in silence for some time, Brenna at her embroidery, Raymond staring in moody concentration into the fire.

"Catholicism, you know, is the religion to which those in grievous trouble have recourse—"

"Raymond, must we gnaw at this bone?"

"Aye, we must!" he said, his voice nearly a shout.

"Very well."

He leaned forward, wringing his hands, as if to force a calmness. When he spoke again, his tone was normal.

"It is a religion that offers solace as well as salvation to the sinner, no matter the sin...even to the adulterer."

The needle in Brenna's hand flew faster. "Then your cousin Buckingham should be your prime convert."

Raymond paid no attention. "Why is it, do you suppose, that you are not with child?"

The question brought her dark head up abruptly, lines of puzzlement creasing her forehead. She decided to reply lightly, with a quip. "Perhaps we have not tried hard enough?"

His head whirled and his eyes, blurred by drink, bored into her. " 'Tis part of the test," he intoned.

"Test?"

"Aye. For weeks now we have not lain together.'

"I know, Raymond."

"So when you begin to swell, if you do, the truth will be out!"

"Truth? Truth of what?"

He rose with difficulty from the chair and swayed to where she sat, his tall frame looming ominously over her.

"I know, Brenna."

She looked up into the sunken, haunted eyes of this man who was becoming like a stranger to her. "Know what, Raymond?" she asked, but somehow knew. It was the intensity in those eyes. They seemed to be stripping the clothes from her body and reading the very thoughts in her mind.

"Don't play the innocent with me!" he suddenly raged, his face florid with anger and drink. Brenna feared for an instant that he would actually strike her.

"Raymond, please. Cannot we sit and discuss whatever is bothering you calmly? Surely there is nothing—"

"Nothing? *Nothing?* You call cuckolding your husband behind his back *nothing*?"

"Raymond, what—"

"I know everything, you witch, don't you understand? I know of your secret meetings with the Irishman while at Titchfield! I know of your amours on a bed of filthy straw! I know—"

"You do not know!" Brenna cried, rising and facing her husband, her own anger riled now. "You have only heard rumors. . . and rumors from a source not too reliable, I'll wager!"

"I've seen the letters he has written you."

"Letters? There are no letters."

Suddenly he was lurching around the room, frantically searching. Then he found the object of his search and returned to loom over her.

"The book!" he shouted, thrusting the Bible toward her. "Swear on the book!"

"Swear? To what?"

"That you are not an adulteress."

"I am not!" she wailed in a choked sob.

The room was whirling before her eyes. Raymond's lips curled into a sneer, his whole face seeming to contort. Again he was screaming, his words pounding in her ears.

"On the book—your hand on the book! Swear, swear, swear at the risk of your eternal damnation."

"I swear, I swear!" she cried, placing both hands on the leather-bound Bible.

Raymond gasped. The book fell to the floor with a dull thud. "You have sent your soul to eternal damnation."

"I have sworn. What else would you have me do?"

"You don't even respect God," he moaned, frantically waving his arms in the air.

Sudden anger burned through Brenna's fear of him. She grasped the lace of his shirt and shook him with all the force in her arms. "This is insanity, Raymond. You have listened to them, now listen to me!"

His arm came around in a wide arc, the flat of his hand striking her cheek. The force of his blow spun her backward until she crashed into the wall. When her eyes cleared, she found herself sitting on the floor, gazing up at the shocked expression on Raymond's face.

"Good God, you are mad," she whispered.

IT TOOK VERY LITTLE TIME for Lady Compton to let it be known to town and court alike that the Viscount Poole had taken up residence in Suffolk without the viscountess. Gossips took up the hint, and word spread like fire in a dry meadow that the Viscountess Poole had committed an indiscretion with one of the queen's guards.

Brenna was talked about and stared at wherever she went. She was no longer welcome at court, and the few friends she had been able to make were suddenly not home to her calls.

And so she was not really surprised when a solicitor arrived one day at her door. With half an ear she listened to him drone on.

". . . and the Viscount Poole wishes to live, from this day forth, in seclusion apart from his wife. Because of his former feelings toward his wife, the viscount does not wish a divorce, only a separation. He agrees to provide the means for his wife's day-to-day living expenses, and. . . ."

Brenna gave little heed to the rest. It was over. Lady Compton had won at last. She felt that she, too, had sunk into a morass of near madness.

The final blow came when her own mother started doubting her innocence.

"Very well," Brenna had told her. "If I am to be damned, it will not be without reason."

Hounslow was a quiet, rather desolate village south of London, near the great heath. With the meager means allotted her, Brenna rented a cottage. She employed only two servants and instructed them that they would only be needed during the day.

Months passed. The court and the town found other gossip to occupy their wagging tongues. The Viscountess Poole was all but forgotten. Lady Compton, smug with victory, went on to other persecutions. Buckingham became immersed in trying to woo Parliament to his views.

Brenna at last wrote a long, detailed letter to Rory O'Hara. In it she explained everything that had taken place in her life since Chinon. And she confessed that, not only had her love for him never died, but indeed now burned brighter than ever.

Two nights after receiving the letter, O'Hara rode to Hounslow.

CHAPTER FORTY-TWO

IT WAS AWKWARD, not even like the one brief moment of passion when he had embraced and kissed her months before in the lean-to at Titchfield.

Words came hard. It had been so long, so many years. Then they had been thrown together at court, but forced to deny their feelings, their passion and need for each other.

Now it was there, at hand, possible and boiling. But neither seemed able to make the move needed to ignite the flame.

"I—I feel like a child," Brenna said. She was wrapped in his arms, her cheek against the velvet smoothness of his doublet.

"As do I."

"Kiss me, my darling."

His lips bent to hers. The kiss was tense, strained.

Then, suddenly, a low rumble came from his belly and Brenna pulled from his embrace.

They stared at one another, wide-eyed, until a slight smile appeared on Brenna's lips. It grew to a wide grin, and Rory matched it. Suddenly they both broke into wild peals of laughter.

"You're hungry, m'lord!"

"Aye, I've not had a bite since dawn."

"Stoke the hearth here and I'll prepare something in the kitchen."

"Your wood is low."

"Then chop some, you great oaf!" she giggled. "Would you have me call a servant and have him underfoot. . . later?"

Sheepishly, O'Hara shed his baldric and uniform jacket. Dressed in boots, breeches and cambric shirt, he made for the rear door of the cottage.

"Rory—your shirt."

He turned, pulling at the laces on his shirt front. Their eyes met and his hands stopped with the shirt half open.

"Why is it that you can suddenly make me feel so foolish?" he chuckled.

She turned away. "No more than you make me," she whispered.

He whipped the shirt off and stalked through the door.

Brenna bustled in the cottage kitchen, warming to the sound of ax on wood reaching her through the open window. She heated a hearty beef stew she had prepared earlier. When she heard his boots in the other room, she placed two tankards of ale on a tray and steamed them with the iron warmer from the kitchen's smaller fire.

"I thought an ale—"

As she entered the room, O'Hara had been crouched at the hearth, sparking the fire. It blazed up just as he turned to face her.

She stopped in midstep, gasping at the picture he made before the fire. The muscles of his wide chest and shoulders and his great arms rippled like pond water after a stone had been cast in. His mahogany skin, layered with a sheen of perspiration, seemed to glow from the dancing flames behind him.

Brenna had forgotten how big he was, how godlike that stern face could be, crowned as it was with a mass of dark hair. From across the room she could sense his maleness. It was like a heady perfume that made her head reel, and she felt herself melting with desire.

Rory saw the look in her eyes and stepped forward. "I love you."

There was a hoarseness to his voice that Brenna recognized as passion. The tray left her hands, crashing to the floor as she swayed forward into his arms.

Her lips welcomed his, and she felt the sweetness of his warm breath. His fingers curled into the hair at the back of her head, deepening the pressure of their kiss. She responded eagerly, running her hands over the slick skin of his chest before finding the rippling strength of his back.

Then, as his lips continued to devour hers, his hands began to move on her body, heightening her desire with each new place they touched. Somehow she moved her hands to her breast. Her quivering fingers tugged and pulled at the laces of her bodice until it opened. Then the dress fell away from her shoulders, baring her breasts. They were suddenly on fire as the hardened nipples pressed against his chest again.

She didn't bother unhooking the stays at her skirt, merely pulled until they gave. Then she pushed the dress and petticoats down until they puddled at her feet. She stood, trembling with the near unbearable tension of anticipation.

Rory took a step backward, caressing her naked loveliness with his eyes. "Dear God, you are beautiful."

One step and she was swept into his arms. His boots echoed like thunder in her ears as he moved through the cottage until he found the room he wanted.

Her body sank deep into the feather mattress and seconds later the weight of his own body rolled her toward him. She cupped her breasts and guided them to his eager lips.

His breath was like a hot flame over one nipple before he captured it with his mouth. Brenna curled her fingers in his hair and held him to her, aching with exquisite pleasure.

His hands found every hollow and curve of her body, building her need until she was writhing against him, letting him know that she yearned for more.

"I had almost willed myself to forget how wondrous was your touch," she breathed, nibbling at his earlobe.

His reply was wordless. Breathing harshly, he groaned and covered her body with his. His entrance was gentle yet demanding, sure yet painfully slow, as if he were waiting for her to join him.

And then she did, letting her whole body and being dissolve as one with his.

THEY LAY QUIETLY IN THE LIGHT of a single candle, their naked bodies pressed tightly together. Brenna ran her fingers through the thick mat of dark hair on his broad chest. Rory idly ran his hand up and down the silky length of her hair where it spread like an ebony halo on the pillow around her head.

It seemed that they had made love for hours. All the passion they had been denied for so long had boiled over time and again. Now they lay, sighing with mutual satiation.

"It was as if we had never been apart," she whispered.

"I think we never have been. I never stopped loving you, not for a moment," Rory replied, his hand now moving slowly over the curve of her waist.

"Nor I you," she said, "only I hadn't realized it until this moment."

Rory turned his head until his dark eyes found hers. "Such hell they have made of your life."

"Shhh," she murmured. "The hell is over. I've willed it so."

She writhed her body until there was not even air between them. "Love me again."

FALL MELLOWED INTO WINTER AND SPRING CAME. But inside the little cottage, when they were together, time stopped. They became more daring. No longer did Rory set off for Hounslow only at night.

"We cannot be so lucky as to have this go on forever," he said at last.

"I don't think of anything but this day, each day," she replied. "It is one more day of happiness spent with you."

"Brenna, you have—we have—already flaunted convention. Let us do it further," he urged.

"How so?"

"Come to Ballylee with me!"

"No! 'Tis impossible, my darling, and we both know it. You are not an Irish clansman of old who would drag off another's wife by the hair of her head. And, even though I may be damned for the sin I commit, I am still a married woman. You must think of David and Shanna. If you were to harbor me at Ballylee Buckingham would have all the fuel he would need to move openly against you—as he would dearly love to do."

"Damme, but I can't be content with this," he cried. "I want you to be mine in fact as well as deed!"

"We are together. For now, that is enough," she sighed.

THEY HAD WEEK AFTER WEEK of glorious happiness together. Rory purchased tack and horse for her, a tall bay mare much like the animal that had brought them back together at Titchfield. They took moonlight rides along winding streams and climbed to the tops of hills where they stood arm in arm, watching the sun turn the horizon gold.

They strolled the great heath, oblivious to all they passed. They were lovers, and they had found their time.

In the end, it was Richelieu and not Buckingham or Lady Compton who ended their idyll. The cardinal made peace with Spain and overnight France was at peace abroad. This freed Richelieu to put the second part of his plan into action. He turned his attention to the independent city of La Rochelle, stronghold of the French Protestants. Like the rest of France, he would make these Huguenots acknowledge Louis as their sovereign.

In retaliation, King Charles of England ordered, with no warning, that all of Queen Henrietta Maria's retinue be placed under arrest and sent to Dover, then France.

Rory O'Hara, caught with the rest, managed to smuggle a message to Brenna begging her to join the royal party at Dover. Somehow he would slip her into the group.

Brenna hesitated for only a moment when the hastily scrawled appeal reached her. She knew there would be hell to pay from her family for her actions. But she had thought of her family too often in the past. Now she had thoughts only for herself and the man she loved.

Quickly she gathered what money she had and, without aid, saddled the mare. She also armed herself with a tiny pistol. The roads to Dover would be full of rogues and vagabonds.

She rode through the day and, fearlessly, much of the night. A kindly farmer and his wife took pity upon her when she appeared at their door. They gave her shelter and, true to their word, roused her at dawn.

Fearful that she would ride the mare into the ground, she bartered for a fresh mount. Sadness filled her heart as she parted with the splendid animal, Rory's gift, but speed was of the essence.

At last, near dusk, she sighted the ramparts of Dover Castle. On by the rambling old fortress she rode, directly to the port.

Jaundiced seamen eyed her lewdly as she begged guidance to the port master. Finally she was told where to find him. But instead she found the ornate red-and-gilt coach of the Duke of Buckingham and, inside it, the Duchesse de La Mardine.

Brenna's heart leaped with relief when she saw the perfectly coiffed blond head. The ship had not yet sailed. Why else would La Mardine still be here?

"*Madame, Madame!*" Brenna cried, as she reached the coach's step and frantically tugged at the door until it opened.

"Be gone, girl—oh, *mon Dieu*, it is you, m'lady. I thought you a vendor girl," Carlotta said casually.

Brenna knew her face and clothes were caked with mud and dust from the long ride. She also knew that tears of weariness were pouring from her eyes. She didn't care.

"The ship, *madame*, for France?"

"Why, 'tis gone, dear girl, these two hours past."

"But you—"

"I received a special dispensation from the duke at the last minute to stay in England. He has even sent his coach to fetch me. He's such a gallant and so very handsome!"

A WEEK LATER, from her cottage near Hounslow, Brenna sent word to Paris.

My dearest,

I am with child but do not despair. I am elated, overjoyed that it has happened. When our son is born, for surely it will be a son, I will flee to join you in Paris. Until then, know that I love you and will die each minute until we are together again.

With all my love, Brenna

CHAPTER FORTY-THREE

BRENNA COULD HEAR THEIR VOICES over her own screams of pain, but she could distinguish no words. Beneath her hands the contractions made the skin of her distended belly become taut and inflexible.

A rolling swell rippled along her palms. The child. Rory O'Hara's seed fighting to be born. The pains came one after another now. Her eyes flashed open when there was a scant few seconds' respite from the pain.

Her mother was at Brenna's head, her face a mixture of pity and condemnation. The midwife, her florid face dripping sweat, was between her lifted legs.

Hurry, Brenna's mind cried, *dear God, hurry, for I can stand little more.*

She tensed. Her body screamed in agony as another pain struck, ten times worse than any that had preceded it. She screamed, and merciful darkness claimed her.

"I SHALL NEVER BE ABLE TO THANK YOU," Brenna said, watching the hulking man who was her half brother replace a cooing Robert in his crib.

"Nay, there is no thanks needed," Clement replied, moving to join her on a settee. "'Tis my way of assuaging the guilt I have felt for so long."

How different he is, she thought. *How like all of us, Clement has changed.* He was still called "the fighting Coke," but now he fought with words alongside his father in the House of Commons.

At Robert's birth, it was Clement who had comforted her, while Brenna's mother thought first of the scandal. Before Brenna had even regained her senses, Elizabeth had summoned a rector. Then and there the boy's birth had been registered and he had been baptized and christened Robert Hubbard.

Brenna had objected strongly. "He is an O'Hara, and an O'Hara I will have him named!"

"You will not, you little fool. You would play the whore—admit your sin to the world? I'll not let you!"

"'Twas no sin in my eyes. He is The O'Hara's child, and as soon as I am well enough I plan on joining the boy's father in Paris!"

"So be it," Elizabeth had replied, her wrath apparent on her face. "But in the meantime I will muddy the waters as much as I can to lessen the scandal. The law states that a child born of wedlock in our kingdom is the husband's child. This was the case and, damme, I'll have it so!"

"Dear God," Brenna had stormed. "My mother has become a Puritan, my husband a Catholic and my bastard son made legitimate. Scandal? I tire of it. 'Tis I who have been scandalized my whole life. I will be no more."

But as usual Lady Hatton would brook no argument. She had had her way and, when it was done, had returned to Hatton House confident that her old age would not be tainted by her daughter's folly.

It was Clement who had come to Brenna's real aid. He had brought them to London and given them refuge in his house near Cripplegate. He had hired the best of nannies for the boy and nurses for Brenna.

And he had opened an avenue of communication with Paris.

"You are still of a mind to go when word comes?" he asked.

Brenna nodded. "I will miss England but not its people. And I would not have O'Hara's son grow up ruled by men like Buckingham!"

Clement sighed. "It might be more difficult than you think. The winds of war blow stronger both ways across the Channel. The duke cries for blood. He would be savior of England's glory by freeing La Rochelle from Richelieu's siege."

"He would be the savior of his own glory!" Brenna scoffed.

A carriage clattered to a halt before the gates, drawing their attention.

"Od's blood, will miracles never cease," Clement said, a caustic smile on his lips. "What could possibly bring the great lady to my doorstep?" By the time a servant had escorted Lady Hatton to Brenna's apartments, Clement had slipped away.

Elizabeth mumbled the barest of greetings as she seated herself and then launched immediately into the reason for her visit. "The fat, my wayward daughter, is indeed in the fire."

"How so?" Brenna replied, averting her eyes from her mother's hurt, accusing stare.

"Word has reached Buckingham of the birth. Lady Compton has disowned your son Robert completely. She has gone before King's Council and claimed that he is no Hubbard in fact."

"He isn't."

"Damme, will you listen to reason?" Elizabeth shouted.

Her voice brought an instant wail of fear from the crib. Brenna rushed to the child's side and soon comforted him.

"Would you mind, mother, railing in a whisper?" she retorted at last.

"Perhaps you won't be so calm when you hear my news," Lady Hatton said coldly.

"I'm listening."

"The duke demands you undergo a public trial for adultery and sorcery. He claims access to you by Raymond was impossible, and even if it were, the Viscount Poole could not be the father by reason of infirmity."

"I would agree with that," Brenna said sharply.

Elizabeth stood to her full, glowering height. "You'd best not if you ever wish to call me mother again. You will declare that the Viscount Poole is indeed the child's father. You will deny any liaison with the Irishman. And though it be a wretched name, you will declare your son a Hubbard by blood."

"Have you never in your life made a misstep, mother?"

Elizabeth turned from her daughter and moved to the window. "Aye, I have. And I have paid for it all these years."

"I have made no mistake, mother, yet I have paid all my life. But, as I do love you, I will bring no more scandal upon your house. I will do as you ask," Brenna finished resignedly. She saw her mother's shoulders sag with relief.

"Thank you. And now I must take the boy," Lady Hatton said, still turned to the window, unable to face her daughter.

"Robert. . . . Why?" Panic, like a fluttering bird's wings, began to rise in Brenna's breast.

"Because, my child, the court has made me governess until the trial is over."

"I can care for him right here!" she protested, unconsciously wringing her hands as the import of her mother's words began to register.

Elizabeth turned, her face drawn and nearly drained of color. "But you won't be here. You are remanded to Fleet Prison until the completion of the trial."

LAMBETH PLACE STOOD IN GLOOMY SPLENDOR on the south side of the Thames. As Brenna stepped from the barge, two general aldermen fell in step behind her. They would escort her through the maze of walls and gardens to the courtroom.

She walked with her head held high, even though she was sure the awful stench of Fleet still hung on her clothing and hair. She blinked constantly in the sunlight, for she had not seen any for two weeks.

The window of her dark, dank room had been only a

slit in the thick wall. Her narrow view had been the filth and squalor of Fleet Market. In the two weeks of her confinement, Brenna had watched nine men die on those gallows.

She vowed to herself now as she walked through the larkspur, the roses and the clean air of Lambeth Gardens that no matter the day's outcome, she would never return to Fleet Prison.

"In here!" barked one of her guides.

The courtroom was filled with robed bishops and judges, as well as curious spectators.

Now, she thought, taking her place at the bar, *now I know how Frances Howard felt.*

THE TRIAL WAS A MOCKERY AND A FARCE.

Buckingham had gone to great lengths to ensure his victory, even to bribery. Brenna could not believe the parade of witnesses that passed before the judges. Most of them she had never met. One, the notorious Doctor John Lambe, was well known to be under Buckingham's thumb. Besides being a scoundrel, the man had in the past been tried himself and found guilty of sorcery as well as rape.

And he condemns me, Brenna thought, too amazed and appalled to do more than mutely stand at the proceedings.

By midafternoon it was obvious that only a miracle would save her. The charge of sorcery had been dropped, but the other charges still hung like the headsman's ax over her head.

Despair filled Brenna's heart and it was becoming increasingly more difficult for her to hold her head high, when a sudden hush came over the court. All heads turned to the rear of the courtroom. Brenna turned, too, and gasped aloud when she recognized her husband, the Viscount Poole, walking toward the witness stand.

As he passed Brenna, their eyes met and held for the briefest of moments. Brenna could discern in his look no hate, no flashing madness, no desire for revenge. She saw instead the old melancholy and sadness, deepened now with weariness.

"You would give evidence, m'lord?" the chief justice inquired.

"I would," Raymond replied, and glanced once more at Brenna before continuing. "As to the charges of adultery against this woman, my wife, I cannot say if she is guilty or innocent. Indeed, I care not, for your judgment of her will matter little compared to the judgment she must meet one day at the hands of God. For this reason I would plead leniency for this woman."

An audible gasp rippled across the room. The judges, who had nearly fallen asleep from the heat of their heavy robes and wigs, suddenly became alert.

"And concerning the matter of the legitimacy of the boy, Robert Hubbard, m'lord?"

Raymond cast one quick, sidelong glance at Brenna and then returned his full attention to the robed figures.

"I say that my cousin, George Villiers, Duke of Buckingham, has erred. For at the time of conception I did indeed have access to my wife. M'lords, I do declare Robert Hubbard to be the product of my seed and my lawful and legitimate heir."

It took fifteen minutes for the judges to quiet the clamor in the courtroom. In that time, Raymond had slipped away through a side door.

"In light of the testimony," the chief justice intoned at last, "I think there can be but one verdict. Brenna

Hubbard, Viscountess of Poole, you are judged not guilty of bringing forth an illegitimate heir to a peer. However, we adjudge you guilty of the sin of adultery. How say the church?"

Slowly the old archbishop stood and fixed his eyes on Brenna.

"Viscountess Poole, the church, too, finds you guilty of the sin of adultery. You are hereby fined five hundred pounds, and come Sunday next you will appear at Paul's Cross. There you will be publicly excommunicated. You will then perform the penance of walking barefoot, draped in a white sheet, from Paul's Cross to the Savoy, and there stand for all of London, rabble and aristocrat alike, to hear your words of contrition!"

CLEMENT URGED BRENNA TO SUBMIT, to undergo the penance. Sir Edward sent messages from Sergeant's Inn urging her to think of his position in Parliament. Lady Hatton besieged her daily, on pain of perhaps losing her son and the threat of a return to Fleet Prison.

Brenna had one answer for them all. "Nothing could be more demeaning in my already demeaning life than to carry out this unjust sentence. Verily, on pain of death itself, I refuse to do this penance—now and forever!"

On the appointed Sunday the crowds assembled at Paul's Cross and lined the route, all the way to the Strand. Many of them were in total sympathy with the beautiful Viscountess Poole, but they could not resist the spectacle of a peeress in such straits.

The hour came and went, and the crowds were denied.

Clement returned to Cripplegate.

"Were the crowds large?" Brenna asked.

"Aye, exceedingly so," he replied in disgust. "You would have had more watching you take a Sunday stroll than would have watched the execution of Raleigh!"

But Clement's face showed the concern he felt for his half sister even though his words implied little of it.

"Do not fear for me, sweet Clem. They will yield."

"I think not. 'Tis a matter of prestige now. Lord Buckingham cannot relent."

"And there is no word from Paris?"

"Not yet, but I have a messenger at Dover and post horses waiting between there and here, when word comes."

Buckingham lost no time in exercising his power. Constables arrived at Cripplegate with a summons. It warned the Viscountess Poole that, should she not appear the following Sunday, she would forfeit all her lands and monies and be subject to imprisonment at the king's pleasure.

Brenna shredded the paper and thrust it back into the constable's hand. "What lands and monies? And 'tis Buckingham's pleasure to put me in jail!"

That afternoon, despite the driving rain, constables took up a twenty-four-hour watch opposite Clement Coke's house. Buckingham had his prey in a net, and he was making sure that she didn't sprout wings.

The barrage began again from all sides. Outwardly, Brenna remained calm and steadfast. She refused to entertain any thought of acquiescence. Inwardly, she was deathly afraid—afraid that she would really lose her child, that she would be sent back to Fleet Prison and be forced to remain in that wretched place for who knew how long a time.

As the week wore on her fears invaded her dreams. She could smell the dankness, hear the rats scampering in search of food, see the lower dungeon where those about to die were taken so they could be disposed of quickly when their time came.

More than once in any given night she awoke screaming. And in the morning, every morning, the question was the same: was there word from France?

"Nay, not yet. Have faith, lass," Clement said awkwardly, knowing it was little comfort.

Though they meant nothing to an infant, Brenna sent little notes of love to Robert at her mother's house. She urged him not to worry, not to cry. She told him that the past would soon be forgotten and they would again frolic and laugh together.

She might just as well have addressed them to herself, for it was her own flagging spirits she was trying to bolster.

MONSIEUR FRANCOIS DE BASSOMPIERRE was a tall, graying, distinguished soldier of France, at present Cardinal Richelieu's emissary to England. This he explained to Brenna the moment he entered the parlor where she sat. Then, introductions completed and etiquette satisfied, he moved closer and lowered his voice.

"M'lady, may I speak openly?"

"Of course. We are completely alone."

"M'lady, you have a very powerful friend in England and even more powerful friends in France."

Brenna's heartbeats quickened as her eyes grew wide. For a moment she had trouble speaking.

"*Monsieur*, you bring word from France?"

"Nay, m'lady, that would be improper. I am a guest of the king in this country, and I fear you are not on good terms with Charles."

A puzzled frown creased Brenna's forehead. Why had the man presented himself if he had no word?

"I have merely come to bid you adieu."

"What? *Monsieur—*"

He held up a silencing hand. "I will be departing for St. Malo in France from the Isle of Guernsey come tomorrow midnight."

Brenna's brow furrowed again as she digested his words and then his meaning struck her. A French ship carrying contraband could slip in and out of Guernsey undetected more easily than at Dover.

She smiled slightly. "I do believe I understand, *monsieur*."

"I sail on the galley *Gascogne*," he said, bending over her hand. "And now, m'lady, *adieu*."

"A very pleasant journey, *monsieur*."

Bassompierre was barely in his carriage before Brenna was running toward Clement's study. Her half brother was nodding over a book and came awake with a start at her clattering entrance.

"Clement, Clement! The time is here! Tomorrow night, midnight, I sail from Guernsey!"

Instantly he was alert, and crossing to the door. He assured himself there were no servants within earshot and returned.

"Guernsey, is it," he said, tugging at one end of his mustache. "That means we must leave tonight and travel swiftly."

Only then did Brenna remember the guard stationed outside the house. "Clement, the constables—they will see me leave. If I pass the city gates they will arrest me!"

A low, sardonic laugh rumbled in the big man's throat as he lifted Brenna like a feather and kissed her cheek. "Nay, worry not about those hounds, dear sister. I've already a plan to send them scampering!"

"I must pack," she said breathlessly, already running to the door.

"A light bag, mind you."

"Aye. And Clement, find me a trusted page. I must write mother."

In her own rooms, Brenna set pen to paper.

Madam,

I beg you have pity upon me in my misery. If you have, you will understand that I must do this thing. Remember that I am your daughter, and if I do not flee, will surely be the most afflicted person in the world. Take as much pity on me, dear mother, as you would the poor who ask you for alms.

From Guernsey I leave for France and my happiness come midnight tomorrow. But without my child, my happiness cannot be complete. I beg you to bring Robert, so he can know his rightful father and give happiness to the mother who bore him.

Your humble and loving daughter, Brenna

"PLAY YOUR PART WELL, LAD," Clement said, adjusting the long black wig on the boy's head.

"It's foolish I feel, I tell ya!" the boy replied, scowling down at the dress he wore and then turning a red face up to Brenna.

Their eyes met on a level. He was the perfect height, she thought, and in such huge skirts it surely would be impossible to tell.

"There, this will help as well." She draped a heavy shawl around his shoulders and stepped back to survey the figure that she hoped the constables would see as herself.

"Perfect!" Clement roared, slapping the boy on the back. "The carriage waits. Be off with you now, lad. Do it proper and I guarantee you more coin for this night's work than ye'll make in a year!"

As the lad stepped through the door, Brenna and Clement stationed themselves at windows to watch and pray that the charade was a success.

Looking furtively both ways, as they had instructed him, the boy tripped lightly down the steps and over the walk toward the gate. Across the street, four heads came up at the same time, their eyes peering at the moving figure.

The lad was at the coach door. Then he was inside and the coach was rolling.

"Move...move, you bloody bastards!" Clement hissed.

As if they had heard his words, the four constables moved as one. Horses were hurriedly called for from a nearby alleyway. And then, as if Clement himself were across the street directing the constables, they all took to their mounts and galloped after the carriage.

"It worked, it worked!" Brenna shrieked, gleefully clapping her hands together like a child.

"Aye, it did," Clement grinned, taking her arm, "and here's our carriage heading the other direction. Come quickly!"

Brenna needed no urging. Clement had to sprint to keep up with her.

She was running to freedom, happiness and love.

CHAPTER FORTY-FOUR

O'HARA PACED THE PEBBLY BEACH, weaving between huge, sea-worn rocks. At water's edge, Bassompierre and the captain of the *Gascogne* watched the angry sea and the bobbing small boat.

"Monsieur?" The captain spoke.

Rory changed direction and joined them. "A short while longer, captain," he said, turning his eyes upward to the top of the cliff where Brenna and Clement stood looking inland.

"*Monsieur*, the weather grows worse and the tide—"

"Just a few moments!"

"No longer, *monsieur*. I am sorry, but if we do not leave soon we will not be able to leave at all."

Rory nodded and moved toward the path that led to the clifftop. In moments he was standing silently by a nervous Clement. They both watched Brenna. She stood wringing a kerchief between her slender fingers. Her face was strained and her lips were white where her teeth were biting them.

"Brenna," Rory whispered.

"Moments, my darling. She will come, I swear it—I know it." There was a frantic shrillness in her voice.

"Brenna, the wind changes—"

"A horse. . . . There, a horse!" she cried, running forward, tripping and scrambling to her feet to run again.

Clement and Rory surged forward together. It was a horseman but in the darkness it was impossible to determine if the rider were friend or foe.

The clouds parted briefly, bathing the rider in moonlight.

"Christopher!" Brenna shouted, her feet flying now as she ran with her skirts pulled high above her knees. "'Tis my mother's servant, Christopher!" she called over her shoulder.

"Indeed it is," growled Clement, running beside Rory. "But the lad is alone."

Rory glanced sideways. Clement's wide face looked pinched, the eyes narrowed.

The rider pulled his mount to an abrupt halt and slid from the saddle at the same time.

"Christopher, my mother—" Brenna gasped, grabbing the youth's arm. "Where is my mother?"

Sadness and guilt were to be read in the man's eyes as he pulled a folded piece of paper from beneath his jerkin and handed it to Brenna.

"What is this?"

"My mistress's reply to your summons, m'lady," he answered, averting his eyes from Brenna's face.

She ripped at the paper until the seal was broken. As she read, all color drained from her face and her body began to sway.

"No. Dear God, no. . . not when I was so near—"

Clement caught her in his strong arms as Rory lifted the paper from her hand.

My dearest daughter,

Let me begin by saying that I love you above all others. What you have done is done. What you will do, you will do. I cannot stop you.

But I can stop you from ruining the future of your son. Sir Edward has publicly declared Robert his grandson, as have I. Raymond has filed the necessary papers declaring Robert the heir apparent, Lord Poole. As if this were not enough, Buckingham has had me watched like a common criminal. Even if I chose to flaunt the king's law I would be hard pressed to deliver Robert to you.

If it is to be France for you, dear daughter, then so be it. But remember that your family, including your son, is in England.

Eliza. H.

O'Hara cursed, crumpling the paper in his fist.

"I must go back," Brenna said tonelessly, naught but abject agony filling her features now.

"Nay, lass," Clement said, his arm around her shoulder. "Think of Fleet Prison. There will be no bounds to Buckingham's wrath now!"

"Clement is right," Rory said, taking Brenna by the shoulders and enveloping her in his own arms.

Brenna's body shook but there were no tears now, for she had none left to shed. "She is right. My family is here; my son is here. I must go back."

"I will not let you," Rory said, holding her from him and looking deeply into her eyes.

"He is our son!" she whispered. "Would you have us both abandon him?"

Her words were like a dagger in Rory's breast, but he persevered, knowing that the battle could be better fought from France by the two of them together. "We still have friends here. There is Clement, the queen, and there are others. In time we can get the boy—"

"Nay. As long as there is a Buckingham, he will make sure I never see my son again. And for what I do he will wreak havoc on the rest of my family."

O'Hara's jaw set and his lips became a hard line. Gently he slid his arm protectively around Brenna and guided her a few paces from the others.

"My dearest, let your mind go back, many years ago. You were but a child on a bench in the gardens of Holdenby. A tall man with graying black hair came to visit you."

"I—I can't remember."

"Try," Rory said, fumbling with the gold chain that hung around his neck. "You spent upward of two hours in the garden with the man. And when he left you ran to the carriage after him to give him. . .this." He unclasped the chain and placed the locket in her hands.

One hand went up to rub her temples in concentration as she snapped the locket open with the other. The words and memories came haltingly. "There were. . . others in the carriage. . . ."

"Aye, a woman, a lad and a young girl."

"This was a parting gift from my mother—"

"The woman was Annie Carey. You know her now as Sister Anna, the Abbess of Fontevrault. The girl was Shanna. . .and I was the lad."

Brenna's eyes grew wide as she looked up from the locket. "And the man was Rory O'Donnell."

O'Hara nodded. "He wore that around his neck, near his heart, for the rest of his life."

Brenna suddenly remembered the stares from other women as she was growing up. She recalled the remarks made behind fluttering fans and the veiled accusations from Sir Edward in the heat of arguments with her mother. "No. It couldn't—"

"It is true, Brenna, my darling. Unknowingly, you and I have repeated history."

Suddenly she felt faint. They, all of them, had been living a lie. Was she the reason for the deep-seated hatred between her father and mother? Was this truly the reason Sir Edward had been able to sell her so easily into an unwanted marriage?

She did remember now. Upon returning from the garden that long ago day, she had run to her mother. But Elizabeth hadn't wanted to hear of her conversation with the man in the garden. Indeed, she had broken into tears when Brenna spoke of it.

All the connections were made and washed over her now: her mother's insistence on going to France with them that first time; Elizabeth's many hours spent in The O'Donnell's room at Fontevrault and the look of calm serenity on her face each time she had emerged.

Rory's deep voice broke into her thoughts. "You have as much of Ireland in your veins as I have, and our Robert more than both of us. What say you now, lass—London or Paris?"

Brenna turned and dropped her forehead to O'Hara's chest, allowing him to hold her close. "Paris," she whispered.

Part IV

CHAPTER FORTY-FIVE
FRANCE

PARIS WAS A NEW WORLD FOR BRENNA. She was saddened when war did come between England and France, but the French victories over Buckingham didn't leave her with an expatriate's guilt. For her, Buckingham wasn't England. The more defeats he suffered the sooner would come his loss of power, which could only benefit England.

The duke had been true to his vow. No amount of pleading or pressure, no matter how powerful the source, would make the man relent. The child, Robert Hubbard, was not to leave England.

In an attempt to fill the ache in her heart caused by the absence of her son, Brenna threw herself into Parisian society. She became a favorite at the French court and a friend of the lonely Queen Anne. She also became one of the few women to be accepted by His Eminence, Cardinal Richelieu. Partly this was due, she knew, to the political embarrassment she had caused Buckingham, but she overlooked her status as pawn in hopes that Richelieu would one day be the power she needed to regain her child.

Rory was made a colonel in Richelieu's guard. He leased a house on the Rue St. Antoine and had it completely redecorated to Brenna's taste.

"Oh, my darling, I am overjoyed! But how can all this be done on a colonel's pay?" Brenna had asked.

"It can't," Rory had replied, roaring with laughter. "What will it take to make you realize that I am rich—rich beyond most men's dreams! Talbot has turned Ballylee into a small empire. Worry not, my sweet, we can afford anything our hearts desire!"

There was much laughter and much love between them. Rory retained quarters at the musketeers' garrison out of propriety, but few nights were spent away from the St. Antoine house.

The war was going well for France and barely interrupted their time together. O'Hara was made a garrison commander in Paris, for he had little taste for battle now, and Richelieu respected it.

But there were increasingly moody times as well as the gay ones. They came in spells when Brenna would long for her son and a taste of home. O'Hara, too, chafed to return to Ireland and Ballylee. But both knew their desires were impossible. They tried to keep their moods to themselves.

"Come here to the window. Look!" Rory pointed.

Brenna gasped when she saw the magnificent coach. It was white with gold gilt, and the four matching horses drawing it snorted in harness trimmed in silver.

"Who on earth...?" Brenna stood transfixed, wondering who could be calling on them in such a magnificent equipage.

" 'Tis yours," Rory smiled down at her.

"Dear God, such extravagance!" she cried.

"Nay, 'tis necessary. If I have brought you into exile, I would have you live it like a queen."

A slight shudder passed through Brenna's shoulders. It was she who now held them in exile. If he wished, O'Hara could return to Ireland, and she knew it. But he wouldn't go, not without her, and she was still doomed to remain in Paris. It was the only safe place for her.

"Come, we will ride to the park, and there we will walk and show off your new finery and feathers!"

Brenna giggled like a happy child and took Rory's arm. The coach, the horses and the costly livery of the footmen did indeed make her feel like a queen.

They rode by the Seine and then turned up into the Tuileries. There the gardens were a sea of color dazzling their eyes as they stepped from the carriage.

"They are beautiful, the gardens," Brenna said, drinking in the fresh air laden with a hundred scents that wafted from the blossoming beds.

"As are you, sweet lass," Rory replied, his voice low and husky as he gazed at her.

Brenna flushed and gripped his arm more tightly. "Is it really wise that we should be seen so openly together?" she whispered.

"In Paris we are just another pair of young lovers!" he quipped, giving her hand a gentle squeeze and guiding her down yet another path in the gardens.

After a few more moments walking, they stopped to rest on a stone bench.

"*Monsieur le cardinal* tells me that Buckingham is mounting more ships. He would again try to lift the siege at La Rochelle." Rory's voice was light, with a touch of humor in it.

When Brenna spoke, she matched his tone. "I would think that with all his troubles, the duke would leave off troubling me!"

"So one would think, but we now know that Buckingham is a man driven. Like Richelieu, he will stand for no one in his way, not even a runaway viscountess."

"But unlike His Eminence," Brenna added, shaking

her head, "Buckingham has neither the funds nor the ability to achieve his vast aims!"

"A very wise observation, me young beauty." Rory grinned, leaned over and bussed her on the tip of her nose. "But enough talk of politics. Come, let us see the roses on down the path!"

They moved through the expanse of the rose gardens, stopping now and then to admire a particularly lovely specimen or to breathe deeply of its heady perfume. Suddenly Brenna stopped, her arm tightening on Rory's.

"What is it?"

"I—that man. I see him watching me every time I go out."

Rory followed her stare. The man, tall, with a full head of graying hair, stood on an incline some distance away. He seemed to be merely idling, yet Rory could see that his eyes drifted toward them to stare intensely at Brenna.

"I'd best see what the rogue wants," Rory growled. "Wait here!"

He left Brenna beneath a spreading beech and approached the man. Even at a distance one could see that his clothes, once well tailored, were the worse for wear and that his hair had not been tended for days.

When Rory was less than fifty yards from him the man bolted. He turned and fled at a dead run toward a maze of hedges. It was only then that Rory recognized him.

"René. . . René de Gramont! Wait!"

For five minutes Rory ran back and forth among the high hedges. René had disappeared.

Odd, he thought, making his way back to Brenna. *At least he could have spoken. What can he have to fear?*

Rory searched now for Brenna. She had moved from the sunlight into the full shade of the tree. As he saw her face shadowed by her parasol and the wide limbs, another odd thought suddenly struck him.

Brenna had been spending a great deal of time out of doors since her arrival in Paris. The sun had darkened her fair skin. With her height, her figure and the raven darkness of her hair, she looked from afar almost the twin of his sister, Shanna.

CHAPTER FORTY-SIX
ENGLAND

THE DUKE OF BUCKINGHAM SAT at the end of a long table, brooding over his breakfast. Officers, messengers and orderlies surrounded him. Now and then the duke looked up and through the parlor window.

In the bay, some distance from the house on High Street where he had taken lodging, he could see Portsmouth Harbor and the many ships that lay at anchor. Those ships would make up the second expedition to free the Protestants of La Rochelle from the French siege. The first expedition had been a disaster, and Buckingham still felt the sting of its failure.

It was only one of the things pressing upon his mind that morning. Just before he had left London, his friend Doctor Lambe had been murdered by a mob in the streets. They had followed him from an afternoon at the Fortune Theatre, chanting, "Who rules the kingdom? The king. Who rules the king? The duke. Who rules the duke? The devil!"

Normally the death of any man, friend or foe, would have little affected George Villiers. But the following day the same mob had sung and shouted their way through the streets as they tacked up posters.

> Let Charles and George do what they can,
> The duke shall die like Dr. Lambe.

The Duke of Buckingham shuddered now when he thought of it. Filthy rabble, but their tunes would change when he returned from France victorious!

"Is something wrong with the food, Your Grace?"

"Oh...no, I just have no stomach for it this morning." Gently he touched the left side of his doublet. Beneath the material lay his previous night's work with pen and paper. They were the demands he would make upon Richelieu once the day was England's. One by one he went over the points in his head.

La Rochelle was to be made an independent Protestant state.

All English prisoners were to be freed without ransom.

All the titled exiles in France were to be returned to England.

Buckingham smiled to himself when he reached this one. Once and for all this petty feud with the Viscountess Poole and the Irishman O'Hara would be settled for good. And it would be settled in his, the duke's, way.

"Your Grace?"

Buckingham nodded at the orderly who had appeared at his elbow.

"Your carriage is at the door, Your Grace."

The duke rose. Followed by Lord Cleveland and others of his entourage, he left the parlor and entered the passage leading to the front door. He was nearly to it when a tall, gaunt-faced man stepped from concealment behind a black velvet curtain.

"You!" Buckingham roared when he saw the man. "How dare you—"

"May the Lord have mercy on your vile soul!" the man cried and rushed forward, his withered left hand raised to steady himself.

George Villiers saw the man's right hand rise. Too late he saw the dagger it held. He heard, rather than felt the dagger as it thudded into his left breast.

Around him all was confusion. Lord Cleveland grabbed the duke's falling body. Men surged forward. Buckingham grasped the hilt of the dagger and pulled it himself from his chest.

"Villain!" he cried, tugging at his sword as he lurched toward his attacker.

But it had been a fatal blow. With blood running from the side of his mouth, Buckingham fell against a table and from there to the floor, dead.

The assassin lifted his hat from his head, extricated a note from the hat and calmly handed it to Lord Cleveland.

> That man is cowardly, base and deserveth not the name of a gentleman or soldier that is not willing to sacrifice his life for the honor of his God, his king, and his country....

"And you claim to be such a man, you murderer?" Lord Cleveland shouted angrily.

"I do, m'lord. And not murderer—patriot. My name is John Felton."

CHAPTER FORTY-SEVEN
FRANCE

"It is a sin, and I know it, to rejoice over the death of a fellow human being. But in truth my heart is relieved because of the deed!"

And Brenna's views, according to news they received from England, were widely held. All London rejoiced. Men in taverns drank to John Felton's health. Bawdy songs were composed in his honor. So rowdy were the mobs that Buckingham's interment service at Westminster Abbey had to be held in secret.

But the death of the duke did little for Brenna's cause. His will lived on in the king's mind. Even secret entreaties to Queen Henrietta Maria accomplished nothing toward Brenna's regaining possession of her son.

And Bishop Laud carried on in the matter where Buckingham had left off. Laud meant to solidify the Church of England's power over Puritan and Papist alike. To that end, he considered that Brenna's excommunication and her flight to avoid penance should be made an example.

With the advent of peace, English emissaries again began to arrive in the French court, urging Richelieu and Louis XIII to send the Viscountess Poole home for punishment. When first overtures failed to produce results, more men were sent to France by Laud to serve in person the writ of excommunication against Brenna. It was a necessary step before proceedings could be carried out in England against her.

There were days when Brenna hardly dared to leave her quarters, for they would try to thrust the paper on her no matter where she was found—on the street, in her carriage—once she even discovered them lurking behind a curtain at her seamstress's.

Several times they had tried to bribe her maids. Once, at a time when the servants were away or at their duties in the rear of the house Brenna herself had opened the door. The paper was thrust at her, and she barely got the door closed again, having narrowly prevented the man from pushing his way inside.

Her nerves became more and more frayed, and it seemed that not a day passed when her temples didn't throb with a dull ache. And still these English messengers came, out of every shadow and from behind every tree. Her daily life became a living hell trying to avoid them.

Eventually it began to take its toll on her relationship with Rory. The love they felt for each other couldn't help but be strained. He could entertain no dreams of returning to Ireland with her nor she of ever going back to England. And worst of all, loneliness for little Robert grew to a point at which it devoured Brenna's every waking moment.

No longer was the social whirl of the French court or of Paris itself enough to take her mind off the absence of her son. She grew irritable to all those around her, including Rory. Less and less did she leave the house; for days at a time she would not even leave her rooms.

Rory could see the wedge that was being driven between them, but he was helpless to do anything about it. His own homesick longings were beginning to betray him. The letters begging him to return to Ballylee came almost daily now, their content becoming more and more cryptic.

And then David Talbot arrived in Paris to deliver his plea in person.

DAVID HAD CHANGED VERY LITTLE over the years. The movement of his wiry body was still fluid, and his hooded gray eyes still fascinated Brenna with their intensity.

With great love and, it seemed to Brenna, a sense of awe, he spoke of his wife and children. Aileen had blossomed like a true Irish lass. She gave her father worry, not because she flirted with the lads too much, but because she flirted not at all.

"I swear, methinks the convent had too much influence on the lass! Our neighbors' daughters are already wedded and bedded, and most are five years her junior. She'll be an old maid of twenty soon, and there'll be no lad who'll want her!" David complained to Rory and Brenna.

But Talbot belied his own words when he spoke with reverence and fatherly pride of Aileen's blond hair and the almost magical beauty of her face. It was clear little Maura would follow right along in her half-sister's footsteps as the reigning princess of Ballylee.

"And Patrick, our youngest! Now there's a lad! He has the O'Hara in him, he does. Already he grows in form like you, Rory, and Shanna. Strong as a little bull he is and wily like a fox. I've had to take a cane to him often—gives his mother fits he does!"

Brenna kept swallowing in huge gulps to keep down her emotions. Her heart seemed to turn over as David talked of his family and the small joys and daily pitfalls of raising the children.

Several times as he spoke she was forced to rise and walk to the sideboard. There, with her back to the men to hide the pain on her face, she would make a great show of rearranging goblets and decanters, only to leave them in the same places when she returned to her chair.

Rory, too, felt the tug of family, the son he didn't

have at his side, and the family in Ireland that now seemed so far from him.

Brenna could see it in his dark eyes each time he cast a quick glance in her direction.

Then the conversation turned to politics and Rory squirmed even more.

"I tell you, my friend," David intoned sonorously, "'tis now but a little ripple, but I say 'twill one day soon grow into a giant wave. No one believes me, but I've lived under the English thumb too long and I know."

Rory nodded, idly rolling the goblet he held from hand to hand. "'Tis said that Charles has secretly entreated the Dutch for a loan on the crown jewels."

"I believe it," Talbot replied. "Without money from Parliament, he must get funds somewhere. Our rents and taxes rise weekly, and daily more land is swallowed by undertakers who will pay anything for it in Irish sweat!" Here Talbot sipped from his glass and cast a sidelong glance at Brenna before continuing.

"We have always lived with brigandage, but now the rogues' ranks are swelled by Irish and English soldiers who have been without pay. The lord deputy is constantly on the lookout for more and faster ways to generate money. He now casts his eyes west, O'Hara—toward Connaught, Sligo and Ballylee."

Silence descended like a gray fog on the room. Brenna's eyes never left Rory's face. Her pain was written plainly on her own face, and it multiplied tenfold with Talbot's next words.

"I would arm neighbors and tenants alike, but I'm not sure yet if they would fight as one for a Scot."

The inference was plain, and the tension it caused in the room was palpable.

"Can neither Dublin nor the Irish Parliament do anything?"

"Dublin, Rory, is an English town, and the Parliament is but a tool of the crown." Talbot leaned forward, his voice becoming a mixture of pleading and command. "Rory O'More, Sir Phelim O'Neill and God knows how many others are rumbling like a storm from the mountain Ben Bulben. They see the unrest in England as a way to recover their Irish lands. I preach patience, but they tell me that I can afford patience; we have our land, Rory, if rebellion does come again to Eire, we shall have no choice but to join it."

Rory looked up from his glass. His face was so full of pain and frustration that Brenna was forced to look away, unable to bear the sight.

"Those gray eyes, David. Can they really see so far beyond tomorrow?" Rory slowly asked.

"Aye, they can, my friend. And they see reality. The Irish are dreamers, poets, singers of songs and warriors. It takes a Scot like me or a Dutchman or German—even a Frenchman—to show the Irish progress. But it takes an Irishman to lead another Irishman in battle!"

There was another long moment of silence, and then Brenna shattered it in a voice so calm that she surprised even herself. "Perhaps, O'Hara, you should go back."

"No!"

"For a while, at least. I can go to Fontevrault. Sister Anna—"

O'Hara uncoiled from his chair like a springing tiger. His arm swung forward, flinging the goblet and its contents against the stone mantelpiece.

"No!" he shouted. "And, by God in Heaven, I'll hear no more of it!"

DAYS WORE INTO WEEKS, and still David Talbot stayed on in France. No more did he speak to Rory O'Hara about returning to Ireland. Instead, he turned his attention to Brenna.

Their old friendship was easily renewed. Brenna welcomed it, for so strained now was day-to-day life with Rory that he often stayed away from the house on St. Antoine for a week at a time.

Brenna and David took most of their meals together and enjoyed long talks in the evenings about the past. He once again became her wise older brother and she the little girl who needed a shoulder to cry on. But underneath every conversation was the tension, and it refused to go away.

"You write the Lady Hatton?" David inquired one evening.

"Often now. She keeps me informed of Robert, his growth, his words, how much he would like to know his mama. She says Raymond is good with the boy and does indeed appear to accept him as his own."

"And have you told Elizabeth that you know the truth of your parentage?"

"Nay, I see no reason to do so. I think I have come to understand. O'Hara has told me much of Rory O'Donnell and I see how my mother could have loved him so much."

"Aye, she must have. She loved him enough to give him up. . . give him back to Ireland."

"Please, David—"

"It must be said, lass."

"Could Shanna give you up?" Brenna countered.

There was only a moment's hesitation before he nodded. "Aye, I think she could. She is truly an amazing woman. Ballylee is her life. She loves it even more than I. She is a strong woman, Brenna, almost hard at times, and I love her for it."

"My mother was—is—the same way. She would become a Puritan, I think, just because they oppose the king. Indeed, I fear that she would turn Robert in the same direction. She has great strength, indeed much more than I. But there are times when I am glad of the difference in us, for she has hurt a great many people in her life."

"And you have not and never will," Talbot assured her.

Brenna continued to talk. She knew she was rambling, venturing from subject to subject, but David didn't seem to mind. And for her it was like the confessional, an unburdening of her soul to someone she trusted and who would understand.

Eventually, no matter how indirect the route, their conversations always came back to the same point.

"Is there no hope that you can obtain the child?" David asked.

"None," Brenna replied. "Even Queen Henrietta Maria cannot help me now. 'Tis the one thing the king clings to. He has ruled that Robert shall not leave England. They have at last conceded that all charges will be dropped against me if I return, once and for all, to my family and at least in part remove the smear against the Villiers name."

"Then you have no choice," David said softly, his gray eyes closed to such narrow slits that Brenna couldn't discern the pupils. "Let Rory go, Brenna. For he will surely die if he stays in France."

CHAPTER FORTY-EIGHT

"COME, MY LOVE!" Rory cried, rushing into the room and whirling Brenna in the air. "Dress yourself in your finest silks! Have the maids do your hair to perfection and drape yourself with every piece of jewelry you have!"

"Why, what is it? And put me down, you'll squeeze the very life from me!"

"The private theater in Richelieu's Palais Cardinal is finished. He has invited you, David and myself to spend the evening with him. He will pick us up in his private coach, and like royalty, we will watch the pompous Montfleury attempt to act!"

Brenna sensed that much of Rory's ebullient mood was merely an act to bolster her own spirits, but she did want a change, a chancc to dress and go out. The mood, since David Talbot's arrival, had been one of depression. Anything that would lift their spirits for even a moment was welcome.

She spent the afternoon bathing and scenting her body. Her maids arranged her raven tresses in layered curls atop her head, each one carefully measured to fall just below the ringlet above it.

She deliberated for two hours before she finally selected just the right gown, a pleated silk of a deep crimson that would highlight her hair. The pleats were embroidered in gold, and a narrow ring of fur lined the hem and the low, square-cut bodice.

At last, as the clatter of carriages disrupted the evening stillness at the front gate, she was ready. One last check in the cheval glass pleased her. Just the right amount of bosom swelled enticingly above her bodice; her hair cascaded in elegant curls to frame her face perfectly and diamonds sparkled at her earlobes, catching the light with each movement of her head.

She had matured into a strikingly beautiful woman. There was no doubt of it. She was a wife, a mother, even a mistress. She had endured it all...and she had survived. Leaning forward toward the glass, she saw the tiny lines of age and worry that had begun to etch themselves outward from the corners of her eyes.

"Well," she said aloud to her reflection, "what do you expect? But 'tis the whole that O'Hara loves, and perhaps tonight he will find it again!"

Holding that thought in her mind, Brenna tripped down the stairs in the gayest of moods she had felt in weeks.

Her entrance into the drawing room was grand. To Richelieu she made a deep curtsy. "Your Eminence," she smiled, " 'twill be an evening to remember!"

"And you, lovely lady," the cardinal replied, "are a woman to remember!"

Brenna's mood was infectious, and the others quickly adopted it. By the time the four of them stepped from the house, followed by the cardinal's huge wolfhound, laughter filled the night air. Even the stern face of Richelieu had relaxed into a smile. He waved a footman away and handed Brenna into the carriage himself.

Brenna had barely placed one slippered foot on the carriage step when the nightmare began. It lasted only a few moments, but its result was destined to change their lives forever.

The tall, graying man who had been for so long like a shadow in Brenna's daily life stepped from the darkness at the coach's rear.

Rory recognized him at once. "René, enough is enough—" O'Hara said as he moved to block the man.

De Gramont, his eyes strangely afire with some inner light, pushed Rory aside and moved to face David Talbot. Both hands came up, holding an arquebus inches from David's chest.

Without a word, he fired.

Brenna screamed.

Richelieu, closest to de Gramont, sprang forward to strike the man with his gold-headed staff. René struck first with his pistol, hitting the cardinal on the side of the neck, felling him.

Then he drew a second pistol and raised it toward Brenna. "You will bewitch me no more, Shanna!" René cried.

With growing horror, Rory realized how warped the man's mind had become, so twisted that the mere presence of Talbot and similarity of looks between Brenna and his sister, Shanna, had driven René to this.

O'Hara jumped forward, striking René's arm. The pistol fired. Brenna screamed again as the ball struck the open coach door's velvet padding near her hand.

With a fierce growl Richelieu's huge, Irish wolfhound streaked around Rory. Diable leapt like a coiled spring at de Gramont's throat. The beast made little sound, but went about his deadly task with such ferocity that three of the cardinal's guard could not disengage him from his victim. Finally, Richelieu called the beast back to his side.

Rory knelt over David Talbot's body, his huge shoulders shaking with shock and grief as he held his friend's head in his arms and stared into the lifeless eyes.

Richelieu made the sign of the cross over both dead

men. The only sound was the low monotones of his voice as he prayed.

Finally, Rory's gaze moved from David to René.

When he looked up to Brenna, who stood frozen like a statue on the carriage step, tears were flowing in even streams from both his eyes.

"Dear Lord, I have killed them both," he groaned. "If only I had been able to help René, this tragedy need never have happened. Both their deaths are on my head."

CHAPTER FORTY-NINE
IRELAND

SIR DAVID TALBOT'S LAST RESTING PLACE was one of honor in the tiny chapel at Ballylee. His crypt was placed directly across from Shane O'Hara and his beloved wife, Deirdre.

Rory commissioned a stonecutter to chisel the simple inscription:

Sir David Talbot
Born a Scot
He Died Crying for Ireland's Soul

A fitting sentiment, for his trip to Paris had been just that. He had cried out to The O'Hara to return to the land.

For days after the burial scores of men, women and children came to Ballylee and prayed at the crypt. In death they accorded David Talbot the recognition and reverence as a true Irishman they had withheld from him in life.

Shanna accepted her husband's death with a stoicism that at first puzzled, then angered Rory. But then he came to understand it. His sister was, as Talbot had always said, a strong woman.

"He had a full life and died a good man," Shanna said at the wake. "He gave us two beautiful girls and a strong son. He gave me Ballylee and many fine, loving years. There's not much more a man could ask of life nor a woman of her man."

Aileen took her father's death harder than the younger children, and O'Hara, caring for her like a younger sister, took it upon himself to soften her grief. They spent much time together, talking, walking the hills and heaths. She was a child of many moods, he discovered, one moment able to laugh, the next in the pit of despair, like a true Irishwoman, O'Hara decided.

He found that he enjoyed her company. Like Shanna, she loved the land and never grew tired of talking of it. His sister's letters had been correct as well in reporting her blossoming beauty. Aileen's hair was like wheat, but it held the sheen of gold, particularly when she would run in the sun and it would flow in a stream behind her.

"Why is it," he asked one day, "that you haven't married yet?"

"I've been courted," she replied in a low voice, her face averted from Rory.

"But not married," he insisted.

Her eyes were so frank and bold when she turned them on him that O'Hara was forced to look away. "I've no mind nor passion for the young lads," she said simply.

That evening he spoke to Shanna about her.

"Aye, she's more than ready for a man," his sister concurred.

"Then why—"

"She's waiting."

"Good God, for what?"

"Damme if you're not a fool, Rory O'Hara. Only a man as blind as you, with the weight of the world on his shoulders, could not see what's in her eyes when she looks at you."

"Foolishness!" he shouted. "Damme, she is but a child—and there's already a bit of gray in this head!"

But as he stomped from the house, there was a deep flush on his face.

The signs were all around him, and they became more apparent each day. The solid structure of Ballylee was slowly crumbling. The vast fortune Talbot had amassed was secure, but the fabric that held Ballylee itself together—the people—was beginning to shred. As he had once done all over Ireland, Rory O'Hara set off one day to ride the length of Ballylee.

At the end of that ride, he again sought out the grizzled old herdsman, O'Higgin of the flowing red hair and beard. He found him alone, among his sheep.

"God save all in this place," Rory called the traditional greeting.

"And you, m'lord."

"I am not a lord, O'Higgin. I am Rory O'Hara, the planter on Ballylee."

"To us on the land you're The O'Hara, Lord of Ballylee. Would you share a meal, a cup and a pipe with me, m'lord?"

"I would, O'Higgin."

Rory washed the grime of travel from his body while the old man prepared the meal. It was simple and delicious, with mutton, oatcakes, potatoes and buttermilk.

"You cook well, O'Higgin," Rory muttered appreciatively between mouthfuls.

"'Tis simple fare and easy to prepare," came the gruff but pleased reply.

"How is it you've no wife?"

"I've buried three. At my age, that's enough."

"And children?"

"Eight. Three daughters. They all died birthing."

"And the sons?"

"Dead. Killed—fightin' in the troubles."

The rest of the meal was eaten in silence. When it was over, they hunkered down in the booley's doorway. O'Higgin lit pipes and passed one to O'Hara. Between puffs they sipped strong brew from earthen cups and watched the sun turn the green land to red and orange.

"One day—not soon, but one day for sure—there will be more troubles," O'Hara mused.

"Aye," O'Higgin nodded, his red beard bobbing. "'Tis the way of it."

"The Scot is dead."

"I've heard. He was a good man, I do believe. God rest his soul."

The sun was gone now and the dull gray of twilight spread acoss the horizon.

"The Scot was a Protestant," Rory said at last, "but I believe he was an Irishman at heart."

O'Higgin mulled this over for a long moment before he spoke. "'Tis said that faith is part of the air we breathe. 'Tis faith that gives a man courage and content in life. 'Tis faith that makes us fear not poverty, pain or even death."

"Faith in what, old man?"

"In the land, ourselves and God."

"You're a good man, O'Higgin."

"I thank ye, m'lord."

"Come the morrow I would have you drive your herd near the big house. I'll be gone for a while, and there should be a good man near at hand for the women. Would you do that, O'Higgin?"

"Aye, m'lord. I would."

CHAPTER FIFTY
FRANCE

WITH RORY GONE IN IRELAND and the recent, heart-wrenching loss of her beloved David Talbot, Brenna was totally alone in Paris. She began to feel the tug of England, her son and her family even more strongly.

Why it was, she couldn't explain, but those feelings made her want to return to Fontevrault, as well. She needed desperately to talk to someone, someone who could help her sort out her troubles and perhaps give answers to the questions plaguing her mind and heart.

She sent word to Sister Anna, asking for permission to come to the abbey, and received a quick reply. She left word for O'Hara where she would be and traveled that very night.

Sister Anna had barely aged at all. Within hours, she made Brenna feel as though she had found the most peaceful place on earth. All the storms of her life seemed to fade when she was in the old abbess's presence, and for the first time in what seemed like years, she was able to search for what she thought might be her true self.

She even found herself wanting to know more about her past. Brenna confided to Sister Anna that she knew about her true birth and wanted to hear everything.

"I will pray on it tonight, my child. In the morning we will talk," Sister Anna had replied.

They did, and by the end of it Brenna felt that at long last she understood and appreciated her mother. She knew she would never agree with her, but at least now she understood so many of Elizabeth's actions and the reasons behind them.

During her days at the abbey she gained such an inner serenity and peace that when the letter came from "Viscount Poole to his wife, the Viscountess Poole," Brenna read it with utter calmness. Raymond had regained all his faculties, as well as command of his affairs. He had taken his place in the House of Lords, and had actually turned their means and their properties to a profit.

As she neared the end of the letter she could no longer hold back the tears.

> . . . and so, my darling, I would have you know that I have loved no woman in my lifetime but you. If you can find it in your heart to forget the past, know that I have already done so.
>
> I beg you, dearest Brenna, to return to England, to me and to our son.
>
> Raymond

Brenna read and reread those last lines, until the paper was completely damp with her tears.

A messenger arrived the following afternoon. Rory O'Hara would be at Fontevrault in three days' time.

THEY MET ALONE IN A LITTLE ALCOVE outside the main chapel, and they both knew before the first word was spoken.

O'Hara tried but could not find the words. They choked in his throat and his eyes filled with tears each time he looked at the calm set of her features. Brenna smiled with a serenity he had not seen since those long distant nights in the cottage at Hounslow.

Brenna knew that Rory sensed her inner state, and she was sad that he did not feel the same. She saw the tortured look in his eyes as they met hers and darted away, only to return again. She knew the thoughts that ran through his mind for they were mirrored in his contorted features. But she also knew that somehow one day he, too, would find and feel the serenity that she now felt.

As she stood assembling her own thoughts, the words of The O'Donnell suddenly rippled through her brain so clearly that she could almost mouth them.

All on earth that is worth a man living his life is the love he has for a woman and the love he has for the land. And the land is all a man has to pass on to his sons. Don't ever forget the land, because if the land is not yours to give, then your sons, your grandsons and your great-grandsons will naught have reason to stay.

Then she spoke to Rory, the echo of The O'Donnell's words still sounding in her ears. "It is so very strange, this wondrous thing I have had. In my lifetime I have loved two men—nay, *love* two men. And they have been such different men. One is Raymond, but you are The O'Hara. You had such a destiny that you were a legend the day you were born. I thought, until this day, that I had lived through so much. But now I see those around me, and wonder.

"You saw Ballylee reduced to rubble when you were but a boy. You saw your family decimated, your land and home torn from you.

"You have the name and all that goes with it, Rory O'Hara. You cannot help but be more than mortal man. One day, I can see, you will be forced into it. And when that day comes, my darling love, I know as sure as there is a God, I could not cope with it."

She paused now, dabbing with a kerchief at her misted eyes. But even as the tears flowed, there was a smile on her lips.

"Dear Raymond has been sheltered all his life as an English gentleman, as have I as an English lady. My mother could have coped with a man such as you. In fact she did. And I was the result.

"But I fear I do not have enough wild Irish blood in my veins. I remember when dear David would speak of wild Ireland, I would quake. I fear I do quake, my dear Rory, when you speak of it."

She moved close to him and ever so gently touched his lips with hers.

"I will always love you," he whispered, taking her in his arms one last time.

"And I you. And know this, Irishman. If 'tis in my power, your son will one day know that he has in his veins the blood of the proud O'Haras!"

CHAPTER FIFTY-ONE
IRELAND

RORY O'HARA STOOD ON THE PARAPET, gazing across the heath and rolling hills at the gathering storm. A brisk wind whirled the heavy mantle about his shoulders and the first light drops of rain stung his face.

He had been standing there for hours, just as he had every evening at dusk since his return.

There was the sound of a slipper on the stone steps behind him. He didn't turn, for he knew its owner.

Aileen stood above and behind him, her own cloak wrapped tightly around her body while the wind whipped her long blond hair in swirls about her face. Her thoughts reflected the calm smile of solemn determination on her face.

I am no longer a child, Rory O'Hara. I am a woman with passion in her body and love in her heart. I know the tears you have shed and the heartaches you have endured. And believe me, O'Hara, when I say I can mend them.

Slowly she crossed the walkway until she was at his side. "It is a beautiful land," she said softly.

"Aye," he nodded. "And Ballylee is the most beautiful part of it."

"My father's greatest dream was that there would always be an O'Hara at Ballylee."

"I know," Rory replied. "He said it to me often."

"For that to happen you must have sons, O'Hara."

He turned, bending his head to gaze at her upturned face in the gathering mists. It was there, in the blue of her eyes, and O'Hara could no longer fight it. Indeed, he no longer wanted to.

"I'll never make you forget her, but you'll never regret that I replaced her," Aileen promised.

Rory said nothing. He turned back to look out over Ballylee.

I am The O'Hara and master of all I see.

Slowly his arm slid beneath her cloak and a gentle tug brought her soft body against him.

"We will make good strong sons, O'Hara. Sons of the land."

"Aye, that we will. That we will."

An excerpt from the third epic volume in

THE O'HARA DYNASTY

Watch for it in September 1982
wherever paperbacks are sold!

Ireland, Fall, 1649

THE SHARP RING OF STEEL ON STEEL had stopped and the booming cannon were still. The city of Drogheda was annihilated, the only sounds the agonized cries of the wounded and the solemn cadence of soldiers' boots on the cobbled streets.

Captain Robert Hubbard, of Cromwell's English army, stood on the arch of Duleek Gate, above the courtyard of St. Mary's Church. Flickering lights from the fires of the city played over his shining breastplate. Beneath the visored helmet his face was impassive as he watched defeated Irishmen file under the gate and mill like cattle in the courtyard.

The commander of the Irish force, Sir Arthur Aston, had said, "He who could take Drogheda, could take hell." Well, Hubbard thought, hell had been taken. It would be only a matter of time before the rest of Ireland followed and fell under the Puritan sword.

"Think not of what we do as monstrous," General Cromwell had proclaimed, "for all the blood we spill is done as God's work and in God's name!"

Robert Hubbard smiled at the thought. *Let them all do God's work; I'll do mine,* he mused.

Once again his eyes surveyed the massed crowd in the courtyard and the long line stretching from Duleek Gate nearly to the Boyne River. One by one the people—men, women, children—moved up to stand before a table at the mouth of the gate. Behind the table sat a sergeant, draped in a heavy black cloak. Before him was a huge open book.

The process was unending. Each Irish wretch's name, age and place of birth was demanded and recorded, then his religion was established. Finally, in a bored, sonorous voice the sergeant would tell him to "Step on," and join the other rebels in the courtyard.

At the moment a toddling child of five, perhaps six, stood before the table. Idly, without guilt or remorse, Captain Hubbard wondered how this "rebel" would die: by sword or starvation.

"Do away with their young today, and you'll have no rebels to fight tomorrow!" his superior officers had often said.

Their reasoning has been sound, Hubbard thought, as the child walked under the arch and disappeared in the mass of milling bodies.

Robert was about to retire to his quarters when a broad-shouldered youth with a full head of rust-colored curls stepped before the sergeant.

"Name?"

"Conor O'Hara," came the lad's voice in a booming baritone that stopped Hubbard in midstride.

"Place of birth."

"Ballylee."

"Age?"

"Seventeen."

"Religion?"

"Irish."

"Irish what?" the sergeant growled.

"Irish free man," came the insolent rely.

The sergeant's arm was like a whip as the back of his hand struck the youth's face, sending him sprawling.

In an instant a young girl about the lad's age, with flaming red hair and sharply drawn, beautiful features was kneeling beside him. Tenderly she cradled his head in her arms while the boy blinked and tried to regain his feet.

Cruelly, the boy and girl were pulled apart. The lad, Conor O'Hara, wrestled himelf free from two soldiers' grasping arms and leaped toward the sergeant.

It was a foolhardy move. The larger man merely stepped aside and cuffed the boy to the ground. The girl screamed when a dagger appeared in the soldier's hand.

"Sergeant!" Robert Hubbard called down from his vantage point.

"Sir," the sergeant said, halting the downward motion of his arm, turning the movement into a salute.

Hubbard shifted his attention to the girl. "Your name?" he demanded.

"Margaret O'Hara," she replied, flashing her green eyes upward.

"Are you sister to the lad?"

"Nay, cousins, but we are betrothed. I am of the Antrim O'Hara clan, of Ballyhara."

Hubbard's lips curled into a thin smile and a chill of anticipation rippled through his body. He could hardly believe his good fortune.

"This lad, Conor. Is he the son of Rory O'Hara of Ballylee?"

"Aye," Margaret replied, although a puzzled frown creased her forehead.

"Sergeant!" Hubbard barked. "Put the boy in irons and bring the girl to my quarters!"

The girl was shouting at him, but Robert Hubbard was already descending the stone stairs to the courtyard. His mind was racing ahead to the day when the new, model Puritan army would reach Ballylee.

On that day Robert Hubbard would take what he considered his birthright and the lad, Conor O'Hara, would be on his way to Barbados as a slave.

It will be much easier, Robert Hubbard thought, *to claim Ballylee without my half brother on the land!*

About the author...

An actress for fifteen years, Mary Canon has established a large following in the theater. A few years ago, she appeared on Broadway in the musical "Cyrano" with Christopher Plummer.

Miss Canon, who shares a passion for travel with her husband and fellow-author, Jack Canon, was born in Lewistown, Pennsylvania, but she spent much of her early life in Long Beach, California. The Canons now make their home in North Carolina.

Throughout the past five years she has assisted her husband in the researching and editing of his manuscripts. Finally, with Jack's encouragement, Mary Canon has applied her talents to developing a writing career of her own.

The result is The O'Hara Dynasty, a magnificent saga of the proud and passionate Irish heritage.

Have you missed the first book in The O'Hara Dynasty?

For centuries there had been no love lost between the Irish and the English. But for a brief moment in time, at the court of Elizabeth I, a forbidden love was found... between Rory O'Donnell, a steel-willed Irish spy, and the high-spirited Englishwoman Lady Elizabeth Hatton. Their love created a powerful family, and an even more powerful legend.

Look for the *The Defiant* wherever paperbacks are sold, or complete and mail this coupon today!

WORLDWIDE READER SERVICE

In the U.S.A.
1440 South Priest Drive
Tempe, AZ 85281

In Canada
649 Ontario Street
Stratford, Ontario N5A 6W2

Please send me *The Defiant* by Mary Canon. I am enclosing my check or money order for $2.95 for each copy ordered, plus 75¢ to cover postage and handling.

Number of copies checked @ $2.95 each = $________
N.Y. and Ariz. residents add appropriate sales tax $________
Postage and handling $ .75
TOTAL $________

I enclose________

(Please send check or money order. We cannot be responsible for cash sent through the mail.)

Prices subject to change without notice.

NAME________
(Please Print)
ADDRESS________
CITY________
STATE/PROV.________
ZIP/POSTAL CODE________

Offer expires December 31, 1982 203016453